The Author

HUGH MACLENNAN was born in Glace Bay, Cape Breton, Nova Scotia, in 1907. He took his B.A. (1928) in Classics from Dalhousie University, then travelled as a Rhodes Scholar to Oxford University where he obtained another B.A. and his M.A. (1932); he completed graduate studies in Classics at Princeton University, where he received his Ph.D. (1935).

MacLennan returned to Canada in 1935 to accept a teaching appointment in Latin and History at Lower Canada College in Montreal, which remained his home. In 1951 he accepted a position in the Department of English at McGill University, where he taught for three decades.

Barometer Rising was MacLennan's first novel. His seven novels as well as his many essays and travel books present a chronicle of a Canada that often mediates between the old world of its European cultural heritage and the new world of American vitality and materialism.

MacLennan's many honours include five Governor General's Awards and nineteen honorary degrees.

Hugh MacLennan died in Montreal, Quebec, in 1990.

Hugh MacLennan

BAROMETER RISING

With an Afterword by Alistair MacLeod

McCLELLAND & STEWART

This book was first published by William Collins Sons & Co. in 1941.
New Canadian Library edition 1989

Library and Archives Canada Cataloguing in Publication

MacLennan, Hugh, 1907-1990
Barometer rising

(New Canadian library)
Bibliography: p.
ISBN 13: 978-0-7710-9991-5
ISBN 10: 0-7710-9991-6

I. Title   II. Series.

PS8525.L45B37 1989   C813'.52   C89-093679-X
PR9199.3.M334B37 1989

We acknowledge the financial support of the Government of Canada
through the Book Publishing Industry Development Program and that of
the Government of Ontario through the Ontario Media Development
Corporation's Ontario Book Initiative. We further acknowledge the
support of the Canada Council for the Arts and the Ontario Arts Council
for our publishing program.

Printed and bound in Canada by Webcom

McClelland & Stewart Ltd.
75 Sherbourne Street
Toronto, Ontario
M5A 2P9
www.mcclelland.com/NCL

8 9 10 11 12   10 09 08 07 06

Contents

Foreword

It seems necessary to offer more than a conventional statement about the names of the characters in this book, since it is one of the first ever written to use Halifax, Nova Scotia, for its sole background. Because there is as yet no tradition of Canadian literature, Canadians are apt to suspect that a novel referring to one of their cities must likewise refer to specific individuals among its characters. If the names of actual persons, living or dead, have been used in this book, it is a coincidence and no personal reference is intended.

Nova Scotia family names have, nevertheless, been employed; to avoid them would have been too definite a loss. Since there is no great variety in Scottish given names, the combinations are inevitably repetitious. The characters are, it is hoped, true to their background, and nothing more.

Eight days are involved in the story: Sunday, December second, to Monday, December tenth, in 1917.

Barometer Rising

Sunday

FOUR O'CLOCK

HE HAD BEEN walking around Halifax all day, as though by moving through familiar streets he could test whether he belonged here and had at last reached home. In the west the winter sky was brilliant and clouds massing under the sun were taking on colour, but smoke hung low in the streets, the cold air holding it down. He glanced through the dirty window of a cheap restaurant, saw the interior was empty and went in through the double doors. There was a counter and a man in a soiled apron behind it, a few tables and chairs, and a smell of mustard. He sat on one of the warped stools at the counter and ordered Bovril and a ham sandwich.

"You English?" the man behind the counter said.

"No. I used to live around here."

"Funny, I thought you were an English fella. You been over there, though?"

"I just got back."

He glanced restlessly over his shoulder before he let his muscles relax, but there was no need for caution in a restaurant like this. No one he had ever known in Halifax would be seen in the place.

1

"You been away long?" the restaurant man said. He poured steaming water over the glutinous Bovril essence after he had ladled it into a thick mug.

"Quite a while."

The man set the drink on the counter and began cutting slices from a loaf of brown bread.

"Guess you been in the war, too," he said. "I was in it myself for a while but I didn't get very far. I got to Quebec. My wife thinks that's funny. She says, when you got in the army you started moving backwards before you even began." He pulled a thin slice of boiled ham loose from a pile on a plate and slapped it on the bread.

"What was your outfit?" he said.

The customer stared at the counter without answering and the restaurant man shifted his feet uneasily.

"I was only asking. Hell, it's no skin off my ass."

"Never mind. I was with a lot of outfits, and I didn't sail from here in the first place."

"Mustard?" When he received no answer the man passed the sandwich over the counter. "A lot goes on in town these days. You'd be surprised."

The sandwich was eaten in a fierce silence, then he swallowed the Bovril in one passage of the cup to his mouth. He drew a deep breath and asked for more, and while the restaurant man was supplying it he asked casually, "Are you still in with the army around here?"

"No. They let me out on account of varicose veins. That's why I only got to Quebec."

A tram rumbled around the corner in the gathering shadows of the street and its flanges screamed on the uneven rails. The young man jerked nervously at the sudden noise and cleared his throat. All his muscles had tightened involuntarily, giving him a rigid appearance like an animal bunched for a spring. He remained taut and this physical tenseness invested his words with a dramatic value he did not intend.

"There's a chap I knew overseas," he said. "I was wondering if you'd ever heard of him. Alec MacKenzie . . . Big Alec, we called him."

"I knew a man called Alec MacKenzie once, but he was a little fella."

"Do you know Colonel Wain?"

The man shoved the second cup of Bovril closer to his customer. "How would a guy like me be knowing colonels?"

"I didn't mean was he a friend of yours. I meant, did you ever hear of him?"

"There's one Colonel Wain here in Halifax." He glanced at the younger man's thin and shabby overcoat. "But you wouldn't be meaning him, either. He's pretty rich, they say."

"So?" He picked up the mug and drained it slowly, then stood straight and looked at himself in the mirror behind the counter. The war had made as big a change in him as it seemed to have made in Halifax. His shoulders were wide, he was just under six feet tall, but his appearance was of run-down ill health, and he knew he looked much older than when he had left three years ago. Although he was barely twenty-eight, deep lines ran in parentheses around his mouth, and there was a nervous tic in his left cheek and a permanent tension in the expression of his eyes. His nails were broken and dirty, he carried himself without confidence, and it seemed an effort for him to be still for more than a moment at a time. In England he would have been labelled a gentleman who had lost caste.

He buttoned his coat and laid some coins on the counter. He turned to leave and then turned back. "This Colonel Wain . . . is he in town now?" he said.

"I saw his picture in the *Chronicle* last week some time," the restaurant man said. "I guess he must be."

When he left the café he turned toward George Street and slowly began the climb toward Citadel Hill. When he reached the last intersection he continued across the pavement, then upward along a wavering footpath through the unkempt grasses which rustled over the slope of the hill. He pulled himself up slowly, with a jerky nervousness that indicated he was not yet accustomed to his limping left leg, which seemed more to follow his body than propel it forward. At the top of the hill he stopped on a narrow footpath that outlined the rim of the star-shaped moat which defended the half-hidden buildings of the central garrison. An armed soldier stood guard over an open draw-bridge giving access to the military enclosure. Over it all rose a flagpole and signal masts.

He turned about and surveyed the town. A thin breeze was dragging in from the sea; it was a soundless breath on the cheek, but it made him feel entirely solitary. Though it was early December, the winter snow had not yet fallen and the thin soil had frozen onto the rocks, the trees were bare and the grass was like straw, and the land itself had given up most of its colour.

The details of Halifax were dim in the fading light but the contours were clear and he had forgotten how good they were. The Great Glacier had once packed, scraped, and riven this whole land; it had gouged out the harbour and left as a legacy three drumlins . . . the hill on which he stood and two islands in the harbour itself. Halifax covers the whole of an oval peninsula, and the Citadel is about in the centre of it. He could look south to the open Atlantic and see where the park at the end of the town thrusts its nose directly into the outer harbour. At the park the water divides, spreading around the town on either side; to the west the inlet is called the Northwest Arm, to the east it is called the Stream, and it is here that the docks and ocean terminals are built. The Stream bends with the swell of Halifax peninsula and runs inland a distance of four miles from the park to a deep strait at the northern end of town called the Narrows. This strait opens directly into Bedford Basin, a lake-like expanse which bulges around the back of the town to the north.

He followed the footpath and looked for familiar landmarks, walking around the moat until he had boxed the compass. From here even a landsman could see why the harbour had for a century and a half been a link in the chain of British sea power. It is barricaded against Atlantic groundswells by McNab's Island at the mouth of the outer harbour, and by the smaller bowl of George's Island at the entrance to the Stream. It was defended now against enemy battle squadrons by forts set on rocky promontories running over the horizon into the sea. It was fenced off from prowling submarines by a steel net hung on pontoons from McNab's to the mainland. This harbour is the reason for the town's existence; it is all that matters in Halifax, for the place periodically sleeps between great wars. There had been a good many years since Napoleon, but now it was awake again.

The forests to the far west and north were nothing but shadows under the sky at this time of day. Above the horizon rim the remaining light was a turmoil of rose and saffron and pallid green, the colours of blood and flowers and the sheen of sunlight on summer grass. As his eyes shifted from the dull floor of the distant sea to this shredding blaze of glory crowning the continent, he felt an unexpected wave of exultation mount in his mind. Merely to have been born on the western side of the ocean gave a man something for which the traditions of the Old World could never compensate. This western land was his own country. He had forgotten how it was, but now he was back, and to be able to remain was worth risking everything.

After sunset the hilltop grew colder. The colours died quickly and as the landscape faded into darkness the street lights of the city came on. They made bluish pools at intervals along the narrow thoroughfares that fanned away from the roots of the hill, and all the way down to the waterfront the life of Halifax began to reveal itself in flashes. Barrington, Granville, and Hollis Streets, running north and south, were visible only at the intersections where the inclines plunging from the hill to the waterfront crossed them, and at these corners pedestrians could be seen moving back and forth, merged in irregular streams.

Children were playing a game with a whole block of a George Street slum for their playground. They darted in and out of his vision as they pursued each other in and out of doorways and back and forth across the street. Here and there in the withered grass along the slope of the Citadel the forms of men and girls lay huddled, scarcely moving; they clung together on the frozen ground in spite of the cold, sailors with only a night on shore and local girls with no better place to be.

Halifax seemed to have acquired a meaning since he had left it in 1914. Quietly, almost imperceptibly, everything had become harnessed to the war. Long ribbons of light crossed on the surface of the water from the new oil refinery on the far shore of the Stream, and they all found their focus in himself. Occasionally they were broken, as undiscernible craft moved through the harbour, and he suddenly realized that this familiar inlet had become one of the most vital stretches of water in the world. It still gleamed faintly in the dusk as its surface retained a residual glow of daylight. Ferryboats glided like beetles across it, fanning ruffled water in their wake. A freighter drifted inland with a motion so slight he had to watch a full minute before it was perceptible. Its only identification was riding lights; no one but the port authorities knew its home port or its destination. While he watched, its anchor ran out with a muted clatter to the bottom and its bow swung to the north.

Then the Stream became static. The smoke of Halifax lay like clouds about a mountain; the spire of St. Mary's Cathedral cut George's Island in two; the only moving object was the beam of the lighthouse on McNab's, circling like a turning eye out to sea, along the coast and into the harbour again.

He descended the hill slowly, easing his left leg carefully along the dirt path. Down on the street the contours of Halifax were lost in the immediate reality of grim red brick and smoky stone. In the easy days before the war he had winced at the architecture, but it no longer bothered him. Halifax was obviously more than its buildings. Its functional aspect was magnificent, its solid docks, piled with freight to the edge of deep water, Bedford Basin thronged with ships from all over the world, the grimy old naval and military buildings crowded once more with alert young men. However much he loathed the cause of this change, he found the throbbing life of the city at once a stimulation and a relief.

For twelve hours he had been back, and so far he had been recognized by no one. He stopped in the shadow of a doorway and the muscles of his face tightened again as his mind returned to its endless calculations. Big Alec MacKenzie had returned from France – and so had Wain. The colonel had probably been back for more than a year. The problem was to find MacKenzie before he himself was discovered by Wain. If only he could get to Big Alec first. . . . He began to smile to himself.

When he reached Barrington Street and the shops he found himself in a moving crowd. Girls with English faces brushed by him in twos and threes, sailors from a British cruiser rolled as though the pavement were a ship's deck. Although most of them were walking the main street because they had no better place to go – soldiers, dockworkers in flat cloth caps, civilians – they did not appear aimless. Even their idleness seemed to have a purpose, as though it were also part of the war.

By the time he had walked to the South End where the crowds were thinner, he realized that underneath all this war-begotten activity Halifax remained much the same. It had always looked an old town. It had a genius for looking old and for acting as though nothing could possibly happen to surprise it. Battalions passed through from the West, cargoes multi-plied, convoys left every week and new ships took over their anchorages; yet underneath all this the old habits survived and the inhabitants did not alter. All of them still went to church regularly; he had watched them this morning. And he was certain they still drank tea with all their meals. The field-gun used in the past as a curfew for the garrison was fired from the Citadel every noon and at nine-thirty each night, and the townspeople took out their watches automatically twice a day to check the time. The Citadel itself flew the Union Jack in all weathers and was rightly considered a symbol and bastion of the British Empire.

Grinding on the cobblestones behind a pair of plunging Clydesdales came one of Halifax's most typical vehicles, a low-swung dray with a high driver's box, known as a sloven. This one was piled high with bags of feed and it almost knocked him down as the driver brought it around to level ground. He cursed as he jumped clear of the horses and the driver spat and flourished his whip, and the lash flicked in a quick, cracking arc over the sidewalk. The sloven moved north onto Barrington Street as the horses were pulled in to a walk. Traffic slowed down behind it, a few horns sounded and the column stopped behind a stationary tram.

His leg pained after the sudden pull on his muscles and he walked more slowly until the soreness abated. Images flashed through his mind and out again . . . shell-shock simul-taneous with a smashed thigh and no time to be frightened by either; the flash of destruction out of the dark; who knew until it was experienced how intense the molten whiteness could be at the heart of an exploding chemical? . . . Naked when they picked him up, unconscious . . . and afterwards memory gone and no identity disk to help the base hospital.

The English doctor had done a fine job in mending his thigh and a better one in saving his reason. This, at least, had been no accident; more than twenty centuries of medical history had been behind that doctor. Even though his world was composed now of nothing but chance, it was unreasonable to believe that a series of accidents should ultimately matter. One chance must lead to another with no binding link but a peculiar tenacity which made him determined to preserve himself for a future which gave no promise of being superior to the past. It was his future, and that was all he could say of it. At the moment it was all he had.

A motor horn sounded and he leaped convulsively again. Every time a sudden noise struck his ears his jangled nerves set his limbs jumping and trembling in automatic convulsions which made him loathe his own body for being so helpless. He stopped and leaned against a lamppost until the trembling stopped. Like a fish on the end of a hook, he thought, squirming and fighting for no privilege except the opportunity to repeat the same performance later.

People moved past him in both directions, laughing, talking, indifferent. Were they too stupid to care what was happening to the world, or did they enjoy the prospect of a society in process of murdering itself? Did he care himself, for that matter; weren't any emotions he had left reduced to the simple desire for an acknowledged right to exist here in the place he knew as home? He had long ago given up the attempt to discover a social or spiritual reason which might justify what had happened to himself and millions of others during the past three years. If he could no longer be useful in the hell of Europe, then he must find a way to stay in Canada where he had been born.

He took his bearings when the trembling in his limbs subsided and was astonished to see how far south he had walked. Had the years in London made him lose all perspective of distance? He walked slowly to the next corner and knew he had reached his objective. But now he was here he felt nervous and unreasonably disappointed. He surveyed the cross-street to his right as though he were searching casually for his bearings, but he knew every inch of it and every doorway as far up the hill as he could see.

It seemed to have lost all its graciousness, and yet nothing was actually changed. Then he realized that he had been remembering it as it was in summer with the horse chestnuts and elms and limes towering their shade over the roofs, with the doorways secluded under vine-covered porches, with everything so quiet that it always seemed to be Sunday afternoon. Actually there was little difference; winter had always made it look bare, stripped as ruthlessly as the rest of Halifax. There was no town anywhere that changed in appearance so quickly when the foliage went.

He fumbled for a cigarette and lit it slowly, looking carefully in all directions as though he were deciding which way to shield himself from the wind. Then he began the steep ascent of the hill, his movements furtive and his hat pulled low over his left eye. He stopped at the crest and stood panting, hardly believing that after so much time he was really here, that the red house opposite had stayed just as he remembered it, that the trees still crowded its windows and the high wooden fence shut the garden away from the eyes of passersby.

At least the war had not dulled his trained appreciation of good architecture. Among the many nondescript Victorian houses of Halifax, this one stood out as a masterpiece. It was neither gracious nor beautiful, in a way it was almost forbidding, but it so typified the history and character of its town that it belonged exactly as it was: solid British colonial with a fanlight over the door, about six feet of lawn separating it from the sidewalk, four thick walls and no ells or additions, high ceilings and high windows, and shutters on the inside where they could be useful if not decorative. It had stood just as it was for over a hundred years; it looked permanent enough to last forever.

To cross the street and knock on the door, to take a chance on the right person opening it, would be so easy. Just a few movements and it would be done, and then whatever else he might feel, this loneliness which welled inside like a salt spring would disappear. Spasmodically he clasped one hand with the other and squeezed it hard, then turned back down the hill and followed it to Barrington Street.

There was nothing more he could do today. Sunday was the worst possible time to hunt for Alec MacKenzie or anyone else too poor to own a telephone. He walked north to the junction of Spring Garden Road and waited for a tram. Evening service was under way in St. Matthew's Church and the sound of a hymn penetrated its closed Gothic doors. "O God of Bethel by whose hand thy people still are fed ... Who, through this weary pilgrimage, Hast all our fathers led. ..."

The girls went by in twos and threes, sailors rolled past, evening loafers lounged against the stone wall of the military cemetery opposite, a soldier picked up a girl in front of the iron gate of the Crimean monument. "God of our fathers, be the God of their succeeding race." With a muffled sigh the congregation sat down.

A tram ground around the corner and stopped, heading north. Fifteen minutes later when he left it he could hear a low, vibrant, moaning sound that permeated everything, beating in over the housetops from the sea. For a second he was puzzled; it sounded like an animal at some distance, moaning with pain. Then he realized that the air was salty and moist and the odour of fish-meal was in his nostrils. The wind had changed and now it was bringing in the fog. Pavements were growing damp and bells and groaning buoys at the harbour-mouth were busy. When he reached his room in the cheap sailor's lodging he had rented that morning he lay down, and the sounds of the harbour seemed to be in the walls.

FIVE O'CLOCK

From a window in her office at the Shipyards Penelope Wain
stood watching the evening draw in over the water. It was
invading the Stream like a visible and moving body. It spilled
over from the land and lapped the massive sides of the graving
dock and the hulls of vessels riding at anchor; it advanced
westward from the hidden sea; and because fog was behind the
darkness, the air was alive with the clanging of bells.

She stood quite still, alone in her unlighted office. The
mauve depths of the sky were slashed starkly by the upthrust
angles of the great cranes, by the row of hoppers lining the
dock to the north, by the two masts and three funnels of
the cruiser which lay at the naval dockyard lower down the
Stream. From somewhere in the recesses of the enormous
building at her back came the sound of a closing door. She
turned slightly to listen, but if there were faint footsteps they
receded, and she turned back to watch the harbour.

This assembly of enormous and potent apparatus was so
familiar she hardly noticed it. Yet even while she rested her
eyes on the soft colours of the twilight, she was conscious of
objects that the advancing darkness had partially covered.
There was the long skeleton of the ship under construction,
lying with its keel buried in the night and its ribs caged in
the net of a great gantry. Flat in the open spaces of the yard
under her window sprawled three bronze propellers waiting
to be connected to their shafts. And there was a row of parked
trucks and a line of freight cars standing on a siding, all part
of her work. She handled none of them and had no immediate authority over their disposal, yet ultimately the results
of her daily work became parts of the whole of which these
also were parts.

There was something delicate, something extremely fragile
in the appearance of the girl alone against that angular background of motionless machinery and silent engines. She
appeared slight because the lines of her waist were slim and

her fingers and feet dainty. A second glance would discover definite curves at her hips and breasts, a latent fullness the more pleasing because it revealed itself as a surprise. She had quantities of reddish-brown hair pulled back onto the nape of her neck, but no amount of tidying could hide the graceful manner in which it grew from her forehead and temples. Now, in repose, her face seemed absorbed and private, and because this was the only expression she was able to discover from a mirror, she fancied that she was a plain, average girl of twenty-nine.

But contact with another person transformed her. In conversation her face opened and disclosed a sympathetic and comprehensive mind. She seemed to become part of the experience and emotions of anyone who engaged her interest, and the town was filled with individuals who would like to have found excuses for talking with her. But of this she was entirely unaware. The most striking and piquant feature of her appearance at any time was a lock of white hair running from the left side of her forehead along the temple and over her ear. It set her apart from other women and arrested men's attention by its obscure appeal to their sensuality, though it seldom succeeded in making her thoroughly attractive to them. When they discovered her profession, when they learned that she was a ship-designer with an office of her own at the Shipyards, they kept their distance in fear of the excessively unfamiliar.

She slipped back into the high swivel chair before her desk and turned on the goose-neck lamp at her elbow. It threw a yellow pool over the disarray of papers, pencils, T-squares, and erasers on the desk and shut the rest of the room away in darkness. She began to gather the papers together, checking each one carefully before laying the lot in a lower drawer. A list of figures engaged her attention as she ticked them off slowly with a pencil, and then this paper was placed on top of a pile of blueprints in another drawer.

She dropped the pencil with a clatter and leaned back, stretching her arms. She was tired and knew she should stop, but this was a chronic state with her now that a further speed-up in war work was being pressed, and she welcomed the lassitude as an anodyne to thought. To be a woman and work at a profession pre-eminently masculine meant that she must be more than good. She had to be better than her male colleagues; she had to work longer hours and be doubly careful of all that she did, for a mistake would ruin her. It had taken a war to open such a job to her in the first place, but she was undeceived as to how superior she must be to continue to keep it.

A door opened and shut in the far distance again, but this time she knew the footsteps that advanced along the corridor were coming her way. She glanced at her watch. When old Simon Perry knocked and then came in clutching a grubby paper in his large fist, she smiled and he touched his cap.

"I was about to leave," she said. "I thought you'd decided you didn't need any help after all. Pull up that chair."

"No. I was coming," he replied. And with his cap still on his head and a white forelock projecting stiffly from under its peak, he leaned against the edge of her desk and thrust his paper at her. "I made a drawing. So you can see what I mean."

She had no need of the drawing to understand his difficulty, but from innate politeness she pretended to study it.

"It's no time to be working on the Sabbath Day," he muttered. "But with one like you there's no other way of seeing you. The rest of the days you're too busy. . . ." He paused until she looked up from the paper, and then he said, "That mechanic you sent me is a God damn liar."

"Don't be so cross," she said. "The mechanic made a mistake and you're the boss. Whatever you say is bound to be right, and all you have to do is make him obey."

He took out of his pocket a clay pipe filled with half-burned shag and lit it. The stench made her cough. "He don't think so," he said. "He don't know anything about a ship and so far as I can see he don't know much more about his own trade. He tells me his engine's going to have a certain weight – like you told me – and now I find it weighs nigh onto a hundredweight more. That means I got to set it eighteen inches farther forrad or the craft'll ride like a canoe. He gives me the argument. The shaft don't allow for them extra eighteen inches, he says."

Penelope listened to all this with a grave face even though she was perfectly familiar with Simon's problem. The mechanic had telephoned her about it the day before. But the old man had to be handled carefully. He must be over seventy now; he had been an old man twenty years ago when she first had known him, when he worked as her Uncle John's assistant in his yacht-building yard on the South Shore. Heaven knew how many years before that he had taken part in the construction of great three-masters, of brigs and barquentines which had passed from the seas before she was born. Now he owned a small place of his own where he built light harbour craft, and the cause of his present difficulty was a motor-launch for the use of local naval authorities.

"What did you tell the mechanic, finally?" she said.

"I told him to bugger off."

"Well – he'll have to get a longer shaft, that's all. Tell him I said so, if that's any help."

"You'll fix it up with them naval fellas, Miss Penny?"

"They probably won't even notice the difference."

"Maybe not, but they'll pretend they do. They don't trust nothing except what comes out of a factory." He spat into her wastebasket, making its metal sides clang. "That blueprint you did for me – you still got it around?"

"I've got a copy." She ran her fingers over the edges of a tightly packed file in an open drawer, then extracted the papers.

"Mind you, I never said they were any use to anybody. I'd kind of feel easier if I had a look, that's all."

Like most of the old craftsmen of the province, Simon Perry worked from models of his own contriving, miniatures exquisitely carved out of soft wood and complete to the last detail. But to get a contract from the government the submission of a blueprint was necessary, and Penny had offered to draw one from his model. He did not understand much about gasoline engines and required a mechanic to help with that part of the work, and it was his secret grievance that the engine was perhaps the most important part of his craft. He leaned now over the blueprints he could not understand and tried to look wise, his elbows holding the stiff paper flat and his horny hands on his jaws. The smoke from the shag puffed out, billowing through the pool of light.

Penny got up to escape it. She rested her elbows on the high windowsill, unconsciously repeating the pattern of the old man's posture. Nothing but the contour of the land about the Stream was visible now; the darkness was nearly total.

Simon breathed noisily and stood upright. "You going to change this print now?" he said.

"I doubt if that's necessary. If so, I'll change it. Stop worrying, Simon. You've forgotten more about shipbuilding than the rest of us will ever know. Go ahead and finish the job."

She was thankful that in this case his judgment was right, for it would have been impossible to tell him anything. He joined her at the window and stared gloomily over her shoulder at the stark outlines of the cranes and the long, high lines of the building opposite.

"How the likes of you works in a place like this beats me. In the old days a shipyard used to be something, what with the clean smell of lumber and the tar and the smoke of the open fires. Now what's in it? It ain't natural for a woman to be smart at this sort of work."

When she made no answer he stood off and surveyed her with a calculating candour, even to cocking his head on one side and making movements with his hands as though he were actually feeling the curves of her hips and waist. "You got a figure ought to fill any man's eye, even though it's on the lean side."

She knew that if Simon were twenty years younger he would be attempting to take liberties with her now and decided not to answer. He moved away from the window and pulled his cap more firmly over his stiff hair.

"Well," he said, "I can't say you don't know your trade, even though it ain't natural you should." He hesitated. "I thought John Macrae's boy had his eye on you once, but I guess you lost him, for all that. I guess he couldn't stand it when you started out trying to beat him at his own job. A man don't like that, Miss Penny. Where is he now? I haven't seen Neil in a mighty long time."

Small tight lines appeared about the corners of her mouth and she had to close her lips to keep from telling him to mind his own business. The old man's memory was so hazy he had forgotten that her cousin Neil Macrae was dead.

"Old John Macrae now, he knew how to build a ship. Funny thing him marrying that sister of your father's. Seemed to get on all right with her, too. Seems only yesterday since you and Neil used to stand around and watch us work. That boy was good. It ought to be him here in this office, not you."

Penny made an abrupt movement and again checked the words that came to her lips. She began to roll up the blueprints and hunt rubber bands to hold them, and her breathing became more easy as the current of her mind settled back into its worn channel. Simon was still talking, but she felt immune to anything he might say now.

"What's your father doing around town these days, Miss Penny? I hear he's still running his shipping business in spite of the war and him being in the army. It must be a mighty nice business for him these days. I guess he's better at that than soldiering."

"Simon!" Once more she checked herself and forced a smile. It seemed pointless to object to this old man making a statement with which she agreed herself. "Father's still on active duty, but it's a special sort of job that leaves him free part of the time."

Simon had his hand on the door-knob and stood there with his feet firmly set apart as though he were bracing himself against the roll of a ship's deck. "Well, I guess I better thank you for helping. Maybe if this launch is all right they'll give me something else to do. But I don't like working for the government. There's too much red tape. If they'd just tell me what they want and let me give it to them, things'd be better." He opened the door and stepped across the threshold, then paused again. "Neil went to France, too, didn't he?"

"Yes," Penny said quietly.

"I guess that's why I ain't been seeing him. Last I remember, he was at that engineering school in the Boston States."

"Good night, Simon," she said. "And don't worry any more about that engine. Just send the mechanic over to me if he makes any more trouble for you."

"I can handle the bugger all right," he said, and the door closed behind him. The sound of his heavy boots echoed down the corridor, followed by the muffled slam of a second door; then the cavernous building was silent.

Penny continued sitting at her desk, tense and solitary in the empty room. It was as though a stone had been plunged into the pool of her mind until her memories were surging like troubled waters, and for a few moments her whole body ached with loneliness and a sense of loss. The anaesthetic of hard work could never compensate for the feeling of life and growth that had departed from her; and now, like a man in the desert obsessed by thoughts of green grass and running water, she remembered things as they had been before the war. She saw herself dancing at an Admiralty House ball. She recollected the odour of lime trees heavy in the streets on close summer nights when there were shooting stars, and how those evenings as she walked alone it had been possible to imagine an aeon of tranquillity broadening out like a sea under the sky, herself growing old gently, with children about her, the land where she had been born mellowing slowly into maturity.

And yet she knew that her earlier life had never been especially contented, nor were the things on which she had spent her time calculated to induce any such picture as the one which now filled her mind. She had gone to college and astonished her professors by her ability at mathematics and her precision in the science laboratories. After her graduation she had lived for two years with her family, and being bored by the monotony of it, had ordered the best books on marine engineering she could find and studied them. During the first year of the war she had visited an aunt and uncle in Montreal, but instead of finding a place for herself in the social life of the city, had spent almost all her time at a technical school studying ship-designing.

Now, as she sat alone at her desk looking through the pool of yellow light at the blank face of the window, she quivered at the thought of how helpless her existence had been in the current of forces she had been able neither to predict nor control. Yet, when she examined with detachment what had happened to herself and her relatives during the past three years, she was forced to admit that their experiences had not been unique. The war had taken control of them just as it had of everyone else.

The moment passed and Penny got to her feet, remembering that it was time to go home. Since the death of her mother ten years ago she had tried to be mistress of her father's house while she lived in Halifax, and on Sunday evenings she was expected to supervise the late supper invariably served to those of her relatives who chose to come in after church. She swept her desk clear of pencils and closed the drawers, and then reached for her hat and coat. When she had pulled the hat down over her forehead and stuffed her hands into the pockets of the coat, her face broke into a soft and surprising smile. With an impulsive movement she returned to her desk, picked up the telephone and asked for the number of a hotel.

"May I speak to Major Murray, if he's in?"

She waited minutes, and then Angus Murray's voice sounded at the end of the wire.

"Don't say you're busy, please," she said. "I want you to have supper with me tonight. You know . . . at home . . . the family and everything."

His voice rose in protest. "For heaven's sake! They'd faint at the sight of me."

"Maybe they'd think of it, but on the whole they'd consider it too undignified. Please, Angus . . . I just can't stand them tonight all by myself."

"Where are you now . . . home?"

"No. I'm still at the office. I was just about to leave."

"Then why don't you meet me at the hotel?"

"Can't. That would be asking too much of Sadie. And there's my young brother Roddie. He doesn't like the relatives any better than I do."

"Who's Sadie?"

"Oh, she's our indispensable Newfoundland maid. You've got to come tonight because I want to celebrate. Just you and me, surrounded by aunts and uncles."

There was a pause and she heard Murray clear his throat huskily. "I must say you make it sound attractive! Who's celebrating what?"

"My design. It's been accepted by the Admiralty."

"What design?" She could almost hear him trying to remember.

"I told you all about it long ago. I had a delayed cable from London this morning."

"Oh." His voice suddenly rose in amazement. "You mean – you mean Whitehall's accepted that design for a submarine-chaser you were talking about? The one you finished last spring?"

"Don't sound so upset about it, Angus."

There was another pause, filled with silence this time.

"But, good Lord! That means – that must mean you're really good!"

She thought Murray was reconciled to the fact that she had ability; indeed he seemed to admire her for it. Now she was suddenly sorry she had told him, for it had been her experience that few people know how to be pleased at the successes of their friends.

"Never mind, Angus. It's not very important, not really. They'll probably only test it and reject it. I just became a little too pleased with myself, that's all. You'll come anyway, won't you? About nine o'clock?"

"No, Penny. I know my limitations, and my sense of humour isn't up to an evening with the Wains. Yours isn't either."

She twisted the wires of the telephone extension and a wry smile crossed her face. "Didn't anyone ever tell you, Angus, that I'm supposed to be a respectable girl? People see us together and they tell my family and my family knows you never so much as see me home. Pretty soon there'll be a lot of fine talk going around town."

"Why should you care?"

"The odd thing is, I don't. It's you I'm thinking of. You'd care."

"What do you mean by that?"

"Merely that you're conventional, my dear. Most men are, especially those who think they have a reputation for the opposite. Once you hear the gossip, you'll stop seeing me, and I wouldn't like that at all."

She could hear him grunt and again clear his throat, a frequent and individual trade-mark.

"Pretty shrewd, aren't you, Penny?"

"Have it your own way, Angus." She was laughing now as she teased him. "But the family's awfully partial to a uniform.

If you'll take a stiff drink and chance it, I'll send them home early, and you can stay as long as you please."

"Well . . . I'll think about it. Don't mind if I'm late, though."

She replaced the receiver and stood up. Through the window she could see tracks of lights shimmering across the still water. An inbound cargo steamer slid silently past the end of the graving dock below, on its way to the Basin to await convoy. From this angle, the ferries crossing the Stream and passing each other were two ovals of light, accompanied by their own following reflections in the water. This harbour with its queer congeries of the very new and the very old often depressed strangers, but to her it was so much a part of her life, so patiently and quietly beautiful, that she missed it wherever else she went. Her eye wandered back to the freighter sliding upstream: a commonplace ship, certainly foreign and probably of Mediterranean origin, manned by heaven knew what conglomeration of Levantines, with maybe a Scotsman in the engine-room and a renegade Nova Scotian somewhere in the forecastle. The war had brought so many of these mongrel vessels to Halifax, they had become a part of the landscape.

SEVEN O'CLOCK

When Penny reached home she found everything quiet except for faint bumps that seemed to come from the attic. That would be Roddie playing one of his eternal war games by himself. Since his withdrawal from boarding school a year ago he had become obsessed with the war. She pulled off her old felt hat and dropped it on the hall table, then moved it to see if it had shown up any dust. Sadie was asleep in the kitchen when she opened the door; the girl woke blinking as the light flashed in her eyes.

"Never mind," Penny said. "I just wanted to make sure there was plenty of food in the house. Has the colonel told you how many to expect tonight?"

Sadie got to her feet and rubbed her eyes with a corner of her apron. "Just Mr. Halfred and Mrs. Halfred and Mr. Fraser and Mrs. Fraser," she said. "And Master Roddie and the colonel 'isself."

"All right. And set one extra place. I've asked someone else to come in, too. I couldn't stand an unprotected evening with Uncle Alfred and Aunt Maria, even though Jim and Mary Fraser might help out a little. Not tonight, I couldn't."

"Ho, Miss Penny!" Sadie giggled, and added with a mixture of deference and intimacy, "Mr. Halfred, 'e do heat something terrible!"

"You can't hear his teeth clacking all the way out here, can you?"

"Ho, Miss Penny, wot a thing to say!"

"Well, have supper ready by eight-thirty. They won't be here then, of course. But if church isn't too crowded tonight Uncle Alfred ought to have the collection counted in time to get here around nine. What's the matter with Uncle Cecil? Lumbago again?"

"'E 'as sore bones, Mrs. Cecil said. And she 'as too, today."

"They probably only have colds, but if it pleases them to think it's grippe I suppose we ought to be thankful. Their absence tonight will help a lot."

"Miss Penny – don't you feel well too?"

"I feel all right. Don't take me so seriously, Sadie."

On her way through the hall she glanced into the living-room and saw that the map of Jamaica over the fireplace was hanging crooked again. She straightened it, then gave a cursory look to make sure the rest of the room was in order. The sombre, heavy but comfortable furniture depressed her, but to change it was out of the question. Nothing in this house was ever changed, and her relatives derived a peculiar satisfaction from the thought that in this ancestral establishment even the dust behind the pictures was permanent. She pulled one of the wide, chintz-covered armchairs out of its accustomed position and turned it with its back to the room, so that it faced the french windows overlooking the shadowy cavern of the garden, and then she dropped into it.

Outside, the earth was frozen hard and the flower beds were stiff with frost. It was impossible to see the details of the garden with its stone wall separating it from the street, its great lime trees like buttresses beside the house-walls, its benches and summer-house in the distant corner. The garden was the only part of the property she really loved; to her, the rest of the house was an incubus.

For five generations the Wains had been leading citizens in Halifax and the history of the family was to some extent the history of the town itself. In 1749 a Wain had been a sergeant in one of the regiments brought to Nova Scotia by Cornwallis to found a garrison city against Louisburg, the fortress in Cape Breton which secured the Gulf of St. Lawrence for the French and was a permanent threat to New England. This Wain later fought at Quebec, then returned to the garrison at Halifax, where he died.

His grandson became a privateer in the War of 1812, and with prize money acquired from the American ships he captured, founded the fortunes of the family, built a wharf and a warehouse, and established an exporting and importing business with the West Indies, exchanging dried apples and fish for rum, tobacco, and molasses. From that time until now, the Wain fortune had remained stationary, in the sense that it increased only in proportion to the growth of the family's offshoots, which were fairly numerous.

Wains owned several establishments in Halifax, but the principal one belonged to Geoffrey Wain, the eldest son of the main branch. He was Penny's father and the head of the shipping business. This house which he had inherited stood on the crest of a hill in the South End, in a district no longer fashionable. The years had so mellowed the property that it had acquired a charm rare among the houses of Halifax. The side walls of the house were covered with Virginia creeper and in summer the front was entirely obscured by giant horse-chestnut trees which rose above the third storey. The fragrance of the lime trees in the garden was sufficiently intense to permeate the entire neighbourhood in the dampness of June evenings.

There was nothing pompous about this house, but it was the kind of place which had become too much for its owners. It patterned most of them and held them down, and no matter where any of them wanted to go, it usually managed to call them back. The Wain estates had passed regularly from father to son, each one's will containing the proviso that if the heir should marry a Roman Catholic the legacy was forfeit. The family was not rich by American standards, but by those of Nova Scotia it was opulent.

Penny got up restlessly and went out to the hall. She picked up her hat and coat where they had been dropped and started for the stairs. As she passed the full-length mirror hanging beside the marble-topped radiator her own reflection startled her. She *had* lost weight during the past six months! If she looked to others as fragile as she now appeared to herself, it was no wonder they never believed her capable of the sort of work she did. Automatically her hand went to her hair to try to hide some of the white lock, though she knew it was impossible to conceal it entirely.

Everything else about her seemed undramatically the same. Only this inward process of changing, this increased sense of her vulnerability! And if only her family knew it, the credit for her success did not belong to her at all. The entire idea of the design for the submarine-chaser had been outlined by her cousin Neil before the war. All she had done had been to work out his principles in detail, to check figures of construction costs and the weights of various alloys, to estimate the ratio of horsepower to tonnage, and merge such pedestrian details with her own knowledge of construction and with Neil's general plan. She felt sure that any other engineer could have done as much. The essential design, the conception of the long, wide-shouldered hull with the step in the keel just abaft the fore-quarter, had been contrived in fifteen careless minutes, years before. The pity of it was that Neil had forgotten it just as carelessly.

She reached her bedroom and began to undress. It was impossible to realize that within another six months a product of Neil's brain and her patience would be heaving a seasick crew through the chop of the North Sea. The step in the keel would prevent its bow from protruding out of the water when the vessel was at speed, but in spite of this, enormous sheets of water would be hurled over the nameless, oil-skinned men who manned her. It would convey to the vicinity of invisible Germans a pair of torpedo-tubes, a light, quick-firing cannon, and a considerable number of depth-charges. It would maintain itself away from port for a duration of four days and condemn its crew to cold rations only slightly mitigated by navy rum. It would be the most uncomfortable craft in the Royal Navy.

And yet originally it had merely been a problem in physics, an attempt to solve the dilemma of how to construct a motor boat which would travel fast and yet keep its stem in the water. The use to which such a craft might be put had probably never entered Neil's head. As she stretched out on her bed she decided that so far as she was concerned it would continue to be what it was now in her own mind, an abstraction, a monstrous abortion of an attempt to avoid thinking too deeply about matters she could not control. And then she fell asleep.

EIGHT O'CLOCK

Clocks began striking all over the house, and Penny opened her eyes and got up before the last of their reverberations had died away. She turned on the lights in her bedroom and sat before her dressing-table to brush out her hair. She worked slowly, allowing the automatic motions of her arms to circulate the blood and wake her gradually. Many minutes later she selected a dress and put it on, arranging the belt carefully, and then snapped off the lights and left the room.

On the way downstairs she met her twelve-year-old brother Roddie, who had slicked down his hair with water and wanted her to adjust the stud and tie to his Eton collar. Although it was the second of December, Roddie was wearing short trousers with his knees bare, for it was a matter of pride among the boys in his school to see how long they could go into the winter before covering their knees with knickerbockers.

"Did you hear about the submarine today?" Roddie asked, grimacing as she pressed the back of the stud against his throat.

"Come upstairs to the light." She went up the steps and he followed. "What submarine are you talking about?"

"There was a German submarine off the harbour this morning. Didn't you hear?"

"How do you know there was?" These wartime rumours irritated her, as Roddie dimly suspected. "Don't tell me you saw it from the Citadel!"

"Ouch, Penny, that hurts! Willie Moffat told me. His uncle was on the duty-boat and he saw it."

She squared away from him and studied the tie and collar carefully. His thumbs had made a smudge on one side of the collar, but it was too small to be noticeable. "If Willie Moffat's uncle was on the duty-boat you know perfectly well he didn't see a submarine. The duty-boat never leaves the harbour."

Roddie looked crestfallen, for he was proud of his knowledge of ship movements. Apart from his father, Penny was the hardest mortal he knew to convince of anything.

"Will there be anyone tonight but family?" he said.

"Major Murray will be here."

"Oh." His face assumed a serious expression and his forehead wrinkled. "Penny, *what* does Major Murray drink?"

"Hold still till I get this tie straight. I don't know what you're talking about."

"I heard Uncle Alfred say he drank something terrible."

She stood away and this time looked him in the eyes, but he answered the stare with a bland and innocent expression that was defeated by nothing but its own perfection.

"Roddie, you must be the champion liar of your class."

"But he did say that . . . honest, Penny."

"I'm quite sure he did. Honest, Roddie, and you didn't know what he meant, either."

"Well, does he?"

"You run along downstairs and try to keep your hands clean till supper. Your father may be late and you'll have to be the man of the house until he arrives. And don't stare when you greet Major Murray, either."

At a quarter to nine the doorbell rang, a prolonged jangling sound from the basement as half a dozen bells answered the puller by the front door. Before Penny could reach the hall, Alfred Wain and his wife Maria had let themselves in and were taking off their coats.

"'lo, Penelope," Alfred muttered absently. "Where's your father?"

"He's not back yet. How are both of you?"

"Not very good," Alfred said.

Aunt Maria's voice blared out like a trumpet. "Nonsense, there's nothing the matter with you. Penelope, why weren't you in church? There was a terrible sermon." She squinted at herself in the long mirror and patted the sides of her pompadour with a pair of powerful hands. "I ran into Mrs. Taylor this evening as we came out, that woman I was telling you about in the Red Cross. She's dreadful. People like that shouldn't be allowed to take part in the war."

Alfred was already on his way to the living-room, muttering as he went. "Geoffrey works too much. He's almost as bad as you, though I must say there's some sense to his job." He stood in front of the fire and rocked on his heels, while his hands, cupped behind his back, hoisted the tails of his jacket so that the hot fire could toast his buttocks. He was a gangling man with mutton-chop whiskers and a squeaky voice; he rarely did any work and his chief interest was the Presbyterian church in which he was an elder. There, twice a week and once at Wednesday prayer-meeting, he snored through sermons he later condemned, but he could estimate the collection value of any congregation to within half a dollar.

Aunt Maria stalked into the living-room and sat down in Geoffrey Wain's armchair, which she adequately filled. "Why is your father still working, Penelope?"

"I'm afraid that's one of the things I can't tell you, Aunt Maria."

"Nonsense, you mean you don't choose to. You're all the same. And look at Roddie. I wouldn't be surprised to see him turn out the worst of the lot."

There was a moment in which the room held no sound but the noise of Aunt Maria's breathing, which permeated it. She was a powerful woman with curly grey hair, ruddy cheeks, deep chest and a bosom that projected like a battlement. Although she was always dowdily dressed, nothing less than a crinoline could have concealed the contours of her thighs, which looked potent enough to appease a Hercules.

The clocks ticked noisily; there was a distant moan from the harbour buoys. Then Aunt Maria's voice broke out again. "Cecil has the grippe but Jim and Mary will be here. Who else is coming?"

"I've asked Major Angus Murray," Penny said.

"Who?" Her aunt stared. "Well, of all the things!"

"Eh?" said Alfred. "Who was that?"

"That man," Aunt Maria explained. "That Major Murray everyone knows about." She turned to Penny: "Is this your father's idea of a joke on us?"

"No." Penny got up from the arm of the chair where she had been sitting and moved toward the door. She hoped she had heard footsteps outside. "It was my idea," she said. "I thought he might enjoy it."

But instead of encountering Angus Murray she opened the door to her Aunt Mary and Jim Fraser. These were the two she called her only nice relations. Mary was the youngest of her father's sisters and was unlike anyone else in the Wain family. She was extremely thin and wiry, with quick and vivacious movements; greying hair surmounted a tawny, sun-browned forehead and she had the easy, reckless laugh of a woman who has spent a lifetime in moderate defiance of her environment. She greeted Penny with affection and slipped an arm about her waist, and the two women stood in the hall smiling at their reflections in the mirror while Jim Fraser bent to take off his rubbers.

Mary's warm voice was speaking eagerly in its clear, English-sounding Halifax accent. "It's simply marvellous news, darling! Jim told me about it this morning. Let's look at you properly. Let's hug you. I'm so proud I could burst."

Fraser straightened and grinned. "Here, Penny, got one for me?" He kissed her loudly. "Well, and what did your father say when you told him?"

"Nothing much."

"My God, what a family I married into! Isn't that like Geoffrey."

Penny stood aside from the living-room door to let them pass. "How's Jean today?" she said.

"Wonderful! We fairly had to tie that little brat or she'd have followed us. The way she's growing is almost indecent. When are you coming out to see her again?"

Penny followed them into the living-room. "I've been so busy lately. Each weekend I think the next few days will give us a let-up and they never seem to. But I'll get out this week somehow, I promise."

Alfred Wain greeted them with a melancholy squeak from the hearth. "I never could see why you and Jim want to live at Prince's Lodge. You might as well be at the back of beyond as out there. We've always lived in town."

Jim Fraser, his face a walnut-brown from years on the South African veldt, looking tough and rugged behind a handle-bar moustache, greeted his in-laws and dropped into the nearest comfortable chair. "No, Alfred, I'm damn sure you don't see why we prefer to live out there. There's so much you say you don't understand that sometimes I think you're lucky."

Aunt Maria, disregarding his remark, invaded the conversation. "Did Penny tell you who she's asked here tonight? Major Murray! That man who used to ruin his practice with drink wherever he went."

"Angus Murray?" Jim grinned and looked at Penny in surprise. "I didn't know you knew him. I haven't seen Angus in years. Wasn't he in Geoffrey's regiment?"

"What's that got to do with his coming here?" Aunt Maria said. "I'd like to hear what Geoffrey says when he sees him. I'd like to hear that very much."

Penny might have been listening to empty compliments for all the evidence she gave of minding these remarks. It seemed to her that her relatives had been talking about different sides of the same thing for the last twenty years. "Major Murray's right arm is in a sling," she said. "You should adore him, Aunt Maria. He nearly lost his arm in the service of his country." The bells jangled again and she rose to answer them. "Now for heaven's sake don't stare when he comes in. Roddie's already promised not to."

When she had left the room, Alfred Wain shifted his feet and his face slowly assumed an expression of uneasiness. Jim looked at him in open amusement, for he always enjoyed the spectacle of his brother-in-law endeavouring to think.

"That young woman's too sure of herself," Alfred said finally. Mary broke out impatiently, "Don't be such an old fool! After what she's done all you can think of is to complain because she knows her own mind."

"Stuff!" said Alfred. "She should be ashamed of herself."

Then the room was silent until Penny returned with Angus Murray at her heels. Jim Fraser rose to welcome him and the women looked expectant, but the only part of Alfred which moved was his head. It craned sideways as though its mechanism had no connection with the rest of his body and the worried expression on his face deepened.

In spite of his uniform Murray looked disreputable. He entered shyly, like a long-legged, alien dog in a strange place, his head held slightly on one side. His thinning hair stuck out from the back of his scalp in a short tuft, his tunic had one button hanging by a thread and his trousers palpably had been slept in. His right hand was splinted and swathed in bandages and a sling of black silk hung from his shoulder like a bandoleer.

He bowed to the room, and Aunt Maria broke the momentary silence. "Major, *do* tell us about your work?"

It was a command, and Murray blinked. He tapped his twisted nose with the knuckles of his left hand and under the loose tunic his shoulders were seen to shift uneasily. Then his gaunt face broke into a grin and he glanced at his wounded arm.

"I don't work," he said.

Aunt Maria bulged forward from the armchair. "Of course you don't now. I mean France. I mean the war."

"Oh, that!" Murray's voice was slow and markedly soft, lilting with an overtone of native Gaelic. "That was just one unpleasant job after the other, and the conditions of work were very poor." Seeing Alfred Wain staring at him with the dumb look of an Aberdeen terrier, he added, "The average war wound presents few interesting problems, medically speaking. Unless you're a plastic surgeon, there's not much to be learned."

"But you must have operated on all sorts of people we know," Aunt Maria said. "After all, you were in my brother-in-law's battalion. Or weren't you?"

"Indeed I was, Mrs. Wain. But you know, I can't remember that any of the boys in the dressing station mentioned you. They were usually pretty tired when the stretcher-bearers brought them in."

Penny looked at the clock and the rest looked at their shoes. Then the front door was heard opening and Colonel Wain's step was audible in the hall. Under the weight of his projected presence, their immediate tongue-tied condition was exempted from embarrassment.

When Geoffrey Wain entered the room his presence tightened the atmosphere. He was a tall, broad-shouldered man in his middle fifties. He held himself straight and looked as though he had worn a colonel's uniform all his life. He nodded toward his relatives, hesitated a second as he recognized Murray, then crossed the floor and greeted him with cordiality.

"You weren't in church tonight," Alfred said.

Geoffrey ignored the remark and shook Murray's left hand. "This is a pleasant surprise, Major. I hadn't been aware that you people knew one another. Now that my daughter's a professional woman she's always surprising us. Quite pleasantly, I may say."

Wain's smile showed a row of large white teeth. The effect of it was brilliant rather than pleasant, and something in its quality took Murray aback. He mumbled incoherently, and cleared his throat as he responded to his former chief.

"I heard about your arm," Wain continued easily. "I was told you'd lost it. It's good to know the report was exaggerated."

"It nearly wasn't," Murray said. "Some of my colleagues advised amputation. I had to battle hard to save it."

"You seem to have made a good diagnosis. As usual, if you don't mind a layman saying so. Might I ask when you were wounded?"

"Last June at Lens. Shrapnel splinter just below the elbow. My hand got peppered too."

Sadie entered to say that supper was ready, and no one waited for Penny to lead the way to the dining-room but her father, who continued to look into the fire and talk to Murray as though he had heard nothing. There was something in the man not even his most intimate associates had ever been able to calculate, a discrepancy between the sense of ruthless and indifferent power he radiated and the mediocre record of his achievement. Everything about Geoffrey Wain looked strong, yet his life had been soft and his habits easy. He was broad and burly where his brother Alfred was scrawny. The lines of his face were deeply cut and the flesh between them hard with muscle. His hands were abnormally large, with thick knuckles and a powder of dark hair between the joints. The hair on his head was cropped close, revealing the outline of an evenly moulded skull, and the hair being of a uniform shade of silver, it contrasted oddly with his moustache, which was still black. Everything in his manner indicated an ambitious man confident of his own ability. Yet up to the present neither the ability nor the force with which he had been born had been put to much evident use.

For Murray, the hour spent at the supper table was a dreary experience. It was dominated almost entirely by Aunt Maria, and Penny's efforts to improve the conversation were stillborn. They finally returned to the living-room and it was a relief to be able to smoke. Sadie brought in coffee and Penny sat behind a small table to serve it. Colonel Wain passed around cigars and was complimented on their quality, and Murray had resigned himself to another futile hour of desultory talk when he suddenly realized that the atmosphere of the room had changed. They were discussing Penny's successful design, and Jim Fraser was arguing vehemently with his sister-in-law.

"Can't you people get it into your heads that Penny's not working at the Shipyards just for amusement? To hear you talk, a man would think her work was nothing better than knitting socks for the Red Cross. That craft of Penny's is a revolutionary design."

"Revolution?" Alfred flushed and stuttered. "Stuff!"

Fraser's voice rose. "That's the trouble with everyone around here. This is supposed to be a new country, and half the population —"

Alfred assumed the self-righteous expression of one about to be persecuted for his principles, and sighed heavily. "Yes, I suppose it's a crime nowadays not to believe that the newer a thing is, the better it is."

"Oh, for God's sake, it's not a matter of Penny's work being new. It's a matter of its being good."

"But who says it's good?" Alfred pulled at his whiskers.

Geoffrey Wain's voice, indifferently courteous, interrupted. "I'm under the impression that the British Admiralty believes it's good, Alfred. Do you find it necessary to be shocked at that?"

Mary got up impatiently and handed her empty cup to Penny to be refilled. She seemed to be trying to discover something to say and her mouth opened several times, but no audible sounds issued.

"If it will make anyone feel better," Penny said with the trace of a smile as she filled Mary's cup, "I don't deserve credit for the wretched thing. The whole idea for the design was Neil's."

It was as though she had said something indecent. Murray found himself sitting on the edge of his chair, bracing himself.

He was aware that irritation had developed into an emotion deeper than anger behind the faces he watched. At the mention of this name, Aunt Maria had flushed and Alfred was drumming his fingers together. Fraser looked at his shoes and Mary at the light flush on Penny's cheeks. The colonel's expression had not altered, though his emotions obviously required control.

Then Aunt Maria exploded. "Penelope – you don't know what you're saying! Even if you did, you have no right to mention his name in this house." The varicose veins in her face seemed to spread themselves. "Wasn't it enough that he disgraced the whole family without your —"

"Maria . . ." Geoffrey Wain got to his feet and looked straight at his sister-in-law. . . . "For Major Murray's benefit, don't you think you might spare our feelings on the subject? He doesn't even know that you happen to be talking about my nephew, Neil Macrae. I believe the major knew him personally. As for Penny's statement – Neil ought to have been able to design a good ship. We could never interest him in doing anything else."

He pivoted about and addressed Murray; as he did so, his action and manner seemed to exclude everyone else in the room. "By the way, Murray, do you still have a palate for port?"

"I'm supposed to like it."

"Then come along to the library with me. I'm sure the others will excuse us. Jim, would you care to join us?"

Fraser shook his head tactfully, and the colonel led Murray to the library, closed the door behind them and took two glasses and a bottle of old tawny from the cupboard of a side-table. He poured a little into a glass and sniffed it, then filled both glasses and held them quizzically to the light.

"There is at least one advantage in the shipping business," he said. "One can get good port and good cigars. I think you'll like this. It's very dry. It's almost an Amontillado, in my opinion."

"I wouldn't know the difference," Murray said.

He took the glass Wain offered and sat down, stretching his legs. Wain sat opposite, in a long leather-covered chair on the other side of the hearth. They sipped the wine in silence, and each held his glass once more to the light to savour its colour.

"You must find it pretty dull back here?" Wain said.

"If I had a job it wouldn't be so bad."

Murray went on to explain that he was always pleased to return to Nova Scotia, even though he had never wished to live in the province permanently. Halifax was a city which offered more than met the eye, and there were wonderful places to walk in the near vicinity. He had derived a great deal of pleasure from studying various sections of the city which seemed to him to be homogeneous. One section about a mile long and two streets wide was mostly Irish. In the North End there were districts peopled largely by descendants of English garrison soldiers. He had discovered one street where every inhabitant was a Newfoundlander.

Wain smiled. "I'm afraid I take it all for granted. Really, Halifax is a pretty hopeless place. It has a harbour. It used to have a good university. You don't intend to stay here indefinitely, do you?"

"I've given up making plans, for the duration." Murray gave one of his sudden, shy smiles. "You seem busy enough?"

"A clerk's job," Wain said. "Transportation officer, they call it?"

"I should think that was fairly responsible."

"Some people tell me it is. I still do a fair amount of work at my own business. I shouldn't regret that, but it's not what an officer on active service ought to be doing."

"If the generals had any sense," Murray said, "the war would be over now. At least they could reduce casualties. All they need do is sit tight and wait for the Germans to have a revolution."

"So you think that would solve it, eh?" Wain smiled and drew on his cigar. "No, an outright military victory is essential and it's going to take a long time. Three years, perhaps. Besides, a German revolution isn't desirable. We don't want the rag, tag and bobtail at a peace conference." He studied the smoke circling from his cigar. "Tell me, Murray – what impressed you most in France?"

"The general cowardice of everybody."

"You knew my nephew, of course . . . the one they were just talking about?"

"I wasn't thinking of Macrae when I said that."

"I didn't presume you were. You mean, I suppose, that if the generals had any courage they'd call the whole thing off and admit the war is beyond them? Or that the men would show some spirit? Leave their trenches the way the Russians have done?"

"Something like that," Murray said, watching Wain closely. "I was merely thinking it, not suggesting it."

Wain looked reflective and laid down his cigar while he refilled Murray's empty glass. "There's something in that idea of yours," he said, "though if it ever happens I wouldn't call it an act of courage. The Russian revolution was the last act of a panic-stricken horde. I'm afraid I don't believe the ordinary man is capable of real courage. He's afraid all the time, particularly of his neighbour's opinion. That's the main thing that gets him into the army and keeps him there. When another sort of fear becomes stronger than that one, he panics. I fancy we both know it to be true."

"Frankly," Murray said, "I haven't enough experience of armies to be able to agree with you."

Wain surveyed Murray candidly. "You said you knew my nephew, Neil Macrae. Tell me, what was your opinion of that affair?"

Murray became acutely uncomfortable; he detected an urgency behind Wain's urbanity. What the cause of it was he had no idea.

"If you don't mind," he said, "I'd rather not talk about Neil Macrae. I only knew him casually and he seemed a good fellow. The night he was killed I was busy in a dressing-station. I merely heard the next day that he had been blown to pieces."

"You knew, of course, that he was under guard at the time?"

"I was told so."

Wain seemed disappointed at Murray's unresponsiveness, but he concealed his disappointment almost perfectly. "His arrest was not a particularly pleasant decision for me to have to make," he said. "Now that both of us are out of the battalion I'd like to take the opportunity of saying so to a brother officer. There is no doubt whatever that his flagrant disobedience of my orders in the middle of the attack the day before he was killed was responsible for the failure of the operation. It was perhaps as well that shell found him. A court-martial would have been extremely painful to us all, for it would have been my duty to appear as chief witness against him."

Murray drained off his second glass and rose to his feet. Wain did likewise and the two men looked at each other.

"Your daughter," Murray said slowly, "seems to have a high opinion of his work."

"Yes, it's a great pity about that boy. He had real ability but he was always too unstable to make it count. If it hadn't been for the war he might have outgrown his impetuosity, but . . . he grew up in this house, you know. He was virtually Penelope's brother."

When they reached the living-room they could hear the high voice of Alfred Wain explaining an invention which was going to end the war by next March. It was a secret, he insisted, but he had heard about it confidentially from an itinerant British staff-officer in Toronto.

"Maybe it's Penny's ship," Fraser said, and rose with a glance at the clock. "We'll have to be on our way, Mary. It's ten-thirty."

The whole company rose, and to Murray's surprise, the colonel said he must leave also. As they moved toward the door Penelope slipped her arm through Murray's and whispered, "Please stay a bit."

Murray hesitated and Geoffrey Wain, as though he had overheard Penny's remark, said, "Stay and have some more port, Murray. Unfortunately I must work. The *Olympic* always keeps me busy."

"The *Olympic*?" Murray's eyebrows rose. "She only arrived yesterday."

"So did about a dozen troop trains. Passchendaele is still going on, and the generals are hungry. I'll hope to see you again before long. Good night."

Murray waited in the armchair quitted by Aunt Maria until Penny had seen the others away. Now that the room was empty, he was forced to admit that it fascinated him. The Wain house represented an aspect of Nova Scotia he had formerly seen only from the outside, for he had been born in a farmhouse in Cape Breton. The people in his district were plain and rugged, and they compensated for their poverty by pride and the hope of emigration; and because few of their ancestors from the Highlands had owned property of any sort, few of them had any sense of it. Murray's eyes wandered from the map of Jamaica to the rest of the room. The tables were heavy mahogany and the curtains the colour of ox-blood; there were four models of sailing ships, all reproductions of famous Nova Scotiamen which had once been laded at the Wain wharf. It did not seem to Murray a gracious room, yet there was something proper and fitting about it, and it had dignity. There were no late-Victorian frills. At this moment in its silence he could hear the rhythmic pulsating of the fog signals coming in from the harbour which had given this old house its reason for life.

Finally the outer door closed, and Penny returned to the room and curled herself on the chesterfield opposite the fire.

She looked at him and smiled. "Poor Angus – I'm afraid I've given you a pretty bad evening!"

"At least it's been different from my usual run." He took a deep breath. "No wonder this house has such high ceilings. A good many cubic feet of air are necessary in it."

"Want something to drink?"

"Yes, but not this minute."

He kept his eyes on hers until she looked away, and then they were silent, feeling the comfort of each other's presence and finding speech unnecessary. The room was alive. The periodic moaning of the fog-signals continued to throb through it; there were low vibrations from a steamer's horn and the faint, almost inaudible whine of a locomotive whistle. Mysteriously, all these sounds were creeping in through the crannies of the old house, reminding Murray of eerie noises he had sometimes heard on silent nights on the western front, when the rumble of transport was audible from behind the enemy's lines.

Penny was staring into the fire, and her abstraction made it easier for him to observe her with the detachment he desired. To appraise women, to study their figures and estimate how the planes and curves of their bodies would balance when revealed, had always seemed to him a delightful manner of passing the time. It pleased him particularly to consider shy or diffident girls in this way, for he believed that any sensitive woman had enormous potentialities of pleasure within herself, and the prospects of awakening them never failed to stir his imagination.

"What's going on behind that funny smile?" Penny said suddenly.

"I was thinking about you."

"Oh, Angus – I'd expected a better reply than that."

"If you could see the shape of my thoughts you'd probably think the reply adequate enough. Penny, I suppose you're the most brilliant woman in Canada. That's very nice, but it inhibits me. It's not easy to tell a genius she's adorable."

"It must be awkward." She slipped her legs off the chester-field. "I'll get you a drink. You could probably use something stronger than port."

When she returned she held a decanter in her left hand and a crystal tumbler in her right, but before she could set them down, a bell jangled again. "Here," she said. "Fix it yourself. Apparently I'm on doorbell duty tonight."

He heard a murmur of voices in the hall, and then the sound of feet running upstairs. He filled the glass and sat down. A cold draft of air crawled along the floor from the opened door and with it came the louder sound of the bells ringing in the harbour. The creeping noises of this old town never ceased; for as long as there were wars and she remained the terminus of the longest railway in the world, her back to the continent and her face to the Old Country, she would lie here in all weathers unchangeably the same, and her bells would ring in the darkness.

Leaning back in his chair, warmed by the fire and the whisky, Murray wondered why he felt moved by the thought. The long failure of his life, the inability to alter the nature with which he had been born, had made him a fatalist against all his wishes. And Halifax, more than most towns, seemed governed by a fate she neither made nor understood, for it was her birthright to serve the English in time of war and to sleep neglected when there was peace. It was a bondage Halifax had no thought of escaping because it was the only life she had ever known; but to Murray this seemed a pity, for the town figured more largely in the calamities of the British Empire than in its prosperities, and never seemed able to become truly North American.

Penny's feet sounded on the stairs again, the outer door closed and she returned to the room and her place on the chesterfield.

"Who was that, the police?"

"How did you guess?" Penny smiled. "A light was showing in Roddie's bedroom. He'd turned it on to read with the windows open and shut it off when he heard me coming. What a youngster! He'll always be able to look after himself. He'll never starve when he grows up, but I wish I didn't worry so much about other sides of his make-up."

Murray rose and prowled about the room before settling finally on the chesterfield beside her. She made no movement when the fingers of his good hand slipped about the soft flesh of her inner arm and caressed the skin where the tracery of the veins was visible. The expression on his haggard face, usually strained and ironic, had softened and now his eyes appeared larger.

"Penny – are you as lonely as I am?"

There was an instant's flash of fear in her eyes as she turned to him. "I don't know." Her body seemed to tighten to defend itself. Murray continued to look at her and to caress her inner arm; his manner was candid and there were no overtones of drama. "We're both mature people, Penny. Even if I *am* eighteen years too old for you." He hesitated. "Surely you know what I mean?"

She nodded, and her arm was still under his fingers.

"You probably know I was married before? An American girl. She was much younger than you when she died. The strange thing is, I remember her only as she used to be and myself as I used to be when we were together. I'd be a shock to her now, if she could – I shouldn't be running on like this. I'm sorry."

"Please, Angus – it's all right."

"I married her when I was still in medical school and she died when I was just getting on my feet. I used to blame her death for all those years" – his face twisted as though shrinking from his own words – "those years of drinking and moving around in the States and letting everything slide. But I was wrong to blame anything but myself. It was only a bad habit, letting an old sorrow dominate my whole existence. I found that out in France. Death suddenly seemed unimportant and life seemed everything." He got abruptly to his feet. "Penny, I don't know whether you give a hoot in hell for me, but I do know it's no good either of us going on as we are."

"Do you think I'm doing so badly, then?"

Again there was the flash of fear in her eyes. He returned to the chesterfield.

"I don't know, Penny. Are you?"

"I have my own work, and I like it."

"I had my work, too, and liked it." He shook his head. "No, it doesn't sound convincing. With a body like yours, with that look I see in your face sometimes – no." He got up once again and stared at the map of Jamaica, leaning his elbow on the fireplace. "You could still have your work. With me on your hands you'd probably need it. Penny, I'm trying to tell you I want you to marry me."

A grandfather's clock sounded from the back hall, striking eleven. It was followed by the other clocks in the house, and during the length of their striking Murray remained motionless with his back to the room. When the last note died away he was aware that Penny was beside him and that her arm was slipping about his waist, and his eyes blinked through moisture so that all he could think of was the poignancy of that slim lock of white hair lacing the brown of her head.

"That's the nicest thing anyone has said to me in years," she whispered.

He drew himself away. "Never mind," he said, "I've always been noted for my nerve."

With a quick impulse she put her arms about his neck and kissed him, but his lips let her go almost at once. She returned to the chesterfield and stared beyond him into the fire.

"I didn't mean it the way you think," she said. "I'd rather not dismiss it like this, Angus."

He kicked a falling log back across the andirons. "Yes, Penny?"

"You don't really know me," she said. "If you did . . ."

"I've always estimated myself high as a judge of women. I admit I didn't know how good you were at your job, but that's got nothing to do with your being a woman."

He began to walk about and ended finally in front of the whisky decanter, poured himself a short drink and downed it.

"I'm afraid you don't even know so much about me as a woman, Angus." She smiled at him. "I don't mean that to sound nasty."

He looked at her over the rim of his glass, and his eyes suddenly changed expression as a new idea struck him. "You're not in love with someone else, are you?" He smiled then and cleared his throat.

Seeing that his sense of humour had returned she held out a hand. "Come on back here and sit down. I'll tell you *my* story."

"As you like," he said.

"Would you rather I didn't? I've never tried talking about myself to anyone yet."

Murray sat down in silence, watching her. Then he bent and kissed her gently, tilting her head back with the fingers of his right hand. She answered his gaze and his kiss calmly, and to Murray her manner seemed the only answer he required. He settled back into the far end of the chesterfield and slowly lit a cigarette. "You were in love with your cousin, Neil Macrae . . ." His voice had a delicacy of tone which surprised her. "If you like, you can go on from there."

She waited, looking at her own hands lying in her lap, and the only sound was the fire crackling as another log broke in two. She breathed deeply, and there was a tiny flutter under the skin of her throat. "Yes," she said, "you *are* a good judge of women, Angus."

He made no comment.

"Did you know him well?" she asked.

"Not very. We were both in your father's battalion, of course. But the M.O. in any outfit is in an odd position. I certainly had little time or chance to get acquainted with the younger men."

"Father spoke to you about him tonight, of course?"

Murray looked startled. "Yes," he admitted.

"Was Neil really killed in action?"

He sensed an undertone of apprehension, a state of mind which was not far short of horror. "What the devil do you mean?" he said.

"Father hated him. I think he hated him from the time he was born."

"But —"

"Since Father's return from France I've heard nothing but hints and whispers about Neil. The whole town's heard them, and you must know it. Father never mentions it outright, but it's hardly an accident that everyone thinks Neil would have been shot for cowardice if he had lived and that Father's discharge from active service was Neil's fault."

"Your father wasn't discharged. He was transferred."

Penny smiled bitterly. "Never mind, we both know about that kind of transfer. You haven't answered my question." Her voice took on an urgency that seemed dreadful because it was so unusual in her. "Please tell me – was Neil really killed in action?"

"Penny!" Murray's voice rose and assumed authority. "In this war no one can afford an excessive imagination. If a man's killed, it's a recorded fact. If he's missing, that's recorded too. Mistakes are possible, but they're not probable."

Her hand swept suddenly upward over her hair and she rose from the chesterfield. "It would be as easy to believe I were dead myself."

Murray took both her hands in his and waited until she met his eyes. Even through deep-sprung emotion she seemed able to keep intact her dignity and her power to grasp facts. "I mightn't be so silly," she said, "if someone would tell me what happened that day they say he was killed. Will you?"

Murray eyed the burning end of his cigarette.

"In the first place," he said deliberately, "I only know the story secondhand. Your cousin was put under guard for disobeying an order of your father's in the middle of an attack. He was killed a few hours later in the German counter-bombardment."

"The attack, of course, was a total failure?"

"I rarely saw one that wasn't, in 1915."

"But Father was blamed for it? He was colonel and was sent home to a place where he could do no more harm?"

Murray shrugged and tapped his twisted nose. "I don't know why you're so obsessed with that angle of the case, Penny."

She leaned on the mantel, her cheek resting on her hand, her eyes staring into the fire. "All right, please go on."

"Perhaps I ought to add that your father lost touch with his battalion for several hours that day." She turned quickly to face him, but he continued before she could interrupt. "That's a thing that might have happened to anybody. Don't make too much of it."

"What did Neil have to do with this attack?"

"Well, the colonel had to send up his orders by runner. I think your cousin was the first front-line officer the runner encountered. He may well have been senior officer on the spot, for all the company commanders had been killed in the initial attack and even the adjutant was wounded."

"And then – according to my father – Neil disobeyed that order?"

"Perhaps." Murray's forehead wrinkled and he puffed hard on his cigarette. "Maybe he misunderstood it. Or perhaps it was an impossible order to carry out."

"I don't believe that Neil was afraid. He might have felt fear but I don't believe he could ever have been incapacitated by fear. Either he or my father was wrong. And my father made him responsible."

"Now, Penny" – Murray was beginning to show signs of discomfort – "if I were you I wouldn't put it that way. There are no drum-head court-martials in the British army. All orders are given in writing, and if the boy had obeyed – well, all he'd have had to do in any case was to produce the written order. But no court was held, of course."

Misery clouded Penny's face and Murray stopped talking. Yet, when she finally spoke, her voice was so calm and controlled that the expression on her face seemed an accident, or a trick of the light which fell across it.

"Thank you, Angus. For two years my family has been insinuating that if Neil had faced a court-martial he'd have been shot. In that event, presumably, Father's military career would have marched gloriously on, and he'd not be in Halifax now. They don't mean to persecute me, but that's what they'll never allow me to forget. If Neil had been convicted before he was killed, Father would have been freed of all official responsibility for the failure."

"That's stinking rotten."

Murray stubbed out his cigarette and got to his feet. He felt tired and there were sudden twinges of pain in his bad arm. "Penny, if that's how you feel – get away from here!"

"And leave Roddie to them?"

Murray made a gesture of hopelessness with his shoulders and turned away. He realized that he was no longer young, and that at forty-seven there was no resiliency left in him. Penny continued to talk, and as he listened it seemed unnatural that a girl could carry about such a burden in her mind and still look no older than twenty-nine.

"Neil had such a rotten time in this family," she said. "His mother died when he was born – she was my Aunt Jamsie. And his father could never fit into this menagerie, so he stayed away from us as much as he could. I still remember Uncle John's place where he used to build yachts. When Neil and I were small we used to go there in the summers."

"John Macrae?" Murray looked thoughtful. "He was from Cape Breton, wasn't he? Came from one of the villages? How on earth did he ever meet your father's sister? That's one of the oddest matches I ever heard of."

"That's what my family thought. He met Aunt Jamsie when he was building that yawl Father still owns. I suppose he seemed new and different to her. And with her background she probably seemed glamorous to him."

"Yes," said Murray, "I can understand that. What about Neil? I gather he became a designer, too?"

"Neil was quite out of the ordinary." Penny was trying to be dispassionate, but she was not able to keep the warmth from her voice. "I suppose it's an accident when a woman loves a man and still is able to estimate his work professionally. Neil had that extra something that all the diligence in the world can't make up for."

"But what did your father have against him? It doesn't make sense."

"Father's a peculiar person. You see, Aunt Jamsie was his favourite sister. He loathed John Macrae for marrying into his family and when Aunt Jamsie died – I don't know how to put it. He'd never say anything openly, but he resented Neil. You'd almost think he held Neil responsible for Aunt Jamsie's death."

"But surely John Macrae —"

"Uncle John died when Neil was ten."

"I see."

"Then there was nothing except for Neil to come to us. It's not that Father neglected him. He sent him away to school in Montreal. He wanted him to study law. Father's funny that way. At least he's generous with money."

"What about Neil himself? Did he dislike your father?"

"He could hardly help it. When he left school he left our house, too, and then he only came back on vacations sometimes. He tried several jobs and finally won a scholarship at M.I.T. Then the war broke out and he came back to enlist."

Murray did not attempt to say anything, and for several moments there was silence between them. The fire was smouldering low, and he got up to set more wood across the irons and work on the coals with a bellows. Then he resumed his place on the chesterfield and took his right arm out of its sling and spread the fingers gingerly out along his thigh, manipulating their joints slowly.

"If this war lasts as long as your father thinks it will," he said, "this old hand of mine may see service again."

With an impulsive movement that tossed her hair she leaned against him and her arms went about his neck. He felt the firm outline of her shoulders and her chest tensely strained as she pressed herself against him, and then he was aware that she was quivering and that her cheeks were wet.

"Poor Penny!" He took out a clean handkerchief and awkwardly wiped her cheeks. "There now – it's better, now you've talked it out."

Under the pressure of emotion the soft cadence of his native Gaelic had returned to his voice, and the extreme tenderness of this disappointed, embittered man touched her.

"You're very good to me," she whispered. "I don't know why." She stopped crying and wiped her eyes. Finally she got to her feet and smiled, looking shy and daintily awkward like a young colt. "I ought to know better than this."

Murray felt so tired he could hardly make his legs respond to his will to stand. "If you'll let me," he said, "I'm going to keep on coming around to see you. But now – if you don't mind, I think I'll call myself a taxi."

Monday

T HE STALE, sour smell of the telephone booth bit into his nostrils when he closed himself inside. He thumbed through the telephone book and then called a number. A luxurious feeling of relief passed over him when the impersonal voice of someone who could not see him answered the call. "Military hospital," it said. "What division, please?"

"I don't exactly know," he replied. "I want to locate a man who returned from France a year ago and has probably been discharged. I thought he might have been treated by you. Corporal Alec MacKenzie."

"It may take a while to go through our records. Who's speaking, please?"

"That's not important. I'm a friend of his from over there."

"Hold the line."

There was a wait of several minutes and the receiver at the hospital end caught and transmitted the distorted sounds of people moving in long corridors, of shuffling feet, of nurses and orderlies making enquiries at the desk. He could almost smell carbolic acid.

Then the voice spoke again. "There are three Alec MacKenzies on the lists we have, two privates and a lieutenant. What was the battalion?"

He gave the numeral.

"None of these men were connected with that unit. Are you sure he was registered here?"

"I thought he might be."

"You'd better try the other hospitals. If you don't get anything from them, call the Y.M.C.A. If he's still in uniform all you need do is mail a letter to him, with his battalion number."

"Thanks."

He heard the receiver click, hung up his own and left the booth. He was trembling and his shirt was moist with sweat. His wounded leg ached, yet he felt an immediate desire to run, to move rapidly in any direction in order to feel the motion of his body and escape the throng of pedestrians from which Barrington Street would never be free. The sidewalk ought to be widened, if Haligonians could find nothing better to do than walk up and down this street.

The Parade, a pre-Victorian square fenced in by a stone wall with the City Hall at the end, was opposite the drug store from which he had phoned. He remembered there were benches in it and not too many loafers at this hour in the morning. When he had found an empty bench, he opened his copy of the *Morning Chronicle* and hid behind its pages while he read about how good the spirits of the boys were after Passchendaele.

"For God's sake – Macrae!"

There was no chance of getting away. A man his own age, wearing the uniform of a sub-lieutenant of the navy, was standing by the far end of the bench when he turned around, and as his brain raced with subterfuges he suddenly felt a thrill of elation and then he became calculating. The fellow did not belong to Halifax. Where had they met? A hockey team – that was it, they had been at school together. Years ago, in Montreal.

"Charley Baxter!" He shook hands as though Baxter were the one man he had come home to see. "What are you doing here?"

"Waiting around. I'm due to sail for England any time soon." Baxter shook his head and grinned. "What a chance meeting you here! I could hardly believe it was really you sitting there."

Neil sat down and fumbled to get out some cigarettes, hoping that if Baxter smoked one of his he would also light them both. His hands were trembling even after the smoke reached his lungs, and he dared not risk anyone seeing how they shook. With exaggerated deliberation he clasped them behind his head and leaned back on the bench. But his face felt unprotected against the other man's eyes. The strange thing was that during the past two years his voice had rarely gone out of control; at most for only a few seconds. It was always his hands that bothered him most.

"How's everything in Montreal?" Neil said.

"I don't know," Baxter replied. "Same, I guess. What have you been doing with yourself? I'd have thought you'd have had a permanent job in the Dockyard, the way you used to be keen about ships."

"No, I was in France. Demobbed now, of course. Got hit quite a while ago, back in '15. So you're going to England? Getting a berth in the Royal Navy?"

"Minesweepers, I guess. They have a few around here, but, hell – what's the use of sticking on this side? All you see of the war is bad weather and when you get ashore there's nothing but Halifax to look at."

"Don't know many people, then?"

"Hardly anyone. Old women around the canteens wanting to mother the boys – you know the sort of thing. If I'd known you were here I'd have cashed in on it. You must know all the girls in town."

Neil shook his head. "I haven't lived in Halifax for years. Sorry I can't help you. It's a tough town to find the right sort of girl. They're all one thing or they're all the other. Well, I don't have to worry about that. I'm leaving for Toronto. It's not much better so far as girls go, but it's got better jobs."

Baxter eyed the shabby clothes, the worn shoes and the sharply lined face and wondered. Once they had been in the same class. Once Neil had been one of the natural leaders in the school. He looked at him now and felt uneasy, as though his old friend were a symbol of something ominous.

"So you don't know many people around here?" Neil watched him coolly, his hands still clasped behind his head.

"I thought I'd already told you that."

Now that Neil was sure this meeting with Baxter could make no difference, he became almost reckless in his desire to escape. He got hastily to his feet and put his hands in the pockets of his worn overcoat. "It's damn cold, don't you think? I'd better get along." He held out his hand abruptly. "It was great seeing you, Charley."

Baxter's face showed palpable bewilderment, but he rose automatically and shook hands. "I hope everything goes all right for you in Toronto. Most of the boys are in the army now, but I tell you what – write the Head in Montreal and get a few addresses from him."

"That's a fine idea." He hesitated. "Well, so long, Charley."

He walked quickly with his head bent and his shoulders hunched, and it was not until he was on Barrington Street with the stone wall between himself and further recognition that he relaxed and realized that his shirt was dripping wet once more. His mind was blank and he could think of nothing except a desire to get some place where he would not have to talk again.

He turned the first corner and walked down the hill, and stopped only when he reached Water Street, where the pavement was cobbled and he could smell the docks and see the funnels and spars of the ships. He began to remember Montreal, seeing fragments of it so clearly he might still have been there. It was a Saturday, cold and dry on a winter morning with Mount Royal snow-covered and bulging against a glittering sky. The hockey team was off for the Bishop's game. Then the sheet of ice in the Coliseum, Charley Baxter on the right wing and himself on the left, skates ringing and the puck banging against the boards and the Head standing still as a stork, his long neck gangling over the players' bench. Afterward, lunch in the school hall, its walls lined with the heads of moose and buffalo, and Charley and he trying to get permission from the housemaster to go out that night and watch Canadiens play Ottawa. And then it was night and the trams were jammed along Ste. Catherine Street and the ice on the rink was frozen like grey-yellow oil under the lights and thousands of French-Canadians in the rush-end were shouting, and Vezina in the nets moved easily, loose and slow and then quick like a cat, blinking sleepily every time he kicked a puck away.

"Excuse me —" He snapped around. "'Ave you got a match, guv'nor?"

"Sure." He handed the man several, hesitated, then asked, "You off a ship?"

"Not bloody likely I ain't." He puffed the fire of the match down into his pipe. "Know where a bloke can get a drink around 'ere?"

"There used to be plenty of places right on this street. I haven't been around lately, though."

"It's 'ard," the man began to move off, "to get a bloody thing in this blasted town."

This time there had been no prickly feeling at meeting another human being. The man was too obviously a stranger. A wind began to suck its way down the corridor of the street, baffling slightly but cold and northerly, and his coat was too thin for it. He wished it were spring. But the trouble was that Canada had no proper spring; that season was always skipped when winter leaped right into summer. One week there would be snow-flurries and then, toward the end of May, it would be blazing summer with the leaves unfurling on the trees, and the blackflies chewing your ears off when you went fishing on the Queen's Birthday, and walks with girls in the long warm twilights, and whisperings after dark.

These thoughts and these emotions made no sense. Here in Nova Scotia, right here in sight of docks and shipyards and seamen, he felt rooted and at home. Yet it had been in Montreal that all the good things had happened. There were no fine memories to hold him here, nothing of beauty that had ever been his own; in fact nothing at all but instinct.

A girl came out of a shipping office and crossed the street, walking ahead of him. Her neat, long legs and slim waist made him hungry. He quickened his pace and passed her, glancing sideways. The face was disappointing, for she had a nose like a bird and her lips were thin and mean. A waste, he thought, a waste of a lot of things.

Once he had known dozens of girls in Halifax, but now he had forgotten the names of most of them and their faces and figures were blurred in his memory. Montreal seemed easier to recall. This time it was June. A heat-haze was clamped down over the St. Lawrence valley and the streets shimmered and the leaves were warm and heavy on the trees. He had just been told his transport was to leave the next day; only twenty hours left when he had counted on another week. He had gone out on the crowded tram to Notre-Dame-de-Grâce where she was living with Jim and Mary Fraser, and for the rest of the afternoon they had walked through the humid and sweltering air under the trees on the summit of Mount Royal, seeing the city spread beneath them like a map and the blurred bow of the river curving out from the Lachine Rapids to the thin web of Victoria Bridge. The air vibrated with the faint pulse of the distant traffic. Walking couples moved slowly. The clouds built up an enormous, purple wall over the American border to the south.

As the hours slipped by they had seemed to grow into an intense and aching privacy with one another and to become conscious of nothing else. Her dress was pale yellow, and in her haste to be off with him she had forgotten to wear a hat. Her face was flushed with the heat and their constant movement; it seemed as though they could never rest, for during these hours their whole life was being distilled before their eyes. This day was at the zenith of the season; it should have been the longest day of the year. Yet they seemed unable to hoard it for themselves, and because they could not decide what to do and were afraid to confess what they wanted to do, they wasted the daylight with aimless walking.

And then they were in a restaurant in St. Denis Street and the French-Canadian voices were splashing all around them. White wine stood in a bucket sweated with frost.

Finally, they were in the hot darkness of the streets and only the faintest of glows lingered from the sunset over the roofs. She had decided that they should not marry until he returned. So, after all this, they should not marry. And because his instinct agreed with her, he did not press the point.

In Phillips Square they found an old woman selling peonies and he bought a huge bunch of blooms heavy and drooping on the stem. And almost before he realized it, they had reached the hotel where he had engaged a room for the duration of his leave, and without a word she had gone in, too, and stayed with him.

Dawn entered the room at four in the morning, the peonies he had bought for her stirred in a vase, and he woke and realized that the wind had changed and that now it was cool. She was awake, too, and they were alone in the dawn together, incredibly desirous, and it had not seemed possible that this familiar girl's body could be such an adventure for a man. He could see her hair tumbled on the pillow as the dawn grew, her features becoming distinct, the shadows fading from her opened lips. He could feel the wonder of discovering her so much slimmer than he had imagined, and her limbs as delicately flexible as though they had been contrived purposely for this moment with himself. He could remember the solitary man who had walked up the street from the Windsor Station whistling so clearly they had been able to hear him for nearly five minutes. And still they had felt no need of sleep. . . .

Now he was surveying himself in the plate-glass window of a telegraph office in Hollis Street, in Halifax. The awkward posture induced by his bad leg accentuated the droop which had developed in his shoulders. For a second he dreaded that passersby might be able to guess what a scrawny, weakened frame was hidden by the cheap suit he was wearing. He was tired. He had been tired for two years because his mind was never able to rest. In all this time he had not once wakened up in the morning and looked forward to the coming day.

Behind the plate-glass window was a polished oak counter with pads and pencils ready for people who wanted to say something to someone else who was far away. His mind cleared, only to encounter a sharp sense of loss. There was no one in the world to whom he could send a telegram, even if he should discover something to say. He might as well be dead as the way he was, since the chief loss in death was the ability to communicate.

He turned from the window. A couple of private soldiers approached and his right hand involuntarily left his pocket to wait for their salute. They passed without a glance at his civilian clothes. He turned into a restaurant at the corner, and after taking several minutes to nerve himself, entered another phone booth and called in succession all the remaining hospitals in Halifax. Half an hour passed before he discovered that Big Alec MacKenzie was unknown to any of the military authorities, the hospitals, or the Y.M.C.A.

Eagerness to discover this man had become a torment, yet for the moment there was nothing he could think of doing.

The memory of MacKenzie was clear in his mind: a man about six feet four, but so burly he hardly seemed tall; about forty-five years old, skin freckled and sandy, hair reddish-brown. Alec's movements were slow, his walk had the melancholy rhythm of a ruminant animal, and his wrists and hands were strong enough to bend a steel bar. Neil remembered that he also had a slow manner of talking and that he held the words in his mouth as though they were a cud and he feared to relinquish them, but when the voice finally issued it was hauntingly musical and crowded with Gaelic idioms. English was Alec MacKenzie's second language.

What would he have done had he been in Alec's place, a man with a family, discharged from the army with a small pension? He did not know, for he was not informed of the nature of Alec's wound. Before the war Alec had been a fisherman, and had also tilled a few acres of rugged ground on the Cape Breton shore. If he were still capable of such work, he would probably be back among his own people; if not, he might be living on his pension almost anywhere in Canada. It did not occur to Neil that the war might have changed Alec sufficiently to cause him voluntarily to leave his old trade and take up another.

There seemed nothing to do but wait until he could think of some safe way of finding his man. So he continued his aimless walking through the streets, and their very familiarity introduced into his present mood and situation a sensation of overpowering unreality. It was an effort to force himself to be careful and to walk always against the main stream of traffic so that if he recognized someone approaching he would be able to turn about and escape. It was the sudden encounter he feared, someone he knew stepping out of a shop or a doorway and meeting him face to face. The problem of eating bothered him particularly: if he were sitting in a restaurant when this happened he would be hopelessly trapped.

No one was likely to discover him in the cheap room he had hired in the North End, so he began walking in that direction. He proceeded north nearly half a mile; then he suddenly realized that native Haligonians rarely ate in the station restaurant and would not be expecting to encounter acquaintances if they did so. In the waiting-rooms and restaurant of the station he would be able to sit and read the papers and eat his meals, even to talk with strangers, and allow himself the illusion that he still had a place in the world of the living.

His body felt increasingly tired, and this feeling of exhaustion exasperated him, for he recognized that its cause was entirely mental. His wound was healed. It required a sudden and violent noise to produce any aftermath of shell-shock. His frame was thin and not too well-nourished, but his muscles in themselves were sound enough. These alternating fits of nervous activity and dull apathy spread from his mind to his body, which answered his moods like a parrot. And now he felt physically exhausted and no longer wished to walk. He leaned against a lamppost on the corner just like any other of the loafers with which Halifax, like all seaports, is crowded. He looked straight ahead of him down the funnel of the street to a patch of harbour visible in the gap at its end. While he watched, a procession of five freighters, painted in dazzle-colours and loaded to the plimsoll lines, passed seaward in line ahead. Evidently what he had read was true: the war had made Halifax the third port in the Empire.

Tuesday

THE MORNING was dry and crisp, the ground frozen hard, and white clouds rushed through a glittering sky out to sea. Dust blew through the streets and made people turn their faces aside as the wind eddied around corners, and the dingy buildings in the downtown area looked outrageously unkempt as the brilliant light sharpened their outlines and mercilessly disclosed their need of new paint. On the streets there was the sound of marching men and the music of bagpipes and military bands, and occasionally from the harbour there came a booming sound, deeper than thunder, from the horn of a great ship. Halifax was alive this morning and there was no person in the town who did not feel the change in the air. The *Olympic* was about to sail with another cargo of troops.

ELEVEN-THIRTY O'CLOCK

Angus Murray, walking toward the waterfront with a captain of engineers whom he had met casually a few weeks before, found the activity depressing.

"Living in this town is like being quartered in a railway station," he said, as they waited on a corner for a battalion to pass. "Four months of it. You're lucky; you've only been here since October."

"I don't mind it so much." The engineer was from Ontario. "Must be a lot worse around here in peacetime, though. The war's done a lot for Halifax."

No, Murray thought, any more than the war has done a lot for physics or chemistry. The war and the prospect of wars to come is what keeps the place fundamentally the same through the years. He preferred to remember Halifax as he had found it when he had first come here to college years ago and this had been the largest city he had ever seen. He liked to recall its English gardens in summer: the lazy and affable existence of its inhabitants who seemed to assume that nothing they could do in peacetime could possibly matter to anyone; the way Halifax had of seeming not so much a town as a part of the general landscape; its chameleon-like power of identifying itself with the weather. There were fine days with westerly winds and you could smell the odour of spruce trees in the downtown streets and the atmosphere of the place was like a tonic. But there were almost as many wet days when Halifax was worse than any town he could remember, when the fog isolated it from the ocean and the forests until there was nothing to see but streaming pavements, and the bells moaned in the distance and the stained old buildings seemed to expect the bad weather to go right on to the end of the world. The worst of it was that one knew Halifax did not really care about this. It seemed willing to lie out in the wet forever, to take what other people and powers prepared for it; and no matter what happened, Murray realized, it could never change its nature. It would do its duty by the English as long as there was an England left.

The battalion passed finally, and Murray and the engineer followed it with the crowd to the head of Pier Two, where the *Olympic* was berthed. The Shipyards lay just beyond, but Penny would not be finished with her work for at least another half-hour. He decided that he might as well stay here as anywhere else; troops embarking on the *Olympic* made a spectacle in spite of the familiarity of the sight.

Directly in front of him towered the sharp bow of the *Olympic* with soldiers' heads protruding over the coaming like a row of coconuts. The engineer pointed: "Nice target for a Vickers. Wouldn't that be something to get inside a beaten zone!"

Murray grunted. "Pretty mind you've got. I suppose that would be just another technical problem, so far as you were concerned? Or would it be even that?"

"You needn't get so serious about it."

"That's what I've heard ever since this war started. Don't get serious! Don't interfere with the experts' war. Don't say anything to spoil their fun."

The engineer grinned. "What's the matter? The whisky I gave you last night sour on the stomach? The trouble with you is, you can't take your liquor any more."

"Smith – did you by any chance ever live in a really big city?"

"I worked in Detroit once."

"I thought so."

"Only for a few years, though."

"They must have been mighty important years. I have a theory and you'd make a beautiful example of it."

"You've always got a theory," Smith said.

"I've a theory this war is the product of the big city, and that everything —" Murray became aware that a bicycle tire was brushing the back of his leg and that its owner wanted to be recognized. He turned around. "Hullo! Roddie, isn't it? What are you doing here?"

"Hullo, sir."

"Why aren't you in school?"

"Well —" Roddie suddenly pointed to another boy his own age, a shabby youngster in a roll-neck sweater with a tough, freckled face who also had a bicycle. "This is Willie Moffat. His father was in a German submarine."

"What's that got to do with your not being in school?" Murray grinned amiably. "Don't tell me you have a holiday?"

"Not exactly. But it's all right if we get back by two."

"I'll bet it isn't. Do you want me to tell your sister that we met and it's all right if you get back by two? I'm seeing her in half an hour."

"Oh, sir!" Roddie looked uneasy, but brightened almost immediately. "Willie has a cousin on the *Olympic*. Do you think we can get on board?"

"Not a chance. I couldn't get on myself."

"Well, I guess we better be moving on. I guess we better get closer so we can see better." The boy shifted away. "Good day, sir. You won't tell Penny, will you?"

Murray grinned and looked back at Smith.

A dark green dory, heavy with many years' accumulation of oil and brine and dirt, glided out from a nearby wharf. A longshoreman was sitting on its gunwale sculling over the stern with a long, flat oar, while another sat astride the central thwart as though it were a saddle. They were staring up at the *Olympic*.

"Germans got a bounty on her," one of them said, "like she was a wolf or something."

"They don't get her," his companion said.

"One of them fellas was telling me th'other day they don't take the same course twice going across. Last time he says they went pretty nigh on to Bermuda before they headed north again."

"That's what they say." A moment of silence, then the man added, "Them naval fellas!"

"When I hear about the Germans getting some of them tubs been coming in here lately it don't make much difference, I says. But I'd feel pretty bad if I heard they got this one. She's sort of part of the place, you might say. I'd miss seeing her around. She ought to be convoyed through. One of these days they're going to get her."

"She's too fast for them ordinary convoys. She takes care of herself."

"Yeah. I guess that Captain Hayes is all right."

TWELVE O'CLOCK

The shipyard was flooded with sunshine and the air reverberated with the savage striking of the riveting machines, punctuated occasionally by a ringing clang of heavy metals knocking together. The outlines of the ship they were building were gaunt and uncouth in this merciless light, and the workmen moving about her looked so small it was hard to realize they could be doing anything that mattered.

Penny looked out of her window at this familiar scene and felt alien to it. After her talk with Murray on Sunday night it had been impossible for her to settle back into the groove of her profession. This morning she had spent two hours in the loft, that gigantic room where the plan of the ship was marked out full-size on the floor; her mind, filled with figures, had recorded information with the efficient precision of an adding-machine, had played with their totals and given them out again in a different combination. The loft-foreman had said it was all right. What was all right? Estimates, combinations of angles, balances of stresses and strains, abstractions which had no reality in themselves and never would have reality in anything else unless other experts approved of them. Then they would be translated into steel of a peculiar construction and the sum-total would be an ungainly, high-bowed, high-sterned freight carrier which would only have a life-significance when a crew her builders would never meet had filled it with the smell of bacon grease and dishwater, hung up their dungarees in cabins unkempt with their own living habits, and blown tobacco smoke into the thrice-breathed air between its decks.

She glanced at the clock and saw she was due to meet Murray in less than half an hour. Her morning's work was done, and she began to clear up her desk. One of the junior superintendents entered as she was closing the last drawer.

He smiled genially. "I thought you'd like to have a look at these," he said. As he handed her the papers his eyes ran over her shoulders and he smiled again. "Those mass-produced vessels they're building in the States. When I was in Wilmington in the fall that was all they were talking about." He continued to slide his glance down her arms, though there was nothing directly impertinent in it.

Penny took the papers and laid them on her desk. "Don't tell me we're going to start that sort of mass production here!" she said.

"No, we haven't come to that yet. But the Yanks are smart." His eyes left her waist and focused out the window. "Look at that ship out there. What's the point in being particular about its construction when it has a one-to-five chance of getting itself sunk the first voyage it makes?"

She thumbed through the papers methodically, ignoring the remark. After waiting a few minutes, he left her. She continued to examine the details of these strange new craft which the builders knew would never last more than a few years but which could be made and launched inside a few months. The idea of building ships this way appalled her. The worst aspect of it was that the principle was sensible. What was the use of quality in a world like this? In God's name, what was the use of a person like Neil Macrae with his dreams of excellence which he had never satisfied? If the war continued much longer they would be forced to build like that up here, and what was left of the old Nova Scotian tradition of shipcraft would disappear entirely. It was going fast enough as it was.

Fifty years of governmental neglect, years in which the politicians had turned their backs on the rest of the world in their eagerness to make money out of the West, had reduced British North America from her rank as the fourth mercantile seapower of the world to insignificance.

She got to her feet and reached for her coat, impatient at herself for yielding to generalizations and equally helpless to steer her mind into duller channels. It was the end of ships if they mass-produced them. A good ship could never be duplicated exactly. Vessels in crates, and the devil with quality; men like John and Neil reduced as the assembly line! It was coming. Craftsmanship was already being apologized for, these days. The real skill of the future would be the manipulating of men, and ever-increasing dexterities would be developed to fit masses of men into the moulds produced by the designers.

She opened the door and set out down the long corridor. After her talk with Murray the other night she was almost reluctant to meet him now. Some moments she regretted her confidence, other times she was glad she had trusted his understanding. At least she was aware of feeling alive again, for since Sunday night the restless gnawing in her mind had refused to be quieted.

The departure of the *Olympic* was one of the few events in Halifax sure to draw a crowd. Although its sailing hour was never publicized, it could never be entirely concealed, for it was invariably preceded by a march through the streets of thousands of soldiers, who were accompanied by considerable band music and swarms of children. The Citadel was already dotted with spectators, and hundreds were gathered in the narrow streets near the dock. Haligonians had seen the *Olympic* come and go so often during the past few years they had acquired a personal affection for her. Yet each time she returned, she was strange as well as familiar because her pattern of camouflage was repeatedly altered. This voyage she was painted black and grey and white, with vast sweeps of colour going up and forward in a crazy rhythm from the plimsoll line to the first promenade deck, then veering around as though a wind up there were blowing the colours backwards. Sometimes her stern was blacked down to the wake and the picture of a tramp ship was painted amidships on her hull. But her cargo had remained the same on every voyage since the beginning of the war: three bars of khaki lining the rails, five thousand Canadians travelling in bond, going to Europe with nothing to declare.

Perhaps some scientist of the future, Murray thought, would be able to analyse the nature of the chain which bound Canada to England. Certainly no one could do so now, for the links were tenuous. Hardly anyone in Canada really understood the legal obligations of his own country to England. Hardly anyone cared. Yet the chain was stronger than the sceptics guessed, for twice within the last fifteen years it had pulled Canada into England's wars, and Canadians had offered their lives without question.

A pipe band, invisible in the dock shed, was playing *Lochaber No More*, and the music was making every nerve in Murray's body quiver. This was the lament the village pipers had played a hundred years ago when the clansmen who were the ancestors of half the people in Nova Scotia had left Scotland for the New World. Now Nova Scotian pipers were playing their men back to the Old World again. Was this another of England's baits, or did the pipers really feel their music? He did not know; as he thought about it, it hardly seemed to matter, because he felt the music himself, felt his fingers clenched and a salty constriction behind his eyes. Reason had nothing to do with his feelings; reason had nothing to do with anything that happened until it had become a fact which could be analysed. By reason he disapproved of the war, of Canada's participation in it, of three-quarters of the governments which made the policies for the British Empire. He was irritated by most of the Englishmen he met, and liked Americans better. Yet, in spite of all this, nothing could alter his intuitive belief that the best in England was the finest the world had yet seen, and that a world without England would be intolerable.

They were playing the lament over again. By God, that at least had no place in a war like this! He remembered his father in old-fashioned black serge reading the Bible on the Sabbath in the farmhouse where he had been born, his mother speaking in Gaelic to his sister, and the whole family on their knees each morning before breakfast. Oh, give thanks unto the Lord, for he is good, for his mercy endureth forever!

He glanced sideways at Smith, still examining the *Olympic* with a professional eye. The unbelievable and blind stupidity of this man, coupled with his unquestioned ability and decency, seemed to Murray terrifying. His attitude toward the war was that of a well-brought-up and precocious child playing with a set of Meccano. The only difference between Smith in war and Smith in peace was that now he had unlimited funds at his disposal.

For Roddie Wain, the departure of the great ship crystallized all the impressions he had formed of the past few years, what he had seen and read and what he imagined the purpose of the world to be. The purpose of the world was doing things, and doing them better than the other fellow. It was troops passing schools on route marches, and bugle calls from the Citadel each night and morning, and sudden surprises which turned an ordinary moment into a significant date, and Halifax filled constantly with the shuffle and movement of men wearing the same kind of clothes and doing the same kind of things.

Sometimes when the sound of night practice from the forts woke him he would lie in bed with visions: ships plunging in total darkness through storms in the North Sea with surges washing the decks and sailors clinging to stanchions as the green water leaped over them, while he clung to the coaming of the bridge and guided the ship toward an unseen enemy, uncomfortable but dauntless; shells bursting and Germans pouring across wasted land into the whip of the machine-gun which he, a solitary survivor, directed against them. Sometimes the visions were impersonal. Sometimes it was nothing but a rhythm, a tread of millions of unseen, tired feet moving in time all over the curved surface of the globe. Sometimes he remembered a picture he had seen of Dover headland under the moonlight. The waves rolled in against it and the waves broke, the sea washed slowly away but the headland remained; and behind it were small villages with thatch for roofs and smoke mounting upward in the twilight and fields which were greener and trees more lush than in any other land on earth: England, whose preservation was the reason and the justification of all that happened here in Halifax.

He pushed his way through the crowd to a vantage point. Willie Moffat followed him, and there, resting on the handle bars of their bicycles, they watched the bayonets of the last company sweeping out arcs as the men entered the dock. Roddie wondered why the English used such a short length of steel. German bayonets were longer and those of the French twice as long, and yet they said the British soldier was the finest bayonet fighter in the world. He turned to his friend. "Why do we use such short bayonets?"

"Those don't count, except for something like this," Willie said. "They're just for practice. When they fight they use battle bayonets and grind them sharp. I know. My brother's in the Twenty-fifth." Willie turned and jogged a strange man's elbow. "Mister, when does she sail?"

"Pretty soon now, son."

"That man *I* was talking to is a major," Roddie said. "He was wounded, too. He's a friend of my sister."

"That's nothing. My cousin got gassed at Vimy Ridge and he was killed."

"I had a cousin that was killed too."

"The first Canadian soldier that was killed lived on our street."

They tried to get closer to the entrance of the dock, but a policeman pushed them back; so they continued to stand where they had been, open-eyed and delighted and slightly afraid in the centre of all this excitement, conscious of the noises of feet and the music of the pipes, of the smell of the water, the pressure of the crowd, and the eddies of cold air blowing past them under the sun.

Exactly at twelve the horn of the *Olympic* coughed, then plumed itself and roared, making the air shudder. Longshoremen on the tugs shouted to sailors on the steamer's deck and there was a jangle of bells signalling the engine-room. Then two floods of dirty water raced along the ship's flanks and burst hissing against the sea-wall fronting her prow. The liner began to back slowly out. As the people watched her, someone started a cheer and a flurry shook the crowd like wind in the leaves of a tree. Then silence fell on them all and they watched dumbly as the ship drew away.

Another surge broke from the port screws and churned the sleek waters of the harbour. This manoeuvre swung the ship broadside on and she looked gigantic.

A man standing near Roddie became informative and said to his neighbour, "She'll likely anchor out there in the Stream and wait. That's what she often does. They say not even Captain Hayes knows his course till he clears port. They say he doesn't even know when he's to sail till the last minute."

But this time the captain must have had his orders, for the *Olympic*, under heavy steam, began to belch out smoke and give warning blasts on her horn. Another gurgle sounded from the stern and a mound of white and hissing water was spewed out. A wave appeared at the cutwater and built itself up, and then a great murmur rose from the watching crowd in a sigh, like an involuntary suspiration of mingled relief and anxiety.

Roddie turned and pushed his bicycle through to the fringe of the crowd. Having escaped Willie Moffat, he mounted and set out for the South End of town. By hard pedalling he managed to reach the park on the nose of Halifax peninsula before the *Olympic* had cleared the submarine nets. She was standing seaward a mile beyond him and travelling at full speed; in the wide spaces of the outer harbour even this ship looked dwarfed.

He dropped his bicycle and watched. Behind him lay the park and behind that, the city. Hidden by trees on his left, the waves made by the ship were crashing noisily on the shores of the inner harbour. In the space before him he could see the bow-waves marching in long lines at right-angles to himself across the reaches of the outer harbour toward the bluff of York Redoubt and Sandwich Battery. Somewhere on those hills were 9.2 cannon, guarding the town. He thought they were invincible.

For half an hour the boy stood looking seaward until the *Olympic* was hull down. Soon nothing remained of her but a scroll of smoke, singularly purified by the wind and the sun, drifting across the horizon. And then at last he remembered that he was late for school and he felt empty and alone. The waves breaking lightly on the smooth stones of the shore were like an unearthly laughter, and their sound was constant and all-pervading, wiping out the reality of what he had just seen and filling his mind with an unreasonable sense of disenchantment. He picked up his bicycle to return to school, without being aware that in doing so he was moving back into the continent.

THREE O'CLOCK

The entrance to Wain's Wharf had been built during the War of 1812 and looked like the gateway to a colonial fort. A warehouse of cut granite ran for about fifty yards along a bend of Water Street and its blackened walls were broken at intervals by narrow, grilled windows. In the centre of this wall a deep Roman arch led to the wharf itself, and divided the warehouse into two separate sections. Directly above the keystone hung the faded legend *Charles Wain & Sons, Shippers.* Over this, again, was a window behind which Geoffrey Wain sat at his work. The whole establishment was as solid as it had ever been, its stone and mortar were in excellent condition, yet it managed to give the impression that at some time in its past it had been besieged.

Wain's office above the arch was a long rectangle with long windows on either side and a floor of planked hardwood like the deck of a ship. One of the end walls was covered with dusty maps no one had examined for fifty years; at the other end was a partition of frosted glass behind which three girls were busy at typewriters and filing-cabinets so high a stepladder was used to reach the topmost drawers. At the window overlooking the wharf two desks faced each other, one belonging to Wain himself, the other to his secretary. Although he was on active service with full pay, his duties as transportation officer kept him busy only in spurts and he still had time to manage his own firm, which was busier than it had been in a century.

This afternoon Wain had come to his office two hours after the departure of the *Olympic* and there had found a pair of visitors he had not expected, one wearing the uniform of a staff-colonel, the other an American major of engineers. The colonel had known Wain in France, and he shook hands with the hearty violence of a man who deems it a privilege for others to meet him, but is determined to be democratic about it.

"Is everyone around this port as busy as you are, Wain?" the colonel said. "I've been trying to get you for hours. This is Major Thomson – of the American Army."

Wain shook hands and motioned the visitors to chairs, then opened one of the lower drawers of his desk and produced a bottle of whisky and three glasses. The men made themselves comfortable.

"I thought you were still in France, Eliot," Wain said. "Just get back?"

"Via New York." Colonel Eliot grinned. "This war gets bigger all the time – and better. A different proposition from 1915, I can tell you. It's become a permanent career."

"I heard some time ago about your staff appointment," Wain said. "Like the work?"

"You bet. What a bit of luck to be in the States while the rest of them are stuck with Passchendaele! Wonder who they'll make the goat for it." He glanced sideways at the American and lowered his voice confidentially. "Between ourselves, some of them hadn't the slightest idea of the conditions for that battle. It serves them damn well right. There'll have to be some changes over the winter." Then, raising his voice once more and smiling contentedly, he changed the subject. "Major Thomson's up here on business and I told him you're the man he's come to see."

The American leaned forward and cleared his throat nervously as Wain, with his habitual air of distant courtesy, indicated that he was listening.

"We're going to establish a seaplane base up here," he said, and paused as though waiting for help. As Wain's expression did not alter, he continued unassisted. "You see, the problem at the moment seems to be one of supplies. The colonel here tells me you're the only active-service officer in Halifax with a business on the waterfront."

"That's more or less true." Wain's lips altered slightly into a position that might pass for a smile. "Do you want building supplies?"

"Well, not exactly. Food, mostly. We don't want to bring up an entire army-service unit for the small number of men involved."

Wain blinked and glanced toward Eliot, but the colonel was looking out the window. He looked back at Thomson. "That's hardly a problem, is it? I could undertake a certain kind of provisioning for you, of course. But the whole question would solve itself when your men arrived. Might I ask if that is all you have to settle on this trip?"

The American looked exceedingly uncomfortable and unsure of himself; it seemed as though he had only a vague idea of why he was here at all. "I thought you might give me some advice about the actual site for the base," he said.

"Oh." Wain held his glass against the light and cocked his eye at the milky movement of the whisky in the water. "But surely that's a matter for the government, not for me?"

"Thomson's visit is supposed to be more or less unofficial," Eliot remarked.

"That's it exactly," the American said quickly. "The colonel here tells me you know these parts well enough to show me the best prospect. Maybe if we find our place before it gets around we want it, the price'll be cheaper."

"I doubt it," Wain said. "And with the war on, who cares what anything costs?" He opened another drawer and took out an old telescope, which he carefully removed from its case. The two men watched him sight along the barrel with the interest of a pair of children being shown a new toy. "You can see the best location in the province from here," he said, and guided his visitors to the window. "Look across there."

He pointed down the harbour to the place where McNab's Island curves in toward the opposite shore. The American tapped the telescope and set it against his eye, looked for a few moments and passed it on to Eliot. "Is that a refinery over there?" he muttered.

"A subsidiary of Standard Oil. Just seaward are several acres of fields. I think you could rent them for next to nothing if the government were agreeable."

Eliot was playing with the telescope, sweeping it back and forth across the waterfront. "This is a nice glass," he said. "I can see a hole in a sailor's drawers hanging in the rigging of that Dutch ship out there. Right in the crotch, too. Bloody uncomfortable for him, eh?"

"What's that cove back of the island called?" Thomson asked.

"The Eastern Passage."

"It seems pretty far away from things."

Wain's eyebrows rose slightly as he took the telescope from Eliot and snapped it shut. "We could hardly build an air-base in the centre of town, could we, Major? You see, that bight of water back of the island is about the only stretch of the harbour we're not actually using. It's open to the sea and there are no surface obstructions, but it's too shallow for navigation. A Confederate cruiser escaped through it during your Civil War, but I believe she had the assistance of several dozen rowboats to haul her over the bar."

"I see." The American's face looked brighter. "I heard about that place somewhere."

Wain glanced at Eliot with the trace of a smile. "I don't own that land, you know."

"Well —" Eliot grinned. "You might, mightn't you?"

"I'm sorry. . . . No." Wain looked coldly at his brother officer as he said to Thomson, "If you want to inspect the place I can arrange to have a naval launch take you across. We could have it surveyed for you, I suppose. Really, the whole thing is outside my province. The Harbour Commission might help you, but I can't."

"Thomson only wants a look around," Eliot said distantly. "You know how it is."

"Yes, I know how it is."

Ten minutes later, when the American had left in a naval car for the Dockyard, Wain poured out two more whiskies and laughed silently. "I'm not interested in money," he said.

Eliot drained the whisky with a single gulp. "I don't blame you, seeing you've got enough. I met Thomson on the train and thought you might be, that's all. You got a raw deal in France, as I remember. I thought —"

"Who's responsible for Thomson," Wain interrupted. "Our government or his? If the Americans really want this base, all they have to do is ask for it."

"God knows. Things get more and more devious the longer the war goes on and the more fingers get into the pie." He grinned sympathetically. "You sound pretty fed up. Things slow around here?"

Wain made a slight sucking sound with his lips and teeth and looked out the window. He had rarely felt more in a mood for giving orders than he did at this moment. During the last three years he had seen more misfits in important posts than even his low opinion of human ability had considered possible. Eliot had formerly sold insurance. Thomson looked like an estate agent. The war was a game with them and they were incapable of understanding the first thing about its possibilities. To him it was the greatest power-bonanza in the history of mankind; he saw it continuing indefinitely. And here he was in Halifax, a transportation officer doing the work of a glorified clerk with permanent authority over a batman and a pair of army stenographers!

Eliot reached for more whisky and said, "What are you wasting your time here for?"

Wain's face was a dark and muscular mask as his eyes matched the other man's.

"You shouldn't be stuck in a spot like this," Eliot went on. "Why don't you raise hell until you get a staff job?"

"How long do you think the war's going to last?" The voice was nonchalant. "Or do you know any better than the rest of us?"

"About two years more. It all depends on the lengths they're prepared to go. Maybe three."

"I should guess three at the least."

Wain rose and went to the window. The prospect below might have been satisfying if he had not taken it completely for granted for so long. Two freighters were lying at his wharf, one on either side of the long central shed, and he could hear their donkey-engines clank and their winches bang and occasionally the guttural cry of a stevedore directing the movement of the cranes. A frosty evening was drawing in with all the brilliant colours of a Canadian winter. The sky was a translucent globe of pale blue and the shadows cast by the docks looked stark on the water of the harbour. A vessel flying the tricolour was gliding out to sea a few fathoms from the end of his own wharf, and as he studied her lines and the way she was trimmed he guessed her cargo was munitions. He estimated her tonnage and tried to gauge the volume of her freight, and from this point his mind busied itself with a series of figures as he added up totals of munition-shipments over a period of months. Without turning, he said sharply, "My God, but the generals are wasting shells!"

"Eh?"

"Up to a hundred thousand tons of munitions must go out of Halifax every month, in one form or another. I said they're wasting shells."

He sat down heavily and toyed with the telescope, while Eliot poured himself another whisky and sprawled in a straight-back chair with his knees apart, breathing heavily and studying his own fingernails as though he had just discovered them. One of the typists became a darkened blur behind the frosted glass and opened the door. There she hesitated, a small and diffident figure in the long expanse of the outer office, and when Wain gave her no notice she went back to her work, carefully closing the door behind her.

"Look" – Eliot suddenly forgot his fingernails – "you and I were together at brigade that night before the wonky attack that broke you? Or am I wrong?"

"You aren't."

"The attack was your idea, if I remember rightly? You practically planned it."

"It was."

Eliot drained the last of his whisky and eased his belt. He glanced at the bottle to make sure it was dry, and cleared his throat in resignation. "That attack was one of those things. If it had been successful you'd have had a brigade before the year was out." The toneless voice hesitated, then resumed its droning as though talking to itself. "And by now you'd have had a division at the very least. You're a man with ideas."

"Well?" If Wain was tense there was nothing in his voice to suggest it.

"I've been thinking. The trouble was, your men retreated before they got killed. If they'd been killed a quarter of a mile farther ahead it would have been all right."

Wain shrugged his shoulders.

"But they weren't farther ahead because one of your subordinates got cold feet – that was it, wasn't it?" Eliot looked straight at Wain. "Why didn't you court-martial him?"

Wain said nothing and Eliot resumed the study of his fingernails. "Then it was true, the man was a relation of yours?" he said, without looking up.

"The officer in question was killed the night after the attack."

Once more Eliot was unable to detect any overt emotion in Wain's voice. "So that was it," he said. "Well, no one can court-martial a corpse. You know, I'd almost forgotten that angle of the case. Two years is a long time in a war like this, and everyone else has forgotten about that mess by this time." He rose abruptly. "I've got to be going. How would you like a staff job – in France?"

"Are you making an offer?"

"I haven't exactly the power to make an offer, but there are plenty of strings that can be pulled. The smell of that old affair wasn't too good while it lasted but it's died out now. I think I can promise you a brass hat, if you want it?"

"I want it," Wain said.

"Good! I forgot to say I'm on my way to Ottawa now."

After Eliot had gone, Wain stood for many minutes staring out the window at the glow of sunset reeking over the sheds and spilling on to the flat water of the harbour. He wondered why Eliot had bothered to look him up and decided that the man was so impressed by the position the war had given him that the ability to appear as a benefactor flattered his vanity. It was a humiliating thought. The trouble with himself was that he was proud, and resented having to ask or receive favours. Eliot was a fool to have thought he might have been interested in making some petty graft out of a seaplane base. It was an insult both to himself and to the American, who probably was honest and who certainly didn't know Eliot well. But one thing was certain: if a man like Eliot could maintain himself as a staff-colonel a man like himself could do a lot better. The trouble was in getting started again.

He went back to his desk and began to study the papers that lay in a neat pile before him, and for nearly half an hour there was no sound but the ticking of a clock and the muffled clatter of the typewriters behind the glass. Then the phone rang; it sounded twice before he picked it up, and when he heard the voice of his sister-in-law he took the receiver from his ear and eyed it distastefully. When it had ceased to vibrate, he said, "Maria, is there really anything important you have to say to me?"

The receiver crackled. "It's about Penelope."

"Oh?"

"I simply must talk to you about her. I've been trying to get you all day."

"A certain large vessel, which shall be nameless over the telephone, left port today and I was busy. Well, what about Penelope?"

"You've got to do something about her. People are talking."

"What people?"

One of his typists opened the door again, but drew back as she saw the dilation of his nostrils. It was his only palpably animalistic reaction. Its appearance was rare, but she knew it well enough to be afraid of it. She closed the door discreetly and he looked back at the telephone. "Just what people are saying what, Maria?"

"There's no use your trying to bully me, Geoffrey Wain. You practically insulted us by allowing that Murray man in your house last Sunday, which was bad enough. But now I hear your daughter is keeping company with him and that's too much. You know it is."

Wain tapped the receiver against the desk, a gesture which brought a clamorous outbreak from the other end of the wire. Then he said, "What do you know about Major Murray?"

"Why, everybody knows about him."

"Do they, now? It's been my experience that few people know anything about anything. Suppose, in fifty words, you try to say what *you* know about him. I'll hold the line and you can have a minute to think about it."

He set the receiver down, and leaning back in his chair, tapped a hand-bell. One of his girls appeared with a sheaf of papers in her hand and without speaking he took them from her. She remained standing awkwardly in front of him and he studied her casually for a moment before glancing at his watch. "It's nearly five," he said. "If you and the other girls are finished you can go for the day. I'll stay and check these invoices."

"Thank you, Colonel Wain."

"Did Miss Phillips say when she'd return?"

"I think she said something about being back at four-thirty, sir."

"All right." He adjusted his pince-nez and began skimming the edges of the papers with his fingers. "On your way out, step over to the shed and ask Mr. MacKenzie to report to me at once."

The girl went back to her section of the office and he could see the shadows of the other typists rise from their desks as she spoke to them. Meanwhile cracklings had been sounding intermittently from the idle receiver on his desk. He picked it up and said sharply, "Maria, you're a persistent woman. Now, tell me who has been talking to you and – if you know – what they said."

He held the receiver away from his ear while she told him what she thought of his rudeness, and only replaced it when she grew quieter.

"They've been seen taking long walks with each other," she said. "They've been together more than once."

"And what difference does that make?"

"What difference! Either Penelope is misbehaving or else she ought to be warned. Does a man like that Murray trouble his head over a young girl just for – just for – you know very well what I'm talking about."

Wain bit his lip delicately, and his voice became unpleasantly polite. "I think that's quite enough. But let me warn you. If I find you've been saying anything about Penelope to a soul in this town I'll make you sorry for the tongue in your head. A woman your age ought to have more sense. Goodbye."

He hung up the receiver and turned back to the invoices, but a cold anger grew in him. His large hands opened and closed spasmodically and he sat very still as his eyes ran over the papers without taking in the least sense of their contents. He could not understand why he was so angry. The situation was not serious and his sister-in-law was a fool. But being reprimanded about such a matter somehow diminished his stature in his own eyes and made him appear petty to himself. Mingled with this emotion was an intense and sudden dislike of Murray, of whom he already had no good opinion. Probably what Maria said was true, and if it was, then he would put a stop to Murray's flirtations at once. The decision was not caused by any fear for Penny's virtue but by a habit of aloofness and a commanding sense of insult when other people stretched out a hand toward something belonging to him.

He reached toward a humidor and drew out a cigar, lit it and leaned back in his chair until the anger subsided. Before a quarter of the cigar was in ashes the door of his office opened and his wharf-foreman, Big Alec MacKenzie, stood there with his cap in his hand.

"You would be wanting to see me?" Alec said.

The Gaelic accent was thick enough to cut and the face looked an anachronism from primitive times. It was like a cross between a Presbyterian minister and a Scotch terrier.

"Are those ships nearly finished loading?" Wain asked sharply.

Alec reflected. "Well now, that English one has been doing fine. But those Eyetalians – my glory, they've been here since —"

"Will they be out of here in time?"

Big Alec's jaw bulged as he shifted a wad of gum from the path of his tongue. He shuffled his feet and reflected again. "I would think so," he said finally. "The English one is ready now."

"I suppose everything went all right today?"

"Indeed yes."

"Then before you go, look in the storeroom and take out two cases of whisky you'll find there. Give them to the captains with my compliments."

Alec bent stiffly to tighten a shoelace, displaying an enormous width of shoulders and backside as he did so. Presently he straightened up and looked at Wain with an expression of deep concern.

"Well, MacKenzie – what's the matter?"

"I was thinking about them Eyetalians. It's an awful pity to waste the whisky."

"Then don't think about it. Just give it to them."

"The likes of them would not be drinking whisky."

"What difference does that make?" Wain snapped out the words in irritation. "They must have their gratuity. Try to think, MacKenzie. Will those ships be on their way before dark for the Basin or will they be spending the night here?"

"Well, the English fellas —"

"I know about them. I mean the Italians."

"In about half an hour now, if everything goes all right, I would say the Eyetalians would be ready."

Wain looked away to hide his growing exasperation. "You might have said that in the first place. Anyway, go home as soon as they've cleared the wharf. You've had a long day."

Big Alec still seemed to be waiting for something else.

"Never mind," Wain said, "whether the Italians drink whisky or not. Give a case of it to the skipper. If he wants to sell it when he reaches Genoa he can buy spaghetti with the proceeds."

"It's an awful waste," Alec said, as he went out.

Now Wain was alone in the office, sitting in the gloom beyond the glow of his desk lamp. His mood had changed, and the satisfaction left him by Eliot's last words had almost evaporated. His contempt for loneliness, which he imagined to be the most commonplace ailment in the world, was so great that he refused to acknowledge its presence in himself. He tilted his chair farther back into the darkness of the room, and with slow and almost studious movements carried the cigar to his lips and away again, trying to savour the tobacco. The smoke eddied across the light and disappeared each time until he renewed it. Gradually his body relaxed.

He glanced at the calendar and wondered if years from now he would remember this date in his career. He was pervaded by a quiet and unquestioned confidence that the present had pulled adrift from the past and that his future held unlimited possibilities. Here in Nova Scotia his family had gone as far as the limitations of the province permitted. He had been born at the top of things with no wider horizon to aim for; it had required nothing less than a war to better his prospects and give him a zest for advancement. His first attempt to escape his milieu had been a failure; the next time there would be no mistakes.

Yet as he reflected on this he was conscious of disappointment, of resentment because he had for so long been under a sense of failure. He laid down the shortened cigar and put his hands on his hips and pressed his powerful fingers against the wall of muscles guarding his abdomen. Their resilient ridges resisted the pressure firmly. He was still in good condition; indeed he had never been physically better in his life. Like many men his age he was thankful that the war had found him neither too old to profit by it nor too young to hope for a guiding position. If the war lasted another three years anything might happen in his career. It was not reasonable to suppose that general officers who had been under full responsibility from the beginning could endure the strain indefinitely without replacement. Generals wore out as well as lieutenants.

One of the freighters blew its horn and Wain rose to watch it back away from the wharf. Big Alec had sent the last crane-load aboard the Italian ship and now was walking up the slide with a case of whisky clamped under his arm. Wain puffed a lungful of smoke against the windowpane. MacKenzie was the only man in the world capable of upsetting his apple-cart, of cancelling out all the patient work he had done in Halifax since his return from France. But the big man had no notion of this. When he had accepted the job and brought his wife and family to Halifax he had never guessed that it had been Wain's motive to make him a dependent. Even if Alec had been incompetent, Wain would never have risked his being unemployed. As it was, Big Alec had become the best wharf-foreman he ever had.

The door leading to the outside hall opened behind him, and as he heard the tapping of high heels he turned around and moved back to his desk. "You've been quite a while, haven't you?" he said casually. "What did Harrigan finally say?"

After dropping her hat and coat on a chair, the girl leaned against the edge of the desk. "Mr. Harrigan said to tell you that the railroad accepts your suggestion *in toto*. He says he'll be writing to you shortly. What does *in toto* mean?"

He surveyed her figure as it emerged behind the veil of smoke he had blown in her direction, his eyes passing coolly along the curve of her thighs to the contour of her upper arms, exceptionally plump in so slight a girl. The muscles under his cheek-bones hardened as his lips parted into the beginning of a smile. "You aren't trying to tell me you were away three hours just for that?"

"You told me to get his answer, didn't you?"

"I did, my dear Evelyn. And I also told you I'd be waiting for it."

She shrugged her shoulders and began to search for something in her handbag. Her expression contained a paradoxical mixture of deference, indifference, and condescension, but her manner toward him was obviously intimate. He ceased smiling and with an abrupt movement picked her up and swung her into the air as though she were a child, then rested her on his knees with her face tilted upward under his own.

"Ow!" she said, frowning angrily. "You know I don't like things sudden."

His hand tightened against her thigh, then moved slowly with a hard and even pressure, feeling the flesh warm under its palm and curving gently upward toward the hips.

"Right *here*?" she said.

"Did I say anything?"

"Ouch – that hurts! Do you have to be so —"

She stopped talking and closed her eyes, for she knew that a protest would not affect him and that he liked to enjoy her without talking about it. Under the pressure of his stroking hands her face grew set and concentrated, and though her expression seemed to indicate pain, it was evident that the pain was at least as welcome to one part of her mind as it was repulsive to another. Hers was the satisfaction of knowing that with so small a body she could tame this man of wealth and position and physical strength, but she was humiliated because he was always the one to choose the occasion. Whenever he made love to her he seemed to be studying the effect he produced, and she knew that the basis of his desire lay in the fact that her perfectly formed body was as diminutive as a miniature, that it was easy to hurt, and that he could goad it into the convulsions of a pleasure she could rarely control. If he would only talk more, it would be fun; but as he never did, she usually managed to make him pay for it.

"My, but you've got a gleam in your eye!" She looked up at him without expression. "You like it, don't you?"

He said nothing, and making a gesture of annoyance she wriggled free.

"I wish you wouldn't love me up so sudden," she said. "It's not decent."

He winced at her vulgarity, then pushed her away so sharply she nearly fell to the floor. She recovered herself and stood upright with her legs apart, smoothing her dress. "I'm hungry," she said.

"It's not six yet. Didn't you have any lunch?"

"I'm hungry just the same."

"Well – there's not much we can do about it here."

She left him and turned on the lamp over her own desk. "Guess what? I got a letter from my mother today."

"Was it interesting?"

"She wants to come to Halifax. Will that be all right?"

"No," said Wain.

"I don't see why not. She says it's on account of my father."

"Your what?"

"Oh, he's been gassed or something. Anyway, he's coming home and Mamma wants to be here when he gets off the ship."

"Evelyn" – his voice sounded nasty – "you're a damned little liar. You told me a year ago your father was dead."

She shrugged her shoulders and resumed her perch on his desk, swinging her legs.

"What did your father do?" he said. "Before the war, I mean?"

"He was a fisherman," she said sullenly. "And he needn't think he can get me back to the village just because he's home from the war."

Wain's nostrils dilated as he placed the papers before him in a filing basket. Her remark revealed a situation he well understood. Firms like his own had done much to cause it, and he took it for granted that she was taunting him with the fact. Few fishermen in Nova Scotia made any money because they could not easily market their catches, and prices paid by wholesalers like himself were infinitesimal. It was steadily becoming more difficult to persuade members of the younger generation in the fishing towns to stay there. In her native village a girl like Evelyn would have had some standing in the community; in Halifax nothing but his patronage had elevated her beyond the status of a domestic servant.

"So your dead father was a fisherman before he became a soldier?" He watched her steadily. "And you've become too good for him?"

"He never makes any money. None of them ever do."

"I suppose you know men like your father are about the finest seamen in the world?"

"Where does that get them?"

He laughed harshly, and she disliked the sound of it. "The queer part of it is, my dearest Evelyn, that you're really quite a competent secretary. Yes, you've learned a lot."

"What are you looking at me that way for? Let me tell you something —"

He puffed a cloud of smoke at her. "Well, why don't you go on? I'm waiting."

"I guess I didn't mean anything," she said sullenly. But her eyes were crafty. It didn't get you anywhere saying what you really thought. "What about my mother?" she said.

"She can do what she likes, but I don't want her in your flat. Tell her to go to a hotel. I'll pay for it."

"But Mamma wouldn't let me do that. She thinks I'm poor. She wouldn't come at all if she had to stay in a hotel."

"So you really care what your mother thinks about you?"

"No use bothering folks, that's my motto. Besides – well, I say she's got it coming to her, working like she does."

"Yes." Wain's voice was urbane. "Mrs. Phillips deserves better luck. You can tell her to come at the end of the week. I happen to know that there won't be any soldiers returning before Saturday at the earliest."

He got up and put on his coat, somewhat surprised at the unusual confusion of emotions which the girl's remarks had roused in him. For Nova Scotia he had no real respect; he merely felt it was a little less inferior than the rest of North America. Yet there were certain qualities he expected to find in his province and was disappointed whenever a fellow-provincial lacked them. It seemed proper and natural that Nova Scotians should be unimportant, but unnatural for them to be cheap, and Evelyn's remarks grated on his sensibilities. Men like her father faced danger every day in the foggiest and stormiest tract of the entire Atlantic, and apart from the Scandinavians they were almost the only seamen still left under sail. "He's been gassed or something. . . . He never made any money. . . ." Wain felt personally hurt by these remarks. On the other hand there was little he could do about it. To find a satisfactory mistress in Nova Scotia was difficult and in this respect Evelyn was admirable; her poverty had made her shrewd and in her eagerness to escape from it she was willing to do nearly anything he wished. After all these months, no one in the office seemed to suspect their relationship, and he was prepared to give her some credit for this.

"Will you be coming around tonight?" she said, as he opened the door for her.

"Perhaps." He opened his wallet and gave her a five-dollar bill. "Here, go to a moving picture if you like. But you'd better be back by nine-thirty. I may want to see you then."

FOUR O'CLOCK

The living-room of the house where Jim and Mary Fraser lived in Prince's Lodge was like an album of their lives. It was quiet, simple, and spacious; it never lacked the odour of wood smoke and it managed to preserve something of the freshness of the forest on the edge of which it was built. The room was dominated by a huge hearth made of stones removed from the excavation of the house itself, and its ceiling was supported by beechwood beams cut from the forest. A moose head with fourteen points in its antlers stared glassily from about the mantel.

Although it was the room of a man who liked to live out of doors and of a woman who enjoyed making him comfortable, the photographs hanging from the walls showed that Jim Fraser was not a professional sportsman. There were pictures of him as a mining engineer in South Africa, pictures of galleries in the actual mines in the Rand, pictures of him in uniform, pictures of the mess of the Royal Canadian Regiment and a framed drawing of the company in bivouac before Paardeberg. There were also snapshots of the Wains in dreary family groups and one of Mary herself looking gaunt and awkward in blouse and bloomers, lunging with a fencing foil at a dummy which still hung in the gymnasium of her old school.

Now it was early evening. Darkness would soon convert the unshuttered windows that looked on Bedford Basin to mirrors reflecting the warmth and ease within. Had anyone been able to look into the room from the outside, it would have seemed like an oasis of yellow light in the brooding and heavy darkness of the forest and the paler, slightly ominous sky to the eastward over the Basin. Angus Murray and Jim Fraser lounged in easy chairs on either side of the hearth and Penny was on her knees before it, playing with Jean. Mary's hands moved in quick, birdlike gestures as she cleared away the dishes.

All afternoon Penny had been watching Murray quietly. He had not wished to accompany her to Prince's Lodge; for a time during lunch she had been afraid that her plan to entice him out here would miscarry. But once here he had surprised her, for she discovered that he loved children, and the presence of Jean had made him feel immediately at home with the Frasers. In turn, they had been charmed by his ease with their adopted daughter. Earlier in the afternoon they had gone walking through the woods, Jean perched on Murray's good shoulder and Penny moving alongside to steady her. The forest was silent and empty in the hush before snow, and filled with daylight like a ruined house. A weasel had chased a rabbit across the path in front of them and beside a pond in the heart of the wood they had come upon the tracks of a moose. Penny had never seen Murray appear so peaceful, and the mood had remained.

"You ought to settle down in the country when the war's over." Jim was on his favourite subject now. "Look at the cost of maintaining a practice in a place like Montreal or Toronto! You'd be doing as well with two thousand a year in the country as with ten in places like that. And you'd enjoy yourself into the bargain."

Murray smiled. "There's not much doubt of that," he said. "I've often thought about it. By the way – you used to play tennis, didn't you?"

"Yes."

"Well, practising medicine is like playing tennis. It's the same game wherever you are but the players are different. You get more fun out of it in the small town but the champions play in the city. I guess we all kid ourselves we'd like to be champions."

Jean's attention suddenly wandered from the game she was playing with Penny. She turned to Murray, spreading her arms wide, and cried out, "Water!"

"But the water was frozen and that made it ice."

"No. Water."

Jim gave Murray an inquiring glance and stopped filling his pipe. Murray laughed. "She's right, you know. Where some animal had holed the ice on the edge of that heart-shaped pond the water was black as a pit. I wonder how a two-year-old can notice a thing like that?"

Jean was tumbling on the carpet now, trying to avoid Penny's attempt to tidy her ruffled hair. "Somefing in mouf," she said.

"Who had something in his mouth?" Penny finally captured her. "You mean your father's pipe?"

"Oh, so she's back on that again!" Mary said. "She can't seem to forget it. Jim went off with her a week ago and when they came around one of those big boulders they nearly ran into a deer. It had a piece of fungus in its mouth. She's been excited about it ever since."

"It's a wonder she hasn't been pointing out the ships in the Basin," Jim added. "That's how she's learning to count. Right now there are far too many in, but when they're no more than a few she can generally add them up after a fashion."

Jean now became clamorous for a story and Penny tried to quiet her.

"She's a lot more sense than we have," Mary said. "It's half an hour past her bed-time." She turned to Murray. "Penny tells her a bed-time story whenever she comes out here. She never forgets and she usually has a new one. She'll be spoiled if we don't look out."

"Nobody believes you, Mary." Penny swung Jean toward the door. "Come on up with us, Angus. I'm putting her to bed. This is a job you ought to be good at."

Murray followed them upstairs to the nursery, a tinted room the colour of an apple blossom in the light of the lamp. Penny moved quietly about, undressing the sleepy baby and humming to herself as she hung up the discarded clothes. Murray sat quietly and watched, feeling well content. The afternoon had been one of those respites in time during which a man feels that although no outward event has occurred, something intangible has taken root in himself.

Now Jean was tucked into her cot and Penny was bending over her, beginning the evening tale. "When the winter comes and Jean goes out in the woods, she can't see a thing but the white blanket of snow that covers everything. But underneath the snow there are all sorts of things happening. The rabbits have cities in the ground with tunnels all made like little streets and big holes where they live, warm like you are now, until the spring comes and the snow melts. And the squirrels live all tucked up in the trunks of the trees and every time they get hungry, all they have to do is go downstairs in the tree and bring up the acorns we saw them gathering this fall. And if you go a long way back in the woods, away back behind all the ponds and on the other side of the ridge where the sun goes down, there you'll find a place where the snow is tramped down into streets with high walls higher than this room, and that's where the moose and the deer live in the winter."

"Bees and bears, Aunt Penny?"

"Oh, when the snow falls they just go sound asleep and they never wake up at all, not till after it all melts away." She paused; the child's eyes were closed. "And all winter long the cruel animals go hungry, because the gentle ones are safe and can't be found. . . ." Jean was asleep and Penny's voice tailed off to a whisper. She rose and picked up the lamp and turned to Murray. "It's silly. I don't know where I get all that nonsense but she likes it and I suppose it won't do her any harm. Tell me – what do you think of her?"

He got to his feet. "It's hard to say. I've got a weakness for all children I guess. So naturally I like this one." He took the lamp and held it high while she tucked in a loose corner of blanket. "Where did they get her?"

"In Montreal." She looked closely at him, then back to the cot. "I think she's going to resemble Mary, don't you?"

"Why should she? She's adopted."

"The Wain characteristics are pretty self-assertive."

"I can't see environment doing that much. Did your aunt know Jean's parents?"

"Very well."

Murray's eyebrows went up in mild inquiry, but he did not seem vitally interested. Penny's hair was golden-brown in the light falling over it, and there were deep shadows under the cheekbones and lips. When he lowered the lamp, the dim glow of the burning wick encased her figure from the waist upward and accentuated the swell of her full breasts and the plane of her chest branching into her shoulders.

"It's funny," she said, "how people change and still stay just the same as long as they live. I remember when Jean was an infant. She couldn't do anything but lie on her back and blink at the light and cry whenever she was hungry, but even then I knew what she'd be like when she grew older. Stubborn, and curious about everything. Even Mary realizes she has more natural charm than any of her other relatives."

"That's right. . . . You *were* in Montreal when they adopted her. That's when you were taking your technical training, wasn't it?"

"More or less." The light quivered as her hand holding the lamp began to tremble. "Oh, Angus — you're not usually so guileless!"

"What are you talking about?"

"Are you going to make me say it? I've been trying to tell you" – her voice broke – "Jean – Jean is my daughter."

Murray stared at her, his face frozen into immobility, and in the uncertain light she was unable to detect any change of expression about his eyes.

"I'm very proud of her," she said.

He remained silent, standing stiffly with the fingers of his left hand automatically manipulating those of his right, his shoulders slightly stooped and his breath heavy in his twisted nose.

Suddenly her face flushed with disappointment. "I'll not bore you any longer. Neil was Jean's father. I'm not ashamed of it. But I had to give her up all the same. I gave her up for ever when Jim and Mary Fraser adopted her."

"I . . . look here . . ."

He hesitated and his voice stuck in his throat. And Penny, her eyes wet with humiliation as the memory of nearly three years of secrecy and abnegation exploded inside her brain, trembled so that she could hardly control her voice. "Never mind. You needn't feel you have to say anything." With quick strides she went to the door, carrying the lamp in her right hand, and Murray followed silently. "A train leaves in a few minutes, and I'm going back to town. You needn't take it unless you wish. At least there'll be several cars on it. You don't —"

"Penny . . ."

She rushed down the stairs without listening and Murray followed as slowly as he could, his left fingers still manipulating the stiff ones of his right hand.

Jim met them at the bottom of the steps. "Well, did you get initiated into nursery tactics?"

"I've got to go now," Penny said shortly. "Jean's asleep. There's no need for anyone to come with me."

"But you've still . . ." Mary stopped as she saw the flush on Penny's cheeks, and ended weakly, "Wouldn't you like us to go to the station with you, dear?"

"No, of course not. . . . Oh, Mary, I didn't mean to sound like that. I'm – I just remembered . . ."

"She's really very tired, Mrs. Fraser," Murray interrupted quietly.

Penny had her coat on by this time and was standing in front of the mirror to adjust her hat. Murray took his great-coat from its hook and slipped his cap carelessly over the thinning hair on the back of his head. He looked almost raffish, standing there with his coat open and his helmet at an angle.

"Are you coming?" Penny's voice was so cold it shocked Jim Fraser, but he could think of nothing to say and quietly opened the door. "There's a later train than this," Penny went on to Murray. "Why didn't you wait for it?"

"I'm coming now," Murray said.

He turned to Jim and Mary and thanked each of them for the afternoon. Then he followed Penny down the path to the road, and they walked in silence to the gate opening on the platform that served Prince's Lodge as a station. The two stood like show-window dummies waiting for the train to arrive.

The sky was bright with stars. Orion and Sirius stood over the forest, and the Bear, stretching a long arm to the north-west, rested above the Basin. The forest was hushed on the verge of winter storms, and the Basin, walled by darkness and illuminated by the stars, seemed filled to capacity with ships awaiting convoy. Their riding-lights flickered like a swarm of fireflies motionless in a void. Here Murray sensed an atomic quietness balanced at the core of constant change, of forces eternal and temporal about to radiate into areas where they would be drowned in a welter of predestined and uncontrollable motion. The cold air was fresh with the smell of evergreens and of salt water, and in the far west there remained, like a tiny island burning with distant fire, a sliver of cloud still reflecting a glow from the sunken sun.

To Penny, standing aloof and silent a few yards from Murray's elbow, the scene had the moving quality of all the beauty she had witnessed in the past three years and been unable to enjoy. Occasionally she stole a glance at Murray's profile, but he gave her no evidence that he was conscious of her presence. He was the only human being besides Jim and Mary who knew her secret. She had looked forward eagerly to being able to tell him. And now he was standing beside her, with nothing to say.

The train hooted from the nearest curve and its searchlight came into view, sending the shadows of trees circling away from the sunken tracks. It ground to a stop and they boarded an empty car, Penny first and Murray following, handing their tickets to the conductor as they entered. She sat in the seat next to the door, and Murray dropped down beside her. The train ground on, gaining momentum.

Then Penny was aware that Murray's hand was on her own and she turned slowly to face him. In bewilderment she realized that his eyes were wet.

"Penny. . . ." His voice was thick and he had to clear his throat. . . . "Will you still marry me?"

She stared at him.

"Aren't you the guileless one now, my dear?" he went on. "I love you very much, you know."

"Oh, Angus!" Her lips parted and she turned back to the blank window, her left hand clenched against her mouth, her right spasmodically closing on Murray's. He said nothing more as he watched the back of her head, waiting for her to gather in the tears and face him again. The train swung heavily on a curve, and the two figures swayed right and then left in unison.

"You're so decent, Angus." Her hat had become pushed back on her forehead and she looked a little girl who has just discovered that a major catastrophe can be only a minor incident to grown-ups. "And I'm so terribly fond of you. I think you and I. . . . But do you mind if we don't settle anything tonight? In a day or two, when I've finished the job I'm working on now. . . ."

"Whenever you like, my dear. I'll always be around, and I've learned to wait."

She yielded to an inner amusement. "Now you see I'm not exactly the girl everyone thinks I am, aren't you afraid I might hurt *your* reputation?"

"I've always been able to see what kind of girl you are, though I didn't know a good many of the details. They only improve the picture."

"There are more if you want to know them."

"Why should I?"

"Father and the rest of the family have never cared what I did, and when I returned from Montreal I had reason to be thankful for it. If they noticed any difference they blamed it on my job."

The train stopped at Rockingham and moved on again.

"You see, Neil didn't know anything about Jean before he was killed," she went on, as though explaining something to herself. "He was going into action for the first time just before she was born."

"Didn't you ever tell him?"

"No. What was the use? He'd only have worried."

"Why didn't you get married in the first place?"

"We were first cousins."

"What of it? Not even the Church of England Prayer Book says cousins can't marry."

"No, but my father did. He hated him, more. . . ."

The conductor opened the door at the end of the car and spat sibilantly into the spittoon between the two end seats, then lurched half-way down the aisle and peered out a window. The train was rattling through outlying freight yards, still on the edge of the Basin.

"Mighty big convoy building up out there," said the conductor. "Makes this run more interesting than it used to be, the war does."

He paused for encouragement, and receiving none, passed into the next coach.

"There's one thing I can't understand," Murray said. "Why in hell did Neil have to enlist in your father's battalion?"

"He didn't. He was transferred just before he sailed. You know yourself it wasn't a Nova Scotian battalion Father commanded."

"I see." Murray made no pretence of his amazed admiration. "And I suppose you thought of that, too, and wouldn't let him take on that added responsibility!"

"Why not? He really wanted to marry me, even then. But it would have been so unfair to him. How could I make his existence as one of Father's subordinates worse than it was bound to be anyway?"

"So your father hated him as much as all that!"

The train swung around the last elbow of the Basin and ran along the Narrows and into town, past shipyards and dockyards, finally coming to rest in the North Street Station. Its exhaust crashed rhythmically in the confined space and its smoke mounted seventy feet to the canopy of heavy glass that covered the platform like a sheet of dirty ice.

Penny felt drained of all emotions, tired but peaceful, and she wanted more than anything else at the moment to be alone. She wanted to be at her desk in the Shipyards for a few hours, alone with the absolute and unquestioning simplicity of figures and the docile beauty of white lines on blue paper. She pulled her hat back over her eyes, and once again she was the capable technician.

"If you don't mind, Angus, I'd like very much to go back to work for a while this evening. It's not late, and there are a good many things pressing to be done. Thank you for giving me this afternoon."

"You're a great girl, Penny," he replied. "If you'll take a taxi, I'll go on to the hotel and leave you. But I'll still be around."

He left her standing at the end of the platform, watching him walk away.

FIVE O'CLOCK

Without remembering how he had come to be there, Neil Macrae found himself skirting the high iron railings of the Public Gardens, peering inside in order to avert his face from passersby. The Gardens were locked for the winter and it was difficult to see through the fence, but he found himself remembering what they were like between spring and autumn, when the townspeople walked their paths as though they owned them. The whole town was transformed in summer. The streets of the South End were long tunnels of trees, elms and maples and limes. No matter how hot the day had been, it was always cool in the Gardens after sunset, and they were crowded with sailors and marines, walking their girls and stopping to look at the flowers. There were beds of delphinium and larkspur, intermingled with snapdragon and edged with candytuft; formal beds of rose-begonia and lobelia; and hundreds of strange and rare old trees with their botanical names stamped on metal disks on their trunks. English swans and Canada geese swam about in the pond at the centre of the Gardens, and when darkness fell and the keepers had whistled home the crowds, the birds could be heard honking and calling for blocks away.

He walked up the flank of the Gardens until he reached the open corner at one side of the Citadel. Here the wind was unobstructed and it was cold. He drew his scarf more tightly around his throat. His muscles were tired with long walking, but the strange sense of peace grew as he watched the sun roll over the line of trees by the Wanderers' Grounds and disappear in fire. Darkness descended in successive waves to the ground, street lights flickered on, and the splintered clouds in the west shook loose one by one from the turmoil of the sunset and began their drift to sea. Even as he stood and watched, the colours were dying, and by the time he had reached Spring Garden Road again it was dark.

As he continued his walking of the pavements he felt at last that they belonged to him, and that Halifax for all its shabbiness was a good place to call his home. The life he had led in Europe and England these past two years had been worse than an emptiness. It was as though he had been able to feel the old continent tearing out its own entrails as the ancient civilizations had done before it. There was no help there. For almost the first time in his life, he fully realized what being a Canadian meant. It was a heritage he had no intention of losing.

He stopped at a corner to wait for a tram, and his eyes reached above the roofs to the sky. Stars were visible, and a quarter moon. The sun had rolled on beyond Nova Scotia into the west. Now it was setting over Montreal and sending the shadow of the mountain deep into the valleys of Sherbrooke Street and Peel; it was turning the frozen St. Lawrence crimson and lining it with the blue shadows of the trees and buildings along its banks, while all the time the deep water poured seaward under the ice, draining off the Great Lakes into the Atlantic. Now the prairies were endless plains of glittering, bluish snow over which the wind passed in a firm and continuous flux, packing the drifts down hard over the wheat seeds frozen into the alluvial earth. Now in the Rockies the peaks were gleaming obelisks in the mid-afternoon. The railway line, that tenuous thread which bound Canada to both the great oceans and made her a nation, lay with one end in the darkness of Nova Scotia and the other in the flush of a British Columbian noon.

Under the excitement of this idea his throat became constricted and he had a furious desire for expression: this anomalous land, this sprawling waste of timber and rock and water where the only living sounds were the footfalls of animals or the fantastic laughter of a loon, this empty tract of primordial silences and winds and erosions and shifting colours, this bead-like string of crude towns and cities tied by nothing but railway tracks, this nation undiscovered by the rest of the world and unknown to itself, these people neither American nor English, nor even sure what they wanted to be, this unborn mightiness, this question-mark, this future for himself, and for God knew how many millions of mankind!

The tram came and he boarded it. Then he sat quite still looking sideways out the window to keep his face away from the passengers, as the car bore him north to his lodgings.

SIX O'CLOCK

After Murray had left her, Penny remained standing at the end of the platform. The sense of relief she felt was so new and wonderful that it was good to be alone in order to enjoy it. She bought an evening paper at the news-stand and glanced over the headlines, and finding nothing of much interest, tucked it under her arm and strolled idly about the station watching the people come and go and listening to the cries of the porters and the bellowing of cab drivers massed behind a railing at the street entrance, bidding for fares. She no longer had any wish to return to her office; just to be alone here amid the flow of people was sufficient to rest her. The train from the Annapolis Valley arrived with its minuscule red engine making a great clatter from the cylinders, and she watched the passengers come down the platform toward the concourse.

"Why, Penny Wain – what are you doing here?"

A uniformed man her own age was facing her, a bag in his hand and a wide smile on his tanned face. "Billy – I could ask you the same question."

"That would be too long a story." He set the bag down. "I got back from France three months ago and I'm still around. My family moved to Bridgetown and I've been down there on leave."

She remembered it had been in her own garden that she had last seen Billy Andrews. He had been one of Neil's closer friends, and on a July day years ago the three of them had gone sailing together, putting out from the Yacht Squadron in the early afternoon and returning late for supper. She had prepared scrambled eggs and bacon and tea, and afterward they had gone out to the garden and sat in the summerhouse and talked on in the dark until the moon rose and whitened the leaves of the trees. She remembered how Neil had sat there on the stone bench scratching patterns with his fingernail on the lichen that dusted the stone, the night air liquid-cool and fragrant from her grandfather's lime trees. Billy had said how lovely it was in Halifax in summertime. It was hardly an exaggeration; the garden had possessed a graciousness common to so many places and things before 1914. As she remembered it now and saw again the details of the scene, it occurred to her it might have happened as easily beside the Yellow River in a remote dynasty when mandarins moved in dark kimonos, praising the flower beds and the vines and talking of wisdom.

Did Billy understand that no one mentioned Neil's name in Halifax any more? Was this why he looked so courteously ill-at-ease? She said, "It's been ages since you were in our house."

"It's been quite a while, hasn't it?" He still sounded awkwardly embarrassed. "As a matter of fact, I'm married now."

"Congratulations! Is your wife in town with you?"

"She's in England. That's the devil of it."

"I hope I'll meet her sometime."

"Yes. She'd like to know you – I'm sure she would."

She looked at him directly. "You weren't in Neil's battalion, I suppose?"

"Who?" The smile left his face and he flushed slightly. "No, I was with the Twenty-fifth."

So he knows, too, she thought; like all the rest of them, he knows something I don't, but won't tell. She forced herself to sound casual. "You didn't happen to see him over there, I suppose?"

"No, I heard he was – Jerry got his number, I heard. Terribly bad luck!"

She put her hand on his arm and addressed him with the easy familiarity one uses toward an old friend. "I wish you'd look me up while you're in town. I see few enough familiar faces these days."

"Righto! I'd love to."

Billy had picked up a clipped, English way of speaking. She remembered he had always been an amiable boy, and unconsciously quick to mirror his environment. Probably his wife was English. "I'll be expecting you," she said. "I mean that, too."

"Rather!" He hesitated and looked over his shoulder. "But as a matter of fact, I'm not going to be here more than another day. It was awfully nice seeing you, Penelope."

He saluted, smiled formally, and sloped off toward the street entrance, not once looking back. And as Penny followed at a discreet distance she was sorry she had met him. She walked slowly down the street, allowing several southbound trams to pass her, and did not stop until she had reached the noisy corner of Buckingham Street, where two tram-lines intersected.

A pair of Clydesdales pulling a sloven laden with casks of salt pork were out of control at the corner, and three men were trying to catch the bridles of the plunging horses. Their hooves crashed and struck sparks on the pavement, traffic was stalled and the driver of a north-bound tram was jangling his bell angrily while the teamster shouted and lashed his horses. Loafers moved from lampposts and store fronts to get a closer look.

The scene was a fairly common one in the steep and narrow streets of Halifax, and Penny watched with slight curiosity. The trolley of the tram had slipped off its overhead wire, and as the woman conductor tried to replace it, the lights in the car flashed on and off and the figures of the passengers inside flickered in alternate darkness and light. Finally the trolley gripped and the tram lights burned steadily.

When Penny saw him, he was sitting by one of the central windows of the tram, his chin in the heel of his hand, his hat on the back of his head, his eyes looking at nothing. She recognized the familiar posture and glanced away, closing her lips tightly. When would this trick of the imagination stop? It had happened so many times before. She would recognize the back of his neck or the swing of his arms or the set of his ears or his manner of walking straight ahead through a crowd; sometimes she would even hear his voice and turn sharply around to find its source. These occasions had never lasted for more than a few seconds but they had always unnerved her. During the last few months they had been less frequent; meeting Billy must have caused it this time, or the peculiar effect of the lights flashing on and off in the car and the bizarre shouting of the teamster.

She looked down at the ground while she waited for the feeling of limpness to leave her limbs. It was worse than silly to get this way over nothing; it might even become dangerous if it continued. The tram was about ready to move on and the crowd was dispersing. Everything seemed normal again. And then she looked up once more.

When she cried his name her voice was drowned by the renewed shouting of the teamster and the clawing of the horses' hooves as they dragged the sloven past. She leaped into the street, but before she could reach the tram it gave a violent jerk and started forward. Someone got in her way; she felt a powerful hand grip her shoulder and wrench her backward, and heard a man's voice scolding her for carelessness. The sloven had rounded the corner at last and the horses would have surged down on her if she hadn't jumped quickly.

"For Jesus' sake, lady, watch your step!"

She stared around into a stranger's open mouth, full of bad teeth.

"Lucky thing for you I got you that time! What do you think them horses were doing out there?"

Why was she waiting while this man talked nonsense? The tram was already across the intersection heading north at full speed. She began to push along the pavement, elbowing pedestrians out of her way until she was able to cross the street. Then she began running frantically, hoping that at the next corner the tram would stop for passengers. But the stretch the car was travelling had no regular stop for nearly two hundred yards, and the vehicle was rocking with speed as the driver let full power into the wheels. By the time it slowed down again she was far behind and breathless. Perhaps he was getting off now. It was an important intersection. Perhaps he would have disappeared before she could reach it. People stared at her as she ran forward. Her skirt and coat hampered her movement, and her lungs, unused to heavy exercise, choked from the effort. She reached the intersection and looked up and down, but in the dim light she could recognize no one. She stopped still, gasping and choking for breath and trying to think what to do.

Then she saw a taxi standing across the street waiting for a passing fare. She crossed to it and climbed in and told the driver to proceed slowly north. Her methodical brain had subconsciously recorded the number of the tram and now she remembered it and told the driver. "It can't be more than five blocks ahead of you," she said. "There's no other tram behind it."

"Yes, ma'am." The driver let in the clutch. "That car's only got another mile before it reaches the end of its run. Then it reverses and comes back. We can't help catching it, if that's all you want."

As the taxi moved north, Penny kept looking out of the windows on both sides and scanning the sidewalks. This had always been a poorly lit district, and since the war it had become as dark as a country road. She could see no one she recognized. Several trams rattled past on their way south, but they were not the right ones. It was nearly fifteen minutes before the driver slowed at a corner and pointed to an approaching headlight. "That's likely the one you want, miss," he said.

Penny paid the man off with one hand while she hailed the approaching car with the other. When it drew to a stop she saw it was empty. The driver was hidden behind a curtain at the front and the girl conductor was standing by the back door beside her ticket-machine. Penny got on and paid her fare, looked quickly into the face of the girl and said, "Did you see a man – a young man – I don't think he was very well-dressed. Did he get off somewhere along here on your way north?"

"I didn't notice," the girl said.

"But you must have! There weren't more than a dozen people on the car. Try to think – please!"

The girl made an effort, but before she could find anything to say the car stopped again and three more people got on board. Penny went forward to a seat and watched the girl make change. As soon as the new passengers were seated she came up the aisle and stopped by Penny's seat.

"A lot of people got off at Cornwallis Street," she said.

"Was there a young man left on board after that?"

"A few more got off around the Dockyard. Before that there was some that left at the Station. There was only one passenger after we passed the Dockyard, I remember."

"Was he young? Darkish – perhaps not very well shaved?"
The girl shook her head. "I don't think so," she said.

Then Penny realized that she herself was unable to say whether the figure she had seen was in uniform or not. She had only received the quickest of impressions, and now she began to have doubts. Surely if it had been Neil he would have been wearing a uniform, and the girl would certainly have remembered a soldier among her passengers.

"Were there any officers on the car?" she asked.

"No, I'm sure of that. There weren't even any sailors."

Penny felt her heart beginning to labour. Of course, if Neil were alive and in disgrace he would be a deserter and would not dare wear a uniform. She looked quickly at the girl and said, "Thanks, thanks very much." The girl left her and retreated to the rear platform, and as the car ran south she kept calling out names of familiar streets. Penny sat still and listened to the singsong voice and heard the clicking of the ticket-machine, and finally she began to relax. It had been a mistake, like all the other times she had fancied she had seen Neil on the streets. It had been some man with a posture resembling his, nothing more. Her case was certainly not unique; she knew a woman in Halifax whose son had been killed nearly three years ago and yet the woman was convinced that only last summer she had seen the boy leaning over the rail of the Dartmouth ferry. Not even the fact that she had searched the decks and found nothing had shaken her conviction. Penny breathed deeply. Surely if Neil were in Halifax she would have heard from him. She could not endure the thought that he was alive anywhere and had not come to her.

Then the withering feeling returned as she remembered her father and the things people had whispered about Neil Macrae for the past two years. She remembered Murray's unwillingness to talk and the sudden embarrassment of Billy Andrews only half an hour ago. But Angus, at least, would have told her if Neil was alive. He could never have brought himself to lie about a thing like that. She had been so sure of his sincerity that his answers had finally dispelled any lingering hope that Neil might still be living, in spite of everything.

The tram stopped at the foot of her street and she got off and began to climb the hill. It was silent and cold and empty on this street where she had lived all her life. The air cooled her brain and slowed her thoughts and her heart to a normal pace. As she began to calculate the situation she thanked God for this gift which never failed her, this merciful power within herself that enabled her to spill cold water over her brain and make it lucid in moments of crisis.

She moved slowly up the hill under the bare branches of the trees until she reached the red house at the crest. A thin wind moaned in the eaves and the empty branches, and faint lines of light ringed the cracks in the shutters. Her father was home, had eaten dinner and was probably annoyed because she was still out. Roddie was home, and was using her absence as an excuse not to do his homework.

She looked at the front door. That heavy rectangle of oak weighted with its brass knocker was a symbol. Her family had shut her in from the world when she was young; it had shut her out from itself when she had ceased being a child. Her body straightened, became erect and rigid, as though to counteract the trembling sensation in her spine which now was spreading to her hands, her knees, and her shoulders.

In that instant she knew unmistakably that Neil Macrae was alive and that she had seen him. She realized this beyond the power of any logic to confute it. Her eyes were trained to recognize what was placed before them; they had often tried to fool her, but after sober consideration, they had never cheated her in her whole life.

The quivering in her limbs subsided. She drew a deep breath of damp air, and slipped her hands into the pockets of her coat. And then she felt saturated with anger and cold determination. No one had ever had the kindness to give her an honest account of what had happened to Neil that day or night in Flanders when they hinted that his cowardice had ruined her father's career in the army. The family had whispered their obscure remarks, and after Jean's birth she had been too shaken and apprehensive to ask many questions. But Neil was alive now and she knew it. He was back in Halifax, and not all the coldness and pride of her father could keep her from compelling him to answer her questions tonight. She closed the door loudly behind her as she entered the house.

Wednesday

A NOTHER FINE MORNING, and Neil Macrae was wakened out of a nightmare by the reverberations of steamer horns sounding in different notes, one after the other. He lurched from bed and looked out. There in the harbour, large and unreal in their proximity, the ships of a convoy were following each other in line out of the Basin and through the Narrows to the Stream, then to the harbour gates and the open sea. The window of his room commanded a long stretch of the harbour and held five ships in view. The convoy moved slowly, each vessel keeping station about three hundred yards behind the one immediately in front, so that during the half-hour he watched there were always five ships visible.

They were merchantmen of all the standard sizes and designs, representing half a dozen countries. Subconsciously he judged each with a professional eye, and condemned them all. Long ago he had decided that the standard designs of most tramp ships were wrong. Builders were so conservative they still insisted on setting the funnel in the exact centre of the vessel. A coal-burner made a direct draft necessary, but now that the navy was burning oil exclusively in its new ships, coal would soon be dropped from all ocean-going craft, and something more utilitarian could be designed if anyone were willing to do it.

He remembered a sketch he had made years ago for a lumber carrier. He had set the bridge and mast far forward over wide bows and a shortened forecastle, and the funnel had been placed astern, just forward of the poop. This left the whole midships free for cargo, with derricks on forecastle and forward of the poop free to load without fouling obstructions on the decks. His freighter had carried the gross tonnage of a medium-sized liner, though most tramp steamers today were under five thousand tons and many were no bigger than coasters. Yet each required a crew substantially as large as that necessary to work a ship twice the size.

He left the window and poured water from a cracked jug into a basin and plunged his face into it, feeling the bristles of his beard grate against his hands as he rubbed. He splashed water over his naked chest and shoulders and towelled them, and then he shaved in cold water and sat on the edge of the bed with his chin in his hands and a cigarette in the corner of his mouth.

There was a dead rat somewhere in the walls. In this ramshackle house of ten rooms there was everywhere the sour odour of corners which had never seen sunlight or a mop, and of thirty inhabitants who slept in their underclothes. His own room, no better than a cupboard in the attic, was one of three usually rented to sailors waiting in port for another ship. At the moment he was the only lodger. He looked at the floor. It was made of softwood boards, dark grey with the impressed dirt of fifty years. Outside his door, the hall and stairwells were loud with the noise of children playing.

He wondered what complacent individual in the South End owned this house. He remembered someone having once said that if a man wants a profit from property he must own something in the slums, because the poor make their own repairs, and twelve renters paying twenty dollars a month are worth more than five paying fifty.

He dressed and got out of the place as quickly as he could. He bought a paper on the corner and walked in the direction of the railway station for breakfast. AMERICA TO HAVE TEN MILLION SOLDIERS WITHIN TWO YEARS – and already there were six million from the Empire, seven from France, fourteen from Germany, God knew how many in Russia, all these in addition to the dead. His mind swung to the time when all these men would return home, ants swarming the surface of a globe in which most of the ant-hills have been wrecked, a million sergeants with no more sections to command.

The gloomy slum buildings of the North End depressed him this morning and he had a distorted image of himself as a Gulliver in this Lilliput wrenching the roofs off houses to discover how many myriads of creatures swarmed under-neath and never saw the light. For this was the disgraceful thing about Halifax, the hurting and humiliating thing about his town, that here, backed by millions of acres of space, there should be slums like these and people dull and docile enough to inhabit them. Children, ill-dressed and half-dressed, brawled about this district with dirty faces and blank eyes. The houses were like cracker boxes standing in rows on a shelf. In some cases the foundations were so cockeyed it looked as though the houses they supported might tip over and sprawl into the street. Their cracked timbers were painted chocolate or cocoa-brown, and these drab colours absorbed all the light that entered the streets, and made them seem even narrower and dirtier and meaner than they actually were.

Sometimes he passed an open doorway, and the interior made him shudder: plastered walls, sticks of furniture that looked like rubbish, everything greasy and hand-touched, sour smells issuing into the streets. In this section of Halifax the noises never ceased all the twenty-four hours of the day. It was a shock to realize how little he had known of the North End. When he had lived here, he had always avoided the dis-trict, and by avoiding it, had contrived to blink at its existence.

It was a relief to enter the station and find it alive with people, brilliant with sunshine filtered through the glass roof and roaring with steam exhausted from four locomotives which stood panting in front of their cars . . . the Sydney train, the Saint John Express, the Dominion Atlantic from the Valley, a local train from the nearer villages. He folded the newspaper under his arm and entered the restaurant where he found a seat in the corner farthest from the door.

"Mind if I sit here? Place is crowded this morning."

He looked up sharply, and with a start recognized the numeral of his old battalion on the cap of a private soldier. For a frozen second he stared at the face, then his muscles relaxed and he eased back in his chair. He had never seen this man in his life.

"Sit down." He passed over the paper. "Want a read of this?"

"Don't mind if I do. Thanks."

The waitress took their orders and the two men kept their privacy until Neil had finished eating his eggs. Then the soldier said, "You look like you were just demobbed. What was your outfit?"

"Toronto Highlanders." The lie was quick enough for anybody. "You been back long?"

"Coupla months. Hanging around hospitals. Guess you know all about that yourself. Got a job?"

"Not yet."

"I bet it ain't so easy, getting what a guy wants. Well, I guess you get a pension, though."

"Some."

"A lot of guys, they're in such a hurry to get out of the army they don't get themselves checked up proper. Now take me, for instance. I'm making sure of mine. A lot of guys, they're going to find themselves without any pension, take it from me."

The waitress took the man's cup and refilled it with coffee, and he went on eating heartily, talking through mouthfuls of food. "You know, those doctors sure want to keep the finger on a fella. I'm supposed to hang around town till they get through checking on me, see. But I fooled them yesterday. Went down to Truro to see the old lady. That train goes so goddam slow I thought I was going to be late. I got another board inside an hour."

"You'll have plenty of time," Neil said. He shifted his plate and his voice was sharp. "I used to know some fellows in your outfit."

"Yeah, who?"

"Big Alec MacKenzie – know anyone of that name?"

"Sure, everyone knew Big Alec."

"Where is he now – in France?"

"No, Alec got smashed up. Not real bad, but – you know, like you and me. Just about right."

"Is he home now?"

"Sure, he's been back quite a while."

Neil's fingers opened and closed with quick, nervous gestures and he had to clench his fists under the table to keep his hands still. "Where's he now?" he said.

"I guess he's around." The man stopped in the middle of a bite. "Funny thing you asking that. I saw Alec a week ago."

"Here? In town?"

"Sure. I wasn't talking to him long. You know, just met him around."

"Is he under examination, or something like that?"

"Not on your life, he's got a job. He's doing all right, too. Got his old lady and kids in town. Foreman on one of the wharves, he said."

"Yes? Which one?"

"Don't remember that, exactly, though he did tell me."

"Is he at Campbell's? Smith's, maybe?"

"I don't remember."

"Maybe he's at Pier Two?" Neil went on. "Furness-Withy?"

"No, it wasn't one of them."

"Wain's?"

The man sat upright, grinning with sudden pleasure. "Say, that's the one! You must know your way around this town. Alec's been working at Wain's on to a year, he said. I ought to have remembered a name like that. His boss used to be colonel of our outfit."

"Isn't he still colonel?"

"No, there was some sort of balls-up and he got sent home. Happened before I went over. I was a replacement."

Neil was breathing heavily and he passed his hand over his forehead, bringing it away moist. He was grateful that the man was so absorbed in his food. Geoffrey Wain was home; Alec was home. That they should now be found in the same place seemed such an inevitability that he wondered why he hadn't guessed it long ago.

The man finished his breakfast and wiped his mouth. "You run into Big Alec in France, you said?"

"Yes."

"Then maybe you were in some of those big attacks before I got there. They must have been pretty bad. When I first went into the line I remember the boys were sore."

"I only saw Alec around the base," Neil said. "I never knew what happened to his outfit."

"I guess no one else did, either, the ways the boys used to talk. For a while they had hardly any officers left. Well, it was better when I was with them, though it wasn't any picnic."

"Maybe the new colonel was better?"

"Maybe. The boys didn't have anything against Wain, though."

When the soldier left, Neil picked up the paper and began turning the pages. Now there was no if and no maybe, for Alec had remembered or he had forgotten, and a word would decide it. As Neil realized this, the back of his throat felt dry and parched even while the moisture from under his armpits seemed to be spreading through his shirt until the linen clung coldly to his skin. "Hell!" he muttered, and rose to pay his cheque.

He walked with exaggerated deliberation through the station waiting-room to the information desk and asked for a city directory. While the girl was looking for it, he admitted to himself that during the past few weeks he had so dreaded the possibility of disappointment that he had almost been afraid to meet Big Alec at all. Otherwise he would have remembered that the name might be in the directory, even if it was not in the phone book. He thumbed through the pages, a quarter of which seemed to be covered with Macs. There was an Alexander MacKenzie on a South End street; that was not his man, for the district was too prosperous. There was another in the North End, but the directory said he was a schoolboy. He snapped the book shut. "When was this directory made up?" he asked the girl.

"It's this year's."

"I'm looking for a man who's been in town just about a year."

She shook her head. "His name wouldn't be in there. A lot of newcomers are in town these days and we get a lot of inquiries."

"I see." He put up his coat collar and began walking toward the waterfront and when he reached the dock area, turned south in the direction of Wain's Wharf.

The old firm seemed busy this morning. Through the archway he could see slovens unloading crates and sacks, and there was a great activity of workmen all over the wharf. He hunched his head into his collar and lounged through the arch. On his right was the doorway leading to Geoffrey Wain's office, directly in front were the shed and the slovens, with horses dropping dung on the timbers of the wharf and rattling their harness and bits as they tossed their heads or were manoeuvred about by their drivers.

MacKenzie was not in sight, and Neil realized that if he was here at all he would probably be working inside the shed. He dared not enter. If any of Wain's old workers were still around he would be recognized immediately. A teamster left his wagon and lumbered across the yard, and Neil spoke as the man was about to enter the door leading to the office stairs.

"Does a man called Alec MacKenzie work here?"

The man jerked his thumb over his shoulder. "Alec's in the shed," he said.

"Know where his house is?"

"No."

The man walked on up the stairs, leaving the door open behind him. Then Neil heard a familiar voice.

"Miss Phillips, I'm expecting a caller. Tell him to wait. I'll be right back."

Neil turned and faded through the archway to the street, his eyes darting like an animal's from side to side. But there was no escape this way, either. Coming down the hill facing the wharf-entrance was a familiar figure in uniform, Angus Murray heading straight for the wharf and apparently in a hurry. Neil turned his head aside and moved hastily back into the middle of the slovens and horses on the wharf. Murray entered the archway without noticing him, and finally Neil gained the street.

He was condemned to wait again, and the thought enraged him. He had suffered too much and too long, and unless there was a reckoning soon, his existence would become a disgrace to itself. Wain was back, comfortable and secure; Halifax was drifting through the war in smug and profitable self-satisfaction, unconscious of the realities he knew. The old men like Wain had been willing to have this war because they were bored with themselves, and now they fancied they were in control of a wonderful new age.

For him, the dreary army routine had given place to a phantasmal existence of hospitals and cities away from the front but still a part of the war, an experience in which nothing had been real but loneliness and nothing knowledge but statistics and newsprint. To continue like this indefinitely would turn him into a ghastly, groping automaton who would ultimately accept an invalid psychosis as a substitute for real life. Another two years of it would finish even the courage necessary for suicide.

He walked on toward the South End, muttering to himself, careless of the whole town recognizing him. To be anonymous in Halifax was worse than wandering unknown through London or Liverpool, for there were people here who knew him, even some who had loved him once. He came to a decision. Why wait to find Alec MacKenzie? There was another person he wanted to see even more.

TEN O'CLOCK

At this hour of the morning Geoffrey Wain's office was filled with sunshine so brilliant that the nickel on the edges of Miss Phillips's typewriter flashed a spot back and forth across the ceiling as the carrier travelled with the lines of the letter she was writing. Murray leaned back in the only comfortable chair and smoked a pipe, speculatively appraising Evelyn Phillips at work. She paid no obvious attention to him, but he knew she was aware of his attention and possibly of some of his thoughts, and he admired her detachment. Her adolescent figure seemed to him more piquant than attractive, but he acknowledged its interest for experiment as he recollected that his own experience had never included a woman so tiny.

After nearly a quarter of an hour, Wain returned full of apologies for being late, and motioned Miss Phillips to leave them alone. She picked up her papers and went to the inner office behind the frosted glass, and almost immediately the sound of another typewriter joined the chorus of three already at work there.

"You seem pretty busy down here," Murray said. "I must say I like the establishment. It doesn't look like an office at all."

"Well, it hasn't changed much in the last hundred years," Wain said. "I hope that's some of my tobacco you're smoking?"

"Don't worry, it is. To have access to tobacco and cigars like yours must make the West Indian trade pretty attractive."

"It's about the only thing that does. I can't say this business ever interested me much."

Murray smiled politely. He was curious, but by no means concerned, to discover why his presence had been requested here this morning.

"My daughter speaks to me a great deal about you," Wain said.

"So?" Murray did not believe it. "I hope what she says isn't too boring."

Wain produced a perfunctory smile. "I'll be very frank with you, if you don't mind. Penelope has begun to worry me. Since her mother's death our house has been pretty lonely. I'm too busy to have many people in, myself. And —" There was a momentary silence during which he seemed not so much embarrassed as at a temporary loss for a sequence of words which would cause him the least bother. "By the way, I'm glad to see your arm finally out of its splint. That's splendid!"

The irrelevancy made Murray laugh. "I doubt if the arm agrees with you. The finger-joints still ache like hell."

"But it's good to know it's improving. After all, you and I are the sole survivors of our original battalion mess."

"I never thought of that," Murray said reflectively.

Wain's hesitation had resolved itself. "Frankly," he said, "I've asked you here on a personal and delicate matter. I hope you'll take what I say in the spirit it's intended. The fact is, I want you to do me a favour. I have a feeling you'll be helping yourself as well. You'll certainly be helping Penelope."

Murray indicated that he was listening.

"You know, our family has been here so long it's supposed to have a certain social position in the town. In the eyes of a lot of people I fancy we're snobs. But you know yourself that

if a family has gained prominence it can't avoid its respon-
sibilities. It's got to maintain itself or go under and lose
everything. Now, a situation has arisen —" He stopped
abruptly, and Murray had the impression that he had been
giving away more than he had intended.

"Is Penelope having any difficulty?" Murray asked.

Wain opened a handkerchief. "I'm afraid she may get
herself into an unholy mess. I admit I'm fairly worried about
it. As you know, she's in some respects an exceptional sort of
girl. She's also a wilful one. I've always respected her for it, and
more or less allowed her to go her own way. The consequences
involved now are far more serious than she can understand."
The colonel blew his nose loudly. "To put it bluntly, she insists
she saw her cousin Neil Macrae last night – on a tram and out
of uniform."

"What!" Murray started so abruptly the pipe fell out of his
mouth. "Macrae – alive!"

"You can appreciate what that may mean to all of us."

"But – man, it's impossible! He's dead. Besides, I was with
Penelope last night myself."

"She says it was after you left her. The tram, I believe, was
northbound on Barrington Street."

"You sound as if you actually believed she really saw him."

"I do."

"But you virtually certified his death yourself."

"Yes, I did. But did anyone see the body? Missing, believed
killed – that was the wording in the casualty list. You were
Battalion M.O. Did you see the body?"

"No, but I saw a hole the size of a church door where you'd
had him put a few hours before."

"And therefore we both assumed he was killed." Wain shook
his head. "Funny things can happen in a bombardment on a
dark night. We went down the line the next evening. I wish I
could remember the name of that North-Country battalion
that relieved us. They might have an interesting story to tell."

"Then you really believe the boy's alive?"

"I don't definitely believe anything. I merely think it's quite probable."

"But for God's sake —"

"Murray – you know my daughter pretty well. Do you think she's hysterical?"

"No."

"When she spoke to me last night, she was absolutely positive."

Murray scowled at the bowl of his empty pipe. It now began to occur to him to wonder at Wain's purpose in singling him out as an audience for this story. "Look here," he said, "I think you're exaggerating everything. It's an obvious case of hallucination. The war has provided hundreds of examples like it."

"I've naturally thought of that," Wain said.

"Well?"

"If any other woman but my daughter had told me this I'd have dismissed it at once."

Murray put the pipe in his pocket and got restlessly to his feet. He could see the panorama of the harbour spreading in the winter sunshine and the ships of the convoy passing down the Stream toward the sea. "Granted then that he's alive," he said slowly, "what of it?"

He turned, the two men faced each other, and Wain's nostrils dilated.

"I have no intention of giving him another opportunity to make trouble for me and my family," Wain said.

Murray resumed his seat and crossed his legs calmly. There was an emergency, and the emergency was Penny's.

"You are aware that your daughter's in love with the boy, of course?" he said.

"What does she know about a thing like that?" The anger in Wain's voice was undisguised and unpleasant, and he seemed to realize it, for he added more quietly. "The boy used to appeal to her sense of pity. She's warm-hearted, I suppose. The sort who's apt to think that every wastrel is the helpless victim of circumstances or villains, and needs her support."

"But your nephew was hardly a wastrel, was he?"

"No, that's overstating it. But he was completely impractical. Like a lot of the Highland Scotch he was shiftless unless he had everything his own way. Not that he didn't have ability, mind you. He could have had a wonderful future, but he'd never be interested in anything he'd get paid for. No one was willing to finance him while he experimented on ship designs that looked like vessels from Mars. Penny was a sheltered girl, and because he always had the gift of the gab, he imposed on her. As if that wasn't enough, he was her first cousin."

"I gather she's been told that." In a spurt of dislike he could not control, Murray jabbed out, "I take it you just didn't like him. But the English aristocracy have a habit of marrying their own cousins, so I don't see what objection a family like yours could have to doing the same."

Coming from anyone else, this would have been hard for Wain to take; from Murray it was almost unendurable, and the man made it worse by watching calmly as Wain closed his jaws to avoid a retort.

"It never was a question of marriage," Wain said finally. "I saw to that. But he was always unsettling us. That's why I sent him to school in Montreal. He put ideas into her head and he had plenty of empty ones. I never bothered to find out, but I suppose he was a socialist, as well." Suddenly aware that he was giving a lot more than he was receiving, Wain lowered his voice and added indifferently, "It was a thoroughly unpleasant situation for everybody, and I haven't any intention of seeing it resumed."

"Might I ask," Murray said, "what Penny thinks about all this now?"

"She's too upset to know what she thinks."

"I can understand that. There's another thing – would you mind being specific about what all this has to do with me?"

"I should have presumed that anything connected with my daughter would be of concern to you."

"What do you mean?"

Wain set his spreading hands on the desk, observing carefully the powerful fingers like talons. "I'm no longer your colonel," he said quietly. "I'm well aware that your affairs are no concern of mine. But my daughter's are. And when a man your age – and with your reputation, Murray – is paying open attention to her – just what am I supposed to think?"

"What you damn well please!" Murray was on his feet. "If that's all, I think I'll say good morning."

Wain's lips parted and the teeth shone brightly under the black bristles of his moustache. Murray realized that the expression was a smile.

"Please, Major! Pay me the compliment of realizing that I'm not quite as stupid and conventional as you seem to assume. I merely mentioned that I knew you were interested in Penelope, that's all. Let's reach an agreement before you go."

Murray grunted and resumed his seat, crossing his legs. "It would be a hell of a lot easier if you'd quit trying to be subtle with me," he said. "I know damn well what you meant."

Wain passed his fingers over the cleft of his chin. "Let's assume for the time being that Neil Macrae is in Halifax. What effect is that going to have on all of us?"

"You tell me," Murray said, "what effect it's going to have on you. That's all you're thinking about, isn't it?"

"I was thinking of the effect it would have on my daughter."

"Well, I can help you there, in case you don't know already. It would be the most wonderful thing that's happened to her in years."

"Even if it means he will now be shot by a firing-squad?"

"What? You —"

"He's still subject to court-martial, you know. What slight chance he might have had to escape sentence is gone now. He's made himself a deserter with a record against his name."

"You'd actually do a thing like that to your own nephew?"

"It would be easier," Wain said with pretended weariness, "if people would avoid the habit of looking for a villain in situations which are merely confused. I suppose I ought to feel insulted by your attitude, but frankly, I don't. I want you to understand me, that's all. I haven't the slightest chance of stopping anything that happens to Neil Macrae if he's found here. The first military policeman he meets will arrest him on the spot – if he knows who he is, I mean. Military law will do the rest. But at the same time, I won't be able to avoid connection with the case. I'll be summoned as a witness. You understand me? *I'd* have to be the chief witness against him! And in Halifax!" He leaned back in his chair and surveyed Murray coolly. "That would be a pretty picture for Penelope to carry through life, don't you think? Her cousin convicted and shot for cowardice with her father the chief witness against him!"

Murray slumped back in his chair and passed a hand over his flushed face. At last Wain had managed to convince him; although he knew that Penny's father would be delighted to see Neil Macrae destroyed, he also realized that his picture of the situation was probably accurate. If Neil were discovered, these things would happen.

"You probably have still more to say," he answered at length, in a low voice. "I'm listening."

Wain tapped his fingers decisively on the desk and Murray was able to catch a flicker of satisfaction relaxing the muscles of the older man's expression.

"In the first place, there must be no court-martial."

"If what you say is true, how can it be avoided?"

"I'll tell you. We must first find the boy. Once he's found – by us – I'm fairly certain things can be fixed. Now, he won't be in a hotel where he's likely to be recognized. He isn't with any of his relations. Why he's here at all I don't know, but I'm afraid he may try to see Penelope. If he meets her before we can reach him —"

Murray shut his eyes. "Go on, I know what you mean."

"It's my guess he's gone to a boarding house. Some cheap place in the North End, probably. There aren't many and I'm having them all checked. That's one advantage of the war. You can give orders without a parcel of fools asking why."

"Why do you think you need me in this?"

"When we find him, I want you to talk to him."

"Why not talk to him yourself?"

"Considering everything, I don't think there'd be much point in that."

"Probably not. Well, what do I say to him?"

"Remember that we must avoid a court-martial. The only way that can be done is for him to leave the country at once. Try to persuade him that no matter what sense of grievance he may feel he hasn't a chance if he remains here. Try —"

"Grievance?" Murray interrupted sharply. "What do you mean by that?"

"Nothing definite. I suppose he feels the world is against him, that's all. He ought to. The world *is* against him."

"All right, go on."

"He could easily lose himself if he went to the States. And with the opportunities over there, he might still have a decent future. He's probably travelling under an assumed name. Tell him to keep it. And one thing more" – again an irreconcilable anger flared into Wain's voice – "tell him if he ever sets foot inside Nova Scotia again, or communicates with my daughter in any way, I'll see to it that the law takes its course with him."

Murray did not move; he sat blinking in the sunlight streaming in through the long window.

Wain became impatient. "In all fairness to me, isn't that the most decent thing I can do under the circumstances?"

"I don't know," Murray said slowly. There was a moment of silence during which the ticking clock was audible. Then he blinked again. "If that's your only message," he said, "you'd better see him yourself."

He unfolded his long legs and got to his feet, put his hands deep into his pockets and walked over to the window, where he stood in silence for nearly a minute, looking down on the wharf and the slovens unloading at the end of the shed. The air whistled audibly through his crooked nostrils as he breathed, and behind his back, Wain's fingers drumming on the desk were like an obbligato to the muffled clatter of the typewriters in the other room. Finally he turned and said, "Does Penny know you're seeing me this morning?"

"Naturally not."

Murray's manner became decisive. "You've told me a lot, Wain, but I don't feel I've heard anything that really matters. Suppose you go back and fill in the gaps?"

Wain's only change of expression was a fixity in the muscles of his face: the movement was slight, but it transformed his appearance. "Just what are you suggesting? I don't like the inference."

"I'm suggesting nothing. I'm telling you I'll have to hear a lot more before I'll have any part in this mess."

"I'm sorry," Wain said. "I should have apologized for mixing you up in what, after all, is a family affair. I seem to have been mistaken. I had thought your interest in my daughter – or your ambitions, to put it bluntly – would have been enough to make you willing to assist."

Murray laughed shortly and shook his head. "We'd better stick to facts. You and I are so different we'd never understand each other in a million years. Come on – what's the real problem? It isn't just Penny's welfare. What is it?"

Wain's lips parted in another smile, and Murray was mildly astonished to see that the man seemed relieved. The impression was corroborated when Wain's chin lifted in a quick laugh.

"You know, Murray, maybe you and I can understand each other better than you think. It's a matter of getting used to things that are taboo in Halifax. It's a matter of admitting them – of admitting them to one's self. You imply that I'm thinking of myself. I am. And as I've always assumed that your motives with regard to Penny were not – shall we say, the motives of a twenty-two-year-old boy – I don't see why we can't reach an understanding."

"Go on," Murray said.

"Evidently you realize that you have some bargaining power, and have sensibly decided to use it. On the whole, I think you can. You may or may not be fond of my daughter, but she has attractions other than herself. Money, for instance. You're no longer young. And with your injured arm" – he glanced pointedly – "as well as with your past record – in short, if Neil Macrae stays dead, I'd be the first to wish you success with Penelope."

Murray was silent. Then he tapped his nose and broke into a broad grin. "You know – I can't remember when I've been so blandly insulted. One thing I'm curious about – did you know you were insulting me, or didn't you?"

Wain said nothing, but the drumming of his fingers on the desk indicated that his patience had almost run out.

"Never mind about my marrying Penny," Murray said. "What's your personal motive in wanting to get Macrae out of town?"

"I've given it."

Murray shook his head. "No. You see, I just can't believe that your affection for your daughter or your regard for your precious family is so strong. It was through him you lost your command, wasn't it?"

However great Wain's growing resentment and humiliation might be, he contrived to keep it out of his voice when he answered the ringing telephone. His answers to the queries from the other end of the line were succinct and crisp and when he replaced the receiver on its hook he continued to talk to Murray with no change of tone.

"Yes, I have a personal motive. Everybody has.... The other night you asked how long I thought the war was going to last. I said three years, and I had good reason for the estimate. That means we're now exactly in the middle of it." He looked up to make sure that Murray was attending. "People around here seem to think this war's merely a matter of beating the Germans. I don't. I think it's the first stage of a revolution. Now then – what state will the world be in after three more years like the last ones?"

"What's all this to do with Neil Macrae?"

"It has a lot to do with my plans, which that young fool can spoil by getting himself arrested. After this war the entire world will be bankrupt. It has already become a military society for purposes of the war. Do you think it will slip back into the old mould again? After this war, anyone outside the army or navy will be a nobody. Therefore the services offer the only sure future an ambitious man can hope to have." His voice rose. "I've counted on that, Murray, and I intend to be in on it. I'm not going to have any two-by-four scandal stop me. I got word only yesterday that I'm to be reinstated in overseas service – but this time I shall be on the staff." His clenched knuckles rapped the desk. "I've wasted a whole lifetime in this hole of a town. Everything in this damn country is second-rate. It always is, in a colony. Now I'm going to get away from it for good. You've asked me for my motive and there it is. You can think what you like and be damned to you."

"If you mean all that," Murray said, "I think you're crazy. Hell, I'm a major myself, and the idea of becoming a colonel like you wouldn't get me excited. Of course, you might become a brigadier, and after that they might make you a major-general and...."

"You can think what you like of my ability," Wain said. "The general staff will be the judges of it."

"Yes," Murray said with a yawn, "maybe they will, at that. You know, the only thing in all this rigmarole that makes any sense to me is that at this particular moment you're all excited about a staff job, and that Neil Macrae has something on you. I should have supposed that if he were successfully court-martialled, your position would be strengthened with the staff. But he'd talk at the court-martial, and that seems to be the rub. How about explaining a little more?"

Wain sighed. "You seem determined to make a mountain out of a molehill. Don't you know how an officer gets on to the staff?"

"No, I guess I was never interested enough to find out."

"Well" – Wain hesitated in distaste – "a man has to have the qualifications, naturally. But influence is very important. Some show of politics is often necessary; especially on this side of the water."

"So the dead rat under the family floor is beginning to smell at last! You not only don't want the boy court-martialled. You don't even dare let him get in calling distance of a court."

"You don't know what you're talking about."

"Young Macrae was arrested on your orders, wasn't he? And a court-martial was never held, was it?" He got up and began to pace the floor. "Your version of the story has spread all over the place, Wain. People have come to take it for granted. Neil Macrae disobeyed your orders when he retired, and half the battalion was wiped out. But I don't remember hearing his side of the story. Where were you that day? If I remember rightly, you lost touch with the whole lot of us. A fat chance you'd have of collaring a staff job if all that stuff came to light in an investigation!"

Wain rose to his feet and the two men faced each other. Both were trembling, Murray with the excitement of an idea, Wain with fury.

"You're hysterical, Murray, and you're being a fool! If you'd done more thinking and less talking in your life, you'd have a little more money in your pocket today."

"I'm doing plenty of thinking right now."

With a great effort, Wain relaxed sufficiently to turn away and resume his seat. When he spoke again, his voice had a sound of weary exasperation.

"I suppose I ought to show you the door," he said. "If there was anyone else" – he shrugged his shoulders – "You seem to have forgotten several things, Major. It was I who committed Macrae for court-martial. In the light of that, I can't understand your suspicion that I have anything to fear from what he might say. It is merely impolitic for me to have a scandal at the present moment. Macrae would be convicted, all right. He disobeyed a written order. Do you think I'd court-martial a man who could produce a signed order from me that would acquit him?"

"What was the order? Something impossible?"

"It would help if you wouldn't persist in regarding me a scoundrel, Murray."

"What was the order?" Murray said.

"I was cut off from the front by the enemy's barrage. You remember that, don't you?"

"I remember the barrage. My dressing-station was in the middle of it."

"Very well. The lines were destroyed, the adjutant was wounded. I sent a runner ahead with a message to the senior officer in charge at the front line. The order was to advance immediately on the second objective. That was a low ridge a quarter of a mile in advance of where the battalion then was. It would have cost some casualties —"

"It certainly would!"

"At least it would have saved the attack from collapsing. Besides that, a retirement into an area selected by the enemy for a counter-barrage would have been the worst possible move, and that was precisely what Macrae did. Why my corporal had to encounter my nephew, of all the junior officers in the battalion, and give *him* the message, I don't know, but —"

"You ought to," Murray interrupted. "The senior officers were all dead by then."

"Anyway, the order was flatly disobeyed. It was the most flagrant case of loss of nerve – or plain cowardice – I ever encountered."

Murray leaned back and stroked his bald spot. He found himself remembering an old tag about the man who convicted himself by constant explanation. But at the same time, he was forced to admit that Wain's story hung together and that every detail seemed to be accurate. His recollection of the affair had cleared, and the remembrance of that afternoon in Flanders filled him with a weary and hopeless anger, a disgust with the fundamental stupidity of men like Wain, with the premises on which their lives and actions rested, with the past few years and his own part in them. That particular attack had been a military crime, but he knew it was futile to waste one's self in generalities about it. The back areas of France were littered with execution notices of men who had broken down in the face of similar staff orders, and yet the war went on and no British soldiers were in revolt against their generals. They wanted to beat the Germans more than to save their own lives. It was easy to criticize the high command for incompetence, but a waste to attack their values, for society shared them through and through.

"If I've been making a fool of myself," he said finally, "I apologize."

"Very well." Wain straightened in his chair. "Let's waste no more time misunderstanding each other. Will you see the boy and tell him what I've told you?"

"I suppose so." Murray was hesitant, and added gloomily, "But first I'd like to know why Neil Macrae has returned to Halifax."

"Animals always come back to familiar places. For all we know, he may have been here some time, living a life of his own and no one else the wiser. But I'd prefer you to save Penelope the necessity of running into him again. A meeting with her would probably start him into the open, and his execution would hardly improve her state of mind."

"All right," Murray said. "Tell me where he is and I'll see him. At least he has the right to tell someone his side of the story before he leaves." He looked sharply at Wain, but there was no mistaking the fact that the older man was confident. "And when he has left," Murray went on, "do you think Penny can be persuaded that she was mistaken about seeing him that night?"

"She can be – by you. Or" – Wain made a gesture of indifference – "she'll eventually realize he wasn't worth bothering about anyway. Once she's safely married she'll forget all about him."

Murray got to his feet abruptly. "And then you'll be safe from whatever's bothering you. God damn you, you're the first man that ever tried to bribe me. I'll not forget it."

"An appeal to common sense is hardly a bribe. Our interests in the case differ, that's all."

Wain picked up some papers and affected to be interested in their contents. Of all the men Murray had ever met, this one seemed able to present the hardest shell to others. But Murray had no illusions about him; he knew that underneath the urbane exterior the older man was seething with anger and wounded pride, with humiliation at the steps necessary to advance his career, with outrage over the need of disclosing so much of his private affairs to a stranger.

He picked up his military cap and set it carelessly on the side of his head. As he turned to leave he muttered, "At least your notion of a military dictatorship in this country is a lot of balls."

"I'll let you know whenever the boy is located," Wain said without looking up. "I suppose you can be found at your hotel?"

Murray left the office without another word. It was a relief to reach the wharf and the biting odour of salt on the blown air, and see the workmen unloading the wagons by the shed. A pack of cumulus cloud was building up over the land across the harbour and the wind was hauling toward the south. He strolled down the wharf to watch the men, and their calm and regular movements soothed him.

He smiled inwardly at himself. It was strange that he, whom most people regarded as a waster and an outsider, should all his life have tried to do the right thing by others. He rarely got any credit for his motives, even from himself. He knew he was not stupid in the ordinary sense of the word; his stupidity was emotional rather than intellectual, and he had no illusions about the harm he had consistently done himself. At the moment he had no clear idea what he was going to do. He was positive that Wain had told him the legal truth and he was equally sure that it would be a ghastly mess for everyone if Penny encountered Neil Macrae now. Even if Neil were in the clear, it would not be an enviable situation. Too much had happened to each of them these past three years, and it had happened to them separately. Neil would never be able to understand or appreciate what Penny had gone through, and now that she was professionally successful, he would find her changed. In this particular, Geoffrey Wain seemed entirely right; Neil and Penny must be kept apart.

He turned and began to stroll back along the wharf. It was useless to argue with himself about a matter of which he knew so little. He knew nothing whatever of Neil Macrae; he cared nothing about Wain. If he were to do anything in this situation it must be done for Penny's sake, and so he must find out as soon as possible what she had really said to her father the previous night, if it could be done without revealing his purpose.

He took a last look down the wharf before turning about, and then double-checked what he saw. An enormous man was coming out of the warehouse with a sheaf of papers in his hand, and the figure was familiar. There was no mistaking the face; it was Big Alec MacKenzie, Wain's former corporal. MacKenzie moved on to the shed, and after a few moments Murray walked back to Water Street.

"I wonder," he said to himself, "why that particular man happens to be working here?"

TWO O'CLOCK

The winter sunlight was like a net thrown over the frozen garden behind the old red house. In the living-room Penny lay on the chesterfield while her father's Persian cat, an aloof cloud of black fur with enormous yellow eyes, played with a ball of khaki wool which had fallen on the floor. Work had been out of the question for her today after a sleepless night, and now she was grateful to be alone, her father in his office, Roddie at school, Sadie given an unexpected afternoon off.

One refrain jogged endlessly through her mind: Neil was alive, Neil still was, and the war had not killed the only eager human being she had ever known. Now she could let herself remember, but the inhibitions she had imposed upon her mind for three years were difficult to shake off. That last night together in Montreal, how shy and delicate he had been the first time she lay beside him and then how his habitual eagerness had made him forget everything except that he wanted her, and she had closed her eyes and left the lead to him as she had always done before, and through her mind had floated the words, "into thy hands I commend my spirit." And then he was gone, and she was left with Jean growing within her, and the pain and terror of bringing a child into the world so that no one should know its identity, and existence suddenly become formidable with nothing to control it but courage and endless discipline.

Now he was alive again. That meant she was no longer alone. But so many leaves had dropped from the calendar since that June day by the St. Lawrence. How would Neil be able to recognize the woman she had become, or even want her again? Now that the requirements of her profession had made her critical, would she be able to discover again her need for a man whom judgment told her was careless and impetuous and over-confident of his own ability to shape the world according to his own design?

The cat had finally tangled himself inextricably in the ball of wool, and with a baffled and desperate dignity was trying to get free. But for two years he had been alive without writing her a word; he had been in trouble and failed to ask her help, he had come home, but not to her. Oh, Neil – why couldn't you have let me know? Just something, so I could have known and talked with you no matter where you were!

She checked her emotion ruthlessly. The problem was not limited to themselves. There were Jean and Mary and Jim Fraser; there was even Angus Murray. And above all, there was her father. She thought she would never as long as she lived forget the look on her father's face when she had told him she had seen Neil Macrae alive in Halifax.

The cat rolled over, clawing frantically. Whenever he extricated himself from one loop he involved himself in another. She watched him idly. There were too many problems to solve now. Only one was urgent, and that was to save Neil from arrest, to get him out of Halifax before he was caught.

The cat made a few more efforts to free himself, and then twisted his paws loose and sat down with the wool encircling his shoulders and legs and belly, and with such dignity as he could still retain, began to wash his face. She wondered if

Angus Murray could help her. She would have to tell him that Neil was alive. The more she thought about it, the more sure she was that he was the only person she dared approach.

The doorbell rang and she decided to ignore it. When it sounded a second time, she regretted her decision to let Sadie go, and went out into the hall to answer it.

Neither of them moved or spoke. Neil's enlarged eyes stared defiantly out of a strained and lined face. The fan of crinkles away from his eyes, furrowed in the past by much spontaneous laughter, were merely marks now, unnoticeable among the deeper lines cut like gashes into the thin flesh of his face. His clothes were cheap and stained and shabby, and his shoes scuffed and rundown. But out of the astonishment of seeing him on the doorstep she felt a quick lift of hope, for though his face was lacerated by worry and suffering, it had not entirely lost its familiar aspect of negligent confidence.

She saw him gulp, and then he said, "I happened to know your father would be out this afternoon," and without waiting for her to answer, he passed by her into the hall.

She closed the door and followed him silently into the living-room, standing still inside the doorway as he stopped in front of the map of Jamaica.

"My God, is that thing still here!"

"Neil!"

She forced the word out, and at the sound of her voice he flashed about. She could see his face muscles loosen and his Adam's apple leap convulsively. Everything in the room blurred, and then she was in his arms, feeling his hands clutching her and slipping quickly over her back and loins and shoulders. He tried to lift her, but knowing his intention, she moved with his body and they lay on the chesterfield. It was minutes before his hands were still.

The clock struck a quarter-hour and he sat up abruptly. His face was flushed but its lines were easier now; they were more diffuse, though the eyes were still strange. They seemed to be constantly staring. He stretched out his hand and touched the white lock running along her temple.

"You didn't have this before."

She shook her head.

"You're still so lovely, Penny."

"Am I, Neil?"

His large eyes ran over the lines of her body and back again to her face. He made a quick movement as if to touch her again, but checked himself.

"God, things are in a mess! I mustn't let myself think of you like this, now!"

She touched his hand, picked it up and traced the length of his fingers. It seemed necessary to maintain a physical contact. His hands were rough, and some of the fingernails were broken. "Neil," she said, "you didn't come back just to tell me that?"

"As a matter of fact, I didn't come back to tell you anything. I'm here to square some accounts. It's a pity I wasn't bright enough to have started long ago, but that's the way it is now."

She watched his face more closely. Some of the old scorn was still in his voice, but little of the enthusiasm. She was hurt by the tone of defiance. How much of it was permanent and how much was caused by his determination to crush back his physical desire for her? There was no mistaking that he wanted her. She had the feeling that his eyes stared right through her clothes and lingered on her body. His desire underlay everything he was saying, and after a while it conditioned her own hearing of his words.

But there was something else in his mind much stronger than bodily eagerness, and its presence was just as obvious. It was something new between them; she did not know what it was.

"Why not tell me about it, Neil?" she said quietly.

"I'd like to." The words were decisive, but almost immediately his expression flicked back to a cautious tension. "But I can't yet. If things turn out all right. . . ." He got up and ran his eyes quickly over the mantelpiece. "Have you got any fags around here?"

"I'll see."

She crossed to a table and opened one of its drawers and returned with a large box.

"Three Castles? Your father still does himself well. I've been glad enough of a Woodbine lately." He lit the cigarette and held it critically away, ironically admiring the fine white ash.

"We thought you'd been killed, Neil."

He looked away and dragged heavily on the cigarette.

"I heard other things, too, but I didn't believe them," she went on. She tried to keep emotion out of her voice but it was no use; the overtones that stole into her quiet words made them more bitter than an accusation. "Why didn't you write to me? I loved you when you went away."

He stared at her while the cigarette burned in his fingers. Then he slumped back on the chesterfield and buried his face in his hands, and his shoulders shook as he broke into terrible silent sobs.

Penny sat quietly with his head hard and warm against her breasts, and for several moments she was still. Then she laid her arm over his shoulders and pressed him against her body.

"Don't touch me, for God's sake!" He twisted away. "I shouldn't have come, only I couldn't stand it any longer thinking you might be here. Can't you see it nearly killed me not to be able to write you a single line? I've been alone all this time. I haven't heard my own name spoken in two years. They were going to shoot me, Penny – do you think I could have told you a thing like that? It's bad enough having to say it now." He swallowed and his face twisted as he looked away from her. "Oh, God – it's impossible! Here you are – living in your father's house, everything the same, nothing different! He'd still have me shot if he knew I was alive where he could get his hands on me."

She watched him as he crossed the room to the window and jerked the curtains apart. "The garden!" He turned and faced her again. "I'll tell you this much, Penny. I didn't come back to see you. I came to see your father – your father and one other man. And nothing on earth is going to stop me."

Now she knew. Her father *was* responsible. Whatever had happened, Neil was being killed by the burden in his mind.

"I don't know what Father has done to you," she said. "I don't know anything that happened over there. But whatever it is, can't *I* help you?" She hesitated. "Have you – have you any chance of proving your case?"

He looked at her sharply, almost with hostility. "What do you mean – prove my case? What has your father told you?"

He sat down beside her again and she leaned softly against his shoulder. "Darling – what does it matter now? Oh, Neil – can't you see I love you still?"

He winced away again. "You've got to let me alone in this. It's something I've got to do myself." His eyes were boring into her, examining, scrutinizing. Then he said sharply, "You aren't particularly surprised to see me."

"I knew you were alive."

"How? Who told you?"

"Yesterday evening I saw you – you were on a tram going north. I followed it in a taxi, but by the time I caught up you weren't on it."

"Does anyone else know I'm here?"

She hesitated.

"Did you tell your father?"

"Yes – I had to."

"My God, I might have known!" His eyes lashed her. "For the love of Christ, Penny, of all the people in this world, why did you have to tell him?"

"Oh, Neil!" The look on his face was intolerable and it was an effort not to hide from it. "What else could I have done? Things have happened to me, too. You're not the only one who's been alone. I've been awfully alone. When I saw you last night and realized you'd stayed away from me for some reason . . . Neil, I had to find out why. I was going crazy."

"Well, did you?"

"No."

He got up and moved around the room looking at familiar objects without recognition. Finally he dropped into an armchair opposite her, and after moving in a sudden convulsion, his face became quite calm. It was only then that she realized he had been shell-shocked. The knowledge seemed good; at least it gave a reason for a change that otherwise would have been unaccountable.

"You couldn't help it," he said. "I don't suppose it was much fun to discover I was alive and hadn't let you know. And I don't suppose it's been pleasant living with all the hyenas in the family prowling around you." He gave a curious laugh and seemed genuinely amused. "Tell me, what did Aunt Maria say when she heard the sad news of my demise?"

"Do you really want to know?"

"I've often wondered. Honestly, I have."

"Well, at first she seemed to think you'd fallen in the line of duty and that was so gratifying to her patriotism she said quite nice things about you. What she thinks now I don't know and don't care. Neil – please tell me something. Haven't you any better clothes than those you're wearing?"

"No," he said, suddenly cheerful.

"Then let me get you some. Have you enough money? I don't want to pry, but —"

"To hell with all that, it doesn't matter! I've got enough for the time being and my clothes will do. I suppose you've been wondering why I'm no longer in uniform. It's a long story and you'll have to wait to hear it later. Tell me, is Uncle Alfred still alive?"

"Of course. And Mary and Jim are living in Prince's Lodge now."

"Whatever made them leave Montreal?"

"That's a long story, too."

The desire to tell him about Jean was overpowering. Hundreds of times, lying awake at night, she had imagined meetings with Neil and planned how she would tell him and what he would say. Now she bit her tongue to keep it quiet.

He smiled at her then, almost in the old way, as his tenseness relaxed. "I haven't asked much about you. You aren't married, are you?"

"Of course not."

"What have you been doing with yourself all this time?"

"I'm working."

"Where, in your father's office?"

"No, in the Shipyards."

"Learn stenography?"

"I learned enough mechanical engineering to design a boat."

"You did *what*?"

"Don't be so surprised. You taught me, didn't you?" She smiled shyly. "I'm supposed to be quite good at it."

"I'll be damned! My young Penny a ship designer!" But he was not taking it seriously. "I saw they were expanding a lot down there. What is it – usual stuff? Buy a few blueprints from the Clydebank and try not to make too many mistakes in following them?"

"I suppose so."

"It must be dull as hell."

"I've done a few small craft of my own."

"You don't happen to be working with the local genius who designed that craft I read about in the paper today?"

"I – in what paper?"

"You know what I'm talking about. Penny – you're blushing! I read the details —" He opened his mouth and stared at her in astonishment. "Jesus Christ! It was *you*!"

She was uncertain whether his reaction showed amazement, jealousy, or commendation; possibly a little of all three. While he continued to stare at her the phone rang and she left to answer it.

"Hello, Penny," said the voice on the other end of the wire. "I'm on my way over to see you."

"Oh, Angus, please! Not now. Any other time, but not now."

"I'm not going to stop to explain why, but it's important. Your father had me in his office today and blew the gaff. I've got to see you right away."

"Wait a minute." She rose from the phone and closed the door softly between the living-room and the hall. She was frightened, but as usual the state of alarm made her appear outwardly more calm. "You can't come now. Just tell me what he said. That will have to do."

"I can't tell you over the phone. No matter what you say, I'm coming over."

"Wait a moment, Angus." She dropped her voice to a whisper. "Can you hear me now?"

"Yes, but —"

"Neil's here. He's in the living-room – now."

Murray swore. She heard the air whistling in his nostrils, and over the wire the sound was more strident than usual. After a moment he said quietly, "I'm still coming. Keep him there till I arrive."

"But that's impossible. He's in trouble."

"Are you telling me!"

"But can't you —"

"No, I can't. I have an idea you may be as much a babe in the woods as he is, and he seems a champion in that class, walking right into your father's house." He paused. "What's the matter, don't you trust me?"

She breathed deeply, and repeated his question over in her mind. Did she trust Angus Murray in a situation like this? For that matter, did she trust anyone in the world besides herself? "Yes," she said finally, "I think I do. But I still don't want you here this afternoon."

His voice rose angrily. "You little fool, you don't know what you're talking about. You've been keeping this to yourself so long you've lost all sense of proportion. I spent more than an hour with your father. He means business. There are angles in this case you don't know the first thing about, and maybe Neil doesn't either. If nothing else will hold him there, tell him I just found out your father's in line for a staff job. He ought to know enough about the army to understand it's not a good idea for a youngster to try to buck that lot in wartime."

Penny hesitated, again calculating. "All right, I'll tell him. Will you be long?"

"No more than five minutes," Murray said.

She put the receiver up and sat still on the chair with her hands folded in her lap. She might have been quietly resting there with her own thoughts. Then she walked slowly back to the living-room and opened the door. Neil was standing with his legs apart in the middle of the carpet staring at her.

"What's the secret?" he said.

She smiled. "I'm going to make you some tea. Nobody will be home the rest of the afternoon, so we may as well be comfortable."

"To hell with tea!" He blocked her passage to the dining-room. "Who was that on the phone, your father?"

"Of course not!"

"I've got to know. Was it important?"

"Yes, Neil, perhaps it was. Do sit down. For heaven's sake." She suddenly exploded at him, "What do you think I'm made of? I want some tea and you need it, too, whether you know it or not."

"Who was it?"

"You're just as stubborn as you ever were. Come on out to the kitchen and I'll tell you. Did you ever meet Major Angus Murray?"

"He was a captain when I saw him last. What's he to you?"

She picked up an old Sheffield tray from a walnut sideboard in the dining-room and carried it with her to the kitchen. Then she filled the kettle and set it on the coal stove, opening the draught and lifting the lid to stir the fire.

"What's Angus Murray to do with you?" he persisted.

"He'll be here in a few minutes."

"The hell he will!" Violent alarm flashed across his face and he gripped her arm fiercely. "Penny, what's the idea?"

"He just called up to say he had something important to tell me. I told him to come over. Now get out of my way and let me make the tea. Everything's going to be all right."

"All right!" He dropped her arm. "He was my battalion M.O."

Neil had not changed as much as she had feared; he was still impetuous, still explosive and oblivious to what other people might be thinking.

While she measured tea in a pot he slumped down on a kitchen chair, straddled it and leaned his folded arms across its back. "I'm sorry, Penny," he said. "You're right. I'm a damned fool. But why does Murray have to come around here just now? I can't stay long. Couldn't he come some other time?"

"He's coming to see you, among other things."

"Oh!"

The quiet, distant sound of his voice saying this single word startled her and she set the teapot down. In the instant his face had grown older, it had drawn into itself and become shrewd and brooding. She felt as though a door had been shut in her face.

"Well, my dear," he said, getting up quietly, "I must be on my way. Apparently I haven't yet learned to be careful enough."

"Meaning?"

"This is where you live. You can ask whom you please to the house. But my plans are too important to be ruined now."

"Neil" – she put her hand on his arm, holding him – "Neil, look at me. I know what I'm doing."

They stood quite still, watching each other, and then his eyes wavered and he turned away as a puzzled expression spread over his face. She knew then that if she chose she had the power in his present condition to control him. Something not even he understood had happened to him since entering the house. The responsibility frightened her.

Again he seemed to be calculating, yet it was evident to her that something beyond himself had made up his mind for him. He pulled in a deep breath like a sigh. "All right," he said, "I don't know what you want, but I'll stay and see."

During the past year Penny had met a large variety of men, some of them important, some officials who held far more power than the public guessed. It had been necessary for her to study them and estimate their aims and the forces that moved them. And now as she studied Neil in the same fashion and heard in her own mind the overtones of his reply, she was relieved. It was not the answer of a weak man, or one with a persecution-mania.

The kettle began to hum. She set out cups and saucers on the tray and cakes on a plate, and led him back to the living-room. "I've something else to tell you," she said quietly. "Angus Murray wants me to marry him."

"Oh, he does!"

"I've not agreed," she said. "But . . . we both thought you were dead."

"It's all right with me."

"And when you meet him, please —"

"Don't worry, I'll behave. I've nothing against Murray. As a matter of fact, he seemed a decent egg, in spite of his reputation for drink. You certainly know how to pick men, don't you? First me, then —" He fingered some magazines piled on a table. "By the way, this isn't an irrelevant question. How's your father keeping?"

"Much the same, I think."

"Still beastly to you?"

"He never was – to me."

He grunted. "You know bloody well he was – but of course, always the officer and gentleman about it. How's his military career making out?"

"He was transferred from France and he's been a transportation officer here for the past year and a half."

Neil grunted again. "Good job for him. I'm glad somebody remembered he had an expert knowledge of train schedules and clearance-papers. Well, he was an expensive officer in France. It's a comfort to know there's at least one megalomaniac brought back here where he can't do any harm."

"Do you really think he's that?"

"Don't you?"

"Of course. I didn't know you saw it too."

"One learns – especially from personal experience."

"Angus just told me something he thought would interest you. Father's been offered a job overseas again – on the staff, this time."

Neil sniffed. "I can't see that altering anything." Then he added reflectively, "On the other hand . . . I see what Murray means. Has the appointment been confirmed yet?"

"I don't think so."

Neil looked relieved, but he made no further comment. The bell rang, and Murray was in the hall before Penny could reach the door. She met him on the threshold, his coat and hat still on, and they looked quickly into each other's eyes.

Neil was on his feet, aloof and careful. The two men shook hands formally, and then Murray removed his cap and coat, laid them on a chair and sat down. Neil remained standing as he had been, his elbow high on the mantel and his back straight. Murray took a cigarette out of the box Penny handed him, lit it and cleared his throat loudly. Then Penny sat down and there was an awkward silence.

Murray surveyed the burning end of his cigarette, took a few more draws on it and laid it on an ashtray before he lifted his eyes to Neil. "I'm going to be frank, Macrae. I'm sorry you found Penny and I'm sorry you're here now. But since you are here, we might as well make the best of it. Have you been in town long?"

"Does it make any difference?"

"No, not particularly. I'd like to know, just the same."

"About four days."

"Where have you been staying?"

"Why should I tell you that?"

Murray rubbed his nose and grinned wryly. "I suppose it's not easy for you to understand that my general idea is to help you out. God knows I don't want to mix up in your affairs. But I'm afraid so many other people are mixed up in them now you've got to get used to the idea they aren't private any more. The important thing is to understand what the situation is. Then we can figure out what to do."

Neil was obviously angry now. "I didn't come here to talk about my affairs to anyone. I came to see Penny. And if you don't mind my saying so, it's none of your business and I don't want your help."

"Sorry," said Murray. "I don't particularly want to help you, either. I just happen to be mixed up in this, that's all. Colonel Wain has given me a message for you. He asked me to find you and say that he doesn't want you in town. In fact, if you don't get out of Canada immediately, he says he'll prosecute you to the limit."

Penny's indrawn breath was audible, and Murray suddenly felt embarrassed. Neil gave a short laugh, but made no further comment.

"I'm remembering what this means to Penny, you know," Murray said.

Neil folded his arms and stared at the far wall.

"You've had a raw deal, Macrae," Murray said. "Don't misunderstand me, I know more about it than you think. I don't want to interfere with you but it looks as though I can't help it." He stopped to catch Neil's eye. "I wonder if you realize just how high the cards are stacked against you?"

"I think I do."

"Well . . . a man can't come back from oblivion and expect to be ignored. You've got to give some sort of account of yourself."

Neil said nothing, but continued in stubborn silence to lean sideways against the mantel and stare without interest at the map of Jamaica.

"Neil," Penny said, "please don't stand in your own light."

He turned derisively and surveyed first Murray and then Penny through a cloud of blue smoke; then he eyed the end of his cigarette and stared into the fire. Penny looked from Neil to Murray and back again, and she felt an irrelevant awareness of the mystery of human attraction, for both these men who loved her had more in common than they knew. Murray was older; failure had made him wiser and more philosophical, and because he had given up the fight long ago, he was now content to understand life, and to leave its control to others. Neil was still defiant, and she guessed that he would always be a harder man than Murray. Yet the two regarded things and people from much the same standpoint, and they valued the same attributes in those they met. She knew they could never become enemies, and wondered if Neil realized this, as Murray appeared to have done already.

"Where were you," Neil spoke slowly to Murray, "the night I was supposed to have been killed?"

"In a dressing-station near the front line."

"Did you see any of the attack that afternoon?"

"I saw some of the results of it."

"Competent performance, didn't you think?"

"I've seen worse."

"You know bloody well you never saw worse. I'm saying this for Penny's sake, mind you, not for yours. Since it's obvious I wasn't killed that night, I suppose she has a right to know what actually did happen. Our colonel was distressed about the failure of his battalion and accused me of ruining the attack he'd planned so carefully. He put me under guard" – Neil's lips twisted unpleasantly – "as soon as he found out where his orders had landed us – as well as himself. Some time in the night a German heavy landed on top of the dugout and it was several weeks before I woke up sufficiently to know who I was. By that time I was in a hospital somewhere in England with my thigh in a cast and a pretty case of shell-shock. My identity disk had been lost and I was registered as one Private Harry Bowman of an East Lancashire regiment —"

"That's right" Murray interrupted quietly, "the East Lancashires did relieve us that time."

Penny knew Neil was watching her, but she kept her eyes on her own hands clasped in her lap.

"As an alternative to certain court-martial I decided to remain Harry Bowman indefinitely. Apparently the fellow had no near relatives – at least, I never heard from any of them. So it wasn't as difficult as it might have been."

"Quite a coincidence!" Murray said.

"You can believe it or not," Neil said without a change of expression. "I'm talking to Penny."

Penny raised her eyes, and Neil looked into the fire again. She felt warm sympathy for the older man. She knew how much he hated involvement with others; he had shown her last night how deeply he had committed himself to her. Now he had to deal with a situation which would be painful for anyone. He would act justly because he could not act otherwise; but underneath everything he did or said would be the sure knowledge that he would either lose her entirely or be forced to see her suffer. She watched his lean face, shadowed by his twisted nose, and knew she had never seen him behaving so true to his own nature as he was at this moment.

"I don't disbelieve you," Murray said thoughtfully. "I think I believe everything you've said. But my personal opinions don't count. You'll have to vindicate yourself to a military court if you intend to stay here and resume your identity."

Penny's eyes shifted back to Neil. If he didn't soon say something positive she felt she could not stand being in the room with him.

"Were you discharged as Private Harry Bowman?" Murray asked.

"Yes."

"Then – surely you realize you can't stay here where everyone knows you?"

"That remains to be seen."

"I wish you wouldn't be so difficult. Military police are searching for you at this moment."

"Are they?" But the information produced an effect, for Neil's face lost its derisive composure. "The colonel's work again?"

Penny rose and left the room, and the two men watched her go. When they were alone, Murray leaned forward and tapped his cigarette into the hearth, then sat back in his chair, waiting.

"It's not easy," Neil said finally, "to speak of Penny's father like this."

"No," Murray said. "But if it helps, I agree with your opinion of him."

Neil's face showed a trace of a smile, and the obstinate expression faded out of it. "For two years," he said, "I've dreamed of the day I'd be able to smash that man. Now I don't want to do it. I don't want to, because all hatred is merely self-hatred. And I don't want Penny mixed up in a scandal."

"Wain doesn't want a scandal any more than you do," Murray said. "He'd let the case stay buried if you'd agree to leave the country for good."

"I'll bet he would!" Neil filled his lungs with tobacco smoke and coughed harshly. Again he seemed to be calculating, and as he did so his wide eyes remained fixed on Murray. "You were born in Nova Scotia, weren't you?"

"Yes, in Cape Breton."

"Then listen. I'm going to tell you something." He hesitated, and his voice softened as he continued. "There's a man I used to know here. He comes from the north shore – Guysborough County. He was born in a house with two rooms set in a barren clearing among the rocks. He never went to school. But he learned how to make boats. When he was a young man he crossed over to Tancook Island and studied how they built those light shore-craft over there. He never was particularly good at building, so he went to sea and finally he became a master. He still is one, if he's living. He can take a ship along these coasts in fog so thick he can't see across his own deck, and he can take it inside the ledges because he knows every breaker from Cape North to Cape Sable by its sound. He's been doing that forty years and his keel has never kissed bottom yet. There's no use telling you his name, for you've never heard it. Judged by standards along these shores, he's not even particularly good. There are dozens more can do the same thing."

The black cat rubbed against his legs. "I'll tell you something else. My father was born in a little village in Cape Breton – like yourself, I guess. He never had much schooling but the Bible. But he learned to build ships, too, and he happened to be more than good. He might have been as good as MacKay if he'd lived earlier. But hardly anyone ever heard of him, either. And when he died it wasn't in Nova Scotia. It was in Boston, where they've long ago forgotten how to breed seamen or build a ship. What I'm trying to say is . . . this province is my home."

Murray continued to look into the fire.

"So you see," Neil went on, "Wain can't avoid a scandal. He let himself in for it the day he put me under guard in France."

"Then you intend to stay in Halifax?"

"For as long as I please."

"I see." Murray sighed. "I wish I knew what to say. Wain's case sounds pretty formidable." He rubbed out his cigarette and got wearily to his feet. "My presence here is superfluous unless you care to tell me where you stand," he said. "You'll need more than plain evidence. I don't mean to imply the trial will be rigged, but things will just be so much harder for you once Wain's on the staff. At the moment I haven't the slightest idea whether you have any evidence on your side or not. As the case stands it seems to be this: you disobeyed your colonel's order in open battle. Regardless of whether it was a good order or not, you've made things infinitely worse by living under an assumed name. In the eyes of any court, that would amount to a frank confession of guilt."

Neil laughed harshly. "Do you think Wain could bring himself to murder me?"

"Don't be ridiculous!"

Murray looked exasperated, but Neil kept his ironical grin.

"If a scandal were to break now," Neil said, "he'd not get on the staff if the war lasted a hundred years. His military reputation would stink even if I was convicted. So it would be logical for him to dispose of me at once, don't you think? And what could be easier – seeing I'm supposed to be dead already?"

"For God's sake stop being dramatic!"

Neil shrugged. "I may be able to prove I didn't disobey his orders after all."

"You still have the signed order he sent you?"

"No, it was lost. But another man who was in the line that day read it, and he may remember it verbatim. Moreover, I've at last found out where that particular man is." He threw away the stub of his cigarette and picked another out of the box. "My God – you should have seen the order that damned fool sent! I couldn't have obeyed one part without automatically disobeying the other, and both parts were stupid."

"Is that all your case rests on?"

"Isn't it enough?"

"Two years ago I'd have said it was ample. But you've let things go too long. And there's your assumed name. It amounts to desertion."

"I couldn't have acted sooner. The man who read that message was reported missing just after I was. It was only a month ago – by a chance encounter in a London hotel – that I met someone who told me he'd been wounded and sent back home." His face twisted. "Life wasn't exactly sweet, living in London all that time and trying to fake a Lancashire accent. I was afraid to open my mouth. And to make matters worse I couldn't get any kind of regular job with that damned Bowman's record hanging around my neck. He was a plumber."

"Well." Murray got up and began to move about the room. The close air of the house seemed to be dulling his brain. "They've still got you for desertion. If I'm not mistaken, Wain will have you arrested and charged with that. In which case you mightn't even be allowed to tell your story."

"I'm medically unfit for further service."

"That would be an extenuation if you could prove it. But damn it, Macrae – there's your assumed name!"

"Haven't you heard of cases of loss of memory?"

"Will the hospital in England certify you as a victim of amnesia?"

"I don't know."

Murray drummed the floor with his foot and cleared his throat. "I hate to say this, but there seems to me only one thing to do. You and Wain will have to agree to compromise. The case can be explained away if you both co-operate in the explaining."

Neil folded his arms. "That's impossible," he said.

"Why is it? I'm sure Wain would agree."

"But I wouldn't. He's blackened my name all over the province to save his own reputation. I intend to live in Canada, Murray. I haven't the slightest intention of emigrating to the States or stewing in my own juice in England. It's going to hurt Penny. It's likely to hurt several other people, but there's no other way. If Wain tries to cover up that day's business now, people will only say he's used his influence to whitewash me. Don't forget – I happen to be his nephew, too."

Penny announced her approach from the kitchen by rattling the dishes on the tray she carried, and Murray with instinctive politeness held the door open for her. He noticed that her hands were unsteady as she set the tray on the table. Her eyes met his, dumbly interrogative, and a pang of loneliness went through him. He helped her set out the cups and saucers on the table.

"We're in need of tea," he said with a quiet smile. "I think everything is going to be all right."

Neil remained motionless in Wain's long chair as she poured milk into the three cups and picked up the teapot. "Do you want to tell me, Neil?"

He said nothing, and looked the other way.

"Perhaps it will be easier if you get the story from me," Murray said.

Neil got to his feet, staring at the stream of pouring tea. "I'm leaving now," he said. "Penny, will you come to the door with me?"

She followed him into the hall, and watched him pick up his worn overcoat and put it on. He tried to grin at her, but the attempt collapsed when he saw the tears in her eyes. The fingers of one of his hands reached out to caress the lock of white hair, and then both arms went around her. "I like it," he murmured. "It's what that scrubby brown head of your always needed."

"It's not scrubby."

"Never mind, it's brown – a dull colour."

"Neil, will you be gone long this time?"

"No, this time I promise I won't." His hands slid along her back. "God – if you knew how you feel to me! Be honest – do you really want to see me again?"

Her only response was the searching of her fingers along the line of his hair behind his head. This hard, unbreakable substance in him! He had always had it and never would lose it, not even if it crushed him and everyone in the world he loved.

He released her and saw that she was crying, and his eyes passing over her body noticed for the first time the dress she was wearing. "For God's sake," he said, "that outfit looks like hell on you!"

"All right, I won't wear it any more." She smiled and dried her eyes. "Let me know this time where you are?"

"Tomorrow," he said. "I promise."

He kissed her quickly and closed the door behind him with a slam, and she heard the rattle of his heels as he hurried down the steps.

When she went back to the living-room she found Murray holding a cup of tea ready poured for her, but she disregarded it and sat down on the chesterfield with her hands clasped so hard their knuckles turned white. She sat there staring into the fire. She wished Jean were here. She wished it were tomorrow.

"Angus," she said, "has he really got a chance?"

"I think so."

"What can I do?"

"I don't think you need do anything." Murray seemed to be speaking to himself. "That boy's not so rash as you think. He told me a lot, but there wasn't a word I could have used against him if I'd wanted to."

NINE-THIRTY P.M.

A growing moon, pale as the inside of an oyster shell, hung over the forests and harbours of Nova Scotia, and in this nocturnal glimmer the edges of the province were bounded by a wavering flicker of greyish white, where the sea broke over the rocks of the coast. On all the solitary points thrusting out into the Atlantic, into the Fundy or the Gulf of St. Lawrence, lighthouses winked or gleamed like fixed stars. Such fishing boats and small craft as still worked after dark were now black shadows rising and falling to the lift of the groundswell as they glided home to their village coves. The highways were empty and dark, and the windows of the farmhouses gave no light but that reflected from the moon. In the north of the province, around the Sydneys, pouring slag flared against the sky and turned the harbour into a pool of ruddy fire, while the blast furnaces trembled under the pressure of armament production. In all other parts of Nova Scotia, silence gripped the land like a tangible force, for in only two of its counties was there the noise of a great city or factory, or the rush of traffic over a road.

In Halifax that night, all work at the docks had ceased. A few ships lay in the Stream, and in the Basin a great cluster of freighters pulled at their anchor chains as the incoming tide swung them. Only a few streets had bound over much life from the day. The rest were becoming empty and dark, splashed only at corners by the bluish flicker of arc-lamps, and in some sections the few pedestrians abroad had to walk carefully to avoid stumbling on the uneven surface of the sidewalks.

The North End had the lifeless, brooding atmosphere common to districts where most of the inhabitants are manual workers who rise and go to bed early, whose only relaxation is to sit on doorsteps in summer and in winter about a kitchen stove. It was an extensive area, spreading fan-wise from the northerly slopes of the Citadel to the Narrows and Richmond Bluff, overlooking Bedford Basin. The wooden houses crowded each other like packing-boxes left out in the weather for years. And in the far North End, beyond the Shipyards at the Narrows, a few streets plunged at headlong angles to the wooden jetties that still survived in that part of the waterfront. On the steepest of these streets, in the ground floor of a chocolate-coloured frame house, Big Alec MacKenzie lived with his wife, his daughter, and his two growing boys.

The dinner dishes were washed and the dishcloths hung against the copper boiler to dry. Alec was seated on a wooden chair beside the kitchen table with his shirt open at the neck, his shoes off, and his feet in heavy army socks that made them look like enormous khaki sponges. A glass containing a mixture of rum and water was half-hidden in one of his hands, but he seemed to have forgotten it was there, for he had been sitting all of ten minutes without moving. The stove in the corner was burning high and all the windows were shut. The hot air of the room had an odour of dishwater and cabbage and the fumes of Alec's pipe. Like most poor folk in northern countries, the MacKenzies hoarded what warmth they had. The plastered walls of the kitchen were bare except for a large calendar donated by a grocery store. They were stained and yellow as naphtha in the glare of the unshaded lamp which stood in the centre of the table, giving Alec light to read his paper and enabling Annie, his wife, to see the socks she was knitting.

Although Alec's huge frame was still, relaxed by a day's work and quiet in its very nature, it was possible to detect a vague restlessness, an uneasy sense of insecurity and disharmony, in the lines of his face. There was no evident cause for this; both he and his wife had reason to feel satisfied with the past year. Alec's wounds had been only serious enough to secure his discharge from the army, and his new job at Wain's was bringing him good money for the first time in his life. His two boys were at school, and his grown daughter, Norah, had learned to be a typist and was now earning, too. Later than usual, Alec's family had begun to follow the traditional pattern of Nova Scotia Highlanders. They had consciously given up the land and the fisheries for a life in the towns.

Yet Alec was missing things he had never thought about before: shadows travelling the steep hills of the Cape Breton shoreline; pockets of mist white as fleece in the sunshine along the braes opposite Boularderie; a feeling that time did not matter much, a sense that when a man planted a field or built a boat he did so to meet a season and not a timetable; a habit of rising with the sun instead of an Ingersoll alarm-clock. In an indefinite way Alec realized that he and his wife were at the close of an era and their children were entering a new one.

His eldest son came in from the parlour where he had been finishing his home work and sat down by the stove. Norman was a tall, high-shouldered boy of fifteen, with red hair and sandy skin. "Do you want coal up from the cellar, Father?" he said.

Alec turned slowly and looked at an exercise book and pencil in the boy's hands. "You keep on with the mathematics. That's more important than coal."

"I've finished. I don't know why I find it easy, but it never seems to take any time. Next term we're starting physics. That may be harder."

"Indeed!"

"Mr. Cross says if I keep on being able to do maths I may become a scientist." He came over with his books and set them on the table. Then he opened a scribbler and displayed a page of his work. The geometrical figures were as neat as a blueprint. "Look, Father – I'll show you. It's as simple! One thing leads right into another. You always know just where you are with it."

He began explaining the problem he had solved, and his father tried painfully to follow him. Finally Alec shook his head. "It must take a terrible smart man to be understanding things like that. I remember a boat-builder back in Cape Breton. He could plan a real big boat all the way from the truck to the kelson and do it all on paper. He never used a model at all. Now me, I have to see a thing. And I can't see the mathematics."

"It's just a kind of knack." Norman put the book aside quickly for fear his father would think he were boasting. His voice had lost its native Gaelic accent; Halifax had flattened it out. "I wish I could remember things in history as well."

Alec looked more interested. "Now that would be something I could understand. You were telling me the other night about them Romans and some of the things they used to do then, and I got to thinking, and it was easy to see why they did them. People don't seem to change much, no matter where they are. And I guess they always had corporals, even in the old days."

Norman closed his books and went down the rough wooden stairs to the basement where he could be heard shovelling coal into a scuttle. Alec took a sip of the rum and water and went back to reading the paper, which he did slowly, following the lines of print with his thumb and index finger. His wife rocked back and forth in her chair, silent, heavy, and absorbed, her eyes fixed on her knitting. Presently Norman came up with the coal and set it beside the stove, looked around and asked his father if there were any more chores.

Then he kissed his mother goodnight, shook hands with Alec and went off to join his younger brother in the double bed they shared. Norah had not come home yet; she had gone to the movies with a soldier from the garrison who was courting her.

"Well," Alec said after many minutes, "it's a fine thing coming to Halifax for the children. Think what would have happened to Norman without the education."

"Indeed!" Annie said.

After this there were no sounds from the room except the draught in the stove and the clicking of the knitting needles and the occasional creak of a board over their heads as the family of Newfoundlanders who lived in the upper flat moved over the floor.

The room was still silent when Neil Macrae found the house in the darkness and knocked on the door of the storm-porch.

That night Geoffrey Wain telephoned home to say that he would be working until morning, making preparations for a sudden influx of troops from the west. He then presented himself at Evelyn Phillips's flat in the North End and informed her he intended to spend the night.

This was something he had never done before. Although there was a double bed in Evelyn's bedroom she had never expected him to stay in it longer than an hour or two, and Wain had never given any indication that he considered this length of time insufficient. Indeed he had never, in the strict sense of the word, slept with any woman but his wife. There was something repugnant to him in the idea of lying unconscious and exposed to others, especially to a person he considered his inferior.

He owned nothing in the flat. He had given Evelyn the necessary money to furnish the rooms, but had refrained from offering any suggestions as to the manner in which it was to be done. He felt that if he betrayed a personal interest in her taste, either in clothes or furniture, it would be an admission that he regarded her place as a home of his own, as well as an invitation to her to consider that their present arrangement might become permanent. And so the appointments of the flat were cheap and gaudy, although the offensive details were numerous enough to cancel out their individual powers of disturbing him.

It was part of Wain's pleasure to allow Evelyn to manage the initial stages of their meetings according to her own desires, for her vulgarity and childishness sometimes enabled him to feel that in her presence he had adopted a new personality. Now he sat in her only armchair, smoking a cigar and waiting for her to emerge from the bedroom. For the moment he was able to consign the resurrection of Neil Macrae to a remote corner of his mind. Its influence was not sufficient to spoil his anticipation of pleasure, but it was at the same time enough to upset his customary feeling of security. And so he comforted himself with the reflection that by the time the war ended, familiar conventions would be broken down entirely, and a new age would be at hand of power and vulgarity without limitation, in which the prizes would not be won by the qualified but by the cunning and the unscrupulous. It would be an age which would accept most of the values Evelyn held now. It would change everything, and it would soon be here. He recognized its approach without regret and without approval.

Evelyn came from the bedroom wearing a silk kimono tight about the waist and hips and open at the neck. With what she considered a whorish candour, she had reworked the lines of this garment so that it cupped her breasts separately, pointing them in such a manner that his eyes could rest on no other part of her person. Her black hair was brushed sleekly away from her forehead and she had secured it by a blue ribbon knotted into a wide bow on the top of her head. This was

Evelyn's touch – the little girl's ribbon and the accentuated, pear-shaped breasts. She lay down on the davenport in front of the fire and half closed her eyes, looking at Wain from under her lashes. And Wain watched her. She was so small, so delicate, yet was capable of such tensity of body and fixity of expression, of such smouldering, expanding but yielding hatred! An odour of perfume, cheap and cloying, pervaded the room as he moved toward her.

That night in Prince's Lodge after Jean had been put to bed, Jim and Mary Fraser sat before the fire and talked. The birch logs crackled and shadows plunged and flickered along the white wainscoting of their living-room, and in the far corners the floor was cold. The shutters were open and the water of the Basin was burnished by the moon, while stars rode on the rim of the hills along the horizon.

"Nothing matters in the world but chance," Jim was saying. "I can't remember a single thing that ever happened to me that wasn't an accident."

"You mean to say that was why you married me?"

"That was because you had a rich father, which was an accident so far as you were concerned." He tapped his game leg. "Look at this – if I hadn't wanted that pipeful of tobacco and picked that particular moment to cross a line of fire, a Boer never would have hit it. Look at the way Jean came into this house."

Mary frowned. "Do you think Angus Murray would make a good husband for Penny? He seems so much older."

"Could be worse. Let's see – he's about as much older than Penny as I'm older than you."

"Oh, Jim! You're younger than he is right now."

Jim laughed and stretched his arms. "What was Geoffrey like when he was young?"

"It's funny, I can't remember. He's always seemed the same age."

"What kick does he get out of life, anyway? Well, I suppose Penny could have a worse father. At least he leaves her alone. My dear, you have a dreadful family."

"Some of us aren't so bad."

"That's just another accident." He got to his feet and yawned again, kicked a log deeper into the hearth and set the screen in front of it. "We have a rendezvous in bed, remember? That's something else I've never been able to understand – why I like to go to bed with a woman who has aunts and uncles and brothers like yours." He pulled her to her feet and put a heavy arm about her thin shoulders, and after a feeble show of resistance she smiled at him.

"We need sleep," she said. "We've got to get up for that early train into town."

"That's why you need me first," he said.

A small troop of cavalry had been detailed to patrol the streets to watch for windows emitting light. There was no good reason for this order except the uneasy state of the official mind, which had resigned itself to the strategic failure of Passchendaele and another winter of war. A handful of men on horses went through the dark streets at a slow trot and occasionally one of them blew a bugle.

Maria Wain heard the bugle and the trotting horses and opened her shutters to look out. The troop halted and a man got off his horse, crossed the sidewalk and rang her doorbell. When they had gone, Alfred Wain, asleep in his armchair before the fire, stirred and sniffed. "Maria, what was that?"

"Soldiers. They said we had a light showing."

"Humbug!" he said, and closed his eyes again.

An hour later, Penelope and Roddie Wain heard the horses' feet and Roddie was careful to turn out his bedroom light before peering out. He looked down on the caps and shoulders of the horsemen trotting past, and saw the glint of moonlight on the bugle of the boy riding beside the leader. After they had passed, he came downstairs with wide eyes to find his sister.

Penelope, tired and worried and unable to sleep herself, told him to go back to bed; then, discovering that he would be certain not to sleep in any case, she made him produce his schoolbooks and went over his lessons one by one until they were all checked and Roddie was heavy-eyed. She then went up to his bedroom and tucked him in, and sat on the edge of his bed listening while he talked about the war. He could hardly remember when it had begun, but he horrified her with his precise and detailed knowledge of it. He could repeat from memory the tonnage and gunnage of every vessel in the navy and was looking forward to six years from now when he would be old enough to enlist. She had noticed that every one of his school scribblers had a picture of a soldier or a sailor on the cover, or a British bulldog standing on a White Ensign draped over the stern of a battleship while a Canadian beaver crouched in the corner and sharpened its teeth. As she heard him talk, she marvelled at the skill of the propagandists. Living in a great nation virtually guaranteed by the United States, the present crop of publicists seemed determined to convince Canadians that their happiness would be lost forever if they should aspire to anything higher than a position in the butler's pantry of the British Empire.

Roddie finally showed signs of sleepiness and she left him alone. The house was still now, so still she could hear in every room the ticking of its many clocks, but over everything seemed to throb the overtones of Neil's voice.

All that night the streets of Halifax remained dark and empty of traffic, and the whole town, this clearing in a forest fronting the sea, was utterly silent. Yet a panorama of history, vital and in the main unperceived, flowed through the minds of the seventy thousand people who at that moment inhabited the region marked on the map as Halifax peninsula.

In beds down the long wards of military hospitals lay hundreds of Canadians, some suffering, some bored, some asleep. They had gone to France from the prairies and the west coast, from Ontario and Quebec and the Maritimes, and soon they were going to be discharged back to the cities and the solitudes. Just as soon as they were well enough to exist without help they would be going home. But the war had altered the vision of them all, breaking some and healing the gashes it had made in others by enlarging their consciousness. They could never be the same again, nor could the land they had returned to inhabit.

On the ships anchored in Bedford Basin, men were talking in most of the languages of the Indo-European and Slavonic systems, playing cards and telling each other how it was in the places thousands of miles away from which they had come. Here in Bedford Basin, if thought had any meaning at all, Stockholm and Haugesund existed, and Rotterdam, Antwerp, Lisbon, Genoa, Marseilles, Odessa, and Cape Town. There were Lascars from Calcutta and Bombay, Latin Americans from Rio and Montevideo, Yankees from Boston, sailors from all the ports and havens of England. They were on ships anchored in an indentation of the coast of Nova Scotia, and they knew that one in every five of the ships was doomed to destruction. They wished they were in a port where there were lights and music and women, where a man could raise a thirst and forget the unreality of his skill; they wished they were almost any place in the world except here, bounded by the stars and the empty, inviolate North American forest surrounding them.

In the lighted offices of the Dockyard and the stately rooms of Admiralty House, and in various unnamed buildings along the waterfront, uniformed men on night duty were at work, tabulating orders and registering information.

The official wireless crackled incessantly, and N.C.O. messengers came and went from the wireless room, delivering slips of paper to various officers. Incoming messages were read and filed, and notes of the movements of enemy submarines were emended in the light of later knowledge. Intelligence knew that a German submarine had just stolen out of the Bay of Biscay and was heading for Hell's Hole, that another was lying on the bottom near Queenstown waiting for the destroyers to go away, that still another was moving westward toward the shipping lane that passed Cape Race. They knew that a small British squadron was advancing into the Atlantic to meet a convoy at a secret rendezvous. The information was noted, tables and charts were checked and positions of shipping revised; minor alterations in projected courses were planned.

And in the consciousness of thousands of the generality of citizens who were still awake there lurked as their constant companion a brooding anxiety they rarely uttered, for they pictured sons, brothers, husbands, fathers, sweethearts somewhere in the lines about Arras or Ypres, and yet all were thankful that they were still able to be worried and that another day had passed without the receipt of a private letter from His Majesty.

The war had changed these people, too, but only slightly; it had merely splashed over their lives a little of the hatreds and miseries of the great cities, for quite unwittingly they lived tonight as they had done for years, with their thoughts and actions mainly determined by the habits they had inherited from their forefathers, from the Loyalists who had come here generations ago from the United States because they preferred King George to the new freedom, from the English who had settled in Halifax when their time of service in the garrison was up, from the Irish who had escaped the potato famine seventy years ago, from the Highlanders who had lost their clans at Culloden. They lived in Halifax in an anomalous permanency, still tied to England, suffering when she did but rarely partaking of her prosperities, unreconciled to be Americans or even Canadians, content for the moment to let their status drift with events, convinced that in being Nova Scotians they possessed a peculiar cause for satisfaction, an excellence which no one had ever troubled to define because no one outside the province believed it existed, and everyone on the inside took it for granted.

In Big Alec's kitchen, after Annie had gone to bed and left Neil Macrae alone with her husband, the two men talked quietly together. Neil's manner was calm, and Alec's face, after recovering from a momentary astonishment when he saw that Neil was alive, had resumed its former immobility. If he realized that helping Neil might cost him his job at Wain's, he gave no indication of it by expression or words.

"This is my situation, then," Neil said. "I shall probably have to call on you to testify for me. Would you do that?"

Alec's heavy face was serious, but he did not try to avoid the issue. He sat perfectly still with his knees apart and a hand spread open on his thigh. The other hand still clutched a half-empty glass. "You would be meaning that message Colonel Wain gave me that day?" he said.

"Yes." Neil looked directly at him. "I know it's asking a lot. It may mean you'll lose your job."

"That's as may be."

This was what he had returned home to get. He had counted on Alec's honesty and clannishness to compel him to speak the truth. It had been his great advantage, and if Alec had shown any hesitation he had been prepared to play on his character with all the force he could bring to bear. But besides this, there was a still more subtle interplay of emotion in Neil's mind. Alec and he stemmed from the same roots; now it was almost as if Alec were about to help him vindicate his father for years of humiliation suffered at the hands of the Wains, as though the fundamental strains in his own nature were for once to be successful over the environment which had previously thwarted them.

This momentary feeling of triumph disappeared as quickly as it had arisen, leaving him cold again, and calculating. "Alec, we've got to be precise about this. Do you remember how long you were with Colonel Wain that afternoon? How long was it between zero and the time he handed you that message to take up to the front?"

"That would be about four hours. It would be maybe four hours exactly."

"And all that time the colonel had no contact with the rest of the battalion?"

"Not quite all that time. But for about three hours he didn't know where in hell you were."

"So he sent you forward as a runner with an order? When you reached the front line you found I was the senior officer surviving and you gave me the message?"

Alec nodded.

"I read it, and said it was contradictory. Then, before putting my interpretation of it into effect, I ordered you to commit the message to memory – is that right?"

Alec nodded again.

"Now – can you still swear to its exact reading?"

Neil leaned forward in his chair while Alec took a swallow of the rum, and thought slowly. His throat muscles contracted as the rum passed through to the stomach. Then he nodded. "I can swear. The order went this way: 'Establish contact with Imperial Brigade on the right, then attack second objective immediately.' That would have been the hill right in front of us." Alec breathed heavily. "My God, but that was a bad day for all of us. After I put that message to memory you sent me back with a reply. I didn't read the reply but it made Colonel Wain awful angry when *he* read it."

Neil let the breath slowly pour out through his clenched teeth as he got up to ease the strain of waiting to hear his sentence pronounced. Now that Alec had finally spoken, the whole matter seemed to have lost stature and become almost trivial. And yet the scene of that afternoon had recurred to Neil's mind so often that every detail of it had seared itself into his consciousness. Now it recurred again, but this time the events seemed slighter, as though they had lost their heat. His sensation was similar to that of a man reading a newspaper years after its printing.

He saw himself crouching in a ditch tired and sweating, and then Alec appearing covered with mud and handing him the message. He read it and saw at once it could not be executed in its entirety. Owing to the direction of advance there was at that moment no imperial brigade on the right. The flank was in the air. The Imperials could be seen firing from a ridge a quarter of a mile to the rear and nearly six hundred yards to the right. To advance directly on the second objective, as Wain was ordering, would have increased the gap on the right flank to almost a mile. On the other hand, to establish contact with the English brigade involved a withdrawal on the diagonal. Withdrawal meant the failure of the day's operation; but advance meant probable annihilation and the certainty of a successful enemy counter-attack.

This was the situation. He knew it and Wain didn't. Whoever had planned the attack had failed to take into account the nature of the terrain, for the general line of advance had been along two sides of a gentle slope, the Canadians on the left and the English on the right, and in the course of action they had lost touch. The slope had divided them further, and the resistance had been much more severe than the staff had anticipated. The whole plan of the attack was faulty, and no front-line officers were to blame. Neither Neil nor anyone else had known at the time that the suggestion for this attack had been Wain's and that his superiors had reluctantly agreed to try it out.

When the day's operation was over and the battalion had retired to its original jumping-off position, someone had to be blamed for such a useless failure. No one could have been more aware of this than Wain himself. When Big Alec brought him Neil's message that he was retiring, his own ignorance of the true position of his men made it impossible for him to realize that to establish contact with the Imperials involved retirement. All he could see was disgrace and failure, and it was easier to blame someone else than to admit that the whole operation had been rash and ill-prepared. For a time he was convinced that a subordinate had ruined his plans by deliberate disobedience; the fact that the subordinate happened to be a nephew whom he had always hated did not improve his disposition or his judgment.

Yet on that smoky day, Wain's moods altered fast. By the time he had reached the front line and had seen for himself the extent of the casualties and heard the men cursing as they crouched under a violent counter-bombardment, his anger disappeared and his fright amounted to panic. He had visions of dismissal for incompetence. A hasty roll-call was taken and showed that he had already lost nearly all his officers. Darkness fell and he was alone in a dugout with the earth shaking around him, and war was now neither a game nor a profession, but something he couldn't control or understand.

It was only then that he had ordered Neil's arrest. Because the counter-bombardment was so severe, the prisoner had been placed in a dugout in the second line, under guard. When the news arrived the next day that his nephew had been killed Wain hardly knew whether to be glad or sorry. Neil had admitted to him that he no longer had the written order; he had passed it on to the officer of the next platoon, and this officer was now lying dead in the German lines. With Neil dead, Wain had no chance of shifting the blame and proving to his superiors it was not his.

As the tangled events of that day passed through Neil's mind it seemed to him that he had become two persons, himself and his uncle Geoffrey Wain. He had re-examined the case so often that he had been able to see it from Wain's point of view as clearly as from his own. And now he was weary of it. He was impatient to have it settled. It no longer had meaning. It bored him.

He resumed his seat and looked at Big Alec again. "Did the colonel ever refer to the business again – after he thought I was dead?"

"No." Alec reflected. "But he seemed to be remembering it."

"I bet he did. What about yourself? I heard you'd been taken prisoner. That's why I never tried to get in touch with you before this."

Alec smiled shyly. "I was, but it was not for very long. I had to hit a German fella awful hard one night. I have often wondered what happened to him."

"I thought you'd been wounded?"

"Indeed I was. But it was a bullet. I was hit on my way back to our own lines."

Conversation lagged between them and Neil found himself trying to resist the conviction that chance and preposterous accident had complete control of a man's life. It had been an accident that Alec had given him the message in the first place, an accident that the shell had blown up the dugout where Wain had confined him, an accident that at the very moment he had first tried to contact Alec the big man was supposed to be a prisoner of war. The final chance had occurred a month ago when he had stepped into the lobby of the Regent Palace Hotel in London to avoid a shower of rain, and had run into the soldier on leave who told him that Alec was not only alive but back in Canada.

And yet not even this evidence was able to convince him that his life's continuance was as problematic as a fly's. Rather it seemed the final degradation of war that it could make a man's life appear so.

Angus Murray was drunk. The walls of the room, the tables and chairs and the picture of the dead duck surged like the sea, flowing against his eyeballs and ebbing away with a motion so steady it destroyed everything but his thoughts, and from these it removed the pain. Whenever he said anything, his words seemed to stand like an entity in the air until someone grasped them and removed their existence. The place was dirty, and three hours ago Murray had been able to smell it.

Across from him, sitting sideways on the edge of a wooden chair with one fleshy arm leaning on the table, was a woman his own age.

"Why the hell don't you fix this place up, Mamie?" Only he knew how drunk he was. "It looks something awful."

"I do all right. Maybe I fix it up and then the cops'll only have me out of it."

"That's not the right attitude, not the right attitude. You ought to keep a home here."

"These fellas that come in off the ships they don't know any better."

"You don't like us, Mamie – or do you?"

"Why should I like these fellas?"

Murray sighed and leaned back into such a sprawl that the woman got up to steady his balance, but with an easy swing forward he recovered himself. "Where did you say you come from, Mamie?"

"What's it to you where I come from?"

"I'm not one that just asks."

Her face softened a trifle, but she got it back to its usual vacancy with what looked like a flurry of embarrassment. "You don't really want to know, do you?"

"Of course."

"Aw, go back to your wife, Major. She'll talk about herself."

He laughed soundlessly, shaking his head, and his blood-shot eyes blurred with moisture. "Thought you'd know better, thought a woman like you'd know a man better than that."

"Why, ain't you?"

"Married? Don't make me laugh!"

"You were once, though. That's something I always know about a man."

"What's the matter – touchy about your professional reputation? Look at me! Think any woman'd want to marry me?"

"Holy Mary, I guess you're speaking the truth for once."

"All right. Now tell me."

"Why?"

"I asked you, didn't I?"

"There's nothing about me a man like you would want to know. I guess I've made some money lately, that's all." She laid her hand over his, but his senses were so deadened he did not feel it. "Why do you come around here, Major?"

"Hell, you ought to know."

"You don't get anything out of it. Those girls of mine, they aren't any good. The trouble is they don't seem to care. They don't like it themselves. Sometimes maybe a nice young fella comes along and one of them – Major, they don't give a man anything."

"Lord, we have toiled all night and caught nothing – that's more than most whorehouses can tell their customers."

She looked annoyed. "You haven't got any need to get to talking that way. What's the matter with you educated fellas, anyway? Why can't you leave things the way they are?"

"Though I speak with the tongues of men and of angels and have not charity" – his voice broke – "Mamie, you're a good girl. You must have been born that way. You don't mean anyone any harm. You just want us all to be one big happy family. Were you born here, Mamie?"

"I told you."

"I've forgotten. And then you went away to the Boston States, eh?"

"Shut up, can't you?"

"And then some fella you thought was pretty good ran out on you and back you came. Just like me. What do you think of this country, Mamie? Everyone comes and goes around here, eh? So, like the wanderer, the sun gone down, darkness be over me, my rest a stone – that's your Nova Scotian, if you've the eye to see it. Wanderers. Looking all over the continent for a future. But they always come back. That's the point to remember, they always come back to the roots, like you and me. When you were a girl you had the Gaelic, didn't you?"

"What are you talking about? I'm Irish!"

"What's the difference? From the lone shieling in the misty island, mountains divide us and a waste of seas —"

"How's your hand, Major? Better now it's out of a splint?"

He lifted his right hand and surveyed it as it swam before his eyes, and the fingers moved stiffly as he worked the muscles.

"It's looking just fine," she said.

"Do you really care what it looks like?"

"Of course I do."

"The last operation it did was on an eye. Couldn't have done that without two hands. The trouble with this war, it's become too natural. We're all getting used to it. What I say —"

"A fine, clever man like you! You ought to have a wife and children."

"Know any good women, Mamie?"

"Sure, of course I do."

"No, you and me are alike. We wanted something different every time. You might as well admit it, Mamie. When you were a girl you were curious about every man you saw. You wanted

to see what he'd be like, didn't you? Well, look at us now. You
run a whorehouse and I come to it."

She got up and put an arm about his shoulders, lifting
him to his feet. He stood upright with ease and watched her,
his long body swaying but his feet in perfect balance, his
whole face distorted by a vague and senseless grin. "What
keeps you going, Mamie? Money?"

"Well, I guess money's something you know where you are
with. I do all right, I tell you." She looked away from him and
added sullenly, "I got a couple of kids. They're living in the
country, too."

"That's the thing to do with them! Make everyone live in
the country and there won't be any more of these goddam
wars. Or maybe there won't." He looked at his hands again.
"Listen, Mamie. This war hasn't finished me yet. I can still
operate, understand? I've got a natural pair of hands that can
do almost anything I tell them. Not original, mind you, but
once I see a demonstration I can do it. Sometimes better than
the demonstrator. Take a mastoid, for instance – a good
radical mastoid. I can —"

"Aw, Major, go on home. What do you have to tell me all
this for?"

"Who in God's name else have I got to tell it to? One of
your girls? One of those morons that hang around the hotel
and talk about a war they've never seen? You know it's all a
swindle, don't you?"

"I don't know what you're talking about."

"You know there's no resurrection from the dead, don't
you? Ever since the first Easter, if a man's dead he's stayed
dead, hasn't he? All right. A man falls in love with a girl. He
dies. The girl nearly dies with grief but she gets over it, she
gets mended again somehow and now she's a young woman
with a mind that's old – old, Mamie, like mine, but with a
young body. She's too old for any of the kids her own age. She's

what I want, isn't she? She's someone I can marry without it being a dirty joke, isn't she? Good Christ, if we have to live through all this misery, why can't a young girl marry a man old enough to show her the road? Someone old enough to appreciate what her youth is worth?"

"Major, you're talking too loud. Please now – I don't want to have any trouble. You used to be one of the steady ones. You never used to get this way on me."

"I've seen a man that's risen from the dead."

"Get out – please!"

"But that's not the part that really matters. Maybe – maybe I've got to send him away again, see? Maybe I've got to make him a wanderer. Jesus Christ, he may turn into a second edition of myself. Only he won't have the right kind of toughness, he won't be able to take it. People like you and me – we've got our pride. We can see what smashes us, so it can never smash us really. *Cogito, ergo sum!*"

He put an arm about her waist and guided her toward the stairway leading up to the rooms of the second floor. "When the barbarians entered the empire they came gradually and no one believed they would really succeed. First one province, then another, one city and then another, and people always said there were plenty of other cities left to take the place of the lost ones. But all the dykes gave way in the end, Mamie. These big cities, these places like Boston you thought was so fine – watch them empty themselves when the invasions come! Watch the big hotels grow cobwebs. Watch the great liners disappear from the seas. Then there'll be fishing-boats in Halifax, nothing but fishing-boats. And the women of Lunenburg and Cape Breton will bring up the looms from the cellars!"

She shook free and watched him closely. And then she smiled, and the wrinkles appeared suddenly about her eyes, and for the first time that evening her face looked kindly, as it must have once when she was a generous and pretty girl.

"Come on up with me, then. You poor fellow – I'll spend the night with you. When I like a man I can make him forget a lot of things. You'd be surprised."

"No," he said.

"Come on." Her voice was almost eager. "I want you."

"It's too close in here. It smells."

She shrugged her shoulders and crossed the room to the hat-rack. Her voice was businesslike when she spoke again. "Then let me help you on with your coat. It's getting cold out – a lot colder than you think." But her softened mood still remained underneath the professional exterior, for she laughed and said in a strange voice, "I can still remember my old dad on winter nights the way he used to come in from the barn with his whiskers frozen. 'Mamie,' he'd say, 'it's cold enough to freeze something mighty important off a brass monkey.' That was his little joke."

Murray reeled toward the door. "It's been a devil of a night, Mamie, but I guess it wasn't your fault. How much do I owe you?"

"Forget it, you don't owe me anything. Hell, you were too drunk to run up any bill tonight."

When Murray reached his room in the hotel his head was clearing. He sat down and leaned over the arm of his easy-chair, fighting back the nausea as his eyes ran along the backs of the books which were always a part of his belongings. There were some ninety volumes on medicine in the finest bindings he had been able to obtain, ranging from a worn Gray's *Anatomy* to the latest publications in his own specialty. But these did not interest him as much as the ones which were almost falling apart from use, the books he had acquired at college, which were always news to him. Years ago they had enabled him to fancy himself a part of a wonderful and enormous heritage, but now their titles made a poignant ring in his mind like the remembrance of a bell heard in childhood from a cathedral which the years of a technical era had blindly emptied.

Plato's *Republic*, the *Nicomachean Ethics*, Rashdall's *Theory of Good and Evil*, Horace and Catullus, Thucydides, Shakespeare and Milton – these and the others crowded through his vision as he hung wearily over the arm of his chair, a man grown suddenly old, with the bar of hope broken in his brain. "I'm glad I know about them," he said to himself. "In spite of everything, I'm glad of that."

"So you knew my father!" Neil was saying an hour later. "Alec, you're almost the only person I've met in years who did know him."

"When he went away from Cape Breton we soon heard he was doing fine. First it was Halifax and then we heard it was Boston. I remember a rich man came up to South Gut, St. Ann's, with his yacht and asked did John Macrae come from this village. And Hector Gillies – that was Donald's son that used to have the grist-mill on the Margaree road – he went to Boston and worked as a joiner there, and he heard about John Macrae, too. Your father could handle his tools light and easy, just like a woman handles a needle."

There was silence between them and an alarm-clock over the stove ticked clamorously.

"When this trouble with me is over," Neil said, "what about your chances of another job in Halifax?"

"Indeed I do not know."

"You still have your land in Cape Breton?"

"Yes, but there's terrible poor prices on fish."

"Why the devil should a man like Geoffrey Wain inherit the earth?" Neil's eyes widened with excitement again. "It's firms like his that have ruined the fishermen in the province. I'd like to see —"

Alec laid a huge hand on his wrist and smiled. "Now, Mr. Macrae, you're not a fisherman yourself and you don't have to worry about the prices. And I do not think it pays to have ideas like that, moreover. It makes it harder. I do not understand very much, but I always have known what it is I have to do next, and if I lose the job at Wain's there will be another one somewhere else. We are told that the Lord will provide, and there would be no use whatever in going to church if a man cannot believe a thing as easy as that."

"That's all very well. But the Lord also helps those that help themselves."

Alec got slowly to his feet. "You must sleep here tonight, Mr. Macrae. Your father has slept with us many a time at home."

Neil felt restless, and suddenly ill-at-ease. "Alec, I'm afraid I'm only bringing trouble into your house. I'm terribly sorry."

"Indeed it's not yourself that would be bringing the trouble but the trouble that would be finding its own way. Your father was one of our own people. And there would be no use in arguing against a thing like that, whatever. So you don't have to explain and you don't have to be thanking me, either."

He led the way to a prim little room he called the parlour. Among other relics of the past century, it contained a sofa of horsehair. "I'm sorry there's nothing better in the house for you than this," he said. "But your mind is easy now and you should rest well."

Alone in the parlour, Neil tried to fall asleep. His name and his future were now secure, but how he could reconcile either with Penny or with her father he did not know. Sleep came to him before the course of future plans could be formulated.

When dawn finally lightened over the Eastern Passage, only lookouts on the ships, intelligence men at the Dockyard, and nightwatchmen at warehouses and the railway station were awake and abroad to see it. Not a breeze stirred. A veil of mist rose from the surface of the harbour and spread like a pool into the lower streets of the town, where it lay until the sun rose and turned it into a trillion points of flashing light.

Thursday

A FTER THE sun rose, the whole landscape shone. The rays of light, first red, then orange, then shining gold like the heart of a fire, poured from the seaward horizon into the harbour and lit up the mist which lay like a liquid over the flat water. The drops of moisture flashed like quicksilver. And through this mist moved the shapes of two vessels, one a British cruiser, the other a freighter with a lean funnel and a high bow, a bulging, sordid, nondescript vessel brought to Halifax by the war.

The men of the cruiser's bridge could see nothing in the Stream but the funnels of a few ships, for the morning mist concealed the hulls. The town itself had a false nobility in this light, a counterfeit of the mist and the sunrise, for only its contours were distinguishable. Sparks of light leaped off the weather-vane of St. Mary's Cathedral and the rising shield of the Citadel was bathed in a golden sheen. Two ferryboats were crossing the harbour so smoothly their movement seemed miraculous, as though it were derived from a cause outside themselves, for with hulls invisible, their funnels and decks appeared to be sliding effortlessly along the top of the mist. On the surface of the ground the night-frost was thawing out, but the air was still cold enough to make noses wet. There was little smoke, for the town had not yet begun to work.

Underneath the mist was a disconnected, various life that in a warmer climate or another town might have sufficed to make its people intense and excitable. A battalion was standing to at the Armories. Thousands of men and women were waking with thoughts of the war. Boys were wheeling out bicycles over lawns and gardens stiff with hoarfrost, to ride down to the waterfront and see what new thing the war might have brought on that day. Workers in flat cloth caps, no collars or ties, were striding along to docks and warehouses and foundries and shipyards, hitting the pavements hard with their heels and leaning backward to check their pace on the steep cross-streets. A long freight train loaded with wheat from Saskatchewan crawled slowly around the corner of Richmond Bluff, the promontory that concealed most of Bedford Basin from the harbour. The train passed the Dockyard and moved on under the lee of another hill crowded with tumble-down houses, until it reached the big shed of Pier Two. There it choked, panted a second, and rested.

By far the most of the town rested, too, for it was the habit of workers' wives to give their husbands breakfast and return to bed, and it was also rare to see a prosperous man in his office before nine. But whistles were blowing, and the *Morning Chronicle* was being bawled from street corners and tossed into doorways, and soon Haligonians would be reading about how hungry the Germans were, and about Cambrai and Bourlon Wood, which the communiques were still calling victories long after the conscripts broke and the Guards stood, and fought, and died in their tracks.

The stillness of the harbour was shattered by a heavy rumble as the British cruiser dropped anchor a little south of the Dockyard, and fathoms of steel thundered down the hawse. The outgoing tide chafed the stern and swung her bow toward the north, and she lay there lean and grey and cruel, pointing straight at the Narrows. The mist quivered and broke as the air grew warmer, then in a flurry of breeze the wraiths climbed toward the sun. Seagulls that had followed the cruiser into port came to rest on the water, and with a creaking of blocks a gangplank dropped over the warship's side. The officer of the watch stood by to receive a pair of officials who already were approaching in a launch from the Dockyard jetty.

Angus Murray woke early and bathed his sore eyes with a solution of water and boracic acid, and then dressed and brushed his thinning hair carefully down on his scalp. His veins were still quick with alcohol and his skin felt stiff, but his stomach was quiet and there was no headache. Indeed he was seeing everything very clearly, seeing himself and his world without benefit of intoxication or self-pity, and for the first time in many years a vision of the truth failed to make him afraid.

He ate a quick breakfast and left the hotel immediately, and forcing his flabby muscles to work, sweated up the hill toward the Citadel, past cross-street after cross-street, meeting people with washed faces on their way to work. He walked until he had reached the footpath circling the moat on the hilltop.

Spread below him, the town lay with the mist concealing every ugly thing, and the splendour of its outline seemed the most perfect, natural composition he had ever seen. He thought now that a man could only know the meaning of peace when he no longer reached after the torment of hope. He had lost Penny, with whom there might have been happiness. Now there was no need to argue or justify himself any more; unhappiness could no longer have meaning, for there was no longer anything positive for him to be unhappy about. There was nothing to worry him. Last night he had relinquished the last thread of ambition which had held worries tight in his mind. But the beauty of the world remained and he found himself able to enjoy it; it stayed a constant in spite of all mankind's hideous attempts to master it.

With eyes blinking in the light he surveyed Halifax fanning away under its bare trees from the rounded base of the Citadel. Almost every street and building held for him a fragment of personal history dating back to the time, twenty-seven years ago, when he had first come as a boy, raw from the farm, to Dalhousie College. The faces of classmates crossed his memory; some were successful in the upper provinces or the States; one was famous; few were left in Nova Scotia.

Even as he watched, the mist was dissolving, and glancing down to the harbour, he saw the British cruiser coasting in to her anchorage. The incisive outline of the ship seemed to emphasize and sharpen the essential helplessness of all small places in the world to resist the impact of the outer world. Murray sighed. The town throbbed with the war, and the people in their hearts were not sorry. They welcomed it the way a doctor welcomes a prospect of a dangerous operation which he alone can perform, for England could not fight the war without this town. The great cities which made the wars and sought to circumvent the nature of things could not do without Halifax now.

He took hold of his injured hand and began to manipulate the fingers. They were stiff with the morning cold, but it was obvious they were recovering and soon would be fit for work. He would still have his trade. That would have to be enough from now on.

He glanced at his watch and saw it was nearly eight o'clock, and then began walking down the slope of the hill to the streets. His mind filled with recollections of the scene between himself and Penny and Neil Macrae the previous afternoon. This brought back his conversation with Geoffrey Wain, and then he remembered how he had seen Big Alec MacKenzie come out of the shed on Wain's Wharf. A sudden thought struck him. In what company of the battalion had Alec served? Methodically he checked a mental list of the old N.C.O.'s of the battalion, but could not place him. Then a scene in France flashed into his mind: himself standing by the door of a farmhouse and Geoffrey Wain inside at a table with Big Alec standing beside him. "God damn it!" He quickened his step involuntarily. "So *that's* why Wain remembered to give MacKenzie a job!"

He went straight down the steep street toward Wain's Wharf. The colonel himself would not be there so early, but his foreman might be around any time now. He walked boldly through the arch and continued along the wharf to the central shed. Its door was open and the interior was piled high with crates and barrels and it smelled of raw lumber. No ships were alongside and only a few men seemed to be working. He approached a thin man who was sitting in stolid silence on an upturned hogshead, smoking a clay pipe and spitting in occasional long arcs over the curb of the wharf into the water.

"Is MacKenzie here yet?" Murray said.

"No."

"When do you expect him?"

The man fumbled under a jersey and pulled out a watch. "Mebbe half an hour." He replaced the watch and spat again. "Ain't much work to be done today. Mebbe he don't arrive till later."

"Where does he live?"

The man gave the number of the house and the name of the street; then, as though seeing for the first time that he was addressing an officer, he got off the hogshead and touched his cap. "Do you know where that street is, sir?"

"Yes," said Murray, "I know."

He went up to Barrington Street and boarded a tram, and he did not get off until it had reached the end of its northward run.

The mounting sun flashed into Penny's bedroom and struck her pillow, then crept to her face and across her eyelids. She wakened and blinked, looked at the clock and sat upright with a jerk, her eyes hurting and her limbs numb with nervous exhaustion. It seemed only a few minutes since she had last seen the clock. That had been at four in the morning.

She lay back on the pillow and closed her eyes. She could hardly remember what it had been like in the old days before the war when existence had been relatively simple and people had not found it necessary to live on short-term credits. She had gone through a ridiculous life during these past few years, trying to outwit the Almighty by handing over her daughter to a kindly uncle and aunt, pretending that her sole ambition was to succeed in a man's profession. She thought of the design of her launch, that neat blueprint on which she had spent so much work, the long research that had preceded the formulation of the plan. She remembered how indulgently the engineers and regular designers had smiled at her, then the change to unconscious resentment as they realized she was as good as themselves, then the grudging admiration when finally they were forced to admit that her work had a quality theirs could not equal. So now the Admiralty in London wanted to use a craft of her design, of Penelope Wain's, who had lived most of her life in Halifax. No wonder Angus Murray had been amazed. No wonder Neil had not credited it.

Familiar sounds were in her ears. She heard Roddie's footsteps on the stairs as he went down for breakfast and then the noise of the front door opening. That would be Roddie getting the morning paper from the front porch. The headlines, the war, insanity past human comprehension projected into newsprint and constituting a new world there! Two years ago it had been possible to look forward to the time the war would end. Now it seemed not to matter when the guns stopped. If everyone were as tired as she, they would be unable to do anything but lie torpid and wait for the next calamity to overtake them.

She sighed and turned over, burying her face in the pillow. Had the strain of the past three years been entirely senseless?

A woman could reach a point in which want of normal things became so chronic that her organism rebelled against a change from the familiar privations. Neil was alive and well; he was even sanguine. The war had bruised him but he had not broken under it. It had not even made him forget her. The lack was not in Neil, but in herself. She was like a starving person suddenly confronted with food and unable to consume it, and as she remembered his eagerness she was frightened by the prospect he offered her. After all this time she would never be able to equal his desire.

Footsteps again sounded on the stairs and there was a knock on the door of her bedroom. Sadie announced that she had overslept. She answered briefly and got out of bed, went to the bathroom and plunged her face in cold water. She looked up and saw herself lined and frowning. "You're tired out," she told herself. No, it was much more than merely being tired. There were too many tangled threads to be sorted out. Neil's case was simple compared to hers. She hardly dared contemplate the confusion into which she had landed her life: Neil and her father, Neil and herself and Jean – ever since Jean's birth she had longed for the sight of his face when he first saw his daughter. How could she tell him about Jean now? Jean no longer belonged to her.

The force of habit reasserted itself and she straightened her back and tried to arrange her thoughts for the coming day. One thing at a time. That was what everyone was telling himself nowadays.

She went down to breakfast and found Roddie looking self-satisfied behind the paper. Usually he had to peek at its headlines in the scant moments when his father held the paper up in order to turn the pages. He gave his sister a searching look and set the *Chronicle* down beside his plate. "Where's Father?" he said.

"He had to work all night."

"Why?"

"I don't know." She felt she could keep the balance in this house no longer. "He's simply – he's busy, that's all."

"Is it about the war?"

"I suppose so."

"Tell me, Penny. I won't let on to a soul."

"You'd better go off to school or you'll be late. Do you remember your lessons?"

"I should hope so, after what you put me through last night!" He pointed to the clock and grinned. "Somebody else better hurry today. I bet they give it to you when you get down there late. Or doesn't being late matter when a person gets old?"

Sadie brought in half a grapefruit, two slices of toast, and a pot of tea. She ate quickly and went to the kitchen to check orders and give Sadie instructions for the day. When she returned to put on her hat and coat, she saw Roddie in the living-room still buried behind the paper, and the sight of him sitting with his feet on the chesterfield exasperated her. "Will you never do anything unless you're made to? Get out and go to school!"

He got up, startled by her vehemence. "Gee, Penny —"

But Penny did not wait to listen to his excuses and went out, slamming the door behind her. If nothing delayed the tram on its run to the North End she would probably reach the Shipyards a few minutes before nine.

To Geoffrey Wain, the sunlight coming in through Evelyn's faded lace curtains and splashing over the crocus-coloured eiderdown on her bed was vaguely insulting. He sat up and rubbed his eyes, and then looked at the girl beside him. Evelyn had fallen asleep naked, too lazy to put on the nightgown she had discarded over the side of the bed. She was still asleep and the cold air reaching her skin as he lifted the bedclothes raised a pattern of goose-pimples. She stirred uneasily. The deadness of expression caused by sleep robbed her of all attractiveness. Her slightness which last night had appeared so provocative now seemed a defect. She was so thin that her breast-bones were like ranges of mountains rising against her white skin. After a night of sleep, her breath had an odour of acetone which displeased him too, although it never occurred to him that in this respect he was the greater offender.

With a jerk he swung out of bed, and the movement woke Evelyn. She opened her eyes and surveyed his back, but when he turned to look at her again she closed them. He crossed to the window and surveyed a prospect of untidy backyards and a couple of garbage-men wheeling barrels toward the lane beside the house. He stretched and entered the bathroom.

As he shaved, he decided that a night like the one past would never occur again. Evelyn stood for disorder, for the state of mind which is prepared to let everything take its course, and she spoiled his dreams of greatness. He had discovered that while it was possible to enjoy Evelyn for a few minutes without losing prestige in his own eyes, he was incapable of spending a night with her in bed without admitting, tacitly and inwardly, that she was necessary to him.

EIGHT-FIFTEEN O'CLOCK

Jim and Mary Fraser ate breakfast together in sunlight so bright it dazzled their eyes, for their breakfast nook overlooked the Basin, which now angled the reflected beams of the sun directly at them. After eating they watched Jean set out up the forest path with the maid for her morning's outing. Then they put on their hats and coats and went down the road to the station to catch the local train into town.

The unwonted brilliance of the day and the quietness of the air delighted Mary, and she began to speak of returning home for a lighter coat. "It's almost like Indian summer," she said.

Jim looked at the treetops, motionless in the still air, and then he sniffed loudly. "There's east in that wind."

"Nonsense, there isn't any wind at all."

They were still arguing good-naturedly when they boarded the train for Halifax.

There was now only one vessel moving north toward the upper harbour, the French munition ship *Mont Blanc*. An ugly craft of little more than three thousand tons, she was indistinguishable from thousands of similar vessels which came and went during these days. She was inward bound, heading for Bedford Basin to await convoy. Moving very slowly, she had crawled through the opened submarine net and now was on her way up the Stream, past the breakwater, George's Island, and then the South End docks. She had been laden a week ago in New York with a cargo consigned to a French port, but only her crew, the Admiralty authorities, and the captain of the British cruiser in port to command the convoy, knew what her main cargo was.

Men on the motionless ships in the Stream watched her pass and showed no interest. The previous day they had all received orders not to move until further notification, but none had been told they were giving sea-room to a floating bomb.

The cruiser's captain came on deck to watch the *Mont Blanc* pass and estimate the speed she would be able to produce. He was about the only person in the vicinity of Halifax to take any overt notice of her passage up the harbour.

The *Mont Blanc* moved so slowly that her bow seemed to push rather than cut the water as she crept past the cruiser. The pilot was proceeding cautiously and the cruiser's captain observed this with satisfaction. What was not so satisfactory to him was the manner in which the cargo was stowed. Her foredeck was piled with metal canisters, one on top of the other, held down with guy ropes and braced at the sides by an improvised skeleton of planks. The canisters and visible parts of the deck glistened patchily with oil. The after-deck was clear and some sailors in dungarees were lounging there out of the wind.

"I wonder what she's got in *those things*?" the captain muttered to his Number One. "Petrol?"

"More likely lubricating oil, I should think, sir."

"I doubt it. She's not a tanker, after all. Might be benzol from the colour of it. How much speed would you say she's got in her?"

"Ten knots at the most, I'd say."

"Doubt if it's even that. I wish they'd realize that a munition ship ought to be faster than the general run of ships. I can't have a cargo like that keeping station with the rest of them. She's got to cruise on the fringe, and she needs about three extra knots to do it."

But the *Mont Blanc* glided on up the harbour with little sound or evidence of motion except for a ripple at the bows and a thin wake. She was low in the water and slightly down by the head. A very sloppily-laded ship, the cruiser's captain decided. She passed awkwardly onward, the pilot pulling her out to the exact centre of the channel as the harbour narrowed. The tricolour flapped feebly from her stern as she floated in, and as she reached the entrance to the Narrows, bells sounded in the engine-room calling for a still further reduction in speed.

EIGHT-FORTY O'CLOCK

Big Alec MacKenzie was putting on his hat to leave for work when Murray knocked on the door of his stormporch. Too courteous to show surprise, he admitted his visitor and offered to help him off with his coat. Murray declined. And at that moment Neil appeared from the back room, flushed with annoyance.

"Murray – what the devil are you doing here?"

Alec looked from one man to the other in bewilderment.

"You're a little late," Neil said. "I've already found my witness. So you can go back and tell Wain to go to blazes."

"I haven't been seeing Wain," Murray said. He looked inquiringly at Alec. "Could you spare a few minutes, MacKenzie? I've just come from the wharf, and I can tell you there's no need for you to get down there for another hour. Wain isn't expected till late and the watchman told me there was nothing to do."

"Look here, Murray," Neil interrupted. "Wherever I go you seem to be around. What's the idea? I thought I told you yesterday what I intended to do."

Murray glanced at Alec and made a slight clicking sound with his tongue. "Please don't think I'm intruding, MacKenzie. I saw you at Wain's Wharf yesterday, and this morning I guessed you were the man Mr. Macrae had come home to find. As I didn't know where to locate him this morning, I came to you instead." He turned to Neil. "I may be able to help both of you, if you're willing to let me."

"How?"

"That's what I'm here to tell you. Wain, yourself, and I are the only survivors of the original battalion mess. Think a minute, Macrae. When your case is called, I'm certain to be made a witness. Won't it be easier if we confer first?"

Neil hesitated; Alec looked from one to the other with a grave and expressionless face.

"All right," Neil said. "Let's get done with it."

The *Mont Blanc* was now in the Narrows and a detail of men went into her chains to unship the anchor. It would be dropped as soon as she reached her appointed station in the Basin. A hundred yards to port were the Shipyards and another hundred yards off the port bow was the blunt contour of

Richmond Bluff; to starboard the shore sloped gently into a barren of spruce scrub. During the two minutes it took the *Mont Blanc* to glide through this strait, most of Bedford Basin and nearly all its flotilla of anchored freighters were hidden from her behind the rise of Richmond Bluff.

Around the projection of this hill, less than fifty fathoms off the port bow of the incoming *Mont Blanc*, another vessel suddenly appeared heading for the open sea. She flew the Norwegian flag, and to the startled pilot of the munitioner the name *Imo* was plainly visible beside the hawse. She was moving at half-speed and listing gently to port as she made the sharp turn out of the Basin to strike the channel of the Narrows. And so listing, with white water surging away from her fore-foot, she swept across the path of the *Mont Blanc*, exposing a gaunt flank labelled in giant letters BELGIAN RELIEF. Then she straightened, and pointed her bow directly at the fore-quarter of the munitioner. Only at that moment did the men on the *Imo*'s bridge appear to realize that another vessel stood directly in their path.

Staccato orders broke from the bridge of the *Mont Blanc* as the two ships moved toward a single point. Bells jangled, and megaphoned shouts came from both bridges. The ships sheered in the same direction, then sheered back again. With a violent shock, the bow of the *Imo* struck the plates of the *Mont Blanc* and went grinding a third of the way through the deck and the forward hold. A shower of sparks splashed out from the screaming metal. The canisters on the deck of the *Mont Blanc* broke loose from their bindings and some of them tumbled and burst open. Then the vessels heeled away with engines reversed and the water boiling out from their screws as the propellers braked them to a standstill. They sprawled sideways across the Narrows, the *Mont Blanc* veering in toward the Halifax shore, the *Imo* spinning about with steerageway lost entirely. Finally she drifted toward the opposite shore.

For a fraction of a second there was intense silence. Then smoke appeared out of the shattered deck of the *Mont Blanc*, followed by a racing film of flame. The men on the bridge looked at each other. Scattered shouts broke from the stern, and the engine-room bells jangled again. Orders were half-drowned by a scream of rusty metal as some sailors amidships followed their own inclination and twisted the davits around to lower a boat. The scurry of feet grew louder as more sailors began to pour out through the hatches onto the deck. An officer ran forward with a hose, but before he could connect it his men were ready to abandon ship.

The film of flame raced and whitened, then it became deeper like an opaque and fulminant liquid, then swept over the canisters of benzol and increased to a roaring tide of heat. Black smoke billowed and rolled and engulfed the ship, which began to drift with the outgoing tide and swing in toward the graving dock of the Shipyards. The first trembled and leaped in a body at the bridge, driving the captain and pilot aft, and there they stood helplessly while the tarry smoke surrounded them in greasy folds and the metal of the deck began to glow under their feet. Both men glanced downward. Underneath that metal lay leashed an incalculable energy, and the bonds which checked it were melting with every second the thermometers mounted in the hold. A half-million pounds of trinitrotoluol and twenty-three hundred tons of picric acid lay there in the darkness under the plates, while the fire above and below the deck converted the hollow shell of the vessel into a bake-oven.

If the captain had wished to scuttle the ship at that moment it would have been impossible to do so, for the heat between decks would have roasted alive any man who tried to reach the sea-cocks. By this time the entire crew was in the lifeboat. The officers followed, and the boat was rowed frantically toward the wooded slope opposite Halifax. There, by lying flat among the trees, the sailors hoped they would have a chance when their ship blew up. By the time they had beached the boat, the foredeck of the *Mont Blanc* was a shaking rampart of fire, and black smoke pouring from it screened the Halifax waterfront from their eyes. The sailors broke and ran for the shelter of the woods.

By this time men were running out of dock sheds and warehouses and offices along the entire waterfront to watch the burning ship. None of them knew she was a gigantic bomb. She had now come so close to the Shipyards that she menaced the graving dock. Fire launches cut out from a pier farther south and headed for the Narrows. Signal flags fluttered from the Dockyard and the yardarms of ships lying in the Stream, some of which were already weighing anchor. The captain of the British cruiser piped all hands and called for volunteers to scuttle the *Mont Blanc*; a few minutes later the cruiser's launch was on its way to the Narrows with two officers and a number of ratings. By the time they reached the burning ship her plates were so hot that the seawater lapping the plimsoll line was simmering.

The *Mont Blanc* had become the centre of a static tableau. Her plates began to glow red and the swollen air inside her hold heated the cargo rapidly toward the detonation point. Launches from the harbour fire department surrounded her like midges and the water from their hoses arched up with infinite delicacy as they curved into the rolling smoke. The *Imo*, futile and forgotten, was still trying to claw her way off the farther shore.

Twenty minutes after the collision there was no one along the entire waterfront who was unaware that a ship was on fire in the harbour. The jetties and docks near the Narrows were crowded with people watching the show, and yet no warning of danger was given. At that particular moment there was no adequate centralized authority in Halifax to give a warning, and the few people who knew the nature of the *Mont Blanc*'s cargo had no means of notifying the town or spreading the alarm, and no comfort beyond the thought that trinitrotoluol can stand an almost unlimited heat provided there is no fulminate or explosive gas to detonate it.

Bells in the town struck the hour of nine, and by this time nearly all normal activity along the waterfront had been suspended. A tug had managed to grapple the *Mont Blanc* and was towing her with imperceptible movement away from the Shipyards back into the channel of the Narrows. Bluejackets from the cruiser had found the bosun's ladder left by the fleeing crew, and with flesh shrinking from the heat, were going over the side. Fire launches surrounded her. There was a static concentration, an intense expectancy in the faces of the firemen playing the hoses, a rhythmic reverberation in the beat of the flames, a gush from the hose-nozzles and a steady hiss of scalding water. Everything else for miles around seemed motionless and silent.

Then a needle of flaming gas, thin as the mast and of a brilliance unbelievably intense, shot through the deck of the *Mont Blanc* near the funnel and flashed more than two hundred feet toward the sky. The firemen were thrown back and their hoses jumped suddenly out of control and slashed the air with S-shaped designs. There were a few helpless shouts. Then all movement and life about the ship were encompassed in a sound beyond hearing as the *Mont Blanc* opened up.

NINE-FIVE O'CLOCK

Three forces were simultaneously created by the energy of the exploding ship, an earthquake, an air-concussion, and a tidal wave. These forces rushed away from the Narrows with a velocity varying in accordance with the nature of the medium in which they worked. It took only a few seconds for the earthquake to spend itself and three minutes for the air-expansions to slow down to a gale. The tidal wave travelled for hours before the last traces of it were swallowed in the open Atlantic.

When the shock struck the earth, the rigid ironstone and granite base of Halifax peninsula rocked and reverberated, pavements split and houses swayed as the earth trembled. Sixty miles away in the town of Truro windows broke and glass fell to the ground, tinkling in the stillness of the streets. But the ironstone was solid and when the shock had passed, it resumed its immobility.

The pressure of the exploding chemicals smashed against the town with the rigidity and force of driving steel. Solid and unbreathable, the forced wall of air struck against Fort Needham and Richmond Bluff and shaved them clean, smashed with one gigantic blow the North End of Halifax and destroyed it, telescoping houses or lifting them from their foundations, snapping trees and lampposts, and twisting iron rails into writhing, metal snakes; breaking buildings and sweeping the fragments of their wreckage for hundreds of yards in its course. It advanced two miles southward, shattering every flimsy house in its path, and within thirty seconds encountered the long, shield-like slope of the Citadel which rose before it.

Then, for the first time since it was fortified, the Citadel was able to defend at least a part of the town. The air-wall smote it, and was deflected in three directions. Thus some of its violence shot skyward at a twenty-degree angle and spent itself in space. The rest had to pour around the roots of the hill before closing in on the town for another rush forward. A minute after the detonation, the pressure was advancing through the South End. But now its power was diminished, and its velocity was barely twice that of a tornado. Trees tossed and doors broke inward, windows split into driving arrows of glass which buried themselves deep in interior walls. Here the houses, after swaying and cracking, were still on their foundations when the pressure had passed.

Underneath the keel of the *Mont Blanc* the water opened and the harbour bottom was deepened twenty feet along the channel of the Narrows. And then the displaced waters began to drive outward, rising against the towns and lifting ships and wreckage over the sides of the docks. It boiled over the shores and climbed the hill as far as the third cross-street, carrying with it the wreckage of small boats, fragments of fish, and somewhere, lost in thousands of tons of hissing brine, the bodies of men. The wave moved in a gigantic bore down the Stream to the sea, rolling some ships under and lifting others high on its crest, while anchor-chains cracked like guns as the violent thrust snapped them. Less than ten minutes after the detonation, it boiled over the breakwater off the park and advanced on McNab's Island, where it burst with a roar greater than a winter storm. And then the central volume of the wave rolled on to sea, high and arching and white at the top, its back glossy like the plumage of a bird. Hours later it lifted under the keel of a steamer far out in the Atlantic and the captain, feeling his vessel heave, thought he had struck a floating mine.

But long before this, the explosion had become manifest in new forms over Halifax. More than two thousand tons of red hot steel, splintered fragments of the *Mont Blanc*, fell like meteors from the sky into which they had been hurled a few seconds before. The ship's anchor soared over the peninsula and descended through a roof on the other side of the Northwest Arm three miles away. For a few seconds the harbour was dotted white with a maze of splashes, and the decks of raddled ships rang with reverberations and clangs as fragments struck them.

Over the North End of Halifax, immediately after the passage of the first pressure, the tormented air was laced with tongues of flame which roared and exploded out of the atmosphere, lashing downward like a myriad blow-torches as millions of cubic feet of gas took fire and exploded. The atmosphere went white-hot. It grew mottled, then fell to the streets like a crimson curtain. Almost before the last fragments of steel had ceased to fall, the wreckage of the wooden houses in the North End had begun to burn. And if there were any ruins which failed to ignite from falling flames, they began to burn from the fires in their own stoves, onto which they had collapsed.

Over this part of the town, rising in the shape of a typhoon from the Narrows and extending five miles into the sky, was poised a cloud formed by the exhausted gases. It hung still for many minutes, white, glossy as an ermine's back, serenely aloof. It cast its shadow over twenty miles of forest land behind Bedford Basin.

NINE-TEN O'CLOCK

The locomotive was still panting. Little puffs of dust spurted out from the piles of rubble and broken glass about its wheels and fell in a powder on Jim Fraser's face as he lay on his back. What had a few minutes before been a dirty roof of glass was now a pall of smoke dissolving into open sky. Sunlight shot through breaches in the brick and cement wall of the station like searchlights cutting paths through darkness, and the dust of shattered mortar danced in it.

He heard a groan and tried to move. Instantly an agony racked him as though a saw had been drawn across the bones of his spine. He tried to lift his hands but they were helpless. There was a film over his eyes and he shook his head to clear it away. Where was Mary? It was going to snow tonight, it was going to be a very cold winter. What had happened? The shock of concussion and the unbearable noise of the station falling – and that heavy glass roof, thousands of spikes and arrows of glass hurtling nearly seventy feet to the platforms!

The film momentarily cleared from his eyes and he saw bubbles of blood breaking and forming and breaking again. They were directly in front of him. They came from his own mouth. What was that triangle beyond? The square on the hypotenuse of a right-angle triangle equals the sum of the squares on the other two sides. He tried to lift his hand again and saw another bubble break. He was wet through. Where did the apex of that triangle end? That glass triangle with the smoke smudge on its face?

The locomotive continued to pant and stir the dust. It was easier to remember now where he was. He had been passing the driver's cab heading for the news-stand at the end of the platform and Mary had been hoping he would not buy a paper because she hated hearing the war news.

"Mary – what the devil has happened?"

Silence, except for the panting of the engine, except for a queer sound somewhere in his own chest. Silence; the sort of silence that is all a man's own when he is falling asleep and hears the street noises of a strange city pass the window of his hotel.

The film cleared from his eyes again. The triangle of glass was an arrow and its apex was buried in the lung beside his heart. What a way to die, bleeding to death in North Street Station beside an idle locomotive!

He twisted his head and the pain nearly blinded him, but he saw Mary and knew that her eyes were closed and her face composed under a film of dust. Her hat was over one ear and the feather on its side flicked back and forth under the impact of the engine's exhaust. He heard a faintly hoarse sound which seemed to be his own voice calling her name, something stirred beside him and he saw her head waver through the haze, then turn over and settle like a cut flower on its stalk. Somewhere nearby a large sheet of broken glass toppled over with a puny, tinkling sound.

These things Jim Fraser perceived with a peculiar and distant curiosity before his vision darkened and all perception ceased. The locomotive continued to pant and blow dust over his face. And at the same time billions of moats of pulverized mortar began to float down through the sunbeams and settle over all the human beings who had been in the North Street Station when it crumbled.

Roddie Wain sat himself down very carefully on a cement curb fifty yards from the grounds of his school, and left his bicycle sprawling in the street before him. Everything was utterly silent. Now that the great wind had passed, there was no movement except for a pendulum-like waver in the leafless branches of trees as they swayed slowly back and forth through shorter arcs to equilibrium. What had caused that monstrous, roaring crash, the spasmodic sound of unknown objects whizzing through the air, and then the triple lines of windowpanes in his school disappearing inward in a tornado of wind that had punched him in the back and knocked him off his bicycle and landed him here beside the curb?

He looked at his bare knees. Both were cut and bruised by the fall from the bicycle. He looked at the school. Nothing moved in it. And suddenly he smiled. It wouldn't matter being late for school now, not after all this had happened.

He heard a clatter of hooves and saw a milk wagon coming toward him down the street with the horse in panic, tossing his mane, and the tall, box-shaped wagon swaying from side to side and scattering milk bottles right and left from its open doors. The bottles broke on the pavement and the milk foamed out and spread in blue-white patches, but the horse came galloping straight on and a driving hoof plunged through the spokes of Roddie's bicycle wheel. The bicycle was pulled upright as the hoof tore clear and the horse stumbled; then the following wagon smashed the bicycle down again as it passed over it, and the wagon went on down the street leaving Roddie's machine ruined.

"Hey – look out where you're going!" He was on his feet, shouting. But almost immediately he closed his mouth again.

The wagon had no driver. He watched it sway down the road and finally turn turtle as the horse, instinctively following its regular beat, turned a corner at top speed. He looked at his shattered bicycle and his first sensation was one of bewildered relief. Penny could not say this accident was his fault. It was going to take a lot of explaining, but Penny always believed him when he spoke the truth.

He dragged the bicycle out of the street and along the side-walk to the school grounds, and there he leaned it against the trunk of a young maple tree. Now perhaps he could find out what had caused such a peculiar disturbance in the nature of things. Everyone in the school must be afraid to come outside to look, and this gave him the advantage over them all. He observed far to the north a huge white cloud shining in the sun. It had not been there a few moments before. Then he caught sight of a twisted object sticking out of the withered circle of lawn in front of the main door of the school, and crossed the wide school-yard to examine it. It looked like a jagged piece of metal weighing about twenty pounds, and he saw that the grass about it was blackened as though by fire. He bent to touch it, but drew his finger away at once; the metal was as hot as a stove-lid. He stared, and wondered if it was one of those meteorites he had heard about in school a few weeks ago.

Then the front doors of the school were suddenly thrown open and the children came running out in the regular lines of a fire-drill. Some of them were cut and bleeding. A wave of nausea swept over him as he saw a tiny spike of glass pro-truding from a small boy's cheek. He waited until his own class reached the yard, hoping that no one would observe him. Willie Moffat was the last boy out and he slipped over and stood beside him. "What's happened?" he whispered.

Willie paid no attention to him. The whole school seemed to be dumb.

"Is the school on fire or something?"

He asked this question in a louder voice, but no one told him the answer. Then he saw that the teachers were following the boys to the yard and that the principal was being supported by one of them, blood streaming from a gash in his forehead. Mr. Jackson, the assistant principal, a stiff man of middle age, marched to the front of the yard and said in a loud voice:

"You will all stand here until we find out what has happened. There is no need for alarm. Those who have been cut by glass will leave the ranks at once and go down to the basement. They will wait there until a doctor comes."

Having said this, Mr. Jackson stood with his hands behind his back like a soldier at ease, keeping the herd of children to their discipline while the injured ones left the lines and entered the basement.

"Guess there'll be no more school today."

Willie Moffat had found his tongue. Everyone heard him and then all the rest of the children began to talk together and their voices rose in a hysterical clamour.

"Quiet – that boy there!" Mr. Jackson bellowed and started forward to the front line, seized a youngster by the arm and led him apart to one of the maple trees which lined the separation of the school-yard from the street.

"Stand there until you learn to be quiet when you're told! There'll be no more talking. School is not dismissed."

"Old bugger!" Roddie muttered.

He was shorter than any of the boys in the line immediately in front of him and the open door was directly at his back. None of the teachers could see him. He stepped cautiously backward, moving on the balls of his feet and keeping his eyes front and his shoulders squared. Then, feeling his heels touch the steps, he turned and bent double and disappeared into the school.

The big entrance hall was empty and his feet echoed as he ran through it to a classroom at the back of the building. He paused on the threshold in amazement and considerable awe. Every window was broken and the shattered glass was lying in crumbled fragments on the floor or sticking like spits out of the blackboard and walls. A plaster bust of Sir Wilfrid Laurier had a spike of glass six inches long protruding from its mouth and the effect was obscenely bizarre.

"Gee!" Roddie whispered.

He tiptoed over the broken glass on the floor and looked out the empty casement. No one was in sight on this side and it was a drop of only six feet to the ground. He cleared the windowsill of glass with his handkerchief and dropped over, then ran for the fence at the back and clambered into a neighbouring garden. He ran quietly through this and along a path beside the house until he reached the street. Then he paused to straighten his tie before setting out for the centre of town.

The street was empty of traffic and the sidewalks still had no pedestrians. Every window he passed was blown in and the houses on the south side of the street had lost their doors as well. He reached an intersection and saw a tram half-way down the block, stalled and windowless, with no one attending it. He shivered, and continued walking. He passed the car and continued into the next block before turning to head east for Barrington Street. One of the houses on this corner was vacant and only this morning on his way to school he had observed plasterers at work behind its unshuttered windows. He looked up curiously. There were no windows left now and the ceilings inside had fallen to the floor.

Then he heard a low moaning behind him and stood still, trying to locate its source. No one was in sight, and yet the moaning continued. It seemed to be issuing from the drain by the corner. He crossed the grass and then he saw a bundle lying there in a pool of blood. It was one of the plasterers in overalls that were now soaked and red. The man's jugular was severed. Even as Roddie watched, his legs shaking under him, the moaning stopped.

He turned and tried to run, but his knees were too weak. So he turned his back on the gutter and leaned against an iron fence. There was a sudden roar from the street and a truck tore past with a man sitting on the tailboard clutching his face with both hands and blood coming out from between his fingers. Then suddenly the empty street became crowded with people, as though the truck had summoned them. Women poured out from shattered doorways and rushed into the streets with aprons flying, and a confused shouting, wild and exciting and dangerous, began to rise about him. He wanted to escape. He wanted to be back in school again. He wanted Mr. Jackson to punish him. He wished anything would happen to break the continuance of this horrible mystery, this paradox of silence and sudden death and the awful women who now were screaming hysterically and clutching one another and asking what had happened.

Neil Macrae could see nothing but a blazing light behind his own eyes and could hear nothing but the thunder of explosions in his head. He was reeling around and stumbling over objects which he did not know were in his way. His mouth was opening and closing without making any sound. Things were hitting him from every direction. Even the solid earth was smashing at the soles of his feet. The blazing whiteness at the heart of the explosion, the whirling nose of the approaching shell, my own number inscribed in German on its nose *nummer sieben hundert tausend acht hundert* –

He felt something sting his cheek and heard, as from a great distance, Angus Murray's voice. "Snap out of it! You're not hurt – come on out of it!"

Murray slapped his face again, sharply; under the eye and across the nose.

"What in hell's the matter?"

He did not hear Murray's shouted answer, but the roar of the explosion was lessening now; it was like the echo of a cannon shot reverberating among distant mountains. He opened his eyes. "What's happened – a dump gone up?"

Murray's voice seemed excessively loud. "That ship must have been filled with munitions."

The immediate landscape, wildly distorted and irregular, looked like floating wreckage seen from the porthole of a heaving ship. Neil moved toward something solid protruding from the ground and sat on it. But immediately he leaped up with a yelp of pain. It was a section of Alec MacKenzie's stove, still hot from the morning fire.

He felt Murray's arm across his shoulder.

"There's nothing the matter with you. You're an old soldier. When that ship went up you went flat on your face. Dove right off the doorstep into the street. Now – do you remember?"

"Yes, I remember now."

"We've got to dig Alec out – he's buried under the house somewhere. His wife's there too."

Neil smelled smoke and the acrid stench of an unfamiliar gas. Murray's twisted face lengthened and shortened in front of his eyes and then gradually quivered into steadiness as he recovered his focus. Murray was covered with dirt and his coat and uniform were torn, but he was uninjured. The street had disappeared. It was almost impossible to tell where the MacKenzie house had begun or ended. Every building in a space of three hundred acres had been smashed and hardly a single wall was standing. Alec's house had no intact planking larger than a door; it was split to kindlings and deluged with a fine dust of pulverized plaster. The main roof-beam stood upright, straight as a flag-pole in the heart of the wreckage, and by some vagary of the shock, the horse-hair sofa on which Neil had spent the night was standing on its four legs on top of an upturned bath-tub which had been hurled through the toppling wall of a neighbour's house and now was resting twenty yards from its original position.

"Alec – where are you, MacKenzie?" Murray was already looking under broken beams and trying to heave some of the loose timber free. Neil's eyes ranged dizzily over the slope of the hill. It was a devastation more appalling than anything he had witnessed in France. The wooden houses had been punched inward and split apart, some of them had been hurled hundreds of feet; furniture, clothing, and human bodies were littered in swathes and patches among this debris. The trees and lampposts lining the street had disappeared, some of them uprooted and flung, others shorn or snapped jaggedly and lying where they fell, still others tangled with the general wreckage.

"Where are we, in front of the house or behind it?" Murray was looking in bewilderment at the wreckage.

Then Neil remembered that he and Murray and Alec had just been leaving the house, Murray and himself on the sidewalk and Alec still indoors.

"The place is catching fire! We've got to get a move on!"

"I'm all right now," Neil said. Where had these flames come from? With a sound like bracken igniting in thousands of campfires, the entire North End was taking fire. He felt sore places on his own scalp and along the back of his neck and saw that Murray's hair was singed. The flames – they had come from the sky, sharp torches spouting downward out of the atmosphere. But the fire was on the ground now. A flame three feet high was crackling in the wreckage of Alec's house.

Murray lifted his arms and let them fall limply to his sides. He turned back wearily to the wreckage to see if some of it could be cleared away.

Neil's ears were now hearing separate sounds and distinguishing them, the crackling of the flames and the cries of hidden voices, women and children screaming from under smoking heaps of timber and plaster and bricks. From a pile of rubble twenty feet off he saw a human hand wave feebly, then sink back and be still. And blackened figures were emerging everywhere, some of them crouching in the ruins and others crawling clear on hands and knees. They were like ants suddenly scrambling into daylight after their hill has been overturned. They were like soldiers crawling out of shelters into the smoking, heaving earth after a bombardment has passed.

Then suddenly he felt all right. It was as though the prospect of shock had torn at his nerves all these months and now he found his nerves better than he had hoped. The most appalling shock a mind could conceive had come and passed and he was all right. He leaped forward to the edge of the flames, and Murray grunted as he reached his side.

"I think he's under here. Help me lift this beam. Bloody hand of mine's useless."

Neil bent and heaved on the beam but it would not give. Some of the sidewall still pinned it at one end. He picked up a heavy board that once had been a door-jamb, inserted it under the beam and pressed. The beam yielded, lifted a few inches and slithered to one side, making a triangular gap four feet across at its base. Neil crawled through the aperture; his legs slipped and he dropped on all fours to the cellar floor. The place was filled with smoke and dust and he could see nothing. He shouted once and heard an answering groan. Then Murray's muffled voice came down from above. "Don't get yourself trapped down there!"

The dust was choking him and wherever he moved he stumbled over something. He reached in his pocket and pulled out a match and struck it against the seat of his pants. Immediately an arrow of flame darted away from him; there was a quick flash and shock and a noise like thunder. Gas escaping from a broken main had entered the foundation and formed pockets in the wreckage and his match had touched off the train. The ruins jerked upward and separated, then settled back noisily with a sound of cracking wood. Something knocked him to his knees but he was not hurt. As he rose, he saw patches of daylight above him and realized that the exploding gas had scattered some of the wreckage.

"What the hell are you doing down there?"

He heard Murray's voice, near and urgent, shouting from above, and squirmed out through a jumble of planks, tearing his clothes and his skin. He was almost back at the street level and Murray was sweating at the same plank they had tried to lever before. Then a low moan sounded near them and when Neil had cleared out a few loose boards he saw Alec's face.

The big man was crouching like Sampson, with spread arms holding apart two beams which crossed over his shoulders like a pair of shears. His face was distorted and the sweat was already washing a tide of dust down to his neck. He moved his head and seemed to be nodding toward something under his feet. Murray came over and together he and Neil pressed the beams farther apart. Then Neil crouched and got into the space between Alec's legs and found Annie lying there unconscious. Getting his feet under her arm-pits and lying on his back, he pulled backward with his elbows as props until he had drawn her clear. There was no visible wound on her body and she was still breathing.

Then he turned to help Murray and for a second the two men were immobile as they strained on the beams which sheared down on Alec's shoulders. All around them the ruins were on fire and the flames were already close about Murray's legs. Neil finally gave a lurch forward and the shears yielded. As they slithered sideways off Alec's back, the big man's face twisted and he gave a low cry, and then fell forward insensible. "God," Murray muttered. "There was a spike in one of those beams! It got his lung."

They pulled Alec and his wife clear of the fire and Murray cut the coat off Alec's back with a piece of broken glass. It was a deep wound, and the blood looked arterial. Murray gestured toward Annie and Neil bent and tore off her skirt. Murray ripped it into sections and made a pad which he bound across the wounded back with Alec's own belt. Then he sat back on his haunches and rubbed the sweat off his forehead. "If we move him we'll probably kill him. If we leave him here, he'll burn. Oh, Christ – is there anything on wheels around here?"

Neil sat still and panted. Figures of stunned and wounded people were crawling and stumbling in and out of foundations and ruins, appearing and disappearing in the smoke. There was no sense or direction in their movements and their number never seemed to change. He shook his head and coughed. "Where's the nearest hospital?" he said.

"God knows if any hospitals are left."

"Most of these houses have a wheelbarrow. If we could find a whole one it would be better than nothing." Neil got up and skirted the flaming ruins to what had been the backyard. There, filled with rubble, was a wheelbarrow. He pulled it around to where Murray crouched beside Alec and Annie. "If we make a door fast to the top of this we can carry them both."

"Both? Who do you think you are – Sampson?"

"The slope of the hill will be with us." He knocked the sides off the barrow and laid the former front door of the MacKenzie house across its floor and handles, and while he was balancing it, Murray got up and foraged the street for something to secure it to the barrow's frame. There was no need of looking far, for the street was littered with torn sheets and blankets and wires. They lashed both Alec and his wife to the door and Neil lifted the handles of the barrow while Murray steadied it at the side.

If the ground had been level they never could have managed it, for Alec and Annie totalled more than three hundred pounds; but the hill was so steep that the barrow rolled forward under its own weight. There were dead bodies of horses and human beings lying in the street, and so much debris that Murray constantly had to go forward to clear a path. Once they passed a burning fire-engine lying upside down with its wheels still rotating. By the time they had covered the length of three blocks they were in a crowd of other survivors going out in the same direction. The way improved as they neared the harbour, for on these lower levels there were patches where the explosion had simply swept the ground clean. Finally they reached a tram-line and stopped.

Here they first got an idea of the magnitude of what had occurred. Broken ships and the remnants of jetties were piled like driftwood on both sides of the harbour and the water had the appearance of a river after a log-jam has broken. The cruiser moored at the Dockyard might just have come out of heavy action, for it was shorn of its masts and its upper works were bent and twisted. A lumber schooner had been blown out of existence and some of its cargo was now on the warship's foredeck, where sailors were heaving logs over the sides. Smoke was rising from the shell of a foundry and there were heavy fires at the Shipyards, although the metal cranes and the gantries and the shorings of the graving dock still seemed intact. Looking farther down the slope they saw wet ground and puddles left by the tidal wave and long runnels of dirty salt water trickling back to the harbour, and rowboats and launches lying broken in the street.

Murray bent over Alec's head and waited to catch the sound of his breath. "He's tough," he said. "He's still with us."

Neil took his bearings and realized they were on the northerly continuation of Barrington Street. It was already crowded. The dead and wounded were being laid out on the remnants of the sidewalk and policemen whose injuries were not severe already had the crowd in control. Smoke eddied and baffled in the windless air and the noise of coughing was mingled with the phantasmal cries of the wounded. Neil noticed the inordinate number of eye and face-wounds caused by flying glass. Almost everyone he saw was hurt and there were so many stretcher cases that an artillery brigade would not have had the transport necessary to evacuate them. He looked at Murray, then at the wheelbarrow. "We've got to get something else. Wait here till I take a look around."

He pushed his way ahead through the crowd until he reached the next cross-street. He looked both ways and saw what he wanted. An empty delivery truck was just around the corner, standing on two wheels with the foot-spike of a lamp-post plunged through the van behind the driver's seat and the post itself supporting the car. It was almost perfectly balanced, and a single heavy shove sent it lurching back on all four wheels. The foot-spike tore clear, leaving a wide gash in the van's tin side, but that and a broken windshield seemed the extent of its damage. He reached in and turned the key, set the throttle and spark and went in front to crank. The motor was warm and roared immediately, and then he got in and backed the truck down to the main street.

Annie recovered consciousness as they shifted her, but she was too weak to stand and they swung her over the tailboard and laid her inside. One of the policemen helped them shift Alec on the door, and after he was safely stowed, a line formed behind the truck and began lifting other wounded inside. Murray stowed them crosswise, bending their knees to make them fit. Two walking cases were allowed on the seat in front before Neil finally got the truck under way.

It took over half an hour to make three miles, for they were stopped on every block by people carrying wounded. Murray stuck his head out each time through the hole left by the spike and shouted that there was no more room. Sometimes Neil had to stop to clear wreckage out of the way, and the going continued bad until they reached the bend where Lockman Street becomes one with Barrington. Here there was nothing to stop them but the congestion, for while buildings were battered and windowless, they were still on their foundations, and there were no fires.

They began to meet ambulances and private cars running fast to the north, and once a military car hurried by with a soldier in the back shouting directions through a megaphone.

When they finally reached the hospital they found the driveway and streets about it lined with trucks, private cars, garbage carts, bread wagons, slovens, and, at rare intervals, an ambulance. A chain of volunteers lifted the wounded out of these vehicles onto stretchers and doors and anything flat that would hold their weight. Alec was still breathing when a pair of interns carried him in.

Neil was about to turn the car about and head north for another load when he realized that Murray had entered the hospital. He moved out of line to make room for incomers and parked the car fifty yards around a corner, then went back to the hospital. It was a large military establishment with acres of ward-space. The windows were blown in, but this was the only visible damage it had received.

He reached into his pocket and took out cigarettes, surveying the package as though its survival were a miracle. His shirt was wet with sweat but he felt no fatigue, and his hands were steady. A doctor came running up the drive with an instrument-bag in his hand, glanced at him and said, "Hello, Neil," and hurried on. Neil blinked. It was only then that he realized that he no longer cared who recognized him. Even though he was still subject to court-martial, his personal danger had ceased to matter.

Then he remembered Penny and ran up the steps of the hospital. Murray, pushing his way out with a large bottle of colourless liquid in either hand, met him in the vestibule.

"Chloroform and ether – ready mixed," he said. "Let's get going."

"Where's Penny?" Neil said.

Murray looked at him sharply, and began to run down the steps without answering. Neil followed. "I said, where's Penny?"

They reached the truck and Neil started the engine. "Penny said something yesterday about having a job in the Shipyards. Is that a fact?"

"Yes. It is."

"Then we'd better go and get her."

"Listen" – Murray set the bottles on the seat and laid a hand on Neil's knee – "I'm supposed to be a doctor and a quarter of the population of this town is wounded. Camp Hill is the largest hospital this side of Montreal and it's filling up already."

Neil swallowed and stared through the windshield.

"In the first place, you'd never find her. She's being looked after by someone else if she's been hurt. Meanwhile I'm going to turn the Wain house into a hospital and you've got to help me. The military are already commandeering the public buildings in the South End, but it's my guess not even those will hold the overflow."

Neil put the truck about without answering and ran fast along the back streets. He reached the old red house within five minutes and was across the sidewalk and up the steps before he saw that the front windows had been blown in.

Aunt Maria met them in the hall. She was standing with beads of sweat at the roots of her wiry grey hair and a dustpan and broom in either hand. She stared at Neil and stiffened, then her eyes went large and her bosom expanded, but she stood her ground and the dustpan and broom were clenched more tightly than ever. "God bless my soul!" she said.

"Never mind being surprised," Neil snapped at her. "Where's Penny?"

"You!" She flushed angrily. "You stay away from me!"

There was something immortal about Aunt Maria's power to irritate him; it survived even the explosion.

Murray stepped between them. "All right, Neil!" he said, and turned to Aunt Maria. "Mrs. Wain, I have authority to turn this house into a hospital. I need your help. I want all the furniture cleared out and beds set up in every room but the kitchen and bathrooms and library. Go to the neighbours and take all the beds they'll let you have. We'll need a lot of pans and hot water, so keep up a big fire in the stove. I'll use the dining-room to operate and I'll want it ready inside an hour."

She began to shake the broom and dustpan at them and her mouth widened at the corners and increased to a rounded cavern as she tried to think of something to say. Neil pushed by her and ran upstairs, and some of the breath wheezed out of her as she turned to stare after him.

"The report of your nephew's death was exaggerated, Mrs. Wain," Murray said. "As you see, he's quite himself again."

"God bless my soul!" she said.

"I have no doubt He will, but – did you take in what I just told you or do I have to go all over it again?"

With an amused and grudging admiration, Murray watched her fight for poise. And at last she saved it. "What's all this nonsense about?" she said.

"An ammunition ship blew up in the Narrows. It's pretty bad in the North End."

"They had no right to bring a ship like that through the town."

Neil came running down the stairs and stopped long enough on his way to the door to glare at his aunt. "Penny left for the Shipyards this morning. Why the devil couldn't you have told me?" He turned to Murray. "Come on! We're wasting time."

Murray gestured to him to keep quiet. "Mrs. Wain – I'm counting on you as one of the most efficient women in Halifax. Please now – this is no laughing matter."

She pointed at Neil, standing impatiently in the doorway grinding his heel on some broken glass. "What are you doing here? What do you mean – you – you —"

"Mrs. Wain!" Murray interrupted loudly. "Save the family quarrel till later. You're under orders now. When I return, I expect to find beds in every room in this house."

He followed Neil out to the truck, and almost immediately they were charging down the hill toward Barrington Street. When Neil headed north it was like steering a canoe upstream against a torrent.

"That bitch!" Neil said.

"She can't hear you," Murray said. "Take it easy."

"I abhor the sight of her."

"Forget it." Murray suddenly laughed. "That old woman's going to be in her element in the next hour. I bet she loots the beds out of every house on the street."

"She isn't funny," Neil said. His fingers drummed on the wheel. "God – if Penny was in the Shipyards, that boat blew right into her face!"

"Do you want me to go with you?"

Neil looked at him quickly. "She might be hurt."

"All right. Stop at my hotel on the way. If the place is still standing my instruments are there."

Neil turned into Hollis Street and found the going just as bad. After fifteen minutes of stopping and starting, all movement forward bogged down in a traffic jam at the corner of Duke Street.

"It's hopeless," Murray said, and got out. "The hotel's just a block away. I'll be right back."

Neil went around to the back of the truck and probed the tank with a yardstick he had found behind the seat. There was only an inch of gasoline; probably enough for another twelve miles. He climbed in again and lit a cigarette.

By this time the streets had become like the channels of slow, solid-moving rivers. Sidewalks on both sides were so crowded no one could move at a faster pace than a slow walk, and the long columns of pedestrians presented a ghastly spectacle: women with torn clothes, men helping wounded, children staggering along with blood unwiped from hands and faces, people pushing baby carriages and wheelbarrows. Down the centre of the street crawled a line of carts and trucks and ambulances heading south, while the northbound vehicles stood still in a packed and throbbing line, with horses champing and horns sounding and men standing on runningboards and shouting to the cars ahead.

Neil saw a military car stalled alongside him with an officer shouting something through a megaphone at the crowd. No one seemed to pay the slightest attention.

Neil recognized the officer and remembered they had once played tennis together. He got out and crossed the street, putting a foot on the runningboard of the military car.

"What's it all about, Dan? What are you telling them?"

The officer looked around without surprise. "Hullo, Neil. Powder-magazine's on fire in the Wellington Barracks. I'm trying to make these people get a move on in the other direction."

"That's nice. What's the chance of getting the fire out before it goes up?"

"About even." The soldier driving the car was sounding a horn and the officer had to shout over the noise. He looked incongruously neat sitting there with his uniform all brushed and pressed and his cap jaunty over his left ear. "Well, if it does go up, we won't have to worry about this bloody traffic. Going north?"

"Yes."

"Then get off this street. It's solid."

His car started forward and he slumped back with a jerk. Neil went back to his truck and found Murray climbing in the other side with a doctor's bag in his hand and his cap on the back of his head.

"You ought to see that hotel," Murray said. "Jesus!"

"We've got to get on to another street. Hold tight a minute." He backed against the radiator of the car behind him. The driver stuck his head out the window and cursed, but Neil pivoted the truck and ground out the man's right head-lamp, then turned sideways. There was a momentary break in the traffic on the other side of the street, and with horn going he plunged into it and stopped with his bonnet across the sidewalk and through the shattered windows of a store. Then he backed around once more and headed south. "We've got to get around on the other side of the Citadel. By the way – I just heard the magazine's on fire in the Barracks."

Eventually Neil manoeuvred until the truck was on the grass on the western slope of the Citadel, for every one of the streets skirting its base were jammed. Under the grass the ground was hard and the tires gripped and the car plunged upward along the uneven surface with the pan bumping every time the wheels hit a hole. They continued until they were three-quarters of the way to the top, moving on a long diagonal and heading consistently north. Then Neil straightened the wheels and began to descend the long northerly slope toward one of the minor streets where the traffic was lighter.

From this height the catastrophe took on a cosmic aspect. The whole population seemed to be moving, and it was difficult to believe that Halifax could have held so many people. Far to the north the sky was a rolling mountain of smoke, shot through with flashes of fire. Twisting veils of lighter smoke rose in puffs from the nearer streets, hiding their details until they looked like tunnels fuming after the passage of a train. The air shook with a steady, low-toned vibration: the roar of distant fires and the softer rumble of the nearer traffic. The slopes of the Citadel itself were dotted black with people, and the hill was like an island, for the stream of traffic circumscribing its base had no end or beginning but flowed like a lazy river drifting out of the smoke and winding southward along the channels of least resistance.

"You don't look like a shell-shocked man to me," Murray suddenly said.

Neil glanced sideways in surprise. "Why do you say that?"

"I thought you'd been shell-shocked in France."

"I was. But I feel fine now." They were nearing the bottom of the hill and the truck was swaying drunkenly. "Watch for the ditch. Here we go!"

The machine bounced and broke its muffler, gave a vicious heave forward, and crashed over an earthen sidewalk into the street. Neil bullied his way across it through the traffic and immediately entered a narrow and smoke-ridden thoroughfare pointing north. This whole district seemed to have been evacuated and gaping windows and fallen walls revealed the contents of every house they passed. The smoke grew thicker block by block and there were isolated fires with no one to attend them.

Neil heard Murray coughing beside him. They began to bounce over wreckage in the road and once a figure staggered out of a whirl of smoke in front of them and disappeared. And then it was hot and the fires were all around them. Neil slowed down and put up the side window, to find that its glass had been shattered. "I suppose the Shipyards are somewhere beyond this?" he said.

Murray nodded and stared ahead at the road, and they went on. The wheels kept lifting and falling over burning planks and broken masonry, and the roar of the fires was almost drowned out by the thunder of their own exhaust. Finally they turned east and ran downhill until they crossed a tram-line. Neil stopped the car at the curb and got out. Through thinning smoke he could see the twisted funnels of the cruiser at the Dockyard, and the harbour shaking behind waves of heat and drifting smoke and dust. The Shipyards lay at the foot of an embankment directly below him. Sailors from the Dockyard were clearing debris and the dead were already laid out under sail cloth in a double line on the packed cinders of the yard.

ELEVEN-THIRTY O'CLOCK

Everything was suddenly quiet, and the air smelled clean. From where Penny was lying she could make out her father's Persian cat as it arched its back and yawned. Sunlight was pallid along the bark of the lime streets in the garden. Not a muscle stirred in her body; she lay quieter than she ever did when she was asleep. A voice seemed to whisper in her head,

"I can't fight any more, I can't keep it up any more, I don't care any more what happens." Pain gnawed at her left eye, but it was so steady and unchanging that she hardly noticed it.

Whatever had to be done in the house would have to be done by someone else now. She was past caring. The whole place seemed full of strangers this morning. She could hear the sound of heels moving ceaselessly overhead, and Murray's voice rising and falling as he talked to Sadie in the kitchen, and Aunt Maria speaking at the top of her voice to someone in the hall. It was all queer; it was a revolution in the nature of things; it was probably a part of the war. But none of it seemed to matter.

She opened her right eye and raised herself slightly on one elbow. She was on that old sofa they always set up in the garden in summer and kept in the storeroom in winter. So that was where Neil and Murray had laid her when they carried her in! How could those two men have found it? A shiver shook her body and she huddled back on the sofa and closed her eye as she remembered the concussion of the explosion, the sudden stab of glass into her face, the floor lurching and heaving like a ship breaking up on a rocky shore, the atrocious, cracking roar as the building broke from its foundations and shifted with indifference, crumbling out from under the ceiling and slithering down and inward with a noise like hard, unmuffled thunder. When had that happened? How long ago since Neil and Murray had shouted from what seemed such a great distance and she had pulled a hand loose, somehow, to answer them?

"How's everything now?" Neil was bending over her, his face dirty but smiling. Strange . . . whenever they were together he always seemed the stronger; it was only when they were separated that she felt in command of herself. She tried to smile back, but the cheek tightening up under the eye hurt too much. A noise was bothering her. It was an insistent, rhythmic series of abrupt crescendos. "What's that?" she said, her face wincing.

"Aunt Maria's having fun. She's got a crowd of women in there tearing up sheets to use for bandages. We've turned this place into a hospital. You're the first patient."

"Oh!" She felt his hand fondling her right cheek and passing over her hair. Then he lifted the handkerchief from her eye and she watched his face alter as he saw the wound. "Do I look awful?"

He shook his head; his face blurred and his voice came from a long distance. "You'll soon be as good as ever. But I wish Uncle Alfred could see his wife today. The way she's welcoming strange men who come to the door, you'd think she was madam of a whorehouse."

"Darling!" But she seemed to lose sight and sound of him. The morning Jean was delivered, the trees on Mount Royal were covered with late spring snow that was bluish white and shone in the sun. Each time I came out of the chloroform I thought how cold those trees must be, and I thought of rabbits hopping about their boles. Never mind about the rabbits, the doctor said. There aren't any left on Mount Royal these days. You haven't a thing to worry about. You must make an effort – just once more, now – there, that's better! "– Neil!"

Her voice was urgent. A face blurred lower over her own. She had to speak to him now, she had to ask him something. She must find out if he liked children.

"Penny!" That wasn't Neil's voice. The blurred face was familiar, but it wasn't Neil's. Where had he gone? How long had she been here alone?

"You must make an effort, Penny. I've got to do an operation on that eye of yours. It's nothing to worry about, but I can't leave it untended or you'll lose the sight of it."

She sighed and grew limp. Neil had gone away again, as usual. He was always going away. Always, as long as they lived, he would be going away. Now it was only Angus standing over her, wearing a white outfit that looked like a night-shirt. He had lifted the handkerchief from her face and was washing the skin about her eye.

"It's what I thought," he said. "The iris is prolapsed. The lid is cut as well. Does it pain badly?"

"I don't know," she said. "Please, Angus – I'm so tired."

"Yes, Penny – I know."

"What happened this morning?"

"Hasn't anyone told you? A munition ship blew up in the Narrows and knocked hell out of Halifax."

"Oh, yes, that ship. They wanted me — What is it I'm supposed to do now?"

"You'll have to sit up for a few minutes, my dear. Just put your arms about my neck and we'll soon have you comfortable."

"Does it matter that much? Can't you let it go?"

His face blurred again and she felt herself sinking back into a tide of weariness, a lapping darkness that enveloped but never touched her, a nothingness.

Murray bit his lip and frowned, then replaced the bandage lightly over Penny's eye and looked about the room. In the last hour Aunt Maria and her women had transformed it. A deal table stood under bright lights in the middle of the floor and his instruments were set out neatly on a small stand beside it. Bandages were piled on the dresser. All he needed now was an experienced person to assist him, and Aunt Maria had even promised that. "Mrs. Wain," he said. A chair was knocked over in the next room, and then she came in followed by a buxom woman her own age who was wearing a white dress and apron and tying a veil over her hair.

"This is Mrs. Stevens," Aunt Maria said. "She's been a nurse and she'd like to help us." She bent over her niece, but Penny neither moved nor recognized her. "Poor child! We might have known a thing like this would happen to her – working in a place no woman ever ought to have been."

Murray appraised Mrs. Stevens, and felt reassured when he saw her cross to the stand and pass her eye over the instruments. "Have you had operating-room experience?"

"Yes."

"This is an iridectomy." He nodded toward Penny's limp body. "She's pretty well exhausted. You'll have to steady her."

Between them they lifted Penny and set her in position under the lights. She revived with the movement and opened her eyes. Murray surveyed her critically and turned to her aunt. "Mrs. Wain – if I knew another man who was free and competent to do this operation I'd give him the case. You know that, I presume?"

"I'm not a fool, Dr. Murray. Can I help?"

"No, thank you. It will be better if Mrs. Stevens assists."

"Very well." She hesitated, then looked directly at him. "I have every confidence in you, Doctor."

Murray nodded. He had heard this remark hundreds of times, but the words took on a ridiculous meaning as they came from Aunt Maria. She left the room, closing the door behind her. He reflected that the explosion had been one thing Aunt Maria hadn't been able to bully out of the way.

Now there was no chance of turning back. His hand would have to do its work, and if it failed, no one would be able to repair the damage. His forehead was moist with sweat as he anaesthetized and washed out the conjunctival sac. Then he paused for the anaesthetic to take effect and observed that Mrs. Stevens had laid out the instruments in their proper order. This was good, for if he broke down she might be of some help to him. From another point of view it was bad, because she would know enough to be critical. His fingers drummed the table nervously. To hell with her, he thought. Me – worrying about what a nurse may think!

She handed him the deWecker's scissors and he took them with his right hand and tested the strength and steadiness of his fingers. The movement hurt exceedingly, but the fingers were able to apply pressure and close the blades firmly. It would be a short operation. He had done dozens of prolapsed irises and used to think nothing of them. The trouble was that one had to use several instruments simultaneously. He had done it without help several times in France and he would do it now. He would be able to accomplish most of the preliminary work with his good hand and that would rest the weak one. There was a faint smile around his mouth as he inserted a speculum into the eye and secured the lids with a pair of fixation-forceps. Penny stirred and tensed herself.

"Good girl!" he murmured. "Just a few moments now, and it will be over."

NOON

Neil entered the military hospital and pushed through a noisy crowd until he reached a captain seated behind a reception desk at the far end of a long corridor. The man's florid face and white moustache were familiar, but since the explosion Neil thought he had seen a dozen faces he knew, faces which looked older and subtly changed, but he rarely remembered the names that belong with them. He did not recall this man's name now. The captain dismissed an orderly and looked up with a harried expression. Neil asked blandly if the hospital would let him have some medical supplies. The captain's eyes opened wide and so did his mouth and he was about to say something unpleasant, but his mouth remained fixed. Then he found his voice, "My God, Macrae – did this explosion blow the hinges off hell? When did you come alive?"

"Last night, if it matters. How about letting me have a dozen hypodermic syringes and some morphine?"

"Are you crazy?"

Neil sat on the edge of the desk, blocking the approach of an orderly. "Major Murray sent me over. He's setting up an emergency hospital in Colonel Wain's house and it's filling up already."

The captain stared. "*Murray – Angus Murray?*"

"I'm not fooling. He says his hand's fit again. If you'd seen what I've seen this morning you'd know this hospital will be turning them away before afternoon."

"We're nearly full already," the captain said, and frowned. "What kind of work is Murray planning to do over there?"

Neil looked disgusted. "Is that a sensible question?"

"No." The older man grunted and pressed a button. A dozen people were waiting for his attention. "You can have whatever you want provided we've got it to spare. I'll have an orderly take you to the quartermaster's stores. And tell Murray to keep in touch with me – if he can stay sober. I want to know the whereabouts of every medical man in town."

Twenty minutes later, as Neil arrived with the supplies he had been given, he met Murray and Penny coming out of the dining-room into the hall. Murray was supporting her, and his eyes flashed a signal for aid. A pad held by a bandage was over her left eye and her face was pallid. Either she did not see Neil or was too weak to show it.

"It's all right," Murray said as Neil came over. "She's only exhausted. Help her upstairs, will you?"

Neil handed Murray the package of supplies and picked Penny up in his arms. Holding her there, surprised at her lightness, he glanced at Murray and the two men appeared to be examining and reappraising each other. Months seemed to have passed since the previous afternoon.

"How's your hand?" Neil said.

"It seems to have been adequate."

Penny stirred in Neil's arms and tried to turn her head. Without saying anything more he carried her upstairs. His leg flinched, but was equal to the task, and he got her into her room without difficulty.

When he set her down in her own wide bed she lay thankfully; the walls surged against her consciousness, receded and flowed inward again. Jean's face appeared in the darkness, then Mary's and then her father's; they circled about silently through the soft noises of her mind, through the welling waters of her exhaustion, and what they would do to her in the future or she to them no longer seemed of much importance. "I'm so tired!" she whispered.

"Of course you are. Poor darling – all you have to do is rest now. It's all over and you're going to be well in no time. I know you are."

That was Neil's voice. How could he know? He was outside her now, outside in the light of the sun, vigorous and confident and concerned with his own problems. Herself . . . what she had tried to do and the things that still remained to be done . . . these were no part of him. They never could be a part of anyone so confident and hard and sure.

She felt his hand stroking her own and moved a finger lightly to let him know she was conscious of his presence. Oh, Neil . . . don't leave me here. . . . I'm so lonely, and I mustn't ever let anyone know. . . .

When he saw that she was asleep he drew an afghan over her and went down to the dining-room, where he found Murray cleaning up for another patient. "Was it really successful?" he said.

"Yes. Her eye's going to be as good as ever in a few weeks." Murray's voice was defiant, answering a deep-seated hesitation in his own mind.

"Thanks to you," Neil said, looking directly at him. "The military hospital's full already," he went on hurriedly. "The captain I met over there asked you to keep in touch with him."

Murray nodded. "You'd better bring your next truck-load here. I can handle them now. If you find any stray doctors we can use them, too."

Neil left him readjusting the lights of the dining-room. He went into the library, ignoring the women who had commandeered it to sort and roll bandages they were making from old linen. He searched until he found a box of his uncle's choice cigarettes and filled his case with them. Then he passed the box among the women without explanation, and when they all refused by nods or stares, he lit a cigarette and emptied the remainder of the box into his pockets. As he puffed the rich Turkish tobacco he wondered what Wain would say when he returned and discovered him in the house, but he spent little time in speculation. They would inevitably meet soon, and circumstances would have to settle the conversation between them.

He went to the street and looked over the truck, examining the tires and lifting the bonnet to make sure no wires were loose. The engine had missed frequently when he drove it down from the North End, but there was nothing superficial the matter with it. Probably the plugs were dirty. The car's essential need at that moment was gasoline.

He climbed into the driver's seat and looked at his watch. It was nearly half-past twelve: a little over three hours since the ship had blown up. During that time Halifax had come to look like a city caught in the fulcrum of a battle. It was already evident that there would be neither doctors nor hospitals enough to handle the situation, for all the younger surgeons were on active service in England or France.

Had the explosion occurred in the South End, at the tip of the peninsula, the refugees could have moved back into the province, special trains would already be carrying them to inland towns and the congestion would disappear before evening. But the threads tying Halifax to the continent were never more than a single main highway, a railway track, and a string of telegraph wires. And all these had gone out through the bottleneck of the North End. The explosion had blown the town in on itself, and if a strong wind should fan the flames southward, they would have a good chance of ultimately driving the remainder of the population into the sea.

Neil poked his head out of the car to look for chimney smoke to tell him the lay of the wind. There was a thin drift from the east. That meant the South End was safe unless the magazine blew up in Wellington Barracks. But an east wind always brought bad weather, and if it continued in its present quarter there would be rain before nightfall; if it shifted to the northeast there would be snow. Already the sky had a greyish tinge and the sunlight was filtered. Neil grunted; the dullness in the atmosphere was not caused entirely by smoke.

He released the brake and allowed the car to run down the hill, letting in the clutch so the engine could start itself. He would have to leave Penny in Murray's care and hope for the best. Already he had forgotten about Geoffrey Wain, and whether or not Alec MacKenzie would be able to testify in his behalf. He remembered a garage on a street near the foot of the hill and drove to it. The doors were wide open and no one was about. A torn-down engine was lying on a floor hard and black with oil and there were tools spread around on a work bench. He hunted around until he found a barrel of gasoline in a corner and drew off three bucketsful for his tank, pouring them in through a funnel. As he was about to leave, he noticed a map of the city tacked on the wall over the work bench and took it down. With a pencil he marked a double line about the area he knew to have been totally destroyed. Between this line and the Citadel most of the houses had been evacuated but were still on their foundations. South of the Citadel nothing much had been destroyed but plaster, windows, and doors. On the whole, the catastrophe had been respectful to the middle-classes.

He thrust another of Geoffrey Wain's Turkish cigarettes into the corner of his mouth, lit it, and frowned through the wreathing smoke at the map. Even though the town was already under military authority, the work of evacuation still lacked system. From what he had seen, people were leaping to do the first thing that occurred to them as individuals, and no one had begun to organize the flow of wounded into the South End.

The map showed five main arteries running from the North End to the south: one of these passed along the waterfront with several bad bottlenecks on the way, another was Barrington Street and its extension, two more passed the roots of the Citadel, the fifth lay farther west. Between these main streets was a network of shorter ones, and owing to the oval shape of the peninsula some of them were not straight. Where each of these main arteries led out of the fire-belt, clearing stations had been extemporized, but these would never suffice to evacuate such a broad area. There ought to be a station at every corner in the North End, all the way along the line of the fire. Otherwise the same ground would be worked by different parties and hundreds of lives would be lost as a result of time wasted.

On his way back to the North End, Neil tried to plan a way in which he could be of most effective use. He was stopped by a section of soldiers who wanted to commandeer his truck, and there was much argument before he convinced the sergeant in charge of the party that he was himself an officer and had no intention of yielding it. After five minutes of bluff and some minor intimidation, Neil had his way and drove off with a dozen men piled in behind him.

He explained his programme in detail to the sergeant, who was sitting beside him on the front seat. "We're going to set up a clearing station on the edge of the fire-belt and as soon as we find a good place, you've got to organize your men into search-parties. We'll commandeer any private vehicles we meet – along with their drivers. I don't suppose we can do anything now but evacuate wounded, but later on doctors are bound to get through to us from some of the other towns. Then maybe we can do some field-dressing on the spot."

The sergeant nodded; he said he was on leave from France and knew the military routine in his sleep. Then he became talkative and wanted to know if Neil thought the Germans were responsible for the explosion. "My lieutenant, he thinks it's German spies, all right. He's mighty sore at Jerry. Funny thing, though. I met a fella that swore he heard shells in the air this morning. Maybe there's something in it, at that."

"Did *you* hear any shells?"

"No, sir, but queer stuff sure has happened. They say the master of one of them ships out there in the harbour was blown a clear mile and woke up naked on the top of Fort Needham. They say the angle of the hill was the same as the course he was taking through the air and he just sort of skidded to a stop along the ground. Nothing left on him but boots and cuffs." The sergeant spat out the window. "I'd sure like to meet that fella and ask what it felt like."

The smoke grew thicker and they had to stop at a corner where trucks, slovens, and delivery wagons were jammed so tight none of them had room to turn around.

"Another thing I heard," the sergeant said. "A fella told me when that ship went up he lay flat on the ground and when he looked up he saw a whole procession of people sailing through the air over him. First it was a naked woman and then it was an old man looking sort of bowed over and then it was a dory with a couple of fishermen sitting in it holding the oars just like they were when they blew out of the water."

"Get out behind," Neil said, "and tell the driver behind to back up. If he's not going anywhere in particular, tell him to follow me."

By the time Neil reached the fire-belt he was heading a caravan of five trucks and two wagons. Smoke swirled around them but the flames were lower than they had been an hour ago and most of the fire seemed to be lying along the ground. Much of the wood had already burned to cinder and individual foundations were like isolated garbage heaps with smoke winding up from the charred embers and bricks lying on them. The hideousness of the scene was heightened by foul smells issuing from it, and as Neil's nose contracted, he decided that some of the odours wouldn't bear analysis. A few people were poking about helplessly in the wreck of a house fifty yards away, but otherwise the district was deserted. Some dead were on the street, one almost under the wheels of the truck; the body of a woman oscillated slowly from the only lamppost standing on the block. She had been thrown against its top and the cross-beam had skewered her bunched clothes and held them. The only house within sight which could afford any shelter was a ruined fish-market. Neil got out to inspect it: the upper floor had fallen on one side and held on the other, so the structure now was roughly the shape of a triangle. Hundreds of haddock, cod, halibut, and mackerel lay on the sloping counters spitted by glass and powdered by dust.

Neil called the sergeant. "Those counters will have to do for places to rest the wounded. Get your men in here and clean it up. And don't throw the fish away. Half the town is going to be hungry soon and we may find a way of sending them south."

TWO O'CLOCK

The military who had taken charge of Halifax had finally been forced to admit that for the time being the town could rely on nothing but itself. Telegraph riggers had gone out through the fires of the North End and repaired some of the wires running along the shore of the Basin, but the distance between Halifax and other cities of Canada was so great it was obvious that no help could arrive that day. It would take twenty-four hours at least for a train to arrive from Montreal or Boston and twelve hours for help to come from Saint John or Sydney.

This was only one difficulty. The principal railway yard had been blown to pieces and only a few live locomotives had been found. Cars were shunted in from the suburban yard and a hospital train sent up the line to Truro. All organization had to extemporize and depend on inexperienced individuals and impaired facilities. No one yet knew the extent of the casualties, and as the cars and trucks kept pouring into the South End, estimates had to be changed hourly. The Citadel and Commons were black with people driven from their homes. They lay or sat on the grass and built fires to keep warm, and even after the danger of a second explosion had passed with the quenching of the fire in Wellington Barracks, most of them refused to move. Halifax was now like a countryside after a dam has burst and flooded it; sediment was beginning to settle and familiar channels were becoming discernible.

By early afternoon, individual citizens were establishing food-kitchens in churches and private homes, and units of the Army Service Corps set up so many tents on the Commons that the area looked like a military camp. Martial law was proclaimed, but so far as anyone knew, nothing had been looted but a brewery. As the afternoon wore on, crowds began to shift from the Citadel and the situation seemed more controllable. Halifax was cashing in on a century of unconscious self-discipline. Yet there was no end to the processions of wounded coming out of the North End. They kept dragging steadily out of the smoke, moving more slowly as the horses grew tired but always flowing on in a sort of weary perpetual motion, with drivers crouched silently on their seats and the heads of horses drooping lower after each journey. Cars and trucks which had run out of gasoline were stalled on all the principal north-bound streets.

Roddie Wain had spent the morning prowling around the South End, after his fright had developed into a sense of importance. This was the real thing, and he was in on it. As it didn't occur to him that anyone he knew might have been injured, he went home only when he felt hungry. As he approached the house, he decided that its appearance was on the whole satisfactory. It was just sufficiently damaged to look as though it had played its part in events.

He went in by the back door and found the kitchen stove covered with pots of boiling water. Sadie was moving about doing unusual tasks and wearing a scared face, and he heard peculiar sounds coming from the dining-room. He slipped across the floor and opened the door to look, then closed it with a jerk.

"What are they doing in there?" he said to Sadie. "All those lights and someone lying on the table?"

"Get out of my way," Sadie said. Then recognizing him, "Master Roddie – you should have been back long ago! Miss Penny, she's just 'ad a hoperation and Dr. Murray an' 'em's making the 'ouse hinto a 'ospital and you should've tol' somebody where you was."

"Where's Penny now?"

There was no answer, so he ran up the back stairs and stared at the unrecognizable place the upper hall had become. It was crowded with cots, and bundles of people were lying on them; women in white aprons were moving about and two men were carrying a girl up the front stairs on a stretcher. He edged along unnoticed until he reached his own bedroom, where he found three women with bandaged faces lying on cots. Then he went to Penny's room, and in the first moment it was a relief to see her. He noticed that she was asleep, and this seemed strange. He approached the bed and saw that one of her eyes was bandaged.

She stirred as he bent over her bed. "Roddie – is it you?"

"Gosh, Penny – I didn't know." He peered gingerly. "Is it bad?"

"I've been so worried about you!" Her voice was weak and expressionless. "Where have you been?"

"In school."

"Oh, Roddie – why do you have to tell me something like that? Listen – you'll have to find a place to sleep and eat. Go to Uncle Alfred's. Everything here ——" Her voice tailed off.

Roddie looked at her for nearly a minute, then drew in his breath in a quick and nervous gasp and slid out of the room on tiptoe.

Aunt Maria encountered him in the upper hall. "Bless my soul, what are you doing here? Are you hurt?"

"No. I was just ——"

"Get along with you! This minute! Go over to our house and get something to eat. The idea of you being here! Get along. You'll have to sleep over there tonight, too."

"Is – is Penny all right?"

"She's just tired. Now don't you worry about her. Her eye was cut, that's all."

"Where's Father?"

"How do I know where your father is? He's probably with the military somewhere. Everybody's doing things they've never done before. Now get along with you and stop asking questions."

Roddie went out the front door and watched an empty truck start off down the hill. He was sure the stains on its running-board must be blood. When he reached his Uncle Alfred's house he found a queue of refugees waiting at the front door for food, and so he went around to the back, intending to enter by the kitchen porch. He discovered his uncle puttering among the frozen flower beds. The old man looked up when he saw Roddie and coughed.

"Where's your father?" he said.

"Nobody ever knows that."

"They never should have allowed this to happen. I'm going to talk to your father about it. Not a pane of glass in the front of the house! I don't know what's going to become of us all. Your aunt's sent a bevy of women in here and they've turned me upside down. There's no good in that." He coughed again, and he looked bowed and old to Roddie as he stood there talking in bewilderment. "What are you here for?" he added.

"Aunt Maria told me to come here to get something to eat."

Uncle Alfred waved toward the back door and shook his head. "House full of strangers. All the rag, tag and bobtail of the town. I can't even get a policeman to see they don't steal."

"Our house is a hospital now," Roddie said. "Have you got a soup-kitchen here?"

"Soup-kitchen? Stuff! Go and get something to eat."

Roddie soon discovered that members of his aunt's chapter of the Imperial Order of the Daughters of the Empire had commandeered the entire house. One of them mistook him for a refugee and gave him cold ham and potatoes on a paper plate in the kitchen, and while he ate, she asked solicitous questions about himself and his parents. Roddie decided to oblige her, and she listened with horrified fascination while he told her that his father was buried in Flanders and his brother drowned at sea and his mother lost somewhere in the debris of the North End. Everything was going well until she asked where he had lived. He tried to remember the name of a street in the far North End and found he didn't know any. So he bolted his food and got out while she was attending to someone else.

From here he went to Willie Moffat's house. Willie lived on a street that had been fashionable seventy years ago but now had a dubious character. Half its houses had been divided into cheap flats and the remainder were occupied by mechanics, stevedores, railwaymen, and clerks. One brown house in the centre of the block, a dreary mansion of three storeys and great girth, was inhabited by two old maids no one ever saw. They were rumoured to have a hundred thousand dollars in the bank; as they also owned an apple tree Roddie and Willie had frequently visited their backyard during the autumn.

Willie announced that he had just eaten his lunch, and this was easily credible since traces of bread and molasses were left on his face. He was now sweeping broken glass out the front door onto the sidewalk.

"Where have you been to?" he said. "You missed something."

"I've been around."

"Bet you haven't been up to the North End."

"I bet I have."

"I bet I saw more dead people than you did."

"Go on. I saw the explosion and that's more than you did. I can prove it, too. You were in school when it happened and I wasn't."

Willie put the broom inside the porch. The front door had been blown in and Roddie heard Mrs. Moffat's voice calling to her son to look for a hammer and nails to fix it.

Willie disregarded her. "I been looking for you all morning," he said. "I need some men to help me. I'm going to get a horse and team and I'm going to get up to the North End and get working."

"Where can you get a horse and team from?"

"Never mind." Mrs. Moffat's voice rose again and Willie cocked an ear cautiously. "Come on, or the Old Lady'll keep us hanging around here all day."

Roddie followed him to the back of the house and over the fence to a neighbour's yard. There was a small stable in the corner, a pile of manure against the fence and the sound of a horse moving in a stall inside the barn.

"Old Swicker's horse!" Willie said in a whisper. "He's not been around all day. Maybe he got killed or something."

"Where's the wagon?"

"He keeps a sloven inside with the horse." Willie looked truculent. "You're in on this, see! You better not forget that."

"Who's forgetting it?" Roddie said.

Willie looked over his shoulder and quickly unlatched the door and entered the stable. The horse shuffled in its stall and neighed, lifting its neck and showing teeth.

"Chuck the nag some hay while I get the harness," Willie said. "Old Swicker don't feed him right."

Roddie pitchforked some hay into the stall and lifted the shafts of the medium-sized sloven which occupied most of the barn.

"What does Old Swicker do?" he said.

"He drives this cart around," Willie said.

Unlatching the gate of the stall, Willie approached the horse diffidently, but the animal had his head down in the hay and made no movement whatever while they fitted on the collar. Then they backed him out of the stall and between the shafts, and after ten minutes' experimenting, they completed the harnessing and drove off, Willie swinging the whip while Roddie glanced over his shoulder to make sure no one observed them.

"I guess Old Swicker's dead," Willie said, as they headed north.

They were soon in the middle of heavy traffic, and a policeman directed them west. After twenty minutes they passed between the Citadel and the Commons and then they were in streets where the houses were uninhabitable and the smoke hung heavy. All the south-bound vehicles they passed were loaded with wounded. It was not long before they saw a man lying dead by the curb.

Roddie had a recurrence of fright. "Look!" he said.

Willie gave the body a casual glance. "That's nothing. You wait till we get nearer. I bet none of the fellas in the school see what we're going to see when we get nearer."

The horse balked several times as the smoke thickened and Willie laid into him with the whip. The animal whimpered and walked on. Finally they stopped in line behind a long row of vehicles and waited. A sergeant approached, giving directions to the drivers, and when he reached them he was on the point of repeating his order. Then he looked more closely. "Who the hell let you kids up here?" he shouted. "Get back where you came from."

"We been sent up," Willie said.

"Come on – get out of it! You're being sent back right now." There were two men in the cart ahead and he called to them. "You guys there – one of you take this cart. Couple of kids swiped it somewhere and I'm sending them back home."

A thin-faced man with a dirty cap over one ear and a roll-neck sweater came up and pushed Willie off the driver's box. Roddie climbed down, too.

"Go on, son," he said. "Beat it!"

"You better look out," Willie said to the sergeant, and pointed to Roddie. "His Old Man's a colonel."

The sergeant paid no attention and passed on to the vehicles that had pulled up behind them. Willie stared glumly after him. The column started to move and the thin-faced man drove their cart along with it. Roddie and Willie watched him go and then began walking south.

"What's going to happen to Swicker's horse?" Roddie said.

"Gee, I never thought of that!" Willie took a match out of his pocket and began to chew it. "We never swiped it. That sergeant and the guy did. And don't you forget you were in on it, either."

"Who's forgetting it?" Roddie said.

They walked slowly southward, looking into gaping doors and battered interiors as they passed. Once they entered the empty shell of a house and tried to go upstairs but found the steps had fallen in. Roddie wandered out to the kitchen and saw the remains of a breakfast laid out on a table dusted over by plaster and glittering with sparks of broken glass. When he came back to the front room he found Willie opening a drawer filled with silver.

"Finders keepers," Willie said.

Roddie felt uneasy. "This is different," he said.

"How do you mean it's different? I found it, didn't I?"

"The soldiers get you for it. They call it loot and they shoot looters."

Willie slammed the drawer shut. "I don't give a bugger for the cops, but the soldiers are different." He returned to the street by clambering over the remains of a fallen wall, Roddie following. "Come on, let's do something. Let's go downtown and see what's happening."

They turned east and walked for nearly a mile. At the foot of the hill they saw several carts and wagons drawn up before a grimy stone building and soldiers and workmen lifting long, heavy bundles across the sidewalk and carrying them in. They tried to enter the door and were turned back by a policeman. "Get out of here. This is a morgue. It's no place for you."

A woman standing behind the constable whispered something in the man's ear and his expression changed. He put an arm about Roddie's shoulder and led him into a vestibule. "What's your name, sonny?" he said.

Roddie gave it and the woman, overhearing, smiled. "Are you Colonel Wain's little boy?"

Roddie winced. "Yes," he admitted.

"Then you have nothing to worry about. Is your friend – looking for somebody?"

"My father was taken prisoner," Willie said with satisfaction. "The Germans treat him something terrible."

The policeman's face had become serious and he was trying to attract the woman's attention. Failing to do so, he interrupted gruffly. "Son, was Mr. Fraser of Prince's Lodge your uncle?"

"Yes." Roddie suddenly was frightened and wanted to run away, but the policeman's eyes magnetized him. When he looked at the strange woman he felt still more uncomfortable. "Why? What's happened to Uncle Jim?"

"You must be very brave," the woman said.

Roddie said nothing.

"Your aunt and uncle were brought here this morning. They were found in the North Street Station."

"Are they – are they dead?"

The woman nodded.

"Perhaps the boy ought to make the identification?" the policeman said.

"That's been done already."

Roddie's lips quivered. "I've got to go now, I guess."

"You're a brave boy," the woman said. "And will you remember something? Tell your father we'd appreciate it if he'd come down here as soon as he can. There are papers to be signed – he'll understand."

Roddie blundered down the steps and Willie followed him silently. He liked his uncle and was fond of his Aunt Mary, but it was no sense of bereavement that caused his present emotion. Rather it was the abrupt and ruthless impingement of the unseen and the incalculable into his own life, the realization that what had happened today was not an adventure but a catastrophe.

"Gee," Willie said, "that's tough. Well, they can't talk about Swicker's horse now, not after what's happened to you they can't."

Roddie did not answer and they began their homeward walk in silence. They cut west toward the Citadel and then they were aware that it was getting cold.

"Gosh," Willie said, "you should've gone into that place. I bet it was full of dead bodies and corpses and things. I'd like to see a corpse. Gee, we only saw one all day!"

But Willie's heart did not appear to be in his words, for by the time they reached the hill they were both uncomfortable with cold and apprehension. The stream of traffic on the roads about the Citadel had the same consistency as before, but now all adventure had gone out of the sight of it and the people huddled together on the trucks and carts looked miserable and hungry, and this was not a vision transported from France or Serbia or some country that was never immune to such things, but an actual occurrence in Halifax. The sky was greyish-brown in the east and a wind had risen. It moaned now and stirred the frozen branches of the trees. As they raised their faces to the sky they felt the wind sting; for a moment the air looked misty and then it solidified rapidly and they saw it was snow. It slanted down in a thin, wiry mist, hardly visible as it struck the ground but intensely cold and constantly building up its body. The grey air whitened and began to swirl. As they neared home, the rising wind had pegged itself in the northeast and had begun to drive. The streets were shiny black bands on a white sheet, and the sky was darkening into early night. The wind eddying in alleyways took on a fuller tone and howled like a homesick dog.

At the front door of the old red house they watched a soldier come out and get into an empty truck. He looked at the sky and buttoned the collar of his greatcoat. "That's the last straw," he muttered, and drove away.

FIVE O'CLOCK

Angus Murray's back was aching and the fingers and wrists of his right hand had become numb. He fumbled as he adjusted a dressing and the nurse had to help him. Finally the bandage was secured and the patient lifted off the table and carried from the room on a stretcher. Almost immediately the door opened again and another limp form was brought in and laid on the table. Murray and the nurse looked at each other.

"Don't you think you'd better rest, Doctor?" she said. "You haven't stopped for six hours."

Murray spread out his right hand under the lamp; it had begun to swell again and the joints were so stiff he could hardly control them. He looked at the patient: another bad eye case, another hard decision whether to excise the eye or take a chance and try to save it. He looked up at the nurse again. "How many are waiting, do you know?"

"I'll see."

She returned almost immediately. "Mrs. Wain says there are twenty urgent cases waiting operation now and almost thirty needing minor attention."

Murray made a clicking noise with his tongue and looked at his hand again. "I've got to get some help," he said.

The lines on his face were deep gashes and his eyelids were red. As he turned, he had to reach out to the table for support and he waited there a moment, bent over with both hands resting on the flat surface of the table. Then he readjusted his head lamp and examined the patient's eye. He swabbed away the blood and shook his head. Three hours ago, he thought, it might have been possible to save this man's sight. It was a double accident for him to have been brought here now.

"Stand by for a few moments, Mrs. Stevens. I'm going to get a cup of tea."

He picked his way through the crowded hall to the library, found it empty and quiet, and slumped down in an armchair, closing his eyes. "What a surgeon!" he muttered aloud to himself. "Conking out after six hours!"

"Drink this, Doctor."

He stretched out his hand automatically. Aunt Maria was standing beside him with a cup of tea, extended like an ultimatum. He grinned feebly. "Thanks."

She watched him as he drank. Her face was flushed with work, but the experiences of the day had done little to change its expression. It was therefore a surprise to Murray when she said, "There's no sense in not talking about it – you've done wonders today, Doctor."

"Who – me?" He laughed shortly and glanced at his sore hand. "I've merely over-rated myself – as usual." But the hot tea had revived him and he got to his feet. "Thanks for the lift. You know" – he laughed again – "you're not so formidable as I thought. Well, maybe this hand will hold out an hour longer but that's about its limit."

"Nonsense!" Aunt Maria said sharply. "I won't hear of you going back to operate any more."

"Won't you, Mrs. Wain?" Murray tried to grin once more. It was many months since he and Neil Macrae had lifted Big Alec and his wife out of the ruins of their home. It was an age since yesterday. "Who's going to take my place?"

"I've arranged for that. Special trains are being run in from Truro and I've sent two soldiers to meet them. I told them to bring doctors here as soon as they arrived – at least three."

"But the regular hospitals will be short-handed, too."

"If this isn't a hospital I don't know what to call it. Anyway, I'm positive you'll get help shortly."

Murray sat down in the chair again and closed his eyes. He had never been fond of hard work and after six months of idleness and alcohol his physical condition was hardly normal. The floor was swaying like a hammock under his feet and his right arm throbbed with pain. He wondered if he was falling asleep. Was his life always to be a series of dreary vacuums capped by violent crises? Why did he have to be so God-damned philosophical at a time like this? Neil Macrae didn't waste time generalizing. Or did he? And what do I care what he does with his spare time? I am a reed, but I am greater than those things that destroy me. I am a thinking reed. My boredom and my defeats are therefore more significant than the excitements and victories of others because I recognize them for what they are. At least they're significant to me.

He opened his eyes and discovered Aunt Maria in front of him again. This time she held a glass in her hand.

"Here," she said. "You need something stronger than tea. Drink this."

He sniffed and observed that it was brandy. Aunt Maria's face was impassive under her wiry grey pompadour as he drank it down. "That's much better," he said. He pulled himself up and cast his eye over Wain's library of inherited and unread books. "Has the colonel returned yet?"

"No. Now I hope you'll stay here and rest. I thought the brandy —"

There was a knock at the door and she crossed to open it. A soldier entered with snow on his shoulders and stood at attention until Murray signed to him to be easy. He was followed by three elderly men, each carrying a medical bag. Murray recognized none of them, he had no idea of their qualifications or abilities, but at least they seemed to be of the profession.

He rose to shake hands. "You can start in immediately, gentlemen," he said. "You can see for yourself what we're up against."

The doctors took off their coats without more than a few murmurs and opened their bags in unison. Murray observed the supply of instruments and was relieved to note that two of the men were surgeons.

"How did you get into town?" he said. "I thought the line was up?"

"They stopped the train outside – Fairview, I think they call the place. Your two men didn't give us much chance of doing anything but accompanying them. We expected to go to the military hospital or at least to the General."

"There'll be plenty to do here," Murray grunted.

"It looks like it," the second doctor said.

As Murray passed through the hall to the dining-room with the three men following, he heard an unconscious suspiration of relief from the suffering bundles on the floor. It was a strangely exhilarating sound, and it annoyed him to realize that he was moved by it. He left the two surgeons in the dining-room and directed the third upstairs, then returned to a desk Aunt Maria had set up in the back corner of the lower hall. There a woman was keeping a record of the casualties and he checked it over rapidly. With three men besides himself working, it was likely that the present number of patients would receive attention before midnight.

He straightened and complimented the woman on the precision of her work, and as he was about to return to the dining-room he saw Roddie standing by himself just inside the front door. The boy beckoned to him and Murray went over to see what he wanted. Roddie's eyes filled with tears and his throat seemed caught by a sudden constriction and he reached up and clutched Murray by the arm.

"Well, well – what is it now? You're not hurt, are you, Roddie?"

Roddie shook his head and clung tighter.

"Is it Penny?" Murray said. "She's going to be all right, you know."

"No." Roddie's face was haunted by fear of something he did not even begin to understand. "Aunt Mary and Uncle Jim – they're dead. They were in the station."

"Good God!"

An older man should never show alarm to a youngster, Murray tried to tell himself, and he put a hand on the boy's shoulder and guided him through the hall to the kitchen. "I suppose – I don't suppose Jean was with them?"

Roddie gave him a puzzled look as though he could not think who Jean was; then, remembering, he shook his head and the tears retreated from his eyes. "How long is this going to last, sir?" he said.

"What do you mean, Roddie?"

"I don't know, I guess. I mean – how long before things are going to be like they used to be?"

Murray smiled gently and shook his head. "We'd better not worry about things like that, do you think? After all, who'd like things to stay the same for ever?"

"I never thought of that," Roddie said.

MIDNIGHT

It was dark when Penny woke. Her uncovered eye tried to estimate her surroundings, but her room had become an ominous and unfamiliar place. Three cots had been set up close to her bed and three strange bodies were outlined under the blankets. A lamp set on a table near the door had been covered with a green cloth and it gave the room an eerie luminosity. The shadows it cast were faintly rigid on the floor and walls. The room was cold. Outside, the wind howled and there were angry spurts of snow against the beaverboard someone had nailed across the broken windows. Under a particularly heavy impact of wind the whole house trembled and swayed gently like a ship bending to the motion of the sea.

She propped herself on one elbow, and then swung her feet to the floor. Except for her dress and shoes, she was still wearing everything she had put on that morning – was it that morning? She was wide awake now. The events of the day crashed through her mind and for the first time she realized clearly what had happened. Halifax, and with it the rigid, automatic life of her family's hierarchy, had been blown wide apart.

She stood still, shivering. Where was Jean? Had she been frightened when the ship blew up? Had the expanding air struck with equal violence to the northwest? As the crow flew, Prince's Lodge would be less than four miles from the Narrows. Perhaps the house at Prince's Lodge had been flattened too? The expansion would have had a clear pathway across the Basin. But Richmond Bluff would have diverted its violence. There were also contours in the shore of the Basin itself which would lend Jim Fraser's house protection. There were the trees between it and the road.

She went softly to her closet and opened the door. The old hinges creaked and a woman on one of the cots stirred and moaned. Penny felt among the clothes-hangers until she found a warm dress, drew it out and pulled it on. The sleeping woman groaned more loudly and turned over. Penny waited until her breathing became regular. Then she felt for her slippers in their familiar place, pushed her feet into them and tiptoed out of the room, closing the door behind her.

The house was like a cathedral at a watch night service, for all the lights were carefully shaded; a low, rustling sound pervaded the still air, and it was not the echo of the wind outside. As she moved among the cots to the stairhead, a figure crouched by a desk-lamp rose and came to meet her, its shadow gigantic on the ceiling.

"Where are you going?" It was one of the nurses she had seen earlier in the day. As she recognized Penny, she added more quietly, "You should be in bed, Miss Wain."

"I'm better now. Is anyone awake downstairs?"

"Some of the doctors are still working in the dining-room. Your aunt has gone to the next house to rest. There's a terrible storm outside."

"What time is it?"

"A little after midnight."

Penny went down the stairs and found that the cots in the lower hall were empty. She saw a light under the library door and turned the knob without knocking. Murray, his face haggard and his eyes red, was nodding in an armchair and she saw with amazement that an open book was lying across his thighs. She looked over his shoulder and read the title of one of Balzac's novels. There had been a set in the library as long as she could remember. She let herself down into another chair, but as the springs creaked, Murray opened his eyes.

"Yes?" he said. Then, recognizing her, he started up. "For God's sake what are you doing out of bed?"

"I'm sorry I wakened you."

"I wasn't asleep." He yawned, and as he stood up the book fell to the floor. "I've been giving your father's library a little exercise. It needed it. How does your eye feel now?"

"I'd forgotten about it."

Murray pulled a battered packet of cigarettes out of his pocket and lit one. "Mouth like the bottom of a rusty can and I'm still smoking," he muttered. "What's the matter with you? Why didn't you stay in bed?"

"I couldn't. Did you ever wake up in your own room and find queer sounds and strange women in it?"

"Plenty of times. Once I even thought there was a green tiger. But I wasn't sure. Still, I know what you mean."

"Where's Roddie?" she said.

"I persuaded him to go with his aunt to sleep next door. He spent several hours this evening working at the furnace. Are you warm?"

"Yes. Is Neil all right?"

"I haven't seen him since noon, but he seemed better able to look after himself than most of us."

"Angus – I just thought of something and I'm terribly frightened. Do you think – have you heard anything about Jean? Or Mary and Jim? They were coming into town today – or yesterday or whenever it was."

Would this day never come to an end? Midnight, a ruined city buried under the snow, and here was one more crisis he was required to face. Was all the rest of the twentieth century going to be a continuance of this alternation between boredom and violence?

Murray picked the Balzac off the floor and sat back with it closed in his hand. "Jean's all right," he said. "Jim and Mary must have left her at the Lodge with the maid. They were alone when they were found."

"What do you mean?"

He faced her with as much detachment as he could. God damn people like Penny with that tense calm like still water under pressure! The idea that he might have married her appalled him now. That calm, that potential energy in the girl would annihilate him if he ever had to live with it. A stubborn, imaginative, violent man like Neil Macrae would be just the sort to make her do whatever he wanted, make her forget to think, force her into the pattern of his own life without even knowing he was doing it. The next time he thought of getting married, Murray decided, he'd hunt someone capable of hysterics.

"Jim and Mary are dead, Penny," he said quietly. "They were in North Street Station when the ship blew up. I doubt if anyone in the station survived."

Penny received the information exactly as Murray had known she would. She sat up very straight, her backbone rigid and the clenched fingers of her right hand set hard against her lips. She said nothing and made no sound.

Murray got up and looked away. He was too tired to find relief in physical activity, but anything was better than sitting still and watching her insuperable control. He moved to the window and remembered that it was covered with beaverboard. Then he turned back and started forward. Penny had fainted.

All that night the storm grew and the wind drove steadily harder out of the northwest. The wind shattered the snow high in the air and when the flakes reached the ground they had the consistency of sand. Horses and men travelling north moved with hanging heads into the gale that lashed the snow against them and drove it into the horses' eyes and embedded frozen particles in the men's collars and clothing. The temperature dropped steadily and by early morning it was not far above zero. Wagon wheels began to stick in drifts and soon only the heaviest trucks were able to smash through. Many horses had become too tired to pull and their owners had to stable them for the night. Some men had found sleighs, and after dark there was much activity as the wheels were stripped off slovens and replaced by runners.

The snow fell invisibly in the darkest night anyone in Halifax could remember, for the gas lights that illuminated the streets were not burning. In most of the North End there was total blackness, apart from the glimmer reflected from the snow around the occasional glow of a lingering fire. The streets circumscribing the base of the Citadel were outlined by lights that bobbed dimly behind the curtain of falling snow in endlessly moving chains. These were the lanterns and hurricane lamps that swung from the shafts of the sleighs coming and going from the North End. In the South End, most of the windows had been covered by beaverboard or planks or blankets nailed on the inside, and few gave out any light. Here and there at street corners the police had hung out red lanterns.

Now the whole city was quiet. By early morning the rescue workers were too tired or hungry to speak and there was nothing to hear but the wind and the hiss of sleigh-runners gliding over the streets and the constant whisper of falling snow.

The blackened ruins of the North End were buried in drifts and gradually they quenched the remaining surface fires. Yet heat lingered in the foundations and melted the snow which lay directly over them, so that steam rose cold and humid and foul-smelling from that section of the town. Some of the rescuers probing the ruins for human life tried to work in the dark, but most of them had lanterns, and these flickered back and forth through the fire-belt as men kept doggedly at work.

When dawn broke, Fort Needham looked like a long whaleback, pocked with hundreds of hummocks, grey with sooty snow. But a fume of steam rose from the whole of it and blew southwest in the gale, and the thin line of men working methodically across it appeared like the vanguard of an attacking army stopped in its tracks and digging in under fire.

The ships in the Basin were still awaiting convoy and the storm hid most of them. In the dawn the harbour was bleak and steel-coloured, extending into the whitened land like a scimitar with broken edges, stained by fragments of debris drifting with the tide.

Friday

MIDNIGHT

NEIL AND the sergeant stood up to their calves in snow and checked the file of men returning with stretchers to the dressing-station. Most of the stretchers were empty, but a few held prostrate forms. Two hurricane lamps swung from nails in the ruined building at their back, creaking in the wind. Shadows of the approaching soldiers plunged forward in the snow. Behind them, at the rear of the shelter, a cluster of lanterns made a patch of yellow light, and in the centre of it a silent little doctor was dressing a man's wounds.

The soldiers filed in and set down the stretchers, all of them sooty as colliers from the blackened foundations in which they had been working for thirty-six hours. "All this lot seems to be dead," one of them said.

Bending wearily, Neil lifted the blanket from each of the four still forms, flashed his torch into the eyes and raised the lids. When he had completed the examination he took off his cap and beat the snow from it, passed a hand through his hair and sat down on an upturned box. "After the doctor's made sure they're dead you'd better take them out to the sleigh," he said.

The soldiers made no reply. One of them sat down on the floor but the others remained standing with arms limp and shoulders bowed over with exhaustion.

"There's only one sleigh, sir." The sergeant's voice seemed to explode out of the silence.

"That's all you need, isn't it?"

"I told you a while back that horse was too tired to pull," the sergeant said.

"Oh."

Neil got up and flexed his knees, one thigh stiff and devoid of all feeling, pulled his cap over his eyes and went outside. The silent persistence of the falling snow irritated him, as though the flakes had been a swarm of flies. He flashed his torch about and saw the sleigh in the middle of the street, with the horse crouched on the ground between the shafts. He slapped the animal's shoulder, then kicked it gently in the ribs. There was no response. "He'll freeze to death if we leave him out like this." No one answered him. He looked back at the shadows of the soldiers in the shelter, but none of them moved. Perhaps they had not heard him; perhaps they were too tired to care any more what he said. After the panic and excitement of yesterday their work had descended to a killing routine of digging in the frozen earth, heaving away fallen beams, and clearing foundations. The longer they worked, the fewer bodies they found; but because they always found one here and another there, the work had to continue. Most of the bodies brought in within the last six hours had been dead a long while, and all were frozen stiff. The men had not slept the night before and had taken little food. The fish they had found in the market had been sent off to a community kitchen in the South End.

Neil felt mechanically in the pocket of his overcoat for a cigarette before realizing that he had smoked his last one hours ago. He moved slowly back to the shelter. His nerves were numb with exhaustion, but the cessation of physical work was followed by no relaxation. His mind was abnormally active and it refused to allow him to rest.

This was his own city; it had been in North America that this had happened. For more than a century and a half Halifax had existed without violence. Yesterday within a few minutes, he had seen it cease to be a city. It occurred to him how solitary an organism Halifax had been, a diminutive cage of streets and houses illumined after dark, an oval of rocky soil surrounded by sea and forests. Now in the North End nothing remained but snow and anonymous death, nothing but whitened ruins, no lights but an occasional lantern flickering in the darkness. There had been one splendid, full-throated bellow of power: the earth had trembled, houses fallen, fires arisen. There had been a few hours of brave and passionate co-operation of human beings labouring in a single cause; then a mechanical routine; then exhaustion and hunger; then finally the primal solitude of snow drifting like sand over the ruins, of snow obscuring the quick and the dead and all the hideousness of carnage, of handfuls of men too tired to speak standing mutely in a ruined house with their heads and shoulders and hanging arms casting long shadows in the light of hurricane lamps.

He listened. There was no sound but the interminable hiss of the blizzard. He flashed his torch once more down the snow-filled depression that had been a street, nothing moved across the beam but the unending spangles of white. He coughed and buried his chin in his collar, and realized that his whole body was feeble from cold and that his coat was too thin for such weather. He returned to the shelter.

"Sergeant —" The man's head rotated in his direction. "There's nothing else to do tonight. March the men out."

They must have heard what he said, but they did not move.

"They're too tired to march, sir," the sergeant said.

In the back of the shelter the doctor had finished examining the last bodies brought in. "All dead," he said. "We might as well give up for the night."

One of the soldiers moved slightly. "I saw a small furniture store about five blocks south," he said. "Some of their stuff was still whole. Might be a place to sleep."

"Had the roof fallen?" Neil said.

"I don't know."

Neil shook the sergeant by the shoulder. "This is no place to spend the night. Get your men out of here. If we head south we're bound to find somewhere for them to rest."

The instinct to obey reasserted itself and the sergeant came slowly into action. A thought flashed through Neil's mind: I've just learned something. When a man's too tired to eat or speak he's still willing to obey.

"Come on, men!" the sergeant said. "Out of it! You heard what the captain said – get a move on, you there!"

The men shuffled out to the street, instinctively maintaining some form of order, and they went off through the snow with the sergeant leading and Neil and the doctor bringing up the rear. Neil carried one lantern, the sergeant another; the rest of the lamps had been extinguished and left in the shelter. Their stumbling march continued for over a quarter of a mile before one of the soldiers touched the sergeant's elbow. "This looks like the place," he said.

They scrambled through what had been a show-window and the sergeant lifted his lantern to look at the interior of the store. Snow had drifted in, the roof had fallen at the back and most of the furniture was damaged. In the middle of the floor were three brass beds littered with glass and plaster. The sergeant pulled a coverlet off the nearest one and flicked it into the air. There was a rattle of falling glass, and then he flung it over the foot of the bed and sat down, feeling the blanket with dirty fingers. "Sheets and everything! Bloody place's like a hotel!"

Neil looked at the beds. There were twelve men besides himself and the doctor, and the beds would hold four each, if necessary. In a corner he found a small sofa lying on its side and dragged it out. "Want to try sleeping on this?" he said to the doctor.

The doctor sighed. He was a thin, nervous little man, obviously beyond initiative of his own. "What about yourself?" He hesitated, looking at Neil with weary admiration. "You've been on your feet nearly two days."

"I can't sleep now," Neil said. "I've got to see someone in the South End and I might as well start on my way."

The men rolled into the beds without even troubling to take off their boots. Neil went back to the street and trudged southward, the lantern swinging in his hand. The image of a strange girl who still was Penny filled his mind and excluded everything else. He was conscious of wanting to get back to her more than anything else, and he began to imagine what it would be like to be lying with her now, both of them warm and smoothly naked, in bed alone in the dark with the sound of the snow on the outer windowpanes.

But Penny had been wounded. He had almost forgotten that. And Murray . . . was he still working, or was he asleep now, too? Were they all going to forget about what had happened, now there was nothing more to be done and the snow hid so much of it? It was difficult to imagine that anyone else was still alive anywhere in Halifax, this district was so desolate and abandoned.

He held up the lantern and looked at his watch; it was nearly one o'clock. Surely Penny would be asleep now. Murray had said the wound was not serious, but it had required a delicate operation just the same. Odd chap, Murray. He plodded on with the wind driving the snow against his back. The explosion had played tricks with this block. Some of the houses were in total ruin while their neighbours seemed untouched except for broken windows, but the snow had drifted into all alike and they had become caverns through which the wind moaned. Penny had changed. It was difficult to grasp just how she had changed, but something alien had taken root in her mind and whatever it was, it was all her own. She had no intention of sharing it with him. That white lock of hair – that startlingly beautiful stripe retiring over the left temple from the forehead, white from the scalp! He had never meant to fall in love with his own cousin. Not with Penny, of all people.

He remembered the night he returned from his first year in the technical college at Boston. He remembered her face as she caught his look, her eyes dropping as she flushed in alarmed surprise, the immediate knowledge that there was a secret between them and no use denying its existence, the garden after dark and the soft feel of her cheek against his own. He had wanted her even then but had not dared admit it. The old childhood affection and easiness were too good to lose. And afterwards, alone in his room watching the moonlight on the familiar wall, he had known that she was awake in her room also. That was two years before the war; the night in Montreal had merely been a culmination.

He reached a corner and the snow swirled about him like a cape. The blizzard seemed endless; the gale had been blowing for thirty hours and now was stronger than ever. It was as though all the snow of Labrador had blown across the estuary of the St. Lawrence in an enormous migration to the Gulf Stream. His feet clogged in the drifts and his old wound ached, his mind was overcrowded with the dismal and shocking images which had charged it during the past forty hours, and yet he discovered in himself a sort of weary elation. The bitterness of his exile was quite extinguished. No matter what happened to him in the future he would always be able to tell himself that he had survived worse things in the past. *Forsan et haec olim meminisse iuvabit.* Only one who had experienced ultimate things could comprehend the greatness of that line.

He continued walking through the blizzard, his feet dragging in the drifted snow, but the sense of elation did not leave him. He was alone in this desolation and ruin and nothing seemed to matter but a new feeling of enormous and unreasonable joy. He was no longer a wanderer. He had come home and seen his city almost destroyed, yet he knew beyond any doubt that the war was not all powerful. It was not going to do to Canada what it had done to Europe. When it ended, there would be madness in the Old World. Men would be unable to look at each other without contempt and despair. How many in Europe would have the will-power to live naturally under such an intolerable burden of guilt as theirs would be? The war was no accident, but the logical result of their own lives, the inevitable consummation of a willingness to frustrate others at any cost, to smash what they could not equal or understand.

And yet he and his countrymen had been a part of it. Why should Canada escape the results? There were thousands of dead Canadians and hundreds of thousands of living ones fighting over there now. Yes, but though a part of the war, they were innocent of the cause of it. They were explorers of an alien scene; they were adventurers, idealists, mercenaries, or merely followers of the herd. But no matter what the Canadians did over there, they were not living out the sociological results of their own lives when they crawled through the trenches of France. The war might be Canada's catastrophe, but it was not her tragedy; just as this explosion in Halifax was catastrophic but not tragic. And maybe when the wars and revolutions were ended, Canada would begin to live; maybe instead of being pulled eastward by Britain she would herself pull Britain clear of decay and give her a new birth. For that Britain would not endure into the future was unthinkable; she would endure, even if the United States were finally compelled to accept her destiny and balance a world which the Europeans were bent on destroying because they knew in their hearts they had lost it.

Suddenly, like a blow on the back of the neck, physical exhaustion struck him. He could never walk through this heavy snow all the way to the old red house tonight. He peered

at the buildings he was passing. They were empty and windowless, but in much better condition than the places he
had left a half-mile back. Some of them looked as though they
had been punched in by a colossal fist, most were awry on their
foundations, but almost any one of them would give shelter
from the storm. He thrust his lantern through a casement and
saw the snow-covered ruin of a living-room. He continued to
the next house, and the next. The snow had drifted knee-deep
into the ground floors of all these places, for the window sashes
were all set low and now were on a dead level with the drifts
in the street. After five more minutes of searching he entered
a doorway and the lantern disclosed a flight of steps. He tested
them, and finding them firm, went up to the second floor. The
door at the top of the stairs was open and he entered a narrow
hall. The floor was dry and carpeted and the lantern showed
lumps of plaster which had fallen from the ceiling. A telephone
stood on a table and a small stained-glass window set high
above it was intact. A strong wind was blowing from the back
of the house and he went down the hall to investigate its
source. The floor suddenly began to bend and sway under his
feet and he saw there were great cracks between it and the
supporting walls. Moving carefully, he turned into a doorway
and stopped still, for empty space yawned at his feet and cold
air was eddying into his face. The roof and the upper half
of the back wall had been blown down, and only by a vagary of
the shock had the front half of the building been left standing. He crouched and held the lantern so that its light went
down into the chasm. It revealed a welter of beams, of plaster
and furniture caught in a trap by the lower half of the back
wall. Little snow had entered, for it was the southwest side of
the house. By all the normal logic of force, this side ought to
have been the one spared.

His lantern began to flicker and he noticed that the edges
of the wick were red. When he shook it there was no answering sound of splashing oil. He swore, and the light dimmed

and went out. He took the electric torch from his pocket and as he flashed it down into the ruins he thought he saw the outline of a human body protruding from the rubble. He fixed the beam on the spot and isolated a head and a pair of shoulders in the circle of light. He replaced the torch in his pocket, lowered himself over the broken edge of the floor, and dropped. As his hands plunged forward for balance they touched something soft and smooth and cold. He flashed on the torch again and saw that it was a girl's body, entirely naked and exposed. It looked pathetically frail, stretched there in this senseless confusion, but the sight of it was more incongruous than shocking. He played the torch about toward the form that had first drawn his attention, lying face down. He was about to commence the weary routine of digging these corpses out of the debris when he realized that without the lantern he would have only one hand free for the work. The job of composing these strangers for their journey to the morgue would have to wait for the morning.

As he was trying to find a foothold to climb back, a plank broke loose and the man's face was revealed; Neil stood staring as the beam of the torch fell on the frozen, familiar features of Geoffrey Wain. His fingers slipped from the switch and he was in darkness, his knees shaking and the tired blood throbbing through his temples.

Saturday

THE SNOW had ceased to fall, the wind had hauled to the southeast and was pouring inland from the sea under a sky that glistened like wet lead. The boarded windows of the South End looked raw against the lustreless volume of new snow. Occasionally, when the wind opened seams in the roof of cloud, there were brief splashes of watery sunshine and the fresh flakes glittered, but almost immediately the roof would close again. The streets were deep in drifts and gashed darkly by the marks of horses, sleighs, and human feet, and in the downtown districts people shuffled aimlessly through uncleared sidewalks past boarded and half-empty stores, their overcoats appearing so black against the dreary whiteness of the streets and the sooty red bricks of the battered buildings that they all seemed to be in mourning.

The town was silent as a sick man too miserable to move. No trains jangled their bells at corners, there were no sudden sounds of motor horns. The snow was too deep for any car lighter than a truck with chains or a military camion to negotiate it, and many of these had already skidded on the hills and stalled in strange positions. The ships in the Basin remained at anchor; there seemed no life on them and no one gave them a thought. They had become a part of the landscape.

Angus Murray walked down Spring Garden Road, keeping to the middle of the street and watching nothing but his own steps. No one spoke to him, and if he recognized any of the people who passed he gave no sign. Since Wednesday morning he had not had more than six hours' sleep, and although the strain and fatigue and the constant throbbing of his injured arm bowed his shoulders and made him appear like an old man, he was too nervy to want to rest. He wanted more than anything to be alone, he wanted to see something that had not been maimed or destroyed; above all, he wanted to think and to have time to recover the only thing he had left in the world, the sense of his own personality.

He walked as far as the waterfront, perspiring with the exercise, and then continued south until he reached the out-skirts of the Park. It was solitary enough here. The wind had whipped the shore so fiercely that most of the road was clear, and the drifts had accumulated seven feet high among the trees to leeward. The sea-wall was covered by a thin crust of ice through which individual stones were clearly visible, like bricks under whitewash. George's Island was encased in snow and crusted around the edges; on McNab's the trunks and branches of trees scarred the whiteness like a labyrinth of black wires. The harbour was opaque, and wraiths of steam crawled here and there over its surface.

Murray wondered what Halifax would have been like today had there been no explosion before the snow. He pulled a newspaper from his pocket and sat down on the smooth ice-crust of the sea-wall. The war had been relegated to the back pages. Passchendaele seemed to have petered out and there would be little news from Europe before the spring. If there had been no explosion, people in Halifax would now be telling each other what an awful storm it had been and prophesying the worst winter in memory. Geoffrey Wain would have learned that his plans for military glory had been upset and that the hidden resentments of his past life were not worth the bill which had accumulated through the years. And Neil himself, after keeping a hold on life for so long by the hope of revenge and vindication, might now be discovering that in the process he had changed too much to care for those things he had a right to enjoy.

Murray folded the paper and laid it on the sea-wall, then shifted his position and sat on it. Perhaps Neil might still make that discovery. From the little he had seen of Penny and Neil together, he had been unable to find any real common denominator between them. Since the explosion they had hardly seen each other; when Murray had left the Wain house two hours ago they had both been asleep.

He crossed his legs and looked at the landscape; for the moment there was nothing more important for him to do. The town had plenty of doctors now. They had come in on special trains from every town in Nova Scotia, from New Brunswick and Montreal, even from Boston. A major he had just been talking with at the military hospital had expressed fear of an epidemic, but Murray was not inclined to take him seriously. Supplies were needed, and there was a distinct shortage of food, but that condition could hardly last for long. It was rumoured that the Americans were going to send a relief ship from Boston, loaded with food, clothes, glass, and medical supplies. It was a strange characteristic Murray had often observed in Americans, that nothing ever excited them quite so much as the repairing of a disaster, provided it were big enough.

Murray was as motionless as a part of the landscape, his chin sunk in his collar and a fur cap pulled down over his ears. During the past three days he had done good work, and he knew it. He had done better than even his incurable personal optimism had fancied possible. Since Thursday he had performed eleven operations without assistance and done the dressing for nearly fifty more. He had improvised a hospital which had handled nearly two hundred cases and he had seen to it that the work was good. He reflected on this record without pride but with definite satisfaction. Many doctors in Halifax had done more and were still at it, but if they were sensible they would rest now. There were enough fresh men to take their places and weather the emergency.

A solitary tramp ship had entered the submarine-gates and was moving up to the Basin, and the sight of it reminded Murray again of his own part in the war. Just three years ago, almost to the day, he had sailed out of this harbour for Europe and had leaned over the rail of the trooper to watch every familiar angle of shoreline recede from view. So now the glorious adventure was in its fourth winter! Three years had passed and left him an old man. Was this feeling the culmination of a process induced by the war alone? He hardly thought so. Last week he had not felt this way. It was something more personal than an abstract disgust with the war, a revolution more profound than his immediate fatigue. He knew quite simply that the remainder of his life was going to be different from his past. He would never again crave excitement for its own sake, and the thought of alcohol or accessible women had lost any power they once possessed to modify his actions. The explosion, his experience with Penny and Neil and Geoffrey Wain, were undoubtedly connected with this development in himself, but the immediate link he could not discern. The only thing he knew definitely was that the microscopic society in Halifax of which he had felt, even though inadvertently, a part, had been blown to pieces and his own function in it had ceased to exist. Penny no longer needed him. Geoffrey Wain was dead. Alec MacKenzie had died only two hours ago. No one else in this town would even notice his absence.

Murray's twisted face yielded to a slight smile. The catastrophe which had torn Halifax had revealed nothing about its inhabitants that he had not known or guessed anyway. It had merely accentuated their ingrained characteristics. He smiled again as he tried to decide whether or not he really liked Neil Macrae. The boy had his points, but care for details was certainly not one of them. He had apparently forgotten already his original purpose in returning to Halifax. The explosion had been merely a release for his violent natural energy. He had done excellent work, and few others had shown equal resourcefulness. But while Neil had been busy in the North End with his dressing-station, Alec MacKenzie was slowly dying in the military hospital. Neil had forgotten all about him; had it not been for Murray's own initiative, Alec would have died without giving the vital testimony.

Once again the wind was building up to gale strength. It swept raw and cold off the sea and stung Murray's face and pierced the thick wool of his great coat so that he had to rise and begin moving back to town. His eyes left the harbour and wandered among the iced tree trunks of the Park, and the sight of those gnarled, familiar boughs gave him a melancholy pleasure. He remembered a day very like this when he had arrived home for Christmas after his first term in college. There was no road to his father's valley in those days; it had been necessary to go from Sydney by a small coaster which brought mail and provisions to the Cape Breton outports twice weekly. He had left the ship at the jetty and walked the river road three miles to his father's house, arriving just about this time in the afternoon, shortly before dark. His father had taken him out to the barn to cut a sirloin off the frozen carcass of beef that hung there for the winter, and he could still remember the whiteness of the old man's moustache, his soft voice asking questions about college and the life in the city, his gruff manner as he tried to conceal his pride in the fact that his son Angus had the brains to secure a better life than had been possible for his parents.

A better life? If the old man were alive now he would probably still say so, even though in most people's eyes and often in his own Angus Murray was a failure. It was too easy to be sentimental and tell one's self that the pioneers were superior. Murray never shared the current bourgeois view that to be acquainted with the world's culture was a handicap for which a man should apologize. His father had been better integrated than he, but the only choice that had ever confronted the old man was whether to work hard and have a good farm, or take things easy and keep just above starvation level. He had chosen to work hard. Inheriting fifty acres of fairly good earth on the farthest eastern tip of North America, he had cleared a hundred more. He had taken some of the timber to a sawmill up the stream and had it shaped into planks for the larger barns he had built with his own hands. He had educated two sons and sent a daughter to high school. But his children were all he had been able to give the world, and they were his only continuity.

Murray had returned to the little valley just before he went across in 1914. The house had not been painted for twenty years and a stranger lived in it, the land was untidy and one of the barns was not being used, and when he walked up the slope from the river he saw the fences running into a stand of young spruce, and realized that nearly fifty acres of his father's clearings had already reverted to forest.

Why was he remembering all this now? Because only two hours ago he had been at Alec MacKenzie's bedside watching the big man die. His presence had been a peculiar comfort to Alec, for it had made him feel that he was dying, not in the crowded ward of a military hospital, but among his own people. Alec's village had been about thirty miles from the valley where Murray was born. He spoke like Murray's own father, he had the same aspirations, he had lived on into an era he could not understand; he, too, had left the world nothing but a family assured of a better life than his own.

To Murray, the death of an individual was an insignificant event unless it could be reconciled with a pattern possessing a wider meaning. He was still capable of being moved by a village funeral, by the sight of a whole community standing about the grave of someone who had been a part of the lives of them all. But death in a great city seemed to him much like death in the war, an atomic life extinguished finally by an enormous process which had always been its enemy.

The wind began to swing the frozen branches of the trees, gathering a powder of snow from their bark and lifting it howling backward through the woods. It was going to be a bad winter in Halifax, with schools working in double shifts, hospitals jammed, doctors working to the exhaustion point, thousands living in emergency tenements with insufficient heat and no privacy, and the unspeakable hideousness of wreckage left in every street as a reminder of what had happened to everybody. Perhaps it was fanciful to look for any pattern here; the explosion had been blind in its selection. Perhaps if there were a pattern at all it had been here all the time, and it had required this upheaval to enable him to see it.

He turned away from the wind and tried to walk more quickly. There was Geoffrey Wain, the descendant of military colonists who had remained essentially a colonist himself, never really believing that anything above the second rate could exist in Canada, a man who had not thought it necessary to lick the boots of the English but had merely taken it for granted that they mattered and Canadians didn't. There was Alec MacKenzie, the primitive man who had lived just long enough to bridge the gap out of the pioneering era and save his children from becoming anachronisms. There were Penny and Neil Macrae, two people who could seem at home almost anywhere, who had inherited as a matter of course and in their own country the urbane and technical heritage of both Europe and the eastern United States. And there was himself, caught somewhere between the two extremes, intellectually gripped by the new and emotionally held by the old, too restless to remain at peace on the land and too contemptuous of bourgeois values to feel at ease in any city.

We're the ones who make Canada what she is today, Murray thought, neither one thing nor the other, neither a colony nor an independent nation, neither English nor American. And yet, clearly, the future is obvious, for England and America can't continue to live without each other much longer. Canada must therefore remain as she is, noncommittal, until the day she becomes the keystone to hold the world together.

Yet it was characteristic of Murray that before he reached the Wain house he had dismissed these ideas as too artificial to entertain seriously. His scepticism was already accusing the positive side of his nature for inventing an explanation of something which did not exist out of words unrelated to anything in his own experience. He yawned with fatigue as he entered the door and smelled the odour of disinfectant. Then he saw Aunt Maria, as inexhaustible as a machine, walking heavily down the front stairs to meet him.

"Penny's awake," she said, "and she seems to want you for something. For goodness' sake, Major, take off that wet coat first. She's in the library."

Murray found Penny balancing a teacup on the edge of an armchair. She had brushed out her hair and put on a tweed suit which made her hips look broad, and the pleasant composition of her features was ruined by the patch over her wounded eye. But in spite of this, there could be no doubt that she was on the way to recovery.

"Hello," he said. "You look as though you'd had a good sleep. When did you get up?"

"I've been getting up at all hours. First it was dawn. And then I got up when Neil came in." She put the cup down and crossed to the table to pour tea for Murray. "I guess I'm up for good now."

The listlessness of her voice surprised him. He took the cup she handed him and drank the tea standing, then sat down in an armchair opposite her. The heat of the room was increasing his drowsiness and he was about ready to fall asleep. He wished it were a month from now. He wished Penny were well again. He wished he did not have to think of so many things all at once.

"Neil still asleep?" he said.

"Yes, he's sound."

"I suppose they've told you?"

"About Father? Yes."

Murray closed his eyes and sighed heavily. He hoped sincerely no one had told her of the circumstances in which the body had been found. "Things seem to have piled up, don't they?" he said slowly, as though fumbling for words. "The physical shocks – spectacular, I suppose – but they're easier to take than – than a lot of things." He opened his eyes, and saw her looking at him intently. "Try not to have any regrets, my dear."

"Regrets? Why do you say that, Angus?"

"Nothing." He shrugged his shoulders. "A lot has happened in a little while, that's all."

"Maybe I should have – regrets, as you say. But I don't seem to feel anything. What's the matter with me? Am I still in a stupor?"

He knew that if Penny harboured any sensation of sorrow it would not be caused by her father's death, but by his life and the knowledge that he had done little with it that anyone wished to remember. So much the better if she felt empty of emotion now. Once more, he wished it were next month. But there was a routine to go through: Penny must grow accustomed to the idea that her father was dead and that Neil was to be accounted for again, to convalescence from a slight wound and a violent shock, to the cessation of her regular work until the Shipyards were repaired. Like everyone else in Halifax, she would have to spend the winter in a town hideous with destruction in which more than a quarter of the population were mourners.

He sighed and passed his hand over his eyes. It would be a great medical discovery if people could be put to sleep or hibernation for the duration of such a period. The whole world would need a sort of acclimatization drug when this war was over, but they wouldn't get it. They would have to live in the ruins for quite a while.

"Don't worry, Penny. You can't expect to feel otherwise. You've had a hell of a few days."

Her voice continued toneless. "But nothing seems to matter. Other people cry, or look as though they wanted to. I don't want to do anything."

"Not even to see Jean?"

She moved a foot back and forth, and her answer was more disturbing because neither her face nor her voice altered. "I've schooled myself to think of Jean as my niece for two years. I've never let myself imagine her a part of my own life." Her shoulders moved slightly as though to resist an advancing hand. "After all this time – Neil has never once so much as . . . wondered. Now – I don't know – I hardly want to tell him at all."

"Why do you resent his not asking?"

"I know it's silly – why should I? I don't suppose there's any reason to expect a man to wonder about a thing like that."

Murray smiled slightly. "If you think he's forgotten, you know less about men than you imagine." His expression changed. "Where is he now?"

"He's asleep next door. Another explosion wouldn't wake him."

"He needs all the sleep he can get. After another few hours he'll wake up hungry. And then he'll eat like a horse. After that he'll want you. If you take my advice, you'll leave everything to him. He's got survival value. So have you, for that matter, but you've been drawing a lot of cheques on it for quite a while."

Her lips quivered slightly as she watched Murray's tired face grow animated again. She wondered where his vitality came from. Neil was like that, too, apparently exhausted one minute and full of vigour the next; only Neil's body was never still while Murray seldom moved.

"You've been awfully good to me, Angus. It's funny – I can't believe I've known you only a few months. You seem a part of the family – though that's not saying much, considering the family. But now I can't imagine not having you here."

"Don't let your Aunt Maria hear you say that," Murray said absently. He reached into his breast pocket and took out a long envelope. He looked at it a moment, and then handed it to her. "You'd better read this. It concerns you as much as it does Neil."

She opened the envelope slowly and spread out a sheet of official hospital note-paper covered with Murray's awkward handwriting and Alec MacKenzie's large and wavering signature at the bottom. There were two other signatures besides Alec's, witnessing the document.

She looked up at him. "What is it? I don't understand."

"You know why Neil came home so mysteriously, don't you? Why he was afraid of recognition?"

"Oh!" she said quickly.

Murray watched her bend over the paper and saw her fingers clench as she read it through. He had spent a full half-hour of the morning working out the wording of that document, but the only words that mattered were those quoting the message Geoffrey Wain had handed to MacKenzie that afternoon in the middle of the battle, and Alec's signature testifying to their authenticity as placed on this paper. It still seemed incredible to Murray that Neil could be so careless as to ignore the necessity of getting such a document. Alec had not forgotten. He had been so weak he could hardly move, but he had insisted on signing the paper before he died.

Penny looked up, her face colourless. "Did Neil know you were doing this?"

"No, he was too tired when he came in. I didn't bother to tell him."

"But you – you weren't too tired!" She buried her face in her hands and Murray moved awkwardly over to the arm of her chair and put his hand on her shoulder. She started to her feet and her eyes swept the room wildly. "This – this house! I can't ever live in it again! That's it. Where shall I go, Angus? I want to get away from Halifax and everyone connected with it."

Murray smiled and let himself down into the chair he had just left. "I felt like that once, too. The house? Well, maybe. But Halifax! Nova Scotia?" He shook his head and closed his eyes, and then he almost forgot her presence in the room. Nothing but a short time to sleep, and then he would be moving out for good. There was a sound in the air, a plangent ringing that seemed to be in the walls. "I'd forgotten the wind had shifted to the southeast. The harbour bells are at it again. I suppose they'd still be ringing if every one of us here were dead."

His mind clouded. He saw green trees under the sun and heard locusts shrilling at high noon and there was no more snow because it was midsummer; the hay wains were coming up the hill and after sunset the sea-run salmon would be rising in the river.

Monday Night

IT HAD STORMED again over the week-end with rain and sleet, and then the blizzard had renewed itself and turned the atmosphere into a flux of dry snow drifting with a gentle motion out of the east. Now, for the first time in days, the night sky was clear. Everything was buried under shimmering snow so delicately clean that it seemed as though nature had conspired to conceal the misbegotten effects of human ingenuity. The peninsula of Halifax was a white shield curving upward under the sharp-edged stars. The patches of harbour visible where the streets ended at the foot of the hill shone like sections of a river moving in moonlight and flicked by a breeze.

Penny closed the house door behind her and followed Neil across the snow-filled sidewalk to a military truck parked with engine running on the slope of the hill. A soldier inside opened the door and they entered, Neil sitting next to the driver with his knees straddling the gears, Penny on the outside.

"You're sure you can get through to the train?" Neil said.

The soldier let in the clutch and the car slipped forward with a cushioned movement through the deep wool of the snow. "The main street's pretty well beaten down now," he said. "We can try, anyway."

The car surged down the hill in an uncanny silence and the rear wheels slithered widely as they swerved into the beaten level of Barrington Street. It would be almost impossible to return up that hill, Penny thought; and then she realized with a sense of shock that she had left home for the last time. The house would be there for years to come. Spring would revive the flowers in the garden, and by the Queen's Birthday the creeper would have covered the stone wall, and by mid-June the cones of the chestnut blossoms would be nodding by the upper windows. But the familiar intimacy of the house would never return. Her father, the most untouchable man she had ever known, had been capriciously extinguished, and it was as though something profoundly improper had occurred without any adequate reason beyond the physical fact that two ships had met at a point where only one should have been.

She looked sideways as they passed one of the emergency street lights just installed, and saw Neil's profile clearly etched for a second; then it merged with the darkness again, and she was left with the impression of a man who seemed strange and unknown. The lines of his face were like sweeping arcs bound over an enormous spring of energy. They were tense and concentrated. She was tied to this man, and the realization made her shiver. She was a prisoner of his maleness because once she had wanted him and he had refused to forget it.

Turning, and seeing her eyes on him, he slipped his arm about her shoulder and pressed her closely against his side.

"Are you all right?"

"Yes," she said.

"Seems funny, going out to the suburbs at a time like this. Prince's Lodge was just a few houses on the edge of the woods the last time I saw it."

"I suppose it still is."

"This youngster of Jim and Mary's – how old did you say she was?"

"Just about two years." Penny waited for him to make some other comment, but none came. "She can talk a little."

"Is that remarkable at two?"

"Oh yes."

She felt she must cry out if Neil said nothing more. He had not even asked why she was so anxious to go out to Prince's Lodge immediately after the storm, when it would have been reasonable to wait awhile or to send someone else to bring Jean into town. He had asked her no serious questions at all since that first afternoon when she had admitted him to the house. Now when he spoke to the soldier his voice sounded indifferent and practical.

"Is that the Shipyards down there?"

The soldier's reply came back carelessly. "What's left of it. It gets worse farther north. You'll have to walk through a lot of junk to reach the train. That ship blew right into the middle of the railroad yard. It ain't pretty."

The car bumped onward and the Shipyards slipped by in darkness on their right. They drove slowly on through the darkened street, past scattered groups of tired men and women, past sleighs and slovens dragging wearily to the south, and on their left was a dreadful area of emptiness with incongruous bulges projecting along the slope where a few days ago thousands of people had lived.

Neil's hand tightened on her shoulder. He looked down and she saw his teeth as he smiled and then felt his chin harsh on the line where her hair met her forehead.

"This is a good town," he said. "Professional soldiers could have been demoralized by a lot less than these people have taken."

Everything he said seemed to frustrate her. "Neil —" she began.

"Yes, Penny."

"Neil – did you ever think —"

Here in the jolting truck, crawling through the darkness along the slope of Fort Needham, she was no more capable of telling him about Jean than when she had been in the oppressive atmosphere of her own home, with patients filling the upstairs rooms and Roddie and Aunt Maria hanging on every scrap of conversation that passed between them.

"Are you sure you're all right?" His voice was anxious. "Maybe we should go back? If the child has managed to get along all this time without us, another day or so won't make any difference."

"No. No, let's go on. We've got to."

She was in the current now. She had been in it ever since that night in Montreal, except that by synthetic action she had tried to pretend she was safe on dry land, safe with the accumulated weight of her environment to support her. She could see nothing clearly ahead. To force one's self on into the darkness to keep one's integrity as one moved – this was all that mattered because this was all there was left.

Neil's hand was hard against her upper arm. She tried to visualize something of the welter out of which he had preserved himself. She saw him trying to make himself a cog in the machine of the army. She saw him lying like a dead man alone on a patch of tormented earth. She heard the sound of his footsteps echoing bleakly as he wandered like a fugitive through strange cities in England.

Then she knew that it was inevitable for him and Jean and herself to go on together, even if they could do nothing better than preserve themselves blindly for a future she felt to be epitomized by the events of the past few days. She was too much of a scientist to forget that titanic forces once let loose are slow in coming to rest again. Did Neil have any idea what confronted him? By nature he would fight indefinitely to achieve a human significance in an age where the products of human ingenuity make mockery of the men who had created them. He would fight because nothing yet had been too big for his courage. And perhaps he would gain his significance, just as within the last few days he had achieved his dignity.

She relaxed against his shoulder and tried to rest. Then out of the blackness enfolding the landscape they saw the glow of an engine's fire-box and the flickering of moving lanterns, and finally they came in view of a string of coaches with their lighted windows drawing a long line around a gentle curve.

"It's almost like a wrecked ship!"

"A train in the middle of all this!" Neil's voice was eager. "When there are no trains to take people away from the messes they make – then you'll know the lights have gone out for sure."

The truck came to a standstill and the soldier pointed down the embankment to the tracks. "That's your way, sir. The path's been beaten down some since suppertime. I guess the lady'll make it easy enough."

Neil thanked him and jumped to the ground after Penny. They made their way through a confusion of tracks, over-turned and gutted box cars and uprooted sleepers. This yard had been almost totally destroyed, but the snow had buried the worst remnants of the carnage and the moon gave the scene a false peace. The greater constellations were only a little dimmed by the moon, and their lights were hard and clear; the Bear hung over the Basin, Orion at their backs was mounting toward its zenith.

Neil laughed suddenly. "Remember the old tobogganing parties we used to have on the golf links? Do the kids still do it?"

"Oh, Neil!"

"What's the matter?"

"What a thing to think of now!"

"It's not that bad. Some things never change."

"But people do. I've seen the war changing them all the time."

"Maybe that's a good thing." He pulled her strongly forward as she sank into a deep hole in the snow.

"Neil, I'm so tired. I can't think any more about what may happen now."

"Yes, I know. Being tired is the worst part of things like this."

They reached the train and he left her while he picked his way forward to find the conductor. Then he was back almost immediately. "Standing room," he said. "We leave in a few minutes. Let's wait here till they start."

They stood at the rear of the train watching the opposite shore slope up from the black surface of the Narrows. Penny knew that in his own way he was trying to find means of assuring her that she was no longer alone.

He breathed deeply and smiled. "This air – it smells so damned clean! God, it's good to be back! Over on the other side I sometimes thought I could smell the future, but as soon as I got to thinking about it I couldn't tell the future from the past. I wonder how many people realize how fast they're breaking up, over there? It's not a decline and fall. It's just one bloody smash."

"Do you think we're much better here?"

"Better? I didn't mean that. But I'm damn well sure we're different. The trouble with us is, we've been taught to think we're pioneers. We ended that phase long ago, and now we don't know what we are. I tell you, if Canada ever gets to understand what her job in this world really is – well, unless she does, she'll never be a nation at all. She'll just have to look on at the rest of the world committing suicide."

Penny made no answer, but continued to stare into the darkness over the Narrows. Neil knew next to nothing of his own country. He had never been able to see how it was virtually owned by people like her father, the old men who were content to let it continue second-rate indefinitely, looting its wealth while they talked about its infinite oppor- tunities. And meanwhile the ones like Neil, the generous ones who had believed the myth that this was a young man's country, were being killed like fools thousands of miles away in a foreign world.

The conductor came down the line swinging a lantern. "You folks better get aboard," he said. "We're starting."

Every car in the train was crowded. Some were ordinary day coaches, but the majority were old-fashioned colonist cars generally used to transport harvesters and settlers to the West at cheap rates. These had board seats padded with black leather and backs which could be lowered so that passengers could sleep flat with their clothes on and their heads on their kits. The backs of the seats were down now, and wounded lay on either side of the aisles. In each car there was a single nurse.

Neil drew Penny into the door of the rearmost coach and they stood just inside the corner by the drinking-water tank. The interior of the car was in half light and most of the prone forms seemed asleep.

"Neil – apart from the trouble you were in – why are you so glad to be back? What makes you think you'll find things so much better over here?"

There was a muffled blast from the locomotive's whistle; the engine passed a gentle shudder from coach to coach and the whole train began to move forward.

"A man has to think he hasn't got a country before he knows what having one means," he said.

He looked down the car and saw the lines of quiet bodies sway gently with the train's motion. Why was he glad to be back? It was so much more than a man could ever put into words. It was more than the idea that he was young enough to see a great country move into its destiny. It was what he felt inside himself, as a Canadian who had lived both in the United States and England. Canada at present was called a nation only because a few laws had been passed and a railway line sent from one coast to the other. In returning home he knew that he was doing more than coming back to familiar surroundings. For better or worse he was entering the future, he was identifying himself with the still-hidden forces which were doomed to shape humanity as certainly as the tiny states of Europe had shaped the past. Canada was still hesitant, was still ham-strung by men with the mentality of Geoffrey Wain. But if there were enough Canadians like himself, half-American and half-English, then the day was inevitable when the halves would join and his country would become the central arch which united the new order.

The train swung through a long arc and he saw the bodies of the wounded slide gently to the right as the force of the curve pulled them. They were outside Halifax now, going around the foot of Richmond Bluff.

"How long does it take to get to Prince's Lodge?" he said.

"Ordinarily we'd be there in less than ten minutes."

The statement tightened the muscles of her throat. She tried to look at Neil but was unable to keep her eyes on his. She felt his fingers on her wrist as he stood swaying with the train, and with the hundreds of wounded they surged on into the darkness of the continent, wheels clicking over the joints and the echo racketing back from the rock-face. In a few minutes the train slowed at Prince's Lodge.

They paused on the narrow, snow-banked platform and watched the lights of the coaches disappear around the next curve and heard the dying echoes of the whistle reverberating through the forest. A slight wind out of the northwest dragged down the gully of the track, bringing with it the fresh smell of balsam. There were no lights anywhere, but under the moon and stars the snow gleamed faintly out of the woods. Everything was utterly silent.

Suddenly Penny required his tenderness so greatly that it was as though all her life she had been starving for it. She wanted him to take her in his arms and hold her as he had done that unbelievable night in Montreal when nothing had existed but sounds in the darkness and the sense that each of them had been born for that moment. All this she wanted, but the habit of restraint, the cold control she had trained herself to acquire, was still unbreakable.

Neil made no effort to move up the road. He stood watching her, then came close and his fingers touched her hair where it escaped over her temples. He gave a sudden smile, and all strain vanished from his face.

"Wise Penelope! That's what Odysseus said to his wife when he got home. I don't think he ever told her he loved her. He probably knew the words would sound too small."

Tears welled up in her eyes and receded without overflowing, and her fingers closed over his. He looked over her head to the patch of moonlight that broke and shivered in the centre of the Basin, and heard in the branches of the forest behind him the slight tremor of a rising wind.

Afterword

BY ALISTAIR MACLEOD

The Halifax Explosion of 1917 took place approximately twenty years before I was born. Yet in the Cape Breton household in which I grew up, people still recalled it and remembered it quite vividly. They "remembered" it in the peculiar way that people remember events that they did not witness and, at the time, had no way of fully understanding. They remembered the sound which they recognized as being that of an explosion and they said the dishes rattled in the cupboards and the water in the dish-pans and in the standing buckets sloshed back and forth. They said the dogs barked and the hair on their necks stood up. The dogs, they said, reacted as if "a stranger" were coming, a reaction based on a combination of wonder, hostility, suspicion, and fear.

These people witnessed only the effects of an event and had no knowledge of its distant cause. Halifax was some 250 miles away at the end of winding, and often muddy, roads and across the waters of the Strait of Canso. It was still regarded as being "in Nova Scotia," as distinct from Cape Breton, and many of the people in the house had never been there.

Like most people who experience such sound and the moving of the earth, they reacted, after the initial shock, on a fearful and personal level. Closely following the original question of "What was it?" came the corollary: "What does such obvious *bad* news mean for *us*?" At the time my grand-father was working in a coal mine eight miles away in the town of Inverness. The immediate deduction was that there had been an underground explosion and the immediate fear was that he had been killed. In 1917 my grandfather was the only person from that house who worked "for money." The other adults worked either within the house itself or on the land surrounding it. The house, like many in the community, con-tained family members who spanned three generations. Some of the younger children of my great-grandparents were still at home and they were not so different in age from the older chil-dren of my grandparents. My father was a teenager in 1917. All of them had a lot to be worried about when they asked them-selves the question, "What does this *bad* news mean for *us*?"

In 1917 there were no telephones in the country and either boats or horses supplied the transportation. Many of the people walked. Artificial light was provided by candles or kerosene lamps. When the news of the true cause and nature of the explosion finally reached the people of the house, it is not unreasonable to imagine that their fearful sympathy was somewhat tinged with personal relief. When the anecdotes detailing the full horror of the explosion and its aftermath reached them, a portion of the initial shock had already dis-sipated. Perhaps they were occupied with the howling blizzard that followed. During the night of one such blizzard the major window and windowcasing of the house blew in, and only the quick thinking of my great-grandfather prevented the roof of the house from being blown out to sea. Apparently he snatched the mattress from one of the beds and, still in his underwear, held it against the gaping hole in the building's wall. With his hands outstretched against the mattress, he shouted for others to bring him boards and a hammer and nails so that their home might not be lost. Although quite old, he was still a big, strong man, they said. Yet, even so, some-times the howling fury of the snowfilled gusts would push him one or two steps back before he could regain his position with the mattress and re-establish a semi-permanent footing. After they had nailed the boards across the mattress and into the inside wall, he continued to press against the barrier for some time, hoping to keep the wind at bay. Still later slivers from the spruce boards were found in the soles of his bare feet. Perhaps, when the detailed news reached them, they, like the people of Halifax, were immersed in the immediacy of their own situation.

I relate the foregoing in an attempt to illustrate a number of things. The most obvious is that a major event often freezes us in time. It makes us look more closely at where we are in our temporal and spatial journey at the moment of its occurrence. The people who related *their* specific details of the Halifax Explosion to me were in some ways like the many people who remember the rending assassinations which occurred in the United States during the 1960s. Their recall is not only of the event (often distant and, at first, misunderstood, and, only later, more significantly realized) but of what it meant to individuals at its particular moment. Such people recall where they were standing or where they were going and even such small details as the precise items of clothing that they wore. Without such events that directly or indirectly affect us, perhaps we might not look so closely at ourselves arrested and frozen in that one specific moment. It is somewhat like being captured in a candid photograph in the midst of the ordinariness of our lives. "This is what I was doing or what was taking place when *it* happened," such photographic memories seem to say. Sometimes the occurrences that follow such a happening function in a cause-and-effect manner; sometimes they may be merely coincidental, highlighted by the circumstances surrounding their arrival. The blizzard that followed the Halifax Explosion would probably not be so outstandingly remembered if it had not come so quickly and fiercely upon the heels of the earlier devastation. My earlier anecdotes, which are, in strict reality, not *mine* at all, also indicate that in the wake of the big disruptions there is still the desperate ordinariness of what has to be done by those who have survived. Those who survive the physical and/or spiritual movement of their earth must still carry on. Following the eruption of Vesuvius and the destruction of Pompeii there were still surviving people faced with the daily tasks of fetching water and tending to their babies.

To my mind *Barometer Rising* is, among other things, a novel about a city and its individuals captured in the specific "nowness" of their time. The city of Halifax is one of the novel's major characters. It is a character of an undecisive nature limited, perhaps, by both heredity and environment. Dominated by an older English aristocracy, it has become comfortably, if unimaginatively, well-to-do, but still it suffers from a certain static listlessness and the feeling that it is being largely ignored by the larger world. It is not in the mainstream of either European or North American life. "And Halifax, more than most towns," muses Angus Murray, "seemed governed by a fate she neither made nor understood, for it was her birthright to serve the English in time of war and to sleep neglected when there was peace. It was a bondage Halifax had no thought of escaping because it was the only life she had ever known." Speaking more vociferously on the subject, Geoffrey Wain expostulates, "I've wasted a whole lifetime in this hole of a town. Everything in this damn country is second-rate. It always is, in a colony."

Although Geoffrey Wain may bluster more than most, he is not the only one who yearns to leave the listless "bondage" that is Halifax. Angus Murray leaves. The Frasers go to South Africa and to Montreal. Neil is educated in Montreal and at the Massachusetts Institute of Technology, and it is in Montreal that he and Penny conceive their child. Neil's father, John

Macrae, goes to the United States and dies in Boston. Of Angus Murray's classmates, "some were successful in the upper provinces or the States; one was famous; few were left in Nova Scotia." Obviously most of those who are "successful" are somewhere else. The most successful "stay-at-home" person is Penny, and there is constant wonder, bordering on disbelief, that such could be the case. Even Penny herself shares some of this amazement. She is amazed not only because she has been able "to succeed in a man's profession," but also because the London Admiralty really does want to use the design of a young woman "who has lived most of her life in Halifax." At one point she contemplates the heavy oak door of her father's house. She regards it as a symbol of her being both locked in and locked out.

Yet on the eve of the explosion almost all of the major characters have circled back and are in Halifax once again. Each has returned for his or her own particular reasons, and almost all of them comment on how the war has changed the city but somehow the city, in spite of all, has also remained the same. The explosion, of course, changes all of that. The earth moves. The harbour bottom beneath the *Mont Blanc* is deepened by twenty feet. The air concussion flattens almost everything in its path. The displaced waters of the tidal wave roar into and up and through the streets. Then the city, especially the North End with its frame buildings, begins to burn. And finally there is the blizzard. A purgation rising from the unleashed elements of earth, air, fire, and water is about as thorough as it can be. The explosion is a "great leveller" in more ways than one, and it is obvious that Halifax and its surrounding environment will never again be the same.

Barometer Rising abounds in graphic details of people trapped, often quite literally, in their specific moments of time. Roddie Wain sees the plasterer with the severed jugular and the schoolboy with the sliver of glass protruding from his cheek. Big Alec MacKenzie is found in his cellar "crouching like Samson" while supporting the gigantic crossed beams upon his back. In the space between his feet lies his breathing but unconscious wife. At the North Street Station Jim Fraser sees the film of dust that has settled on his dead wife's face – even as she lies beside him. He notices the feather on her hat as it flickers in the breeze. He looks with a sort of wonder at the transparent triangle of glass and the breaking bubbles of blood before his eyes. Just before his death he realizes that the apex of the glass triangle is imbedded in his lung and the bursting bubbles of blood are his own. He had been going to get a newspaper at the time. Geoffrey Wain is found dead in the rubble of his secretary's flat. The secretary, Evelyn, is dead as well, dying naked in the bed she had shared with Wain during the night. When the explosion struck, Wain was shaving and had "decided that a night like the one past would never occur again."

In contrast to such portraits of people pinpointed in their traumatized moments of pain or death, there is the feverish activity of those who are unharmed or, at least, less seriously wounded. Volunteers carry the dead and the wounded, and emergency shelters and temporary hospitals and food kitchens are established. Yet even in the midst of such cataclysmic events, there is the ordinary. Twelve-year-old Roddie Wain is hungry and wants something to eat. He goes first to his house, which, he discovers, has become a hospital, and then to his aunt's, where a lady gives him cold ham and potatoes upon a paper plate.

Still later there is the relative calm born of exhaustion. "Now the whole city was quiet. By early morning the rescue workers were too tired or hungry to speak and there was nothing to hear but the wind and the hiss of sleigh-runners gliding over the streets and the constant whisper of falling snow."

But there is also another concept of time that threads through *Barometer Rising*, this novel which is ostensibly about the events of eight highlighted days. It is a concept that is apart from the static stillness so much railed against by such as Geoffrey Wain and apart also from the stillness of those trapped in the illuminating moments of their deaths. It is apart from the furious activity unleashed by the explosion and apart as well from the almost post-orgasmic exhaustion which follows upon such frenzy.

It is instead the slow but ongoing time of the journey, and it is deep in spatial and cultural memories and reverberations. John Macrae, Big Alec MacKenzie, and Angus Murray all come to pre-explosion Halifax from across the waters of the Strait of Canso, from that Cape Breton which is viewed throughout the novel almost as another country. They come from homes which are mainly accessible by boat and/or the most primitive of roads, and the first language of all three is Gaelic. Unlike Geoffrey Wain, none of the three believes that "Here in Nova Scotia his family had gone as far as the limitations of the province permitted. He had been born at the top of things with no wider horizon to aim for."

Although all three come from the same area, the reasons for coming vary with each. John Macrae, we are informed by different speakers, was talented, gifted, and restless. He is described with awe as a man who "knew how to build a ship" and as one who "could handle his tools light and easy, just like a woman handles a needle." Coming to Halifax to expand his horizons and develop his talents, he is employed by Geoffrey Wain in the building of a yawl and in the process meets Wain's sister Jamsie. Perhaps because "he seemed new and different to her," they fall in love and marry. Wain "loathed John Macrae for marrying into his family," and after the birth of Neil and the subsequent death of Jamsie, John Macrae, we are told by Penny, "could never fit into this menagerie, so he stayed away from us as much as he could." Later he moves to Boston where he dies disillusioned and unfulfilled. The marriage was a "mistake" that Wain does not wish to see repeated between his own daughter and the son of John Macrae. Speaking in exasperation to Murray, Wain mentions the "bad" qualities Neil Macrae has obviously inherited from his deceased father. "Like a lot of the Highland Scotch he was shiftless unless he had everything his own way. Not that he didn't have ability, mind you. He could have had a wonderful future, but he'd never be interested in anything he'd get paid for."

After his wound and his discharge from the army, Big Alec MacKenzie is in Halifax because it offers him the opportunity to "work for money." Unaware that he is part of Geoffrey Wain's larger scheme, he is grateful for his job as foreman at Wain's wharf. He is big and strong, extremely moral and deeply religious. He also possesses "a slow manner of talking . . . but when the voice finally issued it was hauntingly musical and crowded with Gaelic idioms." He is proud that his fifteen-year-old son Norman is a good student who wishes to become a scientist. Norman's "voice had lost its native Gaelic accent; Halifax had flattened it out." Although MacKenzie appreciates the fact that his employment at Wain's provides educational opportunities and financial security for his children, he is often ill at ease within himself. It is often "possible to detect a vague restlessness, an uneasy sense of insecurity and dishar-mony, in the lines of his face." He misses his landscape and the slower time of his past: "shadows travelling the steep hills of the Cape Breton shoreline; pockets of mist white as fleece in the sunshine along the braes opposite Boulardarie; a feeling that time did not matter much, a sense that when a man planted a field or built a boat he did so to meet a season not a timetable; a habit of rising with the sun instead of an Ingersoll alarm-clock." When Neil warns him that the act of telling the truth may cost him his job, he answers simply, "That's as may be." When Neil again raises the issue, he says, "I do not under-stand very much, but I always have known what it is I have to do next, and if I lose the job at Wain's there will be another one somewhere else. We are told that the Lord will provide."

Even Geoffrey Wain is impressed by MacKenzie. Although he hires him as a form of self-protection and although he occasionally bullies him, he has to admit that MacKenzie is "the best wharf-foreman he ever had." On the Tuesday before the explosion, Alec stands cap in hand before an impatient Wain. "Try to think, MacKenzie," snaps Wain in irritation. In the hectic events that follow, it becomes obvious that MacKenzie is capable of thinking – and remembering – quite well.

Angus Murray comes to Halifax to follow the dream of education. His journey from his family's Cape Breton farm begins twenty-seven years before the novel's opening. Successful in his medical studies, he marries while still at medical school, only to have his young wife die shortly after. Haunted by her death, he becomes a restless wanderer, given at times too much to alcohol, "letting an old sorrow dominate my whole existence." He spends time in the United States, goes overseas to France, is wounded, and comes back to Halifax where he lives in an hotel. Although his hotel room contains ninety volumes on medicine, his copies of the classics are the books most worn from use. Never establishing a permanent practice, he at one point compares medicine to tennis. "It's the same game wherever you are but the players are different. You get more fun out of it in the small town but the champions play in the city. I guess we all kid ourselves we'd like to be champions." Filled with nervous energy and curiosity, he is constantly walking through the streets of Halifax, and it is through his eyes that we learn much of what we know concerning the city. Observant and quick, he is, at times, motivated to great action by his "incurable personal optimism." He is also extremely sensitive to "the beauty of the world," and to those who are most vulnerable within that world. He has great compassion for the wounded, shell-shocked soldiers he encountered at the front. In his temporary hospital he is moved by the "unconscious suspiration of relief from the suffering bundles on the floor." Though a childless man, he loves all children and is extremely touched when he understands Penny's true relationship to Jean.

Although Murray has been "a citizen of the world" for twenty-seven years, his deepest vision is still a rural one, rooted in his pastoral past. His most lyrical descriptive memories are those of his father's farm. He is still most at peace in the forest among the gentle movement of animals, or when contemplating the sea or the sky. The playing of "Lochaber No More" makes every nerve in his body quiver and he is still affected by village funerals, "by the sight of a whole community standing about the grave of someone who had been a part of the lives of them all." He has a theory that war "is the product of the big city," and as the barbarians destroyed the ancient cities of the past so will future invasions destroy the cities of the present. To an amazed Mamie, he drunkenly predicts either the end, or the beginning, of a world when "there'll be fishing-boats in Halifax, nothing but fishing-boats. And the women of Lunenburg and Cape Breton will bring up the looms from the cellars."

Although John Macrae, Big Alec MacKenzie, and Angus Murray differ in their aspirations and achievements, they have more in common than might, at first glance, be supposed. And although Neil Macrae is of a different generation and grew up in Halifax, he has more in common with MacKenzie and Murray than he realizes. He flourishes within the crisis of the explosion and is the man of action and the symbol of the new Canada, but he does not act alone. Although he does possess "survival value," it is worth noting that while he is saving the world, these older men are saving him. And they are saving him because of their long shared journey from the deeply felt past.

Angus Murray's encounters with Geoffrey Wain are strikingly similar to Wain's earlier encounters with Big Alec MacKenzie and the Macraes (both father and son). He is viewed as an outsider by the Wain establishment and regarded almost as "curious." If Wain loathed John Macrae for marrying his sister, and is strongly opposed to Neil Macrae's intentions towards his daughter, he is hardly more enthusiastic about Murray as a potential suitor. He changes only when he realizes Murray can be of use to him, and then quite openly offers his daughter as a bribe. The gesture infuriates Murray. Bribery is the same tactic Wain uses on MacKenzie, the difference being that Murray knows he is being bribed while MacKenzie does not.

The first time Murray enters the Wain house, he is ill at ease. His speaking voice, "which was slow and markedly soft, lilting with an overtone of native Gaelic," is obviously different. He finds the conversation uninteresting and the hour at the supper table a "dreary experience." Left alone in the living-room, he admits the room has "dignity" but it does not seem to be "gracious." He is not interested in Wain's selections of port. The later meeting between the two men in Wain's office further emphasizes their dissimilarities. When asked if he understands the ins and outs of military advancement, Murray replies, "No, I guess I was never interested enough to find out." When he begins to realize the significance of Wain's manoeu-vrings and bluntly tells him so, Wain is furious. "You're hysterical, Murray," he shouts, "and you're being a fool! If you'd done more thinking and less talking in your life, you'd have a little more money in your pocket today." The speech echoes elements of his earlier description of Neil as a young man who was not "interested in anything he'd get paid for" as well as his "Try to think, MacKenzie" statement. Murray replies, "I'm doing plenty of thinking right now." Earlier in the conversation Murray says, "You and I are so different we'd never understand each other in a million years."

Once Murray decides to help Neil, there is no wavering in his purpose. As MacKenzie decides to tell the truth even if it will cost him his job, Penny observes that Murray will "act justly because he could not act otherwise." In so doing, she realizes "she had never seen him behaving so true to his own nature." Neil, however, is not that easy to save. Headstrong and impetuous and on occasion given to arrogance, his actions sometimes border on the rashly naive. At one point Murray describes him as "a babe in the woods" and as "a champion in that class." Still, the two men are more similar than they realize. Regarding the two of them together after an angry exchange, "wise Penelope" observes that they "had more in common than they knew" and that "the two regarded things and people from much the same standpoint, and they valued the same attributes in those they met. She knew they could never become enemies, and wondered if Neil realized this."

When Neil visits MacKenzie to make his request, he is again in the presence of more than he realizes. After MacKenzie has listened to the excited young man and agreed to help him, he acts in the manner of a wise and surrogate father. And although he is morally and intellectually sound, he speaks also from the wisdom of his long continuing journey. As he guides Neil to his bed, he says, "Your father was one of our own people. And there would be no use in arguing against a thing like that, whatever. So you don't have to explain and you don't have to be thanking me, either." The sentiment and the language are echoed in Murray's recollection of the moments before MacKenzie's death. Watching the big man die, he knew his "presence had been a peculiar comfort to Alec, for it had made him feel that he was dying, not in the crowded ward of a military hospital, but among his own people."

A few minutes before his death, MacKenzie had signed the document attesting to the orders he had committed to memory at an earlier time. Murray had prepared the format of the document, "but the only words that mattered were those quoting the message Geoffrey Wain had handed to MacKenzie that afternoon in the middle of the battle, and Alec's signature testifying to their authenticity as placed on this paper. It still seemed incredible to Murray that Neil could be so careless as to ignore the necessity of getting such a document. Alec had not forgotten. He had been so weak he could hardly move, but he had insisted on signing the paper before he died."

In *Barometer Rising*, Hugh MacLennan introduces the first of his Celtic people. They come and go throughout his later novels, and they make appearances in his essays as well. They differ from each other as individuals although, as in this novel, in the final analysis their similarities are greater than their differences. Speaking to Mamie, Murray says, "When you were a girl you had the Gaelic, didn't you?" "What are you talking about?" she replies. "I'm Irish!" "What's the difference?" he responds, and then begins to quote the old Canadian/Highland poem about being in one place while looking back to another.

The poem is, in its way, emblematic of the lives of John Macrae, Big Alec MacKenzie, Angus Murray, and even Mamie herself. The last, influenced by the vivid memories of her rural upbringing, has sent her own children to be reared in the country. Of the other three, none, with the exception of Big Alec MacKenzie, inhabits a Halifax house in the traditional sense. As they seem non-permanent within Halifax, so also does Halifax seem non-permanent to them. The private visions of all of them seem to be of another place and another time. They carry echoes of another language, seem curiously indifferent to the standard views of time, employment, and money, and seem quick and/or indolent by turns. They are emotionally moved by "the old sorrow" and "the beauty of the world." It is not surprising that Geoffrey Wain, whose family has lived in Halifax for generations, finds such people to be so frustrating and annoying. And it is no wonder that Murray regards Wain as being "so different" from himself that understanding is precluded.

This is, of course, not to be judgemental or to say that one view is better than the other. Indeed the final statements of the novel indicate that after the purgation of the explosion, a "new world" is on the horizon and new views beckon. The old waters of the smaller tributaries mingle to form the new river of the future. But still, the new river is not totally new nor can it ever be.

Some forty-five years after the Halifax Explosion and some two decades after the publication of *Barometer Rising*, the journey from Cape Breton to Halifax was still a relatively long and complicated one. I think of that particular time because during the years of the early 1960s I frequently made the journey, following the winding roadways of the time. It was true that one no longer had to wait for the ferry across the Strait of Canso. And it was true that the "main roads" of Cape Breton had been paved – although some of them only as recently as 1957. And it was true that the Trans-Canada Highway was actually *there* in certain sections although in others it still belonged to the future. Many stretches of "the old road" were unbelievably narrow and crooked, and it is with a sense of wonder that one regards it now, for sections of it still wind beside the modern Trans-Canada Highway. Much of it has been blocked off; some of it has been reduced to access status or abandoned to the tufts of grass growing through the crumbling remnants of its decaying asphalt. It is hard to believe that so many journeys by so many people were once made upon it.

Sometimes on my journeys of that time, people who were born in my great-grandfather's house would accompany me. We were all lucky, I suppose, that his quick thinking during one crisis in time had preserved his house for all of us. Due to the particular circumstances of their ages and their histories, some of the individuals were often ill, and it was to Halifax that people went to visit certain specialists or to enter certain hospitals. We would leave early in the morning because we would "not be sure what was ahead of us," and although we sometimes stopped at restaurants, more often we took a lunch. The people were often more nervous than they cared to admit and the men would have bloody, little nicks on their chins caused by early morning "accidents" while shaving. Sometimes they carried addresses and phone numbers of Halifax relatives on little scraps of paper in their purses or in their pockets. We would comment on the changes of landscape and of climate; marvelling at how early the spring came to the Shubenacadie Valley or how little snow there seemed on the approaches to Halifax. Sometimes, in winter, our car would be caked in sleet or frozen slush while the local cars and local roads would be relatively clear. On the return winter journeys we would be even more concerned with weather because we would be travelling north rather than south and along the vast expanse of ocean and in an area of high winds. Sometimes, in snowstorms, we would drive, leaning our heads out of the windows, trying to see the centre line on one side and the sloping ditch on the other. Sometimes we could not get through at all and would spend the night fitfully dozing in the car, alternately turning on the engine and the heater and opening the windows, waiting for the snowplough to come through in the morning. Almost all of the people in the car spoke Gaelic as their mother tongue.

I close with these anecdotal memories as I opened with statements in a similar vein. Into the seeming constancy of our time there comes the inevitable challenge of change. And it may come as suddenly as the car skids off the highway or the wind blasts in the window. As suddenly as the explosion that levels the once solid city. And sometimes we know too well and at other times not well enough the impact of such visitations upon our lives. As the barometer indicates changes in the weather, so also does it signal how we might live our lives in accordance with such change. But then there are the changes which it does not predict at all. In *Barometer Rising* Hugh MacLennan begins his journey as a young novelist from a certain region of a certain country at a given period in time. He effects his own changes as he himself is affected by the changes that surround him. But this is his starting point. With a firm step and a clear eye he sets forth towards the future. But, sometimes, like Angus Murray, he hears the echo of "the old sorrow" even as he contemplates "the beauty of the world." This is one aspect of his journey and an important measure of his care.

BY HUGH MACLENNAN

ESSAYS
Cross-Country (1949)
Thirty and Three (1954)
Scotchman's Return and Other Essays (1960)
The Other Side of Hugh MacLennan: Selected Essays Old and New [ed. Elspeth Cameron] (1978)

FICTION
Barometer Rising (1941)
Two Solitudes (1945)
The Precipice (1948)
Each Man's Son (1951)
The Watch that Ends the Night (1959)
Return of the Sphinx (1967)
Voices in Time (1980)

HISTORY
Oxyrhynchus: An Economic and Social Study (1935)

TRAVEL
Seven Rivers of Canada (1961)
The Colour of Canada (1967)
Rivers of Canada (1974)

More Atlantic Canada titles from:
The New Canadian Library
The Best of Canadian Writing

M & S

DAVID ADAMS RICHARDS

The Coming of Winter
Afterword by Rick Hillis

David Adams Richards's first novel, written when he was twenty-two, *The Coming of Winter* reveals an author who finds universal truths in the particular rural setting of New Brunswick's Miramichi Valley. An intensely realistic story with engaging, unaffected characters, the novel provides a window on a world as unsettling, as uncontrollable, and as inescapably authentic as a sudden brawl.

Blood Ties
Afterword by Merna Summers

Blood Ties. For David Adams Richards the expression is an assertion of the reality of life in small-town Canada, where blood ties people in countless, almost unknowable ways to friends, community, and landscape. Using dazzling angles of vision and shifting perspectives, Richards captures the lives of his characters with sympathy and understanding.

Lives of Short Duration
Afterword by Alistair MacLeod

The Terris are engaging people, but they are a family in collapse. In their petty and wasted state, they typify aspects of the larger community, besieged by financial woes and creeping economic and cultural Americanization. Yet while the novel's characters are at times vicious, sleazy, and even outright dim, Richards entitles them to the interest and sympathy of the reader.

NCL A series worth collecting

ERNEST BUCKLER

The Mountain and the Valley
Afterword by Robert Gibbs

Ernest Buckler's affectionate portrait of David Canaan, who comes of age in the Annapolis Valley in the years before the Second World War, *The Mountain and the Valley* captures a young man's spiritual awakening and gradual growth of artistic vision. "One of the great novels of the English language." – Alden Nowlan

ALISTAIR MACLEOD

The Lost Salt Gift of Blood
Afterword by Joyce Carol Oates

The seven stories in this critically acclaimed collection are remarkably simple, yet each piece is infused with a powerful life of its own, a precision of language and a scrupulous fidelity to the reality of time and place, of sea and Maritime farm. "A collection all admirers of short fiction will want to own." – Joyce Carol Oates

As Birds Bring Forth the Sun and Other Stories

Afterword by Jane Urquhart

In this, his second collection of stories, Alistair MacLeod depicts men and women acting out their "own peculiar mortality" against the haunting landscape of Cape Breton Island. In a voice both elegiac and life-affirming, he invokes memory and myth to celebrate the continuity of the generations in the midst of unremitting change. *As Birds Bring Forth the Sun and Other Stories* confirms MacLeod's reputation as a storyteller of rare talent and inspiration.

NCL A series worth collecting

THOMAS CHANDLER HALIBURTON

The Clockmaker
Afterword by Robert L. McDougall

Sam Slick of Slickville, Connecticut, the Yankee clock-peddler of the title, accompanies a visiting English gentleman on an unforgettable tour of early nineteenth-century Nova Scotia. This NCL edition of *The Clockmaker* is an unabridged reprint of the thirty-three sketches that were first published together in 1836, and which established Judge Thomas Chandler Haliburton as a satirical humorist of international renown.

JOHN STEFFLER

The Afterlife of George Cartwright
Afterword by Renée Hulan

This stunning novel, first published in 1992, transforms the real life of an eighteenth-century gentleman-adventurer into a fictional journey that ranges from England to India, from Frederick the Great's Prussia to Labrador. John Steffler recreates a lost time and place, and turns the tale of an enigmatic figure from Canada's history into a telling portrait of our past and a warning about our future.

NCL A series worth collecting

L.M. MONTGOMERY

Anne of Green Gables
Afterword by Margaret Atwood

Anne of Green Gables is Canada's best known and most beloved novel. Its heroine, the spunky and irresistible Anne (spelled with an *e*) Shirley has charmed generations of readers around the world, as has this enchanting and timeless story of real lives and real loves. This NCL edition reprints the original 1908 text and eight illustrations.

The Emily Trilogy
In her celebrated Emily trilogy, Lucy Maud Montgomery draws a realistic portrait of a young girl's life on Prince Edward Island. In these novels we follow the life of Emily Starr as she moves from childhood to adolescence and young womanhood, as the twin threads of bright and dark, love and cruelty, hope and despair intertwine in a pattern as significant as it is enduring.

Emily of New Moon
Afterword by Alice Munro

Emily Climbs
Afterword by Jane Urquhart

Emily's Quest
Afterword by P.K. Page